## PRAIS[illegible]
## *A COSMIC KI*[illegible]

"Wow. I've been reading Samantha [illegible] for years, and she has actually managed to top herself with *A Cosmic Kind of Love*."

—Tessa Bailey, *New York Times* bestselling author of *It Happened One Summer*

"With a premise that shines like the brightest constellation, Samantha Young delivers a refreshing and delicious rom-com about star-crossed lovers event planner Hallie Goodman and NASA astronaut Christopher Ortiz. [With] sizzling chemistry, a tangible connection, and complex characters I rooted for from the get-go, *A Cosmic Kind of Love* did in fact launch my heart into space and left me on Earth, starry-eyed and hoping for my own Captain Chris Ortiz."

—Elena Armas, *New York Times* bestselling author of *The Spanish Love Deception*

"*A Cosmic Kind of Love* will fly you to the moon and leave you stargazing. This clever romantic comedy about two souls brought together by the stars is everything you need in your life, complete with swoons, smiles, and steam enough to power a rocket. *A Cosmic Kind of Love* doesn't just get five stars—it gets the whole galaxy."

—Staci Hart, author of *Wasted Words*

## PRAISE FOR
## *MUCH ADO ABOUT YOU*

"Bestselling author Samantha Young's latest rom-com, *Much Ado About You*, is as cozy as a well-worn blanket." —PopSugar

## PRAISE FOR
# *FIGHT OR FLIGHT*

"A delightfully flirty read full of banter and heat, *Fight or Flight* also captivated me with the depth of its emotional intuition. . . . I was left at the end hugging my copy, both satisfied with the fantastic read and bereft that it was over."

—*New York Times, USA Today,* and #1 international bestselling author Christina Lauren

"[Young's] books have it all—gorgeous writing, sexy characters, heartbreak—I'm addicted."

—#1 *New York Times* bestselling author Vi Keeland

"Funny, witty, sexy, and a little heartbreaking. [Young's] outdone herself with *Fight or Flight*, and that's saying a lot."

—*USA Today* bestselling author Penny Reid

"Utterly delicious and addictive, *Fight or Flight* is Samantha Young at her best. I could not put it down."

—*New York Times* bestselling author Kristen Callihan

"This romance is a knockout. . . . Passionate, pure, and a perfect addition to the genre; a romance with real heart."

—*Kirkus Reviews*

"Young makes the temperature rise in this sexy new novel, which blurs the line between friends and friends with benefits. . . . Readers will finish the novel craving more."

—*Booklist*

## PRAISE FOR *NEW YORK TIMES* BESTSELLING AUTHOR SAMANTHA YOUNG AND HER NOVELS

"Young pens a wonderful romance with lovable, multifaceted characters who want what everyone wants—someone to love them, no matter what."

—RT Book Reviews

"Full of tenderness, fire, sexiness, and intrigue, *Every Little Thing* is everything I hope to find in a romance."

—Vilma's Book Blog

"Ms. Young delivers a character-driven story line that is gripping from the get-go, injecting a beloved enemies-to-lovers trope with intense angst and eroticism."

—Natasha Is a Book Junkie

"A really sexy book. . . . Highly recommend this one."

—*USA Today*

"Humor, heartbreak, drama, and passion."

—The Reading Cafe

"Young writes stories that stay with you long after you flip that last page."

—Under the Covers

"Charismatic characters, witty dialogue, blazing-hot sex scenes, and real-life issues make this book an easy one to devour."

—Fresh Fiction

## Also by Samantha Young

### THE HART'S BOARDWALK SERIES

*Every Little Thing*
*The One Real Thing*

### THE ON DUBLIN STREET SERIES

*Moonlight on Nightingale Way*
*Echoes of Scotland Street*
*Fall from India Place*
*Before Jamaica Lane*
*Down London Road*
*On Dublin Street*
*One King's Way* (novella)
*Until Fountain Bridge* (novella)
*Castle Hill* (novella)

*Hero*
*Fight or Flight*
*Much Ado About You*

# A COSMIC KIND OF LOVE

SAMANTHA YOUNG

Berkley Romance
New York

Berkley Romance
Published by Berkley
An imprint of Penguin Random House LLC
penguinrandomhouse.com



Library of Congress Cataloging-in-Publication Data

Names: Young, Samantha, author.
Title: A cosmic kind of love / Samantha Young.
Description: First Edition. | New York : Berkley Romance, 2022.
Identifiers: LCCN 2022014841 (print) | LCCN 2022014842 (ebook) |
ISBN 9780593438619 (trade paperback) | ISBN 9780593438626 (ebook)
Subjects: LCGFT: Love stories | Novels.
Classification: LCC PR6125.O943 C67 2022 (print) |
LCC PR6125.O943 (ebook) | DDC 823/.92—dc23
LC record available at https://lccn.loc.gov/2022014841
LC ebook record available at https://lccn.loc.gov/2022014842

First Edition: October 2022

Printed in the United States of America
1st Printing

Book design by Daniel Brount

A
COSMIC
KIND OF
LOVE

# ONE

## Hallie

### PRESENT DAY

"So what stupid thing happened to you today?"

I stumbled on one of the concrete steps that led up to my apartment as my boyfriend's question echoed off the stairwell walls from the loudspeaker on my phone.

A flush of irritation made itself known in my cheeks even though George's tone was teasing. "Nothing," I replied defensively as I continued climbing, trying not to sound out of breath.

I struggled to hold my phone and my oversized purse with one hand while I opened the door with the other.

"Come on." George chuckled. "Something had to have happened. It's been almost a week since the last one, so that's, like, a record."

"The sandwich doesn't count." I huffed, dumping my bag onto my small dining table, which doubled as my office desk.

"Eating something that makes you nauseated to please a client counts."

So, okay, maybe I ate several salmon-and-cucumber sandwiches at a client meeting even though the slippery, slimy texture of the salmon made me want to vomit. "Please don't take me back there." I gagged, but the sound softened into a sigh of pleasure as I kicked off my high heels and flattened the arches of my feet onto my cool hardwood floors.

"You're telling me you've gone a full week without something ridiculous happening?"

Perhaps I was merely exhausted and low on a sense of humor, but sometimes it seemed like George only stuck around because he found me entertaining. And not in a good way.

Biting back hurt feelings, I wondered if my defensiveness was less about feeling tired and more about the fact that something stupid *had* happened to me today. "Fine." I cringed. "About thirty minutes ago, I was on the subway and I saw this guy standing across from me who was super familiar, and he kept looking over at me."

"Right . . ."

The mortifying moment was doubly awkward as I relived it. I squeezed my eyes closed against the memory, gritting my teeth. "Well, have you ever bumped into someone who you know but you can't place them or remember their name?"

"Yeah, that's the worst."

"Exactly. I'm thinking, *Oh God, I know this guy, it's probably from college, but for the life of me I can't remember his name.* When he looks at me again, kind of squinting, I'm thinking, *Jesus, he knows me and he thinks I'm so rude for not saying hello.* . . . So I just cover my ass and blurt out, 'Aren't you going to say hello? It's been forever; it's great to see you again.'"

"And?"

I buried my face in my hands, just moving my fingers from my mouth so George could hear my reply. "He looked at me like I was crazy and said, 'I'm sorry, we've never met before. I have no idea who you are.' Well, I couldn't explain to him who I was because I couldn't remember who *he* was, so we just stood there trying to avoid each other's eyes for the next ten minutes, and just as I got off the subway . . . I remembered where I knew him from."

"Where?"

My cheeks almost blistered my fingers with the heat of my embarrassment. "It was Joe Ashley, the news anchor, whom I have never met before but do watch regularly on TV."

There was a moment of silence, and then the sounds of choked laughter came from my phone. George was laughing so hard a reluctant smile curled the corners of my mouth.

"Oh man, oh babe, I'm sorry." George hee-hawed. "I don't mean to . . . but that's hilarious."

"I aim to entertain," I said dryly, switching on my coffee machine.

"Only you," he snorted. "These things only happen to you."

It certainly felt that way sometimes. I attempted to change the subject back to the reason I'd called him. "Are we still on for dinner tomorrow night?"

"Uh, yeah . . . but I was thinking you could come here and I could cook."

A romantic dinner at his place? My earlier annoyance fled the building. How sweet. How unlike him. It *was* our three-month "anniversary" next week. Maybe he wanted to commemorate it. I grinned, my mood lifting. "That sounds great. What time? Should I bring anything?"

"Uh, six thirty. And just yourself."

Six thirty was early for dinner. *Why* so early? I frowned. "I don't know if I'll have finished work by then."

George snorted again. "Babe, you're not a heart surgeon. You plan parties, for Pete's sake. I'm pretty sure if *I* can be here by six thirty, you can."

I sucked in a breath as his words ignited my anger and the urge to tell him to go screw himself . . . but that infuriating piece of me that hated confrontation squeezed its fist around my throat.

"Hallie, you still there?"

"Yes," I bit out. "I'll try to be there at six thirty."

"Then I guess I'll see you at seven thirty," he cracked. "Night, babe."

My apartment grew silent as George hung up and I stared at my phone, taking a couple of deep breaths to cool my annoyance. Lately, my boyfriend had gotten more and more patronizing. I wanted to believe he had the best intentions and that he was only teasing. But if he didn't have the best intentions and he was just kind of . . . well . . . an asshole . . . then I'd have to break up with him.

I made a coffee and pulled my laptop out of my purse, my stomach seesawing at the thought of breaking things off. I'd been dating since I was fifteen years old, and I'd only ever had to break up with two boyfriends in the past thirteen years. The rest had either broken up with me or ghosted me. Still, the thought of having to break things off with George made me anxious.

Maybe I didn't have to break up with him, I thought, as I sat down at my desk and flipped open my laptop. Maybe I could just tell him I found some of his teasing derogatory and he should do better not to be such a freaking tool.

Suddenly my cell chimed behind me on the counter and then chimed again and again and again.

"What the . . ." I turned to grab the phone, some kind of sixth sense making me dread the sight of the notification banners from my social media apps. Tapping one—

"Oh my God." Nothing could have prepared me for the video someone had tagged me in.

The video someone had tagged my mother in for her prominent role.

I'd totally forgotten she was attending my aunt Julia's bachelorette party tonight. In typical Aunt Julia fashion, she'd forced everyone out on a weeknight to avoid the weekend crowds. Aunt Julia was my mom's best friend from high school and had been terminally single for most of my life. Then, three years ago, she met Hopper. He was a couple of years younger than her, divorced with three grown kids, and he and Aunt Julia fell madly in love after meeting in a supermarket, of all places. Now they were finally getting married, and I couldn't be happier for her.

However, my mom, who'd been divorced from my dad for less than two years and had to watch him move on to a younger woman, was in a fragile place right now. So I could be mad at Aunt Julia for allowing my vulnerable, postdivorce mom to get recorded at the bachelorette party giving a male stripper a lap dance while sucking the banana he held in his hand.

Yup.

My mother, ladies and gentleman.

I shuddered.

Noticing all the shares on the video, I came out of the app and slammed my phone down on my desk. Part of me wanted to race out of my apartment, jump in a cab, find my mom, and drag her out of whatever strip club in Newark they were in.

Yet there were only so many times that I could rescue my mom and dad from themselves. This was their new reality postdivorce, and I needed to let go. Maybe if I didn't have a pile of work to get through, I might run after my mom.

Who would undoubtedly find the online video mortifying once she sobered up.

Sighing, I grabbed my phone and called my aunt. To my

shock, she answered. The pounding music from the club they were in slammed down the line.

"Hey, doll face!" Aunt Julia yelled. "I've changed my mind and you're allowed to come! Do you want the address?"

Aunt Julia had decided she wanted a bachelorette party that allowed her to do whatever the hell she liked without feeling weird in front of me or any of her friends' grown kids. I was relieved to be left out of the invitation.

"No," I replied loudly, "I'm calling because that video of Mom is all over social media!"

"What video?"

"The lap dance! The banana!"

"Oh shit," she cackled. "You're kidding? Okay," she yelled even louder, "Who put the video of Maggie online?"

Realizing she was talking to her friends, I stayed silent.

"Jenna, you creep!" Aunt Julia yelled good-naturedly. "Take it down!"

"It's not funny, AJ!" I called her by the nickname I'd given her as a child.

"Oh, it's kind of funny, honey, if you're anyone but her daughter!"

"Just make sure she doesn't do anything else lewd that ends up online. Have a good night!" I ended the call before she could reply.

It was clear they were all drunk. Aunt Julia was usually on my side when it came to calming Mom in any postdivorce antics—I'd never had to worry about my mother in any way until her marriage fell apart and she started acting unpredictably.

However, there was no reasoning with drunk bachelorettes.

"Shake it off," I whispered to myself, willing my pulse to slow. "You cannot undo what has already been done, but you can focus on your work so you don't lose your job."

I was an event organizer. I worked for one of the best event-management companies in Manhattan: Lia Zhang Events, owned by my boss, Lia Zhang. After college, I'd planned to go backpacking across Asia, a lifelong dream of mine, but the reality was I needed money to pay for that. So I'd gotten a job as a manager at a large Manhattan hotel, and when the event planner quit three weeks before a big wedding, I'd stepped in to take over. I'd met Lia at the fourth wedding I planned for the hotel, and she was so impressed by my work she offered me a job. The pay was hard to resist because it would take me closer to my backpacking dream.

Four years later, I was still working for Lia, had been promoted to senior event manager, and almost everyone I knew had talked me out of my backpacking trip.

My latest project was planning Darcy Hawthorne's engagement party. She was a true-blue New York socialite. If we got this right, Darcy would more than likely hire us to plan the wedding.

The issue was that Darcy, an environmental lawyer and elegance personified, was marrying her complete opposite. Her fiancé, Matthias, was a French artist and musician. He wanted a "modern, stripped back, yet artistic party with a rock band" while Darcy was all about traditional opulence. She was a flowers-and-string-quartet kind of woman. It was my job as their planner to find a compromise, so I'd asked Darcy and Matthias to email me images and music for inspiration.

I'd been busy at work finalizing plans for another client's spring wedding, so I hadn't had time to look over their emails. I had a lunch meeting with them tomorrow. Hence the late night.

Slamming back coffee, I opened my email and found the couples' separate replies.

Matthias had sent me a helpful Pinterest board. It had to be the artist in him. Most guys I worked with either didn't care about the minute details of the event or didn't know how to communicate what it was they visualized. Clients who were creative, however, were always a godsend because they usually knew how to tell me what they wanted.

While Matthias's board was straight to the point, I discovered Darcy had sent me a link to an online cloud account where she had several digital folders for me to look at. To my confusion, some folders were named with numbers that read like dates. I opened a folder from a year ago to see it contained a video.

Huh?

Had she sent me YouTube videos for inspiration?

I double-clicked and the video started.

A somewhat familiar man's face took up most of the screen, but behind him I could see a strange, organized jumble of pipes and wires on a white wall. I could hear a loud hum of machine noise in the background.

"Well, here I am, Darce." The man grinned into the camera, a glamorous white-toothed smile that caught my attention as if he'd reached out of the screen to curl his hand around my wrist. "I'm on the International Space Station. I still can't believe it."

# TWO

## Chris

### ONE YEAR AGO

Staring into the camera on my laptop, I tried to picture Darcy at the other end, and it was more difficult than I'd ever expected. Maybe I was still on sensory overload. I'd been on the International Space Station for six weeks, and my excitement still hadn't worn off. I didn't know if it could. All I had to do was look out the window, and I felt a sense of amazement and wonder, like a kid who believed in Santa Claus all over again. My big brother's boyhood dream of being an astronaut had amazingly come true for me. If he was really watching over me from the surrounding stars, I hoped he knew that this was for him. I hoped he was proud.

"I've tried calling," I said into the camera with a little smirk. "But we keep missing each other. Guess that's what happens when your girlfriend is an amazing lawyer. I got your emails though."

Tom, the commander of the *Soyuz*, and my crew had given me this look the last time I tried to get Darcy on the phone and couldn't. Tom was the kind of man who could say a thousand things with just one look. Anton, a cosmonaut and our right-seater on the *Soyuz* had given me a similar look when he'd joined us for dinner the other night. But unlike Tom, who just let a person make up their own mind about things unless their way of thinking would lead to a disaster in space, Anton had said in his thick Russian accent, "You should send a video. Like a letter. People act strange when their loved ones are in a situation they do not understand. Show her what you do here."

The truth was, I was so involved in the daily tasks set by NASA that I didn't really allow Tom's look to sink in until Anton advised me to send a video to Darce. But it *was* strange. In fact, surely it was a terrible sign she didn't answer my first call from the ISS or any of my calls in the six weeks since. NASA had assigned an escort to my family to keep Darcy, my father, and my aunt informed of my continued safety. And our arrival on the station was televised, and I'd agreed to send videos and photographs to NASA that they could share on an Instagram account they'd set up for me. I wasn't a social media kind of guy, but I'd do whatever the PR team thought might bring interest to our mission. They'd posted my arrival to my Instagram. Besides, I had talked to Darcy and my family during a press conference, so they both knew I'd arrived safe and sound.

Still.

It was definitely a little off that Darcy didn't pick up when I called from goddamn space. Her emails arrived regularly, and she explained she was busy with a massive case against a large corporation for noncompliance with their environmental impact. However . . . Christ, even my father had picked up when I'd called. Yet, it was possible Anton was correct. Perhaps Darcy was more afraid of me being in space than I'd considered. Though we were encouraged to talk it through thoroughly with our loved ones while we trained for a mission and while I knew my aunt was excited but afraid for me, Darcy had seemed . . . fine.

Thrilled to tell people she was dating an astronaut.

She'd even come to Baikonur Cosmodrome in Kazakhstan for a few days before launch, though her schedule meant she'd had to leave early.

Did she really have to leave early? Or was that just an excuse?

And shouldn't I care more if it was?

I didn't say any of this into the video. There was no time or space in my life to feel resentful and confused. For now my focus was on the day-to-day tasks and the greater task of staying alive in space. At any moment something could go wrong on the space station, and my focus needed to be on keeping me, my crew, and the other three astronauts on the station alive. Darcy and I would talk about our relationship in four months when I returned to Earth.

*Returned to Earth.*

I grinned at the thought and then remembered I was supposed to be making a video letter. "So that zero-gravity training . . . tip of the iceberg, Darce. It's taken me six weeks to get a handle on moving through the station with some swagger." I chuckled at that. "I've missed handrails, bumped into walls—thankfully not destroying anything because the walls are packed with experiments and wires and pipes. Everything does something. The noise you hear . . . Loud, right?" Hence the reason I had to speak up to be heard. "That's the fans and the pumps. Everything we need to survive. Keeps us warm and provides us with oxygen. Takes some getting used to. Don't know if I ever will, to be honest, but it's worth it for the view. I wish you could see what the world looks like from up here, Darce. The world you're fighting to protect. I get that more than ever now. It's so beautiful. I know you asked me in your emails to describe it. . . . For the first time in my life, I wish I was a writer so I could describe it to you the way Tom can. He writes it all down so that . . . you can almost feel what it's really like to be here. I'll give it a shot for you though.

"Nighttime is my favorite. It's mesmerizing. All the lights . . . sometimes it looks like gold dusted across black marble. Other times the lights are fiercer, like fire burning across the surface of a black river. I think daytime would be your favorite though. Blues and greens and silvers and grays and purples and then suddenly rusts from the desert, smog over the cities, and the rivers of the Amazon can seem like liquid gold. It's an ever-changing landscape. I've been in the Cupola only a few times—that's the observatory module." The Cupola was my favorite place on the station. Through its trapezoidal windows, it provided a 360-degree view of Earth.

"To enter it, you dive into it and then pull yourself up, like diving into a cave. There are cameras in there so we can take photographs. NASA assigned me to take some a couple of days ago, and they posted them to my Instagram so you can check them out. Good thing I got a handle on zero gravity. *Some* of those cameras are expensive." I joked; everything on the ISS was expensive. The station weighed in at a million pounds and was the most expensive object ever built.

"Tom said, on his last mission, they captured a space aurora. I've seen the photos, but I'd kill to see that in real life." The green lights over the planet looked like something out of a science fiction movie.

"You asked a lot about zero gravity. Well, it's like learning to fly, except everything is effortless, you know. It took me a while to get a handle on it because I kept putting too much force into everything. You don't need to. Darce, you'd love it. When we're not spending hours every day on experiments, trying to figure out how to make a spaceship that can venture farther into space while keeping humans healthy and alive, we're having fun."

It was the truth. My father would look down on that. *Nothing in life worth doing is fun.* He'd said that a lot to me when I was growing up. When I was nineteen, I'd finally quipped back, *You've never had great sex, then.* My father didn't care if I was in college. He'd smacked me across the head so hard my ear throbbed for hours afterward.

"Sometimes I'm pulling myself through the ship and I'll look into a station and there's one of the Europeans just tumbling and pirouetting on their downtime." I grinned because it was not uncommon to find me doing the same thing. In fact, four days ago, I'd videoed myself doing just that and sent it to NASA; they added a Bowie track to it and posted the video. It was a hit with social media users. Apparently I'd gone viral two days ago and had accumulated thousands of new followers within hours.

"Here's something cool for you." I reached out for a water pouch I'd strapped to the wall. I'd tucked my feet under a handrail, my back against the wall for support. "I'm in node two," I thought to tell Darcy. "The sleep station. My pod is just down in the floor over there." I pointed off camera at the pod that held my sleeping bag. The bag was tied to the wall, and we just zipped ourselves up in there. "Sleeping in zero gravity is what I imagine sleeping on a cloud is like. It looks weird, like we're wrapped up in a cocoon, but it's the best sleep of my life. Still, enough of making you jealous of my incredible sleeping habitation . . . As requested, water in space."

I chuckled as I carefully opened the pouch and squeezed a little water out. It formed into a bubble that danced in the air in front of me with a wiggle. Placing the closed pouch back on the wall, I gently tapped the water bubble toward the camera and then tapped it back and forth between my fingers.

"Cool, huh?" Then I reached forward and sucked it into my mouth. "I just drank my own piss, Darce. Yes, yes, I did." I laughed, imagining the disgusted look on her beautiful face. "Don't worry, it's purified. Our purification system turns our sweat and urine into water. Clever, right?" I wouldn't tell her I rarely allowed myself to think about the pee part or I might dehydrate.

"Anyway, I could bore you for hours about the work I'm doing up here, but I have to get to node three. That's where we do our mandatory workouts. It's part of our daily routine to strap ourselves into the stationary bike or the treadmill. There's also the ARED, which is a special machine they built so we can do the equivalent of weightlifting and squats. . . . It's my time to work out, and NASA wants me to film it for social media. But I just . . . I wanted you to know I'm okay. I'm better than okay. I might even get to do my first space walk soon. So yeah . . ." I trailed off awkwardly, wondering how to end the video. The disconnection from Darcy suddenly felt more about emotion than the 240 miles between the ISS and Earth's surface.

"I hope you're well." I winced inwardly at how formal I sounded. "That your parents are well and that the case is going great. Let me know how it's going. Send a video back if you have time. But if you do, send it to KateD—all one word—at NASA dot gov. She'll pass it on in a format that's easier to download. I miss your gorgeous face. Talk soon, Darce."

I reached out to stop recording. I emailed the video to Kate, who would pass it on to Darcy for me. While we could email and talk on the phone to everyone outside of NASA via a satellite relay with Mission Control in Houston, our connection was slower than on Earth, so it was just easier to send bigger data files directly to NASA to pass on or upload to our socials.

After stowing my laptop securely in my sleeping pod, I used the handrails to pull me out of node 2 so I could head to node 3 to work out. To do so, I had to pass through the US lab. It was then I remembered Darcy had asked me in her last email if I was lonely, and I hadn't answered her question in my video. It was something

I think many people assumed about being up in the ISS. I didn't have time to feel lonely. I asked Tom about it, and he said he'd never felt less alone than when he was on the station. Maybe that should have been my immediate answer.

I hadn't lied when I said I missed her. Yet, the truth was I didn't miss her the way Tom missed his wife, Pam, and his kids. Sometimes I caught the guy rereading their letters that one of the crew handed to him hours before launch. I wondered what she and the kids said that held him so transfixed and brought peace to his eyes.

I wondered why I didn't feel envious that I didn't get that from Darcy, until I thought of my father and felt a cold splash of reality I'd rather ignore.

My father, Javier Ortiz, co-owner of a multi-industry corporation in Manhattan, eschewed the concept of love. Not just romantic but familial too. Even when my mother was alive, the son of a bitch.

The only affection I'd ever seen my father dole out was to my late brother, Miguel, and some offhand tenderness to my mom when he was in the mood.

There was no affection between us like there had been between him and Miguel.

Although, there was pride. I think he was finally proud of me. Pride wasn't love or affection, but it was better than nothing, and Javier Ortiz was openly proud that his youngest son was an astronaut. Not just any astronaut, but one of only fourteen Latinx astronauts in the history of NASA.

"My father, ladies and gentleman," I muttered to myself as I pulled myself into the training station.

Tom was already inside running on the treadmill. "They scheduled you in here too?" It was unusual for us to be scheduled for a workout at the same time.

My commander didn't shake his head as he ran. Sweat was a problem onboard the space station. With no gravity, sweat expanded across our bodies in wet globs. Any sudden movements could dislodge that glob and hit one of your crewmates. We kept a towel on us during our workouts to soak up the perspiration. Tom wiped his across his forehead. "On my downtime."

And he was working out. I understood that. Anton would laugh at us. He felt it was almost unfair that we had to strap ourselves down a couple of hours a day and force our bodies to move as if we were on Earth. But working out had been a part of my daily routine for as long as I could remember, and as much as I loved zero gravity, a workout was still one of my favorite ways to channel my thoughts and balance my mood.

"I'm just finishing up though. You're a little early."

It didn't surprise me Tom was aware of my schedule. I knew his too.

"Did you send the video?" he asked as he unclipped the harness that pulled him down onto the treadmill.

"Yeah, all done." I held on to a handrail with one hand, video camera in the other.

"Good. Because as much as what we're doing up here matters, it matters because of everyone down there." He pointed toward Earth. "You're focused and you're competent, and I'm glad to have you on my crew, Ortiz. But I still don't know what's driving you. Me, I *love* being an astronaut. I've dreamed of being an astronaut since I was a kid. That love never went away, but I do this now because I love my family, and what we do up here creates progress down there. We're mapping out the future for my kids' kids and their kids' kids, and that matters to me. What matters to you?"

I answered automatically despite his seemingly out-of-left-field question. "Keeping my crew safe, helping my team, while we do all that."

"And that's admirable. But is it enough? We're here for another sixteen weeks. Will your reasons be enough when you haven't had a shower for a hundred and eighty-two days? When you haven't had a fresh meal? When you've had to pee into the funnel for the eight-hundredth time? When you miss sex? And good coffee?"

I was confused but not irritated or defensive about his questions. I'd been training for this mission for the last three years and was used to having my decisions and opinions overanalyzed and questioned and discussed by many people at Mission Control. However, everything he'd asked was situational, and I'd been *trained* to deal with them. "I don't understand."

"My mind is always on my crew and my tasks," Tom elaborated. "But my love for my family and what I've left behind on Earth are what drives me to remain focused."

The light bulb went off. "I'm not the only unmarried, childless astronaut who's ever come up here, Tom."

"No, and those men and women live and breathe being astronauts and have done so since they could say the word. You, Ortiz, considered this career late in the game in comparison. And like I said, you're doing great. I'm thankful you're part of my expedition . . . but I guess what I'm trying to say is that for the rest of us, this is a ride we never get off. We go back to Earth, we stay in Houston, we travel to Star City, we train for the next mission. If that's what you see in your future too, then this conversation is moot."

The conversation wasn't moot.

The next mission.

It was something I hadn't thought about, being so focused on the first one.

Surely if this was a ride I didn't want to get off, I'd have thought about what came afterward more?

My commander gave me one of his looks that said everything without saying anything, and I watched him float by me out of node 3, *now* feeling a little irritated with him.

I set up the video camera, attaching it to the wall in front of the ARED machine, then I pulled the harness down and belted it around my waist. Pulling the bar and attached arms of the ARED over my head, resting the bar across my shoulders to hold me down in place, I wrapped my hands around it like it was a barbell. I paused before I started to do squats. Tom's words rang in my ears.

Forgetting for a second that the video was recording, I exhaled heavily.

"Well . . . fuck."

# THREE

## Hallie

### PRESENT DAY

*I had my first standoff with the PR team, Darce. To be fair, I think I've been pretty easygoing about the social media thing, considering if this wasn't my job, I would never be on those platforms and posting about my life. But when NASA asked me to do it, I thought, Why not? I'm experiencing things that so few humans get to experience, and I want to share that. I want to educate people about what we do up here and do it in a way that's fun and interesting to them. So I push myself out of my comfort zone. And guess what, I even have fun with it. NASA told me I reached over two million followers this week. Two million. That's mind-blowing. And satisfying, and it makes me want to keep going.*

*But NASA wanted Tom to film my first space walk. . . . Darce, I . . . for a moment I thought I might be wrong about this—making a bigger deal out of it than it is—but I want to experience that moment. I don't want to be thinking about thousands of people watching my reaction on Instagram. I want to be thinking about what it feels like to be in space, to have nothing but my suit between me and the stars.*

*Thankfully, Mission Control agreed with me. Spacewalking is dangerous; they need me focused, not thinking about entertaining people. PR was disappointed but eventually agreed. And I'm conflicted, for sure. Should I deprive people of seeing a space walk? I'm not sure I should. But should I deprive myself of true immersion in the moment? It's like how some people can't enjoy a vacation or a day trip somewhere new because they're so busy thinking about capturing the perfect shot or video for their social media accounts that they miss the actual experience itself. That's crazy to me. So I'm doing this one for myself. And Mission Control is doing it this way to keep me safe. Maybe next time. I'm astronaut first, PR vehicle second. For now, saying no is the right thing to do.*

—CAPTAIN CHRISTOPHER ORTIZ, VIDEO DIARY #4

As an adopted New Yorker, I took it seriously that you never meander your way on or off the subway.

However, I was so lost in my thoughts about the man on the video—whom I had identified as Captain Christopher Ortiz, bona fide NASA astronaut—as well as my mother, internet sensation, that I wasn't quick enough at my subway stop that morning. By that I mean, I didn't jump off the train as fast as I should have. The crowd of people pushing to get on was doing a good job of trying to keep me on there with them, and as I shoved my way through, hopping off the train, I didn't realize they caught my trench coat between them.

It was a rainy spring morning, and I'd left my trench open. It was a designer camel trench coat I'd gotten on sale and loved because it was lightweight but had this beautiful fullness to it that set it apart from other trench coats.

That also meant there was a lot of fabric.

And one of the rude morons squeezing past me caught the right side of my coat as they got on the train, pulling it up with them. I knew I couldn't move as I wobbled on the platform, but I couldn't work out why until the doors to the train shut and I saw my coat stuck in between them.

Call it adrenaline, call it my body being instinctively used to bizarre things happening to me, but I dropped my large purse with my laptop in it and spun out of the coat just in time for it to whiz away with the train, the left arm of the coat yanking my shoulder with the force as it was stripped from me.

"Holy shit," I heard behind me. "Fast reflexes!"

I turned to see a group of teenagers I was pretty sure should be in school swaggering toward me, eyes wide, grinning at me.

A boy in ripped tight jeans and a pink oversized sweater hopped toward me, staring at me in awe. "Sis, that was dope!" He high fived me, and I laughed a little hysterically as I high-fived him back. His friends surrounded me, patting me on the shoulders, reaching for their own high fives.

"Right?" I grinned maniacally, still in shock. "So dope." *Why am I saying the word "dope"?*

"Epic as fuck," one girl said. "I so wish we caught it on film."

"Hey," the boy in the pink sweater picked up my bag to hand it to me. "Is that what you're doing?" He glanced around, searching the subway. "You filmin' a stunt show or somethin'?"

"Yeah," I lied, my heart pounding. "Don't do it at home, kids. I'm a professional. Gotta go do . . . more crazy-as-fuck stunts." *Oh, please stop, Hallie.*

They nodded, wide-eyed, asking me if they'd be on the show.

I mumbled something vague and put every ounce of energy into strutting away. Once I was out of sight, my wobbly legs gave up and I slumped into the wall.

*Oh my God, I could have died.* People hurrying downward ignored me because it was New York, and I forced myself upward to the light of day. Every inch of my body shook from my near-death experience.

It wasn't until I was out of the subway, walking through the drizzly city streets and toward the office, that I realized I'd also just lost my favorite coat.

I blamed Captain Christopher Ortiz and my mother for distracting me.

"You told them you were filming a stunt show?" Althea's lips twitched as she stood near the door to my office. "The urge I have to laugh should not undermine my sincere concern for what just happened to you."

"You can laugh. I looked like an idiot high-fiving them."

Althea had one of those contagious cackles so out of sync with her sophisticated good looks that I couldn't help but laugh too.

After a little while, she straightened, wiped tears from her eyes, and forced her full mouth into a serious pinch. "Okay, the last bit was funny. But the bit where you almost died really is not. What happened to you has happened to other people and ended . . . not well. Please be more careful."

The reminder that people had died in incidents like that made me feel mildly nauseated. I couldn't tell George. He would lecture me for days.

"At least my laptop is okay," I said, opening it up on my desk. "Though my poor coat."

"Your coat? You're worried about your coat?"

It was much easier to dwell on the coat than to think about how close I'd just come to death.

"All that matters is that you're alive." Damien, our other colleague, suddenly appeared in the hall outside my office. "You do realize how shallow you seem mourning a coat when your family could be mourning you?"

"Oh please, like you wouldn't be the first one lining up to take her office." Althea glowered at him. "Also, eavesdropping is creepy."

"I'm horrified by the insinuation. About the office, I mean," he replied emotionlessly, then looked around my small space. "Though I'd certainly decorate it more tastefully."

Ever since my promotion to senior event manager, Damien had been a little bit of a shit to me.

Ignoring him, I looked at Althea. "It was a designer coat. I got it on sale. Fifty percent off."

"Ooh, that does hurt."

"So does a train going at fifty miles per hour," Damien quipped.

Althea curled her lip at him. "You're sick."

He smirked at her, his eyes dipping insolently down her long body before returning to me. "Also, that coat didn't even suit you. The train did you a favor."

Out of the corner of my eye, I saw Althea moving closer to the doorway as Damien continued.

"You're really too short for designer pieces like that. You should try—"

Althea slammed the office door shut in his face, and he yelped and jumped back as it almost smacked into his nose.

Althea stared at him through the glass door, smug.

He shot her a murderous look and stomped off out of sight.

I stared up at my friend in awe. "Will you marry me?"

"If it doesn't bother Michelle, then sure." Michelle was her fiancée.

"Why can't Damien be awful-looking to match his soul?" I complained.

"Such is the way."

"You know, you probably hurt his feelings. I really think he genuinely likes you." Althea was Damien's type. He had a models-only rule. Yes, it's true: Damien White was a superficial asshole.

With her perfect umber skin and long slender legs, my friend could have been a model. What she couldn't be was Damien's girlfriend. Althea was way too smart and classy, and way too good for him. And he knew it. Besides, while Althea identified as pansexual, she was seriously taken. She and Michelle met senior year of college, and she'd loved her ever since.

"You're delusional. Besides, I'd have to be desperate to want to date that jerk. He's probably riddled with every STD known to man." She was not wrong. Despite Damien's attractive features, I felt zero attraction toward my ultracompetitive, narcissistic, man whore of a colleague and was truly thankful Althea felt the same way.

"I'm going to make you some tea. A calming herbal one, perhaps?" she offered.

I gave her a look. "Not even a near-death experience will make me break up with coffee."

"Your heart rate must be up. You shouldn't drink coffee. *Ever.*"

"Not going to happen."

"Never say never. I'm getting you an herbal tea." She moved toward the hallway.

"With a dash of milk," I called after her. "And coffee. In fact, just hold the herbal tea altogether!"

"You're yelling, why are you yelling?" Lia strode into my office. "Is it because of the train incident?"

I gaped at my glamorous boss. "How did you hear?"

"Damien told me. And he's wrong about the coat. It was fabulous. I'm sorry for your loss, Hallie. How are things coming along with the Hawthorne engagement party?"

The truth was, I'd hardly slept the night before.

It was clear from that first video I'd opened last night that Darcy had sent me a link to files she hadn't intended me to see. After a quick google, I'd discovered she used to date the astronaut. And by used to, I mean they must have broken up while he was still onboard the International Space Station, most likely because she'd met Matthias. By my calculation (and maybe after stalking his Instagram account of *millions* of followers!) Christopher had returned to Earth around six months ago. I'd found interviews of him on daily and late-night talk shows that occurred for several weeks upon his return. That wasn't usual for most astronauts, but Chris had gone viral with a handful of his social media posts from the ISS and had become well-known globally. As the talk show hosts hinted, his good looks were definitely a factor in his popularity, but they also discussed how he was famous for being only the third Mexican American astronaut in space and had a huge following among the Mexican American community. I noticed in every interview that Chris acknowledged his background and was visibly humbled by the support of the Latinx community, but he also didn't seem comfortable talking about his rise to fame.

Or his hotness.

And that was one hella sexy astronaut.

Which was why he was so familiar to me. I'd obviously come across him in passing.

I'd watched three of Christopher's video letters to Darcy before I forced myself to focus on work.

There was also more than a slight chance that I'd downloaded *all* the videos to my computer.

Feeling sneaky and guilty, I covered it with a benign smile. "Great! They have vastly different tastes, but I think there are ways to bring those tastes together. I've got some ideas to pitch to them today at our lunch."

"Hit me with them." Lia settled down on the velvet occasion chair in my office. My boss had collaborated with one of Manhattan's best interior designers to turn our small offices into chic spaces that exuded our style and attention to detail.

I nodded, throwing Christopher's gorgeous face from my mind.

I replied, "Uh . . . well . . . Matthias would like a rock band while Darcy hates that idea and would prefer a string quartet. Easiest solution I can think of is to have a string quartet play instrumental versions of Matthias's favorite rock songs."

"Perfect, I love it. What else?"

"Well, I like it," Matthias said in his mellifluous French accent.

Darcy looked at her fiancé. Her brow puckered in thought before turning to me.

I tried not to squirm.

Since I'd arrived at our lunch meeting on Sixth Avenue, I'd felt shifty. The Italian restaurant was a ten-minute walk from our offices on West Nineteenth Street, and it was not uncommon to see celebrity faces at the cool spot. It did not surprise me this was where Darcy Hawthorne wanted to meet for lunch. The Hawthornes had been a big deal in East Coast society for more than a hundred years. Darcy's family owned one of the world's biggest hotel chains. Most people had expected her to go into the family business, but not only had she studied law, she was an environmental lawyer trying to make a difference in the world. And despite all her family's gazillions, her legs that went on forever and ever, and the fact that she liked to dine in overpriced restaurants, a person couldn't help but admire the heck out of her.

Besides, she was nice.

Well . . . usually.

Now she had me pinned to my chair with her gray eyes as I nervously awaited her opinion on my music compromise. Her long, thick blond hair was pulled back in a sleek ponytail. Darcy wore flared black high-waist pants and a stunning silk blouse with oversized sleeves. She was so chic, and despite the nontraditional business attire, she also looked like a twenty-first-century professional who could bludgeon my reputation to death with her six-inch heels.

Suddenly she grinned. Her smile was a revelation. It was the first thing I noticed about her when we met—Darcy Hawthorne had the sweetest, warmest smile, completely incongruous to her intimidating looks.

I wondered if her smile had attracted Christopher.

And Matthias, of course.

I relaxed. "You like?"

"Yes." Darcy nodded, turning that smile on Matthias as she curled her hand around his on the table. "I think it's the perfect compromise. It'll surprise my mother when the violinist plays the opening notes to Nirvana's 'Smells Like Teen Spirit.'" Her eyes filled with laughter. "But I'm actually looking forward to that moment."

We all chuckled, and I continued to share more of my thoughts about how we could bring their two personalities together for the engagement party.

It was going well until Darcy commented, "These suggestions are near perfect. You took the ideas we sent you and came up with a plan we just couldn't imagine. You're wonderful."

Guilt consumed me at the reminder that Darcy had sent me a

link to her cloud account that allowed me access to not only her engagement inspiration boards but also those videos from her ex-boyfriend.

"Are you okay?" She leaned toward me. "You look . . . oh God, is it something you ate?" She looked down at her own empty salad plate in concern.

"No, I'm fine. I . . ." I wanted to blurt out the truth. That I'd watched private videos meant only for her.

But a little voice in my head stopped me.

That voice belonged to my boss.

"I just remembered that the musicians I wanted to hire for your party might not be available," I lied, my cheeks unbearably hot.

"Oh no." Darcy looked stricken, making me feel awful.

"It's all right, *mon ange*." Matthias slipped his arm around her shoulders, drawing her into his side. "We will find others."

"Don't worry." I hurried to assure them. "It was just a thought. I could be wrong. I will check that and let you know ASAP."

By the time we finished lunch, the lie between us had drained me. The right thing to do would have been to tell the truth. However, as I pondered my dilemma, I realized that Christopher hadn't really spoken intimately about their relationship in his video letters. The three I'd watched so far were really about what he was doing on the space station. I'd never thought space would be interesting, and I didn't know if it was the superhot astronaut explaining his mission or that his enthusiasm was so infectious.

I think it was both.

Definitely both.

Okay, maybe more of the former than the latter, but still.

Space was fun. And hot. Well, actually it was freezing, but he made it really hot.

I ignored the stupid flutter in my belly as I returned to the office. For goodness' sake, I had a boyfriend. No way should I develop the equivalent of a high school crush on a man I didn't even know.

"I made it!" I gasped for air as George opened the door to his apartment in Brooklyn. While I rented a one-bedroom apartment in Kensington that made me long for the backpacking life, George, my financial manager boyfriend—whom I'd only seen once a week in the last month because of his busy career—rented a top-floor apartment in an attractive brownstone in Prospect Heights. It was so much bigger and brighter and airier than my place, and I really hoped one day he might ask me to move in with him so we could see each other more.

My hope had nothing to do with his master bathroom or the four hundred square feet of extra space. Really.

George stared at me like I was a lunatic. "Why are you sweating?"

I pushed past him into the apartment. "You wanted me . . ." I breathed through a stitch in my rib, holding my side for a second. "Me . . . you wanted me . . . here at six thirty. I think I'm dying." I leaned on his leather sectional for support.

"I didn't say kill yourself to do it." My boyfriend placed a hand on my back. "Jesus, you're really hot."

I grinned through my breathlessness. "Why, thank you. You're not too shabby yourself."

He frowned at me. "Where is your coat? Did you decide to forgo one since you planned on running here?"

Remembering my near-death experience on the subway that morning, I stiffened. "Something like that."

I gazed toward the kitchen. The main living space was open-plan. "What's cooking? I don't smell anything." I turned back to

George. "Are we doing takeout? Oh, and hey!" I hugged him, relieved when he hugged me back, because he was acting kind of weird. Usually the first thing he did when he saw me was hug me. George was six feet four, an entire foot taller than me. We shared an apathy for working out, and I loved that he wasn't muscly and intimidating. He gave good cuddle.

"So yeah, hey." He squeezed me and then set me back. "Let's talk."

Dread filled me as he took my hand and led me to the sectional.

We all knew what "let's talk" was code for. My heart raced.

Once we sat down, I blurted out, "Are you breaking up with me?"

George's mossy-green eyes were his most attractive feature. I loved staring into his eyes. Usually. Not now, while they filled up with pity.

Yuck.

"Hallie, you're great." He gave me a condescending smile and a pat on my hand. "You're cute, and you're fun, and the sex is definitely in my top three, but you're like the kind of girl I enjoyed dating in college, you know. You get into hilarious situations that make us all laugh, and you're always up for a party."

I was?

I couldn't remember the last time I partied.

College, I think.

"But I'm thirty this year and . . . uh . . . well . . . I work for very important clients, and I have to attend a lot of serious, sophisticated events, and, uh . . . well, that's not really your thing."

I gaped at him, stunned. "Not my thing? I *organize* those events."

"Exactly!" He grinned as if pleased I understood.

Understood what?

I understood crap!

"You plan *parties* for a living. Who does that? And you can't tell people what you're really thinking because you want everyone to love you. You eat things you hate eating to please people who actually couldn't give a fuck if you eat their awful canapés, and you end up in these mortifying situations because you can't say no. Yes, it's funny, but it's also embarrassing for me. I need a wife who is serious. A wife with a backbone. A wife with an impressive high-powered job who gets what that's like and understands the seriousness of my work, you know. And, um, I think we've lasted this long because you are very *giving* in the bedroom . . . but I can't keep following my dick. It's time to grow up."

Did he just say what I think he said?

I sprang to my feet, so outraged I felt like I was choking. I could feel my face darkening with furious, fiery blood and a lack of oxygen.

I was fun and cute and *giving* in the bedroom?

I *embarrassed* him?

He'd dated me this long only because I was *giving* in the bedroom?

For a start, three months wasn't that long, and we'd barely seen each other for one month. Oh, and my people-pleasing bothered him? Really? What the hell did he think drove me to *give* in the bedroom when he never *ever* gave back?

No, sirree, he did not.

I'd wasted my best stuff on him.

Only for the condescending asshole to tell me I wasn't good enough to be his girlfriend?

*You are a pompous . . . selfish . . . mundane* . . . "Little man!" I yelled the last part of my thoughts out loud.

George blinked up at me in shock. "I'm six four," he replied inanely.

I raised an eyebrow and crooked my pinkie finger at him. "Yes, and in proportion you are not."

He gaped, his voice high-pitched as he threw back, "Uh! That was hurtful, unnecessary, and just confirms I'm right to break up with you."

*I* had been hurtful? "You just told me I had no backbone, that I embarrass you, and that the only reason you dated me was for sex."

"That last one is a compliment!"

My head exploded. "I have to leave." I spun around, tripping over the corner of the damn sectional as I tried to make my escape.

"I think that's best. You really are too sensitive, Hallie."

Choking back the words I wanted to say because I knew he'd just turn them around on me, I slammed out of his apartment. My fury kept me warm as I marched through the chilly spring evening to the subway. I got off at Church Avenue, and it wasn't until I was safe inside my apartment that I announced in a strong, forthright manner to the empty room, "George, you are a patronizing, derogatory, condescending, toxic man-child. And you're bad in bed!"

Wishing I'd had the guts to just say it, no matter his reaction, I promptly burst into tears.

The tears weren't for George. I could never miss someone who had spoken to me like that. No, the tears were pure frustration. With myself.

"At least you said the thing about his penis," I muttered as I switched on the coffee machine and ordered Chinese takeout on my phone. But I even felt bad about that. What if I gave him a complex about the size of his penis? Honestly, it wasn't even small . . . it just wasn't in proportion to his height.

I called Althea and told her what happened, needing reassurance I wasn't a horrible person.

"And why the hell are you worried about giving *him* a complex? Girl, he basically told you that you weren't good enough for him." My friend snapped angrily. "I hope that comment about his penis haunts him every time he whips it out."

I burst into laughter, feeling tears of amusement prick my eyes instead. "Oh God, I love you."

"I love you too. And whatever you do next . . . do not call one of your college friends to tell them about this, okay?"

I frowned because I had been planning on calling Gabby next. Gabby was not only my college roommate but also my best friend from high school. She worked and lived in Newark, so I didn't get to see her often, but we talked every week. Still . . . maybe Althea was right.

Let's just say George wasn't the only one who had pinned me with a rep I didn't deserve.

Later, I sat down on my couch, laptop on lap, take-out carton in hand, and proceeded to watch the rest of the videos Christopher had sent Darcy. My phone buzzed and binged, but seeing it was missed calls from both my parents, for once I put myself first and ignored them. I'd pay for it in the morning when I contacted them.

By the time I'd watched all the videos of Christopher, I wasn't even thinking about George, which just said it all.

Instead I googled every little bit of information I could find on Christopher Ortiz, looked at a ton of his Instagram posts, and rewatched his talk show interviews.

It wasn't until I thought about the last video letter, the one that had been his most personal yet, that the remorse kicked in bigtime.

I'd watched video letters that weren't meant for my eyes and ears. This man, this super intelligent, charismatic man who exuded joy and kindness, had sent these private videos to his girlfriend and did not know a perfect stranger had watched them all.

And intended to watch them all again.

He deserved to know.

And I should apologize.

George was wrong. I *had* a backbone. I should send a video letter apology to Christopher, a stranger I had a crush on, even though he'd probably hate me after, because it was the right thing to do.

# FOUR

## Chris

### PRESENT DAY

Standing in the prewar apartment Mom left me, I gazed out the large window at the city before me. Most New Yorkers would kill for this apartment. I loved it. Not just for its view or the fact that it was eleven hundred square feet of space in Midtown East, but because it was a piece of my mother.

My father had bought her the apartment. My mom was a server at a party my father's business partner, Benjamin Clairmont, had dragged him to. Javier was a highly intelligent college student on an academic scholarship, juggling multiple jobs, struggling but determined not to fail when he met Ben at college. Their friendship turned into a business partnership, funded by Ben's seed money, but it was my father's shrewd mind that grew it into what it would become. Ben opened doors to the business world via his father's connections, but I don't know if either he or Ben expected the level of success that they achieved. They were just on the cusp of that success when my father met my mother at that party. She was a beautiful, hardworking white girl with grand ambitions, and I think, despite his claims about practicality over passion, he loved her. She told me that she'd confided to him about wanting to live in "an apartment in the sky," and so he bought her the Midtown East place as a wedding gift.

But then they had Miguel and decided they wanted a house outside the city. But the Midtown East apartment stayed in my mom's name, and she didn't want to give it up. Sentimental attachment. With financial backing from my father, Mom had gone back to school, studied interior design, and had launched what would become a very successful interior design company.

She'd taken down two walls in the apartment, turning it into a spacious one bedroom and an open-plan living area with a kitchen, dining, and sitting room, all with a massive corner window that looked out over the city.

When Mom died, he sold our family home and bought a bigger apartment in Manhattan, and Mom left the apartment to me and Miguel. When I turned eighteen, it was ours. We'd kept it as a rental, but after my brother died, I took the money Mom had left us from the sale of her company to cover the monthly maintenance costs and moved in. I'd updated the decor to put my taste into it since it hadn't been touched in years.

My inheritance was being eaten up by the costs on this apartment because I hadn't made any decisions on what to do next professionally.

And I refused to take anything from my father.

I'd made low six figures a year with NASA, but that door was no longer open.

The only decision I'd made so far was to retire from the air force. I'd been a test pilot before I'd applied to NASA.

That had not gone down well with my father. Leaving combat, I mean, to become a test pilot. I'd made captain in four years in the air force, and just as they had honored me with the rank at a mere twenty-seven years old, Miguel died. My brother was the whole reason I'd signed up for military life, applying to the Air Force Academy at eighteen, graduating with my degree in systems engineering. I trained as a tactical fighter pilot. I served my country. And none of it seemed to matter once Miguel was gone. All his life he'd dreamed of being an astronaut, talked about the decisions he'd wished he'd made that would have taken him down the path to applying to NASA. So when he died, I was not only weary of combat, I'd decided my skills were best put elsewhere, somewhere useful. So I'd applied to train at the test pilot school at Edwards Air Force Base with the vision of one day applying for the astronaut training program at NASA. If Miguel couldn't be here to do it, I'd do it for him. I'd impressed them so much at Edwards that I ended up serving as an exchange officer at Patuxent River Naval Air Station as a pilot performing research for NASA.

I just didn't know what I wanted to do with my life. Now that the dream was completed for Miguel.

For months, I'd hung around this apartment, lost. And it wasn't like the world wasn't watching. NASA PR got me on talk shows once I'd gone through weeks of recovery; I'd kept up the Instagram account, sharing with the world what recovery from space travel was like. Then experimenting with sharing random, everyday photos of New York and lunches with friends; my maternal aunt's dog, Bandit; walks on the beach near her home . . . and to my shock, those photos and videos racked up views and comments too. Bizarrely, I still interested people, even in my non-astronaut form.

They weren't the only ones watching the suddenly sleepy pace of my life back on Earth though. My father was definitely watching. Avoiding his phone calls and worrying about the fact that I would soon be forced to move out of the one place that made me feel close to my mother had become my full-time job. If I didn't rent the apartment, it would eventually eat away at my inheritance and savings until I had nothing, and then I'd have to sell it.

The realization was a dull ache in my chest.

Turning from the windows that looked down over East Forty-Sixth Street, I decided to change into my workout gear. I liked to jump on the tram to Roosevelt Island and jog around now that it was finally possible to do it. Three months after my return to Earth, my first week back in Manhattan, I'd gone for a jog. Big mistake. My limbs were heavy, I couldn't catch my breath, and I felt faint. I'd realized with much frustration that despite the physiotherapy and tests we'd undergone upon our return, my heart just wasn't ready for that kind of activity yet and neither were my bones.

Now it was. I worked out every day, and it was good to have my body back. Even though, I admit, I missed zero gravity.

I'd just pulled a T-shirt on and grabbed my keys off the sideboard in the foyer when my cell beeped in the living room. Striding over, I picked it up and raised an eyebrow at the banner across the screen. Apparently I had an email from Kate, my IT contact at NASA.

I tapped it open.

Chris,

I received this video in my email. It's addressed to you. Let me know what you want me to do about it.

Kate

That was cryptic.

When I tapped open the video, a woman with cotton candy–pink hair filled my phone screen. She had huge long-lashed blue eyes, which, paired with the pink hair . . . she looked like a Disney character.

I'd never seen her before in my life.

"Hi, Christopher." She gave the camera a little wave. "You don't know me."

"I know that," I muttered a little impatiently.

"But I'm Darcy Hawthorne's engagement party planner, Hallie Goodman, and she accidentally sent me your video letters from the International Space Station. And I watched them. I'm so sorry! Darcy doesn't know, and I feel just awful—"

I switched her off, feeling a burn of something more than irritation as I tried to remember exactly what I'd said in those videos to Darce. Things a complete stranger now knew. Who did that?

Surely when you opened a video and saw it was private . . . you closed it and deleted it, no? You didn't watch the whole thing and then watch all the others.

I hit Reply to Kate.

> Don't know her. Don't think she should have your email. Make this thing bounce so she thinks your email is dead.

A second later, I got Kate's reply.

> You got it.

---

Four hours later, I was jogging down Lily Pond Lane, a tree-lined street in East Hampton. Hedges that had grown high for privacy hid the beautiful homes, while towering trees spaced sporadically along the street offered even more shelter from prying eyes.

The sun was bright in the midday sky, casting shadows from the tree branches, like delicate lacework across the road in front of my feet.

It was two miles from the train station at East Hampton to my aunt Richelle's house on the beach. I'd jogged it in fifteen minutes, enjoying the sweat that beaded across my skin, the heat in my muscles as my feet pounded concrete. This was much nicer than jogging in the city.

But I'd had to take a train at Penn Station, and it had taken two hours to get here.

I did not know what had driven me to jog to the train station. I just knew that when I stepped out of my apartment building, instead of turning left, I turned right. Jogging past the Chrysler and the Empire State Buildings, I suddenly was at Penn, waiting on the next train that would take me to the Hamptons.

Turning right, down a lane that led toward the beach, I realized how much I'd missed this kind of peace away from the frenetic energy of the city. When I was on the ISS, I'd gotten used to the quiet, the distance from human society. But human noise was also the thing I'd grown to crave by the second to last month of the mission.

Funny how the grass was always greener.

My aunt lived at the end of this lane, her house right on the beach, her back lawn having direct access to the sand. It was a moderate-sized (for the Hamptons) four-bedroom home with a swimming pool. Too big for one person, really, but my aunt was once a big deal in the art world. She and my mom were both extremely creative, and while Mom channeled it into interior design, Aunt Richelle was passionate about her painting. Aunt Richelle said her own success was partly finding the right gallery, the right patron, at the right time.

Aunt Richelle bought the Hampton beach house years ago because she said it fed her artist's soul. While her paintings weren't as sought-after as they once were, my aunt really didn't seem to care. The money from those earlier years had set her up nicely, and she assured me she had all she needed.

I could understand why this was the place she decided to live as I drew to a stop outside the double-door front entrance, breathing in the sea air.

There was no answer when I knocked, so I pulled my cell out of the back of my jogging pants and called her.

She answered on the third ring.

I couldn't remember a time when Aunt Richelle hadn't answered when I called her.

"How are you, sweetheart?" she asked without preamble.

"Well, I'm currently standing outside your front door wondering why no one is answering. Are you out?"

"Are you here?" Her voice rose an octave with excitement.

I grinned. "Yeah, that's what I just said. I'm here."

"I'm on the beach with Bandit. Let yourself in. I'll be five minutes."

Eyes narrowed, I tried the handle on her front door and it opened. "Aunt Richelle, you leave your door open?" I stepped inside the cool home, irritated and concerned.

"Nothing ever happens here."

"Until it does. Promise me, from now on you'll lock your doors." My voice was hard as I moved through the open hallway and staircase into the main living area. A large kitchen, dining area, and living space all looked out on the yard through bifold doors. The sea glimmered beneath the sun beyond the lawn.

Aunt Richelle sighed. "Okay, I promise. Help yourself to a beer. And I just baked a fresh batch of banana bread and cookies."

"I adore you." My stomach growled at the thought of my aunt's famous banana bread.

She laughed, and the line went quiet.

I didn't care. I was already on a mission.

By the time Aunt Richelle returned to the house, I'd eaten two slices of banana bread. I was nursing a bottle of ice-cold beer when she burst through the doors and got hip-checked by Bandit, who tore past her as soon as he saw me.

Bandit was a large white Old English sheepdog named for the unusual black patches of fur across both of his eyes.

"Jesus." I had just put my glass down safely before Bandit launched his big hairy body at me. "Hey, boy." I laughed, lifting my chin to avoid his kisses. I gave him a rubdown as he barked and panted with joy.

"Okay, Bandit, out of the way, out of the way." Aunt Richelle pulled him gently by the collar out from between us so she could envelop me in a hug.

"I'm sweaty—" I tried to say, but it was too late.

"I don't care." She huffed, squeezing me tight.

I returned her embrace, inhaling her familiar scent with a sense of relief as I lifted her off her feet.

Aunt Richelle giggled like a little girl, and I chuckled, finally releasing her.

She pulled back to clasp my face, and she looked so much like my mother, I felt a sharp twist in my chest. "So what brings you here . . ." She glanced down at my attire. "No luggage?"

I shook my head. "Honestly, I don't know how I got here. I went out for a jog, and the next thing I know I'm on a train to you."

I felt her scrutiny for about two seconds before she said, "You have clothes in your room if you need to change. You're welcome to stay as long as you like."

Another reason I loved my aunt. Unlike my father, she didn't badger me with questions or commands. She knew when I was ready to talk, I'd talk.

"Thanks." I leaned in and kissed her cheek. "I missed you."

She beamed, her smile the same as Mom's. There were only four years between Mom and Richelle, my aunt Richelle being the younger sibling. The Wilsons had only each other growing up.

No big extended family. Just my grandparents and Mom and Richelle. My maternal grandfather had been a plumber and my grandmother a nurse.

When I was three years old, my grandparents had gone on a rare vacation to Maine. On the first night in the new lodge they'd rented, they'd died in their sleep from carbon monoxide poisoning from the faulty flue installation of the wood burner in the bedroom.

It had devastated Aunt Richelle and my mother. I never knew my grandparents, but my mom and aunt had told me so much about them over the years, I almost felt like I had. I'd seen photographs, and both sisters were the spitting image of my grandmother when they were younger.

Thick blond hair, eyes as blue as the Caribbean from space. Tall too, at five ten. They were beautiful. Or maybe I was biased. I didn't think so though. I think my mother's beauty was a big part of the attraction for my father. He was a man who liked to procure beautiful things.

As I climbed the stairs to the guest room designated as mine, my gaze passed over the photos Aunt Richelle had hung on the wall of the stairwell. Photos of my grandparents, of the parties Richelle held at the beach house years ago, of Miguel.

I touched his photo. "Brother," I murmured as I passed.

Then I stopped again at a photo I'd seen a million times.

Of my father and Mom at some gala or other.

My mother was stunning in a red gown and my father handsome and severe in a black tux. While Mom smiled at the camera, my father stared stonily ahead, his hand resting possessively on her back.

She died from ovarian cancer when I was sixteen years old.

I never saw my father cry once. I sneered before moving upward.

A photo of Mom sitting on the porch swing of the small house she'd grown up in. She was a teenager in the picture. The sight of her eased my anger.

"*Te amo, jefa.*"

The small amount of Spanish we'd learned hadn't come from our father. Our father didn't teach us anything about his Mexican heritage. In fact, it was the opposite. No, Miguel had learned that "*jefa*" was an affectionate word meaning "boss" that Mexicans often used when addressing their mothers. We loved it because Mom was definitely our boss and had both her boys wrapped around her finger. Whenever we were in trouble, we'd weasel our way out of it by telling her, "*Te amo, jefa.*" Never in front of our father. He'd snapped at Miguel to speak English when he'd overheard him call Mom that.

Staring into her laughing eyes, I missed her warmth. Her support. Her wisdom. She'd been everything to me. For years I'd had focus, I'd had goals, and now that I had none of that, it was like the seventeen years since she'd passed were but months.

"God, I miss you." Fighting back tears of grief, surprised by the ferociousness of it, I retreated to the bedroom. Once in the shower, I let the jets of water pound down on my shoulders, slicking away the sweat and hopefully the bitterness. I thought I'd won that fight long ago.

It had never been more clear since returning to Earth that I hadn't made peace with my father.

That's *why* I'd come here to this house.

There could be no pride or ego or arrogance in an astronaut. An inability to put all that aside and listen to advice, or admit when you needed help, could cost you or your crew their lives. So I knew when to admit that I needed something.

And I needed family.

I needed support to figure out my path forward.

The only person left in my life who could truly give that to me was Aunt Richelle.

---

It was late. Or early. The sun had long set, the hands on the grandfather clock in the dining room had passed midnight. And for the first time in months, I didn't feel restless. Aunt Richelle and I had eaten out back, watching the surf meet the golden shores. We'd drunk beer, talked about my worries, my future, about her paintings, and her neighbor's hatred of Bandit.

A few hours. That's all it took for me to feel like I wasn't so off-balance anymore.

Aunt Richelle had departed for bed before midnight, leaving me on the porch swing out back. I sat for hours in the dark, just listening to the soothing sound of gentle waves lapping at the beach.

The sound of my phone beeping at my side jolted me, and I cursed at the disruption as I reached for it.

I frowned, seeing the notification.

Another email from Kate at NASA.

Chris,

Got another. Do you want me to bounce this one too?

Kate

What the . . .

I opened the attached video, and it was the pink-haired woman again.

Maybe it was my more relaxed mood, but this time I watched the whole thing.

# FIVE

## Hallie

*I got to use the MinION again today. I don't think I've told you about it, but I know you'll think it's clever. It's a portable DNA sequencer, and today I was using it to extract DNA from samples of space bacteria. I am sequencing DNA in space without a lab, just with a MinION. Here's how it works: I take samples of bacteria found onboard the ISS, use the MinION to extract the DNA, sequence it, and see if it's changed or evolved. The results help us diagnose illnesses up here, and we can identify microbes growing on the station and figure out if they might be a threat to our health. These experiments are important for us while we're onboard, but there's a possibility this could be used in the future to identify DNA-based life-forms found in space. It's all very cool. I feel like a mad scientist and . . . I needed the work today, the distraction. Tom said something to me a while back that's been playing on my mind ever since, and the closer I get to returning to Earth, the more I can't stop thinking about it. I'm . . . I'm worried about the future, Darce. I'm worried what I'll do when I get back.*

*Fuck, I haven't admitted that to anyone up here. It seems ridiculous to be anxious about it while I've got weeks to go, so much to experience and enjoy. But I can't help it. I wonder what comes after this. I wonder how I ever move on from an experience like this. I worry that nothing is ever enough for my father. You get that, right? I know you get that.*

*Ah, well . . . I guess there are no answers right now. I have to focus on this current mission. But . . . I feel better for saying it out loud, for telling you. Maybe you'll have some words of encouragement to keep me going, keep me living in the now. I miss you. I miss Aunt Richelle and even that crazy dog. I guess every day can't be all sunshine and roses on the International Space Station—so to speak. But I'm okay. I'm always okay. This helped. Thanks, gorgeous. Talk soon.*

—CAPTAIN CHRISTOPHER ORTIZ, VIDEO DIARY #6

At first, when my email bounced, I felt disappointed. I had so wanted to relieve myself of the guilt of having watched Christopher Ortiz's video letters. However, when I got home that night after an unbelievable day that honestly made this week the most ridiculous week of my life, I saw it as an opportunity.

I realized I had felt so much better when I made the video confessing that I'd watched his video letters. It felt good to put that out there into the universe.

Maybe I didn't need someone at the end of the video to still feel good about venting about my life. I felt like I couldn't vent to my friends because no one seemed to take me seriously anymore. Althea did . . . but I was a little worried if I told her too much, she'd start to see me as a joke too.

I could treat the video like a kind of diary, sending it out into the internet as if it were going to reach Chris, while safe knowing that my private thoughts were still my own. Perhaps that was silly. I said all this into the camera as I sat before my laptop that evening to tell "Chris" about my week.

"It all started with Joe Ashley . . ." I continued into the camera. I went on to explain about my coat on the subway, the teens afterward, and George's cruel breakup. I didn't cry because I was still too angry for tears—I'd wasted three months on that jackass.

"But as if to prove him, and almost everyone else in my life, right—that I am a ridiculous person who has ridiculous things happen to them—my lunch break got really weird. . . ."

"I would come with you," Althea said as I stopped at her cubicle in the main shared office space to ask if she wanted to join me for coat shopping, "but I have to work through lunch. Lia's spot in *New York Style* magazine is under threat because Koy Event Management just booked an event for a Montenegrin royal, and they think that's more exciting than what we've got going on." My friend was one of our marketing coordinators, even though Althea eventually wanted to do what I did. She looked frazzled, and she never looked frazzled.

Concerned, I offered, "Want help? I could go coat shopping later."

Althea gave me a soft look. "No, I got this. Amanda de la Cruz is just a little hard to get a hold of."

"Amanda de la Cruz of *New York Style* magazine?"

"Yeah. She's my contact, why?"

"Well, she hired us two years ago and owes us for talking a VIP client into another venue when they demanded the Rainbow Room on the same date as her wedding last year. A gentle reminder about that might just do the trick."

"You're a lifesaver, Hallie." Althea was already tapping numbers on her landline phone. "Now go buy a coat . . . and one that won't kill you this time."

A few minutes later I was on Fifth Avenue, diving quickly in and out of stores, looking for a trench coat. What? I'd make sure I kept it closed whenever I got on and off the subway.

In all honesty, the hunt for the coat was as much to keep me distracted as it was a desperate need for the perfect spring outerwear. Now and then I'd get flashbacks of George breaking up with me, his horrible words echoing around and around in my head. And then I'd remember affectionate moments between us during the last three months, like snuggling with him after sex and talking to him about my parents' divorce, and I'd cringe at the memories.

I hated that I'd made myself vulnerable to someone who thought so poorly of me.

It wasn't the first time, obviously. I'd been broken up with before. But that didn't make it any easier to stomach.

Forcing the memories out of my head, I zeroed in on my task. Fifteen minutes into the hunt, I walked into a store and was checking through the racks of their coat section when I spotted a camel trench draped over a coat sale rack like someone couldn't be bothered to put it back in its rightful place.

My eyes lit up in delight.

"Please be my size, please be my size; please be on sale, please be on sale." I reached for the coat, frowning at the lack of a tag. Someone had clearly snapped it off while trying it on.

Though somewhat reluctant to try on something that I maybe couldn't afford, I slipped on the trench with its butter-soft fabric. It sat perfectly on my shoulders.

Yay!

Hurrying over to a full-length mirror at the shoe department, I twisted and turned, admiring myself in the coat that was almost identical to the one I'd lost.

Maybe my luck was turning.

"Where's my coat?" I heard a frantic voice in the distance but paid only vague attention. I was too busy searching for a sales assistant who may or may not break my heart by telling me I couldn't afford my new coat.

Spotting a tall, slender man dressed sharply in pants, shirt, and tie, I waved him down. "Hi." I beamed, hoping my cheerful smile might put something like a 50 percent discount out into the universe, "Can you tell me how—"

"That's my coat! Stop her! Thief!"

Spinning around to see who was trying to steal something from the store, I was shocked to find a red-faced, angry woman in stylish thick black glasses storming toward me.

"Thief! She's stealing my coat!" she shrieked hysterically.

And that was when I realized she was talking about me.

Understanding dawned, and horrified, I looked down at myself.

I shrugged out of the trench faster than when mine got caught in the subway doors.

"Oh, no, no, no, no," I held it out to her, pleading with her and the sales assistant who looked at me like a bug he'd quite like to step on. "It was lying over the sales rack. I thought it was for sale."

"Likely story." The woman yanked the coat from my hands and turned to the assistant. "Where is security?"

My eyes widened in panic, my cheeks so hot I swear they could keep me and anyone in the vicinity warm during a New York winter. "Seriously, this is a complete misunderstanding." *Fuck. My. Life!*

The assistant's expression softened. "I don't think security is necessary. It seems like a mistake to me."

"She tried to steal my coat. This coat costs more than everything in your store combined!"

He raised an imperious eyebrow, huffed at the insult, and promptly stalked off.

"Uh, hello!"

"Hey, hey, hi." I grabbed her attention. "I am so sorry. I really thought it was for sale, and I could explain to you about the loss of my own trench coa—" I stopped at her darkening expression and hurried on. "But clearly you're a busy woman, so let me just make this whole misunderstanding up to you. I'll, uh . . . I'll, uh . . ." I glanced around the store, looking for the cheapest thing I could gift her.

What? I was nice, not a Rockefeller.

Spotting a rack of novelty socks, I gestured to them like they were made of gold. "I'll buy you a pair of socks!"

Trench Coat Woman scowled ferociously at me. Then, just when I thought she might start shrieking for security again, she looked at the rack of socks in consideration. "What kind of socks?"

Relief made my body sag. "Any kind of socks you like."

She stalked over to the sock rack and I tentatively followed her. Turning the rack, she surveyed her options. "Any pair?"

Crap, she was so going to choose the most expensive ones. "Any pair."

"How about this pair?" She lifted a pair of bright pink socks with brown kittens on them.

I grimaced without thinking. "Those? Really?"

The woman's face mottled with renewed anger.

*Oh, shit in a sandstorm.* I pulled the socks off the rack. "Cutest socks ever."

She looked like she was plotting my death.

Seriously.

Angry, angry lady.

Seeing another pair of socks in blue with white kittens, I grabbed those. "And I'll even throw in these. So cute." My smile strained with eagerness. "Your glasses are awesome, by the way."

After a few seconds of scowling, Trench Coat Woman's face softened. "They *are* really awesome." She reached back toward the sock rack. "Can I get the yellow pair with the red kittens too?"

"I didn't tell Althea," I said into the camera, still mortified from today's shenanigans. "I mean . . . there's just so much even your best friend can accept as truth. No one would believe a person if they told them they almost died on the subway losing their coat, lied to a bunch of teens that it was a deliberate stunt, got broken up with on the same day, and then accidentally tried on the angriest woman in the world's coat less than twenty-four hours later and got accused of stealing it. And then had to fork over forty bucks for three pairs of kitten socks just to appease her." I groaned into my hands and then flopped back in my seat. "Seriously. I'm exhausted. And I haven't even gotten around to what happened a few hours later."

Concerned that my mom's video might go viral beyond my immediate circles, I'd deleted that social media app for a few days. I just didn't want to know about it if it was out of my control. However, deciding I'd have heard if it had anyway, and that nothing worse could surely happen to me today, I'd reinstalled the app during my commute home from work.

Thankfully, Aunt Julia had gotten Jenna to delete the video of Mom, but clearly not before it was shared with all my friends and extended family. My inbox was full of messages from people asking about it, friends telling me I must be so mortified, family scolding my mom or cheering her on, depending on whose side of the divorce they were on.

I emailed back family members who had berated me as if it were my fault, apologizing if the video had upset them and reminding them my mother had been drunk, and "Hadn't we all done things we regretted when drunk?" *I'm looking at you, Aunt Keira.* She once danced topless on her pool table at a New Year's Eve party *in front of children* . . . and she had the audacity to call my mom an embarrassment to the family.

Done with that, I finally listened to the voice mail message my dad had left me after I failed to answer his calls.

"Hallie Meredith Goodman, I put you through college, young lady. Why am I getting calls and texts about some pornographic video your mother starred in? I shouldn't have to deal with your mom's ridiculousness. I don't want this to get back to Miranda. And call me—Alison wants a pool party for her sixteenth birthday, and Miranda would like your help to plan it. I said you'd do it for free since we're all family. Call me back, Hallie."

"Ugh." I shuddered in irritation, drawing a frown from the guy passing me on my street.

Trying not to dwell on my dad's message, I clicked on the next voice mail.

"Why aren't you picking up your phone?" my mom's voice snapped impatiently. "Are you too busy for me now? I have stretch marks on my stomach that I'll never be rid of because of you, young lady."

Jesus, my parents were so alike, and they couldn't even see it, I thought as I climbed the stairs to my apartment.

"The least you can do is call me back. I know you saw a video that might have embarrassed you, but you're an adult now. And your mother is a single, attractive woman. I get to let my hair down sometimes, you know. If your father can shack up with some bimbo fifteen years younger than him—what a fucking cliché!—then I can eat a banana while sitting on a male stripper's lap. Now your aunt Kiera is rubbing it in my face that twerp he installed in that house in Ridgewood he *cannot* afford is throwing a *family* pool party for that bimbo's sixteen-year-old brat. Are you going? Because Kiera mentioned something about you organizing it, and I know that can't be true. My Hallie wouldn't do that to me. You can be irresponsible and I know you like a party, but you would never willfully hurt my feelings like that. Would you?"

I stared into the computer screen, mentally and emotionally drained as I said to "Christopher," "I'd like to point out that I haven't partied since I was in college, and yet I still have this reputation as the party girl. Planning *events* for people does not make me a party girl. Irresponsible? Where did that label come from? And it feels weird watching my dad move on with someone else and playing father to some strange girl. . . . I'm worried he's taking on too much with his new house, trying to impress Miranda and Alison. And I really do not have time to plan a party I'm not getting paid to plan.

"But I'm Hallie." I smiled sadly at the camera. "So I'll just grin and bear it and try to make it work for everyone else." With a groan, I slumped over, laying my forehead against the desk. I waved at the screen in good night to my imaginary Chris and blindly ended the video.

And then, because something about watching his handsome face and listening to that deep, soothing voice relaxed me, I lifted my head, sent my video letter into outer space, and then clicked open one of Chris's video letters to watch again for, like, the tenth time.

# SIX

## Chris

*The Whipple shield took some debris last night. I felt it. Nothing major, nothing to worry about. Anything big, we'd steer the station out of the way. I was on repairs yesterday and had to overhaul the communications system. That kept me busy. Today I tested the crew's blood samples. And I will not lie . . . before I started this video, Tom and Anton and I timed each other to see who could get from node 1 to node 2 the fastest. And I know you're dying to know who won. I'll give you a hint . . . you've had sex with him. Darce, I miss you. I'm glad everything is going well down there. When I return, I'm going to take you out on the town to celebrate you winning your case. Did you get my flowers? I ordered those flowers from space. There's a conversation starter for you.*

—CAPTAIN CHRISTOPHER ORTIZ, VIDEO DIARY #9

It had taken weeks to get the sound of humming machinery out of my head once I'd returned to Earth. I'd lie awake at night, my luxury mattress like a brick beneath my back compared to sleep in zero gravity, and I'd still hear that humming from the ISS. It was its own kind of silence. The night the Whipple shield took a hit I'd felt the station shake, waking me. But the machinery noise lulled me back to sleep and into dreams of Miguel. Like so many times before, I dreamed I'd lost him and I couldn't find him, my panic rising. I'd woken up soaked in sweat and gasping for breath.

I didn't confide in Darcy about the dream in the video I sent her the next day. She was uncomfortable when I talked about my mother or Miguel. She'd change the subject. That wasn't a problem for me. Besides, I had been psychoanalyzed numerous times while training to be an astronaut. I had thoroughly discussed everything I felt about losing Miguel to war with my therapist.

And still I dreamed of him. As I did last night, and even though my mattress had grown more comfortable over the last few months, I couldn't fall back to sleep again. Maybe I needed those humming sounds from the ISS to help me nod off.

There was no true way to compare life up there to life down here. To compare that unique experience to the beauty of running down the beach, listening to the rhythmic, soothing sound of gentle waves. Of seagulls squawking in the early morning sky. Bandit barking now and then as he rushed to keep up with me.

Sea air filled my lungs as I pumped my body as hard as I could, sweat dripping off me.

Then, suddenly, I could hear *her* as I ran.

Hallie. Hallie Goodman.

I might have googled her.

The search didn't bring up much. Just that she worked in Manhattan for Lia Zhang Events. There were a couple of articles on the company and the extravagant events they'd organized. If the photographs were anything to go by, Hallie and her colleagues were good at their jobs.

No wonder Darcy had hired her.

While it was clear from Hallie's video letter—or perhaps I should call it a diary since *she* was certain that's what she was using it as—that her life was kind of a mess, she was handling it with more grace than I think she knew. She was funny. I hadn't laughed like that in a while. Though she really needed to stop being so sweet to people who were trying to take advantage of her.

As Bandit bounded ahead of me at the sight of my aunt's house, Hallie's eyes filled my mind. She had the most amazing eyes. They were big and adorable, and so expressive. And that cotton candy–pink hair was growing on me. Having assumed no one was going to see the video, she'd tied her hair up into a messy knot on top of her head, donned wire-rimmed oversized reading glasses, and wore an old sweater. There was a coffee spill on it. If she was anything like Darcy, she'd be mortified to know I'd seen her like that . . . but I thought she was cute.

She was messy but cute. And from what I could tell, her life was messy and *not* cute. Just like mine. Though my messy was an empty kind of messy, while hers was most definitely because she had too many things going on.

I'd replied to Kate to tell her to bounce Hallie's email again but to let me know if she sent another.

Smirking to myself as I remembered the way she'd signed off the video, face-planted on the desk, waving at the screen, I jogged up the beach and opened the gate to Aunt Richelle's backyard. Bandit had been waiting patiently for me to let him in, and he rushed up the lawn toward the house as if he hadn't seen my aunt in years.

By the time I got inside, Aunt Richelle had rubbed the sand off the dog before allowing him in.

"Morning." I leaned in to kiss her cheek as I passed. "Just going to take a quick shower."

"I'll make waffles!" she called after me.

"You spoil me!" I called back, and heard her answering chuckle. She needed someone to look after. It was in my aunt's nature to look after people. She'd never left my mom's side when she was sick. And I hated that Richelle was alone now, in this house.

But it was her choice, I reminded myself.

I swiped my cell off my bedside table where I'd left it and saw I had three missed calls from my father and a voice-mail message that was undoubtedly from him.

Gut churning, I threw the phone on the bed and hurried into the shower. Once washed and dressed, I returned to the kitchen to find warm waffles plated on the island. There was whipped cream, maple syrup, and a bowl of mixed berries beside it.

"I might just move in permanently," I joked, salivating as I slipped onto the stool.

Aunt Richelle stood on the opposite side of the island, staring at me.

A little intensely.

I paused in my waffle onslaught. "Everything okay?"

She exhaled slowly and then walked across the kitchen to open a drawer. I studied her stiff demeanor as she removed what looked like a cream-colored card. "I should have given this to you last night, but I just wanted you to relax. But it's yours, so you should have it."

Curious, I reached for the card and saw the elaborate embossed detail on it.

The words *We're Engaged* were scrawled in silver script on the front. A pearl with a loop over it acted as the clasp. Unlooping it, I opened the card.

*You are cordially invited to attend an engagement party in honor of Darcy Hawthorne & Matthias Lemieux.*

The date followed (in three weeks), along with the location and the RSVP email.

I should probably have felt more emotional impact about it than I did.

"I think she must have sent it here because she wasn't sure you were back in Manhattan," Aunt Richelle said. "What is she thinking, sending you an invitation? And who sends actual invitations anymore?" Her voice rose with her agitation. "I thought she was an environmentalist. Hasn't she heard of an e-invite?"

I laughed at my aunt's outrage. While she'd never come out and said it to my face, I'd always gotten the impression my aunt didn't care for Darcy. It had surprised me because, while we were dating, I thought Darcy was a total catch. She was intelligent and strong-willed but compassionate too. Moreover, on a personal level we both knew what it was to feel like we were disappointing our successful families by taking a different path in life from the one they wanted us to take. We'd bonded over the conflict we'd both been through, we understood that we felt disconnected from people in our social circle, though for entirely different reasons, and she was far better at pretending to fit in than I was. There was comfort in our bond. For three years she'd been my sounding board and my friend as well as my lover. But with hindsight, I could see there were things that didn't work. For a start, we were really bad at communicating with each other. She wasn't always the first person I thought of when something happened that upset me or excited me, and I realized it was because Darcy didn't really excite me. Not in the way I realized now she should have. Obviously, she realized that before I did. And I'd genuinely forgiven her and moved on.

Aunt Richelle studied my face in confusion and concern.

Reaching for her hand, I placed mine over it. "I'm okay. We ended it as friends. She's being friendly. Now I'm going to eat my waffles."

Aunt Richelle was unconvinced as I dove into the food. "You're not going, are you? After what she did."

Swallowing a bite of the best waffles on the East Coast (I was not biased, my aunt could *cook*), I opened my mouth to answer in the negative, when the vision of a pink-haired Hallie appeared in my mind. Frowning, I considered my answer and then asked, "Do the people who plan these things attend the event?"

"What do you mean?"

"You know, the event-planner people . . . do they actually attend the event?" My parents had thrown business dinners and parties while I was growing up, but I'd never paid attention to how they came together.

"Sometimes. Usually for big events like this one, yeah. They need to make sure everything runs smoothly. Why? What a weird question." She made a face as she slipped onto the stool beside me.

And since I told Aunt Richelle most things, I turned to her and replied, "Well . . . something *weird* happened."

# SEVEN

## Hallie

*I like the lack of bullshit up here, Darce. We have our routine, our tasks, and we have to be mindful of each other. This place is bigger than people think, but even so, we're stuck up here together for months. If you let the things that annoy you go unspoken, it just builds. It's not like back on Earth, where you let things go because you can get some distance from each other. . . . Up here we speak our minds. We deal with the problem and we move on. No bullshit. It got me thinking, Why can't it always be like that? I like to think I'm an honest guy, up front about things, but if I think about it, that's not entirely true. There are so many different reasons to hide our true feelings: to protect other people's feelings, to protect our own, because we don't think the situation is worth a fallout . . . because we're afraid. How much easier things would be if we could all agree to be honest with one another on the proviso that the honesty comes with the best of intentions? But there's the rub . . . not everyone's intentions are good. Some people use honesty as a weapon.*

*Sorry I'm rambling to you today. It was just something I was thinking about. I'm honest with most people . . . but some-*

*thing holds me back with others. But with you . . . Darce, I promise not to hold back with you if you promise not to hold back with me. Never lie to please me, okay. I always want your truth.*

–CAPTAIN CHRISTOPHER ORTIZ, VIDEO DIARY #8

My knee was currently doing an involuntary bouncing thing. If you've ever had a doctor hit a tiny hammer against your knee, then you'll understand what was happening with mine.

Except there was no tiny doctor hammer.

Just my dad meeting me for lunch, wherein I had to have a difficult conversation with him.

Nervousness had taken over my limb.

I glanced toward the restaurant door, hoping he'd be on time. Because of work, I had only a brief window to eat lunch these days. The butterflies in my stomach roared to life again at the sight of my dad pushing into the restaurant. That stupid knee tried to bounce, but I stood up on shaky legs. This was so weird, I thought morosely, being anxious about having lunch with him.

As he caught sight of me, his face broke into a handsome grin, and I was taken aback again by how much he'd changed in the last year. He'd started running again, like he used to when I was a kid, and started eating a little healthier. It was no lie to say that those changes had taken ten years off him. And Miranda seemed to have influenced his wardrobe choices. No more baggy nineties suits for my dad. They were fitted and stylish. His gray hair was now cut and styled, and I realized as he walked toward me that Dad looked distinguished.

More than that, he looked happy.

Fuck.

I wanted my dad to be happy. I did. He'd been put through the wringer. But I also didn't want him being taken for a fool either.

"Cupcake." He greeted me with a warm embrace.

Relieved he didn't seem mad at me, I accepted the embrace, relishing the rarity of his attention. When we settled down at the table, his blue eyes glittered under the restaurant lights. "You really do look like a cupcake now with that hair."

I fingered my pale pink waves that I'd just had redone, so the color was pinker than ever. "I like it," I replied, a little defensively. Mom already gave me shit about my hair every time I saw her. I didn't need it from Dad too.

He raised his palms. "No, no, I like it. It suits you."

I relaxed a little. "Thanks. And thanks for coming into the city."

"No problem. It was nice to be invited."

I tried not to take that as a pointed comment that I didn't invite him enough into my life, but since he said it in such a pointed tone, it was difficult not to. Not wanting to argue with him that it went both ways, I shook it off.

The waiter arrived to take our order, and as soon as he was gone, I launched into my apology. "I'm sorry for not returning your calls about, well, the Mom thing. I have a lot going on at work. And on that note, while I wish I could help Miranda plan a sixteenth-birthday party for Alison, Dad, I am drowning in work. I just . . . I'm sorry, I just don't have time. And honestly, it really would put me in the middle of things with Mom."

My heart banged in my chest as Dad studied me carefully. I didn't dare reach for my glass of water, even though my mouth was so dry, because I didn't want him to see my hands shake.

For not the first time in my life, I cursed this incessant need to please.

Finally Dad sighed. "Look, I know it's a little awkward, but we need to move past that. You can't let your mother make you feel guilty for spending time with me and my new family."

I tried not to flinch at his words.

"Miranda and Alison are in my life. They're not going anywhere. So we all need to be grown-ups."

He wasn't wrong.

But he also wasn't the one who would have to put up with Mom's constant bitching about the whole thing. Bitching that covered her hurt.

"You're right," I acknowledged. "But, Dad, I'm not lying when I say I'm snowed under with work. I just don't think I have time to plan a sixteenth-birthday party on the side."

He frowned at me and sounded hurt as he asked, "But you have time for that boyfriend of yours, right?"

I stiffened. "We broke up actually."

His expression softened with sympathy. "No doubt because you work too hard." Dad reached over and covered my hand with his. "Take it from me, Cupcake, work isn't everything. Don't push away your loved ones in favor of your job."

Duly guilted, frustration cut off my protestations. I wanted to tell him that George broke up with me because he thought I was ridiculous. I wanted to tell him I was too busy to plan Alison's sixteenth because I worked for one of the most demanding and successful event-management companies in the country. I wanted to tell him that even more so than that I didn't want to plan the party of some girl I barely knew who had only ever acted like a brat in my presence. Who didn't seem to appreciate that my dad was stretching himself to the financial limit to provide her and her mother with a house that made my mom seethe with jealousy. I wanted to tell him I didn't want to plan a sixteenth-birthday party for his "new kid" when he'd never even bothered to show up to mine!

I didn't say any of that. Instead I pasted a smile on my face and agreed to plan the damn party.

# EIGHT

## Chris

Standing on my aunt's sheltered back porch, I watched the rain hit the ocean. Today the sea was a dark grayish purple, reflecting the brooding sky. But as the rain made contact, the water splashed upward in thousands of bursts of what seemed like frenetic joy.

"You're restless, I can feel it."

I turned to my aunt as she walked out of the kitchen and onto the porch. "I'm always restless lately."

"True. But you can usually run some of it off." She handed me a mug of coffee that I accepted with a thank-you. "Sit." Aunt Richelle pointed to the porch swing behind me.

I did as she asked, and she sat down beside me, her gaze on the water.

"I love the rain." She sighed happily. "When we were kids, your mom and I used to sneak out to our tree house anytime it rained. Dad built it and it had a tin roof. We loved the sound of the rain dancing across the top."

Sliding my arm along her shoulder, I pulled her into my side.

Aunt Richelle relaxed against me, and I kissed her temple and confessed, "I miss her too."

"I know," she whispered, her eyes still on the water. "She would have been so proud of you."

That I knew. It was nice to hear it, anyway.

A while passed as we quietly watched the rain together. Until my aunt pulled away from me, searched my face, and abruptly asked, "What are you doing here, Chris?"

"I needed my family," I answered honestly, my tone a little gruff.

Aunt Richelle caressed my cheek, tenderness in her expression. "Sweetheart, you will always have that in me. And you can stay as long as you need. But—and you know I try to give you time to work these things out for yourself—I'm worried about you. You seem lost."

"Maybe I am. Maybe I don't know what my next move is. I do know if I don't make it soon, doors that are currently temporarily closed may never open again."

"NASA?"

I nodded. "They don't want astronauts who aren't fully committed to the job."

Contemplating this, Aunt Richelle settled against the swing again and studied the landscape stretched out before us. "Well . . . I think the place to start is the obvious one. What do you enjoy? What do you still want to accomplish in life? And before you answer, take your father out of the equation."

"He's very much in the equation."

"Right now, he's not even here." Her expression was uncharacteristically stern. "He's not a part of this discussion, so put him from your mind and just think about what *you* want."

Considering it, focusing on my currently itchy feet, I blurted out, "Travel."

"Travel?"

"I know I traveled with the air force, but it's not the same. I always wanted to backpack but—"

"Your father said it was for bums," Richelle interrupted. "I remember, I was there, and it stung. I backpacked, which he knew." She muttered something that sounded a lot like "asshole" under her breath.

I grinned. "Yeah, he's good at that. But I remember you told Miguel and me stories about your travels when we were kids, and even then, I wanted to follow in your footsteps. You made it sound like something everyone needed to do."

"I think it is. I wish everyone had the money to, but I got lucky with my art. I know Mom and Dad worried sick about me the entire year I was gone, but it changed who I was. For the better."

"But you were young. It's kind of expected that that's the time you do it."

"Who cares? When you're old and unable to do anything more rigorous than lift your butt off a seat to fart, you'll wish you had done whatever the hell you wanted. Not what's expected."

I chuckled. "You have such a pretty way of putting things, Aunt Richelle."

She snorted. "But you know I'm right."

I did know she was right. Longing filled me. "When I was up there on the station"—I pointed upward—"I spent so many hours looking down on the world, in awe of it . . . and I realized being up there was one of the few times in my life I had seen it at its best. I'd traveled, but to places torn apart by war and pain." I swallowed hard against the memories, the images that flickered across my vision, which I knew would haunt me for the rest of my life. "I saw the worst in humanity, and, thankfully, there were moments when I saw the best. But for once I just want to experience all of it without constantly watching my back for the enemy."

My aunt grabbed hold of my hand, drawing my gaze to her. Her expression fierce. "Then go traveling. Go backpacking."

I gave her hand a squeeze but released it as I stood, aggravation tightening my shoulders. "It isn't a productive use of my time."

"That's your father talking."

Scowling, I shook my head. "Not just my father. I have skills that should be put toward something useful, something that aids toward progress, that helps people."

Aunt Richelle mirrored my scowl. "You've done that. And you will do it again. But you're allowed to take a break. Sometimes we just need to refill the well, you know."

I shook my head. "It would just be running away."

"That's your father talking again." She stood to face me, fire in her eyes that I'd never seen in my mom's until the end. Mom appeased everyone for the sake of harmony. Perfect for my father, since he didn't want anyone to challenge him. But when she was dying, I remember seeing that fire in her eyes when she begged me to be happy no matter what it was in life that would make me happy. The memory got to me as Richelle continued insistently, "Traveling will help. Experiencing other cultures, you know that changes you, shapes you. I think it would give you the clarity you need to take the next step in your career."

Or drive an even deeper wedge between me and my father.

Because as much as traveling might make me happy, I couldn't deny that, as much as I didn't understand him, as angry as he made me, I didn't want to lose him too.

"I'll think about it," I lied.

Disappointment clouded Aunt Richelle's face. "No, you won't."

"It's not just about him," I told her softly.

Her expression told me she didn't believe me.

"Aunt Richelle . . ."

She gave a heavy sigh, squeezed my shoulder, and said, "Whatever you decide, I'm here."

I watched her disappear into the house before I turned to stare out at the rainstorm. Despite her best intentions, the indecision that rode my shoulders before our talk now felt crushing.

Sitting down on the porch swing, I ignored the chill in the air as the sky darkened. Richelle popped her head out again to let me know dinner was ready, but I told her I wasn't hungry. She said the food was there when I wanted it, and then she left me alone.

Guilt clung to me.

A while later, it was so dark—the moon hidden behind clouds—I could no longer see the ocean; I could only hear it rushing against the shore. There was something particularly soothing about it tonight.

I'd switched my phone on silent because I'd been getting a few calls from unknown numbers, but it meant I'd probably missed another call from my father. Filled with dread but needing to know, I pulled my phone out of my pocket. Sure enough, there were several missed calls and one of them was from him. There were also a couple of new voice mails. However, my gaze snagged on the notification banner from my email. I had another message from Kate.

Ignoring everything else, I tapped on that notification.

Chris,

She sent another. What do you want me to do going forward?

Kate

Something like anticipation filled me as I tapped open the video. Hallie Goodman's face filled the screen, and a smile prodded my lips. This time she looked more put together. Her hair was styled and longer than I realized. It fell over her shoulders and out of shot of the camera. She wore a black silk shirt. Makeup perfect.

"Fuck. My. Life."

Her opening line made me chuckle. "Yeah, I hear you," I muttered.

Hallie blew out air between her lips and slumped forward in her seat, elbows on her desk. That silky pink hair fell into her face as she bemoaned a lunch meeting with her dad.

"Let me just preface this by saying, I love my dad and he deserves happiness after what my mom put him through—"

I wondered what that was exactly.

"But I can admit to feeling pissed at him for three things." She held up a finger. "One, he treats my job with no respect. He asks me to plan his girlfriend's bratty daughter's birthday party for free and acts hurt when I tell him I'm snowed under with work. No respect for my time or how stressful my job is. Two." She held up a second finger, and I saw pain flicker in her gaze. I sucked in a breath, holding my phone closer to my face. "He never even showed up at *my* sixteenth-birthday party. And I don't care if I sound like a whining five-year-old when I say this, but I resent that he's spending all this time with this kid who isn't even his. I don't care about the fancy house or the fancy clothes that she's getting that I never got, I've never cared about that—that's my mom's gig . . . I care that every time I asked him to spend time with me growing up, I got a kiss on the head and an 'I'm sorry, Cupcake, Daddy's gotta work, but we'll do something together later.' Did later come? Did it like hell." She glowered at the screen. "And now I have to give up time I don't have to plan this party for a girl who is the most spoiled little shit I've ever encountered. The last time I had dinner with them, she was rude to me about my appearance, my job, my boyfriend at the time, and she monopolized most of the dinner, begging her mom for fifty bucks to go shopping with her friends the next day. I am not exaggerating when I say she repeated the word 'please' for five minutes straight. It felt longer. And her mom caved. I would have shoved the fifty bucks in her mouth."

I grinned, imagining it.

"That's not true." Hallie threw up her arms in frustration. "That's a lie! I would have given her the fifty bucks and probably three pairs of kitten socks."

Snorting at the reminder of her escapades in the store, I nodded, even though she couldn't see me.

"In fact, I said yes to planning Alison's sixteenth. And here's where three comes in." She held up a third finger. "I'm also mad at my dad for putting me in this position when I told him it would put me in the middle with him and Mom. Did he care? No. And I just had to endure a twenty-minute phone call with my mother as she railed at me for my betrayal. It was so bad, I knew she was just hiding her hurt through anger, so I cried." Her eyes glistened with emotion, and any amusement I felt died. "Upside: my new waterproof mascara might be the first mascara in history to actually be waterproof."

"I'm sorry," I whispered uselessly.

"I just . . ." She stared down at the desk now, and I felt frustrated I couldn't see her expression. "I know she did this to herself, but it's hard to see her in pain. Even harder when she won't admit why she's really hurting. Instead she goes out and does wild and stupid things and I . . . I'm just . . ." Hallie lifted her gaze, and I sucked in a breath as I watched her tears escape. "I'm tired. I'm so exhausted. I spent all this time trying to stop my dad from falling apart, and now he's okay and it's my mom who's falling apart. And I know this is selfish . . . but it's like no one cares that *I'm* falling apart too. Probably my own fault." She swiped briskly at her tears and pasted a fake smile on her face. "George was right. I am a people pleaser. I mean, I knew that about myself, but I never realized just how much it is the reason I end up in ridiculous, uncomfortable situations that inevitably always end badly for me."

"You shouldn't be in this situation to begin with," I said in exasperation, wishing I could talk to this woman. Her dad was an ass for forcing her into the middle. And I knew all about absentee fathers. It didn't matter what age you were, parental neglect hurt, and it never really went away. Therapy had made it manageable for me, but his absence, his lack of affection, his closing the door on our Mexican heritage even as I gained fame as a Latino astronaut, had become a part of who I was.

Just like Hallie's parents' divorce had become a part of her.

I wanted to talk to her. To help her figure out why she felt the need to please people to the detriment of her own happiness.

Why was it that good people always ended up taking everyone's crap?

I knew I'd listened to only a few videos of Hallie's confessions, but I sensed she *was* a good person. If she wasn't, she wouldn't be so softhearted, and people wouldn't have the chance to take advantage of her like they obviously were.

Suddenly motivated, I went into the house and found Darcy's engagement-party invitation on the kitchen counter. "Dammit." I'd missed the RSVP date. Her engagement party was in three weeks.

I considered my options and then, before I could stop myself, I found Darcy's name on my phone.

Hey, Darce, how are you? Look, I just got your invitation, so I've missed the RSVP. But if I'm still welcome, I'd love to be there.

As I waited for a reply, I emailed Kate and told her to keep making it seem like Hallie's emails were bouncing but to also keep forwarding them to me. It was the sneakiest, most underhanded thing I'd ever done. But I didn't want her video letters to stop.

Selfish but true.

My phone chimed.

**Chris, it's so good to hear from you. We would love you at the party. Thank you. Your friendship means so much to me. I can't wait to see you there. XO**

A different kind of anticipation filled me, and suddenly I was starving. Finding the leftovers from dinner in the fridge, I sent up a silent thank-you to my aunt, who was surely an angel in disguise. Then I sat down at the island to eat and watch the rest of Hallie's video.

# NINE

## Hallie

*I've been missing home this week. But two days ago we filmed a short video for a couple of middle school classes. The teachers sent in questions from the kids, and we tried to answer as many as possible and demonstrated our answers where we could. Well, they'd filmed the kids watching our video, and NASA sent us the film today. It was awesome seeing how excited these children were about space and what we're doing here. Sometimes constant routine, no matter how extraordinary the situation, can make you forget the bigger picture. But those kids and their responses reminded me why I'm up here. Why I'm doing what I'm doing and how goddamn privileged I am to be doing it. There was this one kid who reminded me so much of Miguel. He was so excited to see me, someone like him, Latino, working for NASA. He said he wanted to be an astronaut now too and how it really felt like a possibility for him. That's humbling. Exciting to know I've inspired someone. He had Miguel's passion and humor. I could see Miguel when we were little, telling me all about the greatest astronauts and how one day he would touch space. He never got that chance, but I did, and I won't waste a second of it again on wishing it away.*

*Sometimes you just need the reminder that you're doing a good job, that you're appreciated. We all need that, no matter who we are or what we're doing. I feel appreciated today, and I feel appreciative.*

—CAPTAIN CHRISTOPHER ORTIZ, VIDEO DIARY #10

The sound of teens screaming and melodic house music—every single track sounded like the one before it—still pounded in my head as I opened my laptop to vent about my day. I'd changed into my pajamas (a David Bowie shirt and a pair of loose jersey pants), scrubbed off my makeup, and piled my hair on top of my head. Reading glasses on, I curled up on my couch, laptop in one hand, mug of decaf coffee in the other, and began recording my video for my imaginary Chris.

"So today was Alison's sixteenth-birthday party. You can bet it was a very trying day. On the upside, my friend Althea is perhaps the best person I've ever met in my life. . . ."

"Thanks for being here with me," I said to Althea for like the fiftieth time as we decorated the kitchen and the patio surrounding the pool.

The caterers had already arrived and dropped off the food. Miranda was taking care of organizing that while Alison primped in her room.

"You don't have to say thank you again. In fact, I might have to push you in the pool if you do," my friend griped.

Chuckling, I nodded. "Got it."

Althea was just as busy as me, even more since she had a fiancée and a family she actually enjoyed being around, so her dropping everything to be my support today was amazing. I hadn't even asked her. I'd mentioned yesterday at work that when I'd called up my friend Gabby to ask if she'd come to the party with me, her response had been obnoxious and hurtful.

"Oh, Hallie, we're not in high school anymore. I know you don't understand this, because you're not a mom, but most of us don't have time to go to teen pool parties. I can't just drop everything because you're afraid to go alone. And this coming from the woman who wanted to go backpacking *alone*. Can you imagine? You'd either get lost in a jungle or eaten by something, or you'd fall for some strange guy and end up kidnapped by sex traffickers." Gabby'd snorted.

"So that's a no on the party, then?" I'd ignored the sting of her words.

"You'll understand when you have kids, Hallie. The rest of us just don't have that kind of free time on our hands."

Althea had had a few choice words for Gabby's attitude. "Women like her," she had seethed, "give moms a bad name. Some of my girlfriends have babies and you don't see them acting uppity, like the rest of us don't know what hard work is. I'm coming with you to that party."

"You don't have to do that. You're busy. What about Michelle?"

"Michelle will understand. And it's only a few hours, right?"

"Right."

And so here we were. Though I wouldn't say it to Althea because we weren't in high school anymore, she had just been promoted to my best friend. I'd demoted Gabby after that conversation, though truth is I should have demoted her a long time ago.

"Pink?" a high-pitched female voice asked shrilly behind us.

We turned from where we were arranging rose-gold and gold balloons at one end of the pool. In among the ordinary balloons was a rose-gold flamingo and a golden balloon shaped like a number one and another like a number six. We'd wrapped fairy lights around any object we could safely wrap them around.

"What?" I called to Alison.

She narrowed her eyes and flounced toward me in a short summer dress my dad would never have let me wear at that age. "I specifically said no pink!" Alison yelled at me.

"This isn't pink," I told her calmly. "This is rose gold. Very grown-up. A lot of my clients prefer this metallic over others."

"Well, I'm not a bored fifty-year-old housewife." She wrinkled her nose as she looked around the pool area. "I can't believe you get paid for this shit."

"Watch your mouth." Althea stepped up behind me.

Alison's bravado faltered.

"Ladies, how's it going?" My dad stepped out into the yard, beaming at us. "Look at this place." He stopped beside Alison, wrapping his arm around her shoulders. He drew her to his side. "What do you think, Cupcake? Hasn't Hallie done an amazing job?"

It was like getting punched in the gut.

*Cupcake?*

I stumbled back a little and felt Althea's hand on my shoulder.

"Yeah, it all looks fine. I'm going inside. Mom's making me a smoothie before my friends arrive."

"Sounds good." Dad turned and winked at me. "Place looks awesome, Hal."

Watching them walk away together, I tried to ignore the burn in my chest.

"Hey, you okay?" Althea suddenly stood in my path.

Blinking rapidly against an onslaught of unwelcome tears, I nodded, trying to numb myself.

"You don't look okay."

"It's stupid," I whispered.

"Hallie." Her voice was stern.

I met Althea's gaze. "My whole life, my dad's nickname for *me* has been Cupcake. He's never called me Hal. It's like . . . it's like he wants a do-over with her. With them." I shrugged, feeling immature as I turned away to fix the balloons. "It's fine. I'm being childish."

"No, you are not. That's really hurtful. And we do not have to stay. We can leave. Right now."

"No, it's fine." If we left, it would end in a confrontation, and I didn't want to deal with that.

"Okay, if you're sure. But I swear if that kid speaks to you like that again, I'm going to pop her head right off."

A bark of laughter burst out of me, and I smiled in gratitude. It was on the tip of my tongue to thank Althea again, but she'd probably just pop *my* head right off. The thought made me snort, and she cut me a bemused but relieved look.

A few hours later, seeing that the food laid outside by the pool had diminished, I'd left Althea at our spot at the back of the yard to go into the kitchen to replenish supplies.

"How's it going?"

I startled to find my dad's girlfriend in the kitchen doorway. To my annoyance, my dad and Miranda had disappeared into the house with their friends, leaving Althea and me outside to supervise and keep the food coming.

*Your daughter is a spoiled brat and this is the longest day of my life.* "They seem to be having fun."

Miranda gave me a sweet smile. "If I haven't said it already, thank you so much, Hallie. I can't tell you how much I appreciate you putting all this together for Alison. Sometimes she doesn't make it easy to get along with her but—" Something weary, sad even, moved across her eyes. "Her dad has hurt her a lot. I think it's all just coming out now in attitude, and she doesn't trust your father yet and . . . Anyway, I don't want to bore you with all that. All I wanted to do was let you know it means a lot to me that you would take time out of what I know must be a crazy schedule to do this for us. I told your father not to bother you." She gave me a commiserating look. "I don't think he truly understands the magnitude of stress you must be under to pull off the kinds of events you do. But you said yes, and that just blew me away. I've been bragging all week to my friends that Alison's party is being planned by Lia Zhang Events." She flushed, laughing at herself. "You're such a sweet person, and I really hope the more time Alison spends with you, the more maybe she'll see that we're in a good place now."

Dammit. Why did she have to be so nice? "Thank you, Miranda." I was a little choked up, but this time not with frustration. "You have no idea what it means to me to hear you say all that."

By the time I wandered out to the party again, I no longer felt resentful about being there. In fact, I laid out the food and skirted the teens to find Althea to tell her what Miranda had said.

"I swear if one more sixteen-year-old comes on to me, I'm leaving," Althea said before I could speak. She shuddered. "It's giving me the willies."

Snorting, I pulled her up to her feet. "Come eat something while I tell you the lovely things Miranda just said to me."

"Oh, I gotta hear this."

But as we walked along the edge of the pool toward the food, Alison and a friend blocked our path. While her friend was in a bikini, Alison was still in her super-short dress and completely dry. What was the point of the pool party if the guest of honor wasn't interested in being in the pool? Or was the whole point to just flaunt the fact that you had a pool?

"There you are." Alison flung her hands to her hips and stuck her freckled face in mine; I'd never bemoaned my short height more. "This party sucks. Why isn't there live music?"

"You have a deejay."

"Ew." She rolled her eyes. My God, she was a like a caricature. "And the boys are complaining about the food. Why isn't there a grill? We wanted burgers and dogs. If Justin Myers leaves because you're incompetent, I'll—" Her words were cut off by Althea's palm covering her face.

I barely had time to register the move before my friend shoved Alison's head with enough force to send her flying into the pool. Alison's shriek sliced through the music and then abruptly silenced as she fell through the water, sending it cascading over anyone near her.

Thankfully, she hadn't hit anyone as she went in.

Gaping, struggling desperately to stifle my laughter (her friends were not so kind) I watched as she popped up for air, her mascara now all over her face. "What the hell? I was trying to keep my hair dry!" she screamed at Althea.

My friend glowered down at her. "No nasty little Veruca Salt wannabe talks to my friend like that. You're lucky all I did was push you into a pool."

"And that is why Althea will forever be my hero." I practically cackled into the camera. "I try to be compassionate—especially after what Miranda let slip about Alison's dad—but that girl has a mean streak. Hopefully she grows out of it. Althea shut her up for a while, at least. I think too many people have excused her behavior over her dad's neglect and her parents' divorce until now. The only thing I wish was that it had been *me* who shoved her in the pool. But, shh, don't tell anyone I said that."

My phone chimed, and usually I'd ignore it while I was recording my video diary, but it had binged a few times already. With a sigh, I reached across the couch for it.

I had a bunch of social media notifications.

Dread filled me as I opened up the app.

Someone had tagged me in a video.

Another one with my mom. She was with Jenna, the instigator. I watched a little of it and then scrolled through the comments.

"Oh my God." I looked up from my phone at the camera. "I've just been tagged in a video uploaded online of my mom frenching some guy half her age at a club." Embarrassment was the least of my emotions. Jenna had posted it, but my mom had clearly given her the okay because Mom had commented on it! She and Jenna were joking back and forth about her being a cougar. "It just reeks of desperation." My earlier amusement over Althea, Alison, and the pool died. "And that's the truth. I go to a pool party for my dad's new, younger girlfriend's daughter's birthday . . . so Mom goes out, finds a guy barely out of college, and not only makes out with him but also makes sure everyone knows she made out with him. If I thought for a second she was doing this because it truly made her happy, I'd try to get over my embarrassment. But that's not having a good time." I waved the phone at my computer screen. "My mom is hiding how devastated she is. How hurt. And the worst part is that it's kind of her own fault. She—" My chest ached so badly for her. "She broke her own heart and she broke my dad's . . . and now I'm caught in the middle. Every step I take to make this mess better somehow just ends up making it worse."

# TEN

## Chris

I remember on my first space walk how I felt encompassed in an ocean of stars despite their distance from the station. There's no way to describe the endlessness. And I remember thinking how poets talked all the time about the connection between stars and fate. I never really believed in that stuff. Standing among them, the universe a never-ending dark velvet blanket sewn with these stars that glittered like diamonds, I saw the beauty and I saw the science. Never the philosophy.

Yet, I began to wonder now. How my video letters ended up in Hallie's hands. How I felt strangely drawn to her through the ones she sent to me.

And now this.

A week ago, for no apparent reason, other than I didn't know what else to do, I sat down at my aunt's laptop to type up a list of pros and cons of the jobs open to me. Notes, thoughts just poured from my fingers. But not about that. About my time on the ISS, training for NASA. Then I began working backward, sorting out my emotions about the air force and following in my big brother's footsteps. Taking up the mantle of his dream to become an astronaut. I went back even further, to growing up in a very white, privileged world as a mixed-race kid with no connection to his Mexican heritage, who dealt with less racism and bias than other Mexican American kids but still experienced it. And how I felt "other" in the world I grew up in but also so disconnected from any Mexican identity that I felt "other" within the Latinx community. How I never really felt like I fit anywhere. How it was the thing that bonded Miguel and me beyond mere brotherhood.

Me. Writing.

I wasn't a writer.

But there was therapy in it, in getting all the thoughts in my head out on paper and making sense of them.

Never in a million years did I expect a phone call from NASA that morning. When I saw it was a Houston number, I answered.

"Captain Christopher Ortiz?" an unfamiliar female voice said.

"Yes, speaking."

"Captain Ortiz, this is Aleema Ayad from NASA's media relations department. We've had inquiries from several publishers interested in the opportunity to work with you. They rarely reach out like this, but because of your large online following and the media interest around you, the publisher thinks your already significant audience makes you the ideal candidate for an autobiography. NASA agrees it would be a wonderful opportunity for you to continue to promote the program."

I was stunned.

Fate?

Or coincidence?

Was there a fine line between both?

"Write a book for them?"

"Yes. Now, if you're interested, we can certainly help you find a suitable literary agent. . . ."

I barely heard her as I stared at the laptop screen where the words I'd written, words that could easily be rearranged into an actual book, stared back at me. However, I wasn't sure I wanted the pressure of a book deal hanging over my head to finish this thing. I'd started writing purely for myself, and honestly, that's the way I wanted to finish it.

"Can I get back to you on this?" I cut off the publicist.

"Oh. Of course. I'll give you my direct number if you'd like to discuss it."

"Can you text it to me?"

"Absolutely."

After I got off the phone, I sat back on my aunt's couch and stared out at the view beyond her backyard. To my irritation, the first thing that occurred to me was that my father would not approve of my sharing personal details of my life. While he thought my Instagram account and subsequent talk show appearances a smart business move for NASA, I'd never posted anything to the account where I discussed my friends and family.

"You look pensive."

I started at my aunt's voice. She stood in the kitchen, covered in flecks of paint. "NASA wants me to write a book. Apparently some publishers have inquired and they don't usually do that."

Aunt Richelle smirked as she reached into the fridge for a bottled water. "Of course they want a book from *you*."

"What does that mean?"

"Well, as much as I like to keep my nephew's ego in check," she teased, "you have accomplished a lot for someone your age. Besides, how many millions of followers do you have now? Between that and your TV appearances, you generated a lot of publicity. You're the perfect poster child for NASA. They need a continued interest in the program and a good-looking astronaut from a Mexican American background whom men and women alike crush on . . . Yes, they want you writing a book. And then they want you posting to your followers about that book, going on tour with that book, and they want you on talk shows again discussing that book."

I frowned. It wasn't the first time they had trotted me out to the media as some sort of NASA sex symbol and emblem of their diversity. While I'd love to believe everyone following me on social media was interested in space, I knew from the comments on my posts that some people were following me because of how I looked. Not just my so-called attractiveness but because I was Latino. The media coverage always mentioned my background. It discomfited me, and yet I was logical enough to see the sense in NASA buying into it. The federal government funded NASA. Popularity of the program could not wane. It would be fatal to it. They needed the world to view them in a positive light. That they were important, progressive and had a diverse population. I understood it, and I was practical and ambitious enough to forgive the tokenism for the larger cause. That didn't mean that every post-mission interview didn't turn especially uncomfortable when the subject of my ethnicity arose. How I was a leader, a trailblazer. I wanted to be, I wanted to inspire other Mexican Americans, especially kids looking up to me. But I was also very aware that I'd grown up disconnected from that cultural community, that my privileged life in New York, though somewhat diverse, had been mostly white. I felt like a fraud. Yet I knew my position as a Latino astronaut had importance. So I did the interviews, I accepted the love of the community, and I furthered NASA's agenda because the program was important to me too.

"Do you really think I could help promote the program this way?"

"Absolutely."

"I don't know how comfortable I'd be with that, but if it would be a productive use of my time, if it would garner interest from younger people, especially young Latinx—"

"Stop." Aunt Richelle had crossed the room to lean on the couch. Her expression was stern. "You will not write an autobiography, one of the most personal things you could ever do, because it's a productive use of your time and beneficial to the program."

"But—"

"Not *just* for that reason," she corrected herself. "Chris, you've been writing every day for over a week. That's amazing. You did it because you needed to in the same way that I started painting because I needed to. As soon as you introduce outside forces—for me, that's art dealers, critics, and buyers—it messes with the purity of the craft. It can't be helped; it can't be avoided. There are voices in my head now that have warped what comes out of me. And every day painting gets a little harder."

At the astonished look on my face, she smiled reassuringly.

"I still love to paint. It's just different now. This"—she pointed at the laptop—"this needs to be for *you*. Forget about that phone call, forget about what's best for NASA, and just write what you need to explore. You said you've been thinking a lot about your heritage and how feeling disconnected from the Mexican culture and Spanish language has affected you. Write the book to explore those questions. Why don't you take it as an opportunity to finally stop worrying about what Javier wants and actually go out there and look into your paternal background? And if, when you're done, you want to share that with the world, you can do that. But right now, the words just have to be for you."

I stared at her for so long, my aunt frowned. She opened her mouth to speak, but I beat her to it, my voice husky with emotion. "You know, when Mom died, there was this selfish part of me that hated her for leaving me with *him*. I knew I had Miguel, but it differed from having my mom to turn to. At her funeral, I felt so fucking lost. Father wouldn't let Miguel leave his side, and I was just this kid who felt totally unanchored to anything. Like no one would care if I just disappeared. That wasn't true. Not for the reasons I wanted though. If my father realized I was hiding during Mom's wake, he'd lose his shit, see it as an embarrassment.

"But I wasn't alone, was I? You sat down on the couch beside me—in that room filled with strangers who'd come because they needed to foster their business connection with my father—and you took my hand and didn't let go. We never said a word to each other. You just held my hand. And I knew I wasn't alone."

Emotion overcame Aunt Richelle, tears silently slipping down her cheeks.

I reached over and took her hand. "Thank you for always being there for me. And for being so fucking wise."

She swiped at her tears with her free hand and laughed hoarsely when she saw the mascara streaks on her fingertips. "Oh jeez, you ruined my makeup. You owe me. I better get a mention in your acknowledgments."

"A mention?" I grinned at her. "I'm dedicating the book to you." It wasn't a lie.

Fresh tears sprung to her eyes. "Look what you're doing to me," she said, overly dramatic. "I have to leave before I dehydrate."

My laughter followed her out of the room, and my gaze drifted back to my laptop. Aunt Richelle's sage advice had saved me from needing to overanalyze what I was doing. I did want to explore my Mexican heritage, but fear of straining my relationship with my father even more than it was had always stopped me. Maybe Aunt Richelle was right. Maybe I had to stop thinking about everyone and everything else and just focus on what I needed now. Determined to forget about the call from NASA, forget about my father, I tried to find my way back to a natural rhythm with my writing.

Who would have thought it? Me, a writer?

A few hours later, after putting more words on the page, I sat down to dinner with Aunt Richelle. As soon as we slipped onto stools at her island to eat the takeout she'd ordered, my cell rang.

It was my father.

I hit the button on the side that silenced the ringer.

"You know you're going to have to talk to him eventually, or he'll come looking for you, and if you make him come looking for you, he'll be even angrier."

Scowling, I huffed, "I'm a grown man."

"Then maybe answer your phone like one."

She was right, which was even more annoying. Ignoring that she was right, I dug into the Thai food.

"Have you received any more videos from your pink-haired event planner?" She smirked knowingly at me.

I stopped myself from rolling my eyes at her. Sometimes she treated me like I was thirteen, but I didn't need to act like it. "A few."

"Are you ever going to tell me what she talks to you about?"

"No," I replied firmly. "She thinks no one is seeing these videos. It's bad enough I'm watching them."

"You should just call her up instead of attending Darcy's engagement party to see her. The party doesn't seem like a good idea."

"I'm not calling Hallie. I have every intention of telling her the truth, and I can't do that on the phone. It has to be face-to-face."

"Then hire her."

"What?"

"Hire her. Get her to help you plan a retirement party from the air force. Weren't you just saying the other day that you feel you didn't get closure? That one minute you were in the air force and the next you weren't. You could invite friends from the military, if they're home, and your colleagues from NASA. The college friends you still talk to. Maybe having those people in the same room will provide some clarity."

I considered this. "I can't ask people to come to New York for a party."

"Well, have it in Houston."

"A few of my college friends live in New York and Boston, but most of them are scattered all over."

"We'll have it here," she suddenly announced. "And we'll invite your father's fancy friends to keep him placated."

"All so I can meet Hallie?"

Aunt Richelle nudged me playfully. "You're not subtle—I have caught you watching her videos more times than I can count. Meet the woman. See what's she all about. Planning something together will give you the perfect opportunity to get to know her."

As much as I'd like that, I didn't want to have to be the center of attention at a party that involved dragging people out to the Hamptons. "People will feel obligated to come, and they're too busy for me to throw something as frivolous as a retirement party."

"Boo, you're no fun." Aunt Richelle sighed. "Fine, go to your ex-girlfriend's engagement party. Just don't be blinded by her long legs and perky tits."

I burst out laughing. "She's engaged to another man."

"So? Sweetheart, you may be one of the most intelligent people I've ever known, but you're still a man. And when it comes to women, men are stupid. They will happily overlook the cute-as-a-button event planner for the supermodel even if the supermodel is a selfish, disloyal, cheating, uppity society cow."

"You really don't like Darcy, do you?"

"No, I really don't. You being cool with her . . . well . . . that's just too well-adjusted."

Chuckling, I shook my head. "I'm over her, I promise." My thoughts were a little preoccupied by my cute-as-a-button event planner. "I resent the idea that I would overlook a good woman for someone more physically attractive."

"Bah, attraction is all up here." Aunt Richelle tapped her temple. "When I met Akio, we were just friends. I barely even noticed him like that. Then, within days of spending time with him, I realized I was growing more and more attracted to him. One day he didn't give me butterflies, and the next day he smiled at me and, whoosh, butterflies galore." She threw me a sad smile. "You fall in love with the person, Chris, not the face. Otherwise it isn't love."

She never talked about Akio.

Not sure what to say, I repeated, "You're so fucking wise."

Relief glittered in her eyes. "I am. I am goddamn Yoda."

We laughed into our Thai food, but her words stayed with me, just like they always did.

# ELEVEN

## Hallie

*That's what I love about science, Darce . . . there's always a solution to be sought. Always hope that this thing you can't figure out or fix can be figured out, can be fixed. It's not like that with people or emotions. We both know that sometimes relationships can't be mended. There's too much damage. It can feel hopeless. The only thing to do, the only thing that keeps you sane, is to make peace with the fact that whatever it is, is unfixable. Find your hope in something else. Find the next problem to solve, the next solution. Move on. That's so much harder than just being able to fix it. Losing hope. But it's the only thing left for us to do.*

—CAPTAIN CHRISTOPHER ORTIZ, VIDEO DIARY #6

My Sundays were precious to me. Very few of my events fell on a Sunday, whereas I usually had an event at least two Saturdays out of the month. I did not, therefore, want to spend one of my few days off doing something I didn't choose. As terrible of a daughter as it made me, I didn't want to go to my mom's for lunch.

Especially when I was distracted.

A few days ago, Darcy had sent me an updated guest list for the engagement party, and Captain Christopher Ortiz had RSVPed. I did not think in a million years that her ex-boyfriend would show up, and now he was planning to attend. The object of my crush, the man whose privacy I had invaded, would be at the party. In the same room as me.

Every time I thought about it, my heart did this cliché little pitter-patter.

Of course, I'd have to tell him. The voice in my head that sounded like my boss argued vehemently against it, but it was too big of a secret. I had all this guilt, and I couldn't deal with it. The fact of the matter was I had rewatched his videos multiple times. The obsession reminded me of my teen years when I'd watch music videos of Kings of Leon repeatedly. My favorite Followill had been Caleb, but my crush fluctuated between them all, to be fair.

That I was acting like fourteen-year-old me over a guy was embarrassing, but at least only *I* knew about it.

Anyway, long story short, I'd almost memorized Christopher's videos; they weren't intended for me, I'd invaded his privacy, my remorse was all-consuming, and the only way to feel better about it was to confess to him what I'd done (without mentioning the rewatching or crush part). Hopefully, he wouldn't hate me for it.

Nervous flutters rioted in my belly as I strolled up my mom's front walk. Just the mere idea of being within touching distance of Christopher excited me. Ugh, this infatuation was mortifying.

The front door opened before I could even touch the handle.

"Why do you look flushed?" Mom peered at me suspiciously.

"Because I power walked for exercise," I lied impressively quickly as I slid past her and into my childhood house.

"Well, I suppose you can do that in those things."

At her tone, I turned to see her glaring at my Converse.

Rolling my eyes, I dumped my purse on the coffee table and slumped down onto the couch. "Mom, I spend almost twenty-four-seven in high heels. My feet hurt all the time. I just want one day when I can wear comfortable shoes."

"You're too short for comfortable shoes. Iced tea?"

"Please." I ignored her "too short" comment. Mom had been lecturing me on how to overcome my "disadvantages" since before we even knew for sure I was going to be a shortie. And since when was five feet four all that short for a woman? What was with our society's obsession with height, anyway?

"I see your hair is still pink!" Mom called from the kitchen.

Knowing she hated to talk through a wall, I reluctantly followed her into the kitchen and slid onto a stool at the island. "It is."

"Doesn't your boss have an issue with it?" she asked for the one millionth time.

"My hair is stylish, Mom," I replied calmly. Lia didn't even blink at my hair color when I walked into the office with it four months ago.

"It's not very professional."

*Neither is sticking your tongue down a man half your age's throat and then uploading it to social media when you manage a local real estate company.* "I thought you were going through a rebellious phase," I teased. "Shouldn't that mean you approve of pink hair?"

Mom frowned, her green eyes hardening. "What does that mean?"

I huffed inwardly. "Nothing."

Mom harrumphed and set about making our lunch. I studied her as she moved around the kitchen, wondering not for the first time how it was possible for a mother and daughter to be so unalike. My mom was a good few inches taller than me, curvier, had amazing auburn hair and even more amazing tip-tilted green eyes. She was a quintessential Irish American beauty. I took after the women on the Goodman side of the family. Short, blond, blue-eyed, and cute.

When I was younger, I bemoaned the fact that I didn't look like Mom.

But being beautiful hadn't made her any happier.

In fact, I think it kind of screwed with her perspective.

Last year, Mom turned forty-nine and treated the entire process like a loss. She went through the five stages of grieving. Well, truly, she'd circled through the first four in a hurricane of recklessness that had destroyed her life and then she'd skipped acceptance and returned to a mix of stage one and stage two: denial and anger. Though the grieving was no longer about her age. She'd celebrated her fiftieth birthday four months ago without wallowing in depression. No, her grief was about my dad.

I'd failed to help her, to stop her from tearing her life apart.

Now I was stuck in the middle of an emotional war.

As if on cue, Mom slid a sandwich across the counter and said, "It sounds like you're getting cozy with your father's whore."

I blanched.

Something in me snapped.

I couldn't listen to my mom call Miranda a whore anymore. "Mom, you can't call her that. For a start, she's not. For another thing, let's not push the feminist movement back twenty years by perpetuating a toxic narrative that only encourages sexual inequality and has far-reaching ramifications on how women are treated by men across the board."

Mom sighed heavily as she sat on a stool next to me. "Why do you turn everything political?"

"I'm just saying . . . Please don't use words like that, no matter how you feel about Miranda. It's not nice, and you're classier than that." I felt proud of myself for speaking up, but my inner pat on the back stalled at the sight of mom's chin wobbling.

"You like her, don't you? Is she going to steal you from me too?"

Just like that, I felt slapped in the face with remorse. "No, Mom, no, of course not." I slipped my arm around her shoulders and gave her a comforting squeeze. I didn't remind her that Miranda hadn't stolen Dad, because what was the point? It didn't make it any less painful for her. "I'm trying to make this work for us all."

"And what about me?" Tears glistened in those pretty but icy eyes. "What about your mother? Don't you care your father hurt me? Don't you care he shacked up with her and her offspring in a house he never deigned to provide for us?"

"You know he can't afford that house."

"Exactly. He's willing to bankrupt himself for *her* happiness and he couldn't even wait for—" She sucked in a harsh breath and pulled out of my hold. "That's not the point. I'm your mother. I carried you for nine excruciating months, and I deserve more loyalty than you've been showing me lately." Mom stood abruptly. "I'm not hungry."

"Mom," I pleaded.

"It's fine." She gave me a flat smile. "You don't want to take sides. I get it. It's hurtful, but I get it. I just wish, for once, you'd stop straddling the middle of an argument and choose a side. The right side. Your father left me, bought a house he can't afford, and then put a woman half my age in his bed."

Not half her age. Nor did he leave Mom. Anger stifled inside my throat at her rewriting of history.

"That you won't stand by me hurts. But you've always had a weakness of character. You get that from your father." She straightened her dress as if she hadn't plunged her nasty words into me like a knife. "I'm going to change. Jenna and I have a double date for dinner tonight. You can see yourself out."

As she stalked out of the room, I wanted to shout after her, to yell at her she was so blinded by her own mistakes she couldn't see the truth for the trees!

But if she wanted to push me away, then fine. I was done.

I marched into the sitting room, grabbed my purse, and then moved toward the front door, adrenaline pumping, my skin hot. Then my stupid hand stalled on the door handle. The urge to fix this was real.

Out of nowhere, Christopher's face floated across my vision, words from one of his videos in my ears. He spoke of moving on from relationship problems that couldn't be fixed, how sometimes you just had to make peace with it.

I turned to look over my shoulder at the stairs that led to the second floor. I could climb those and beg my mother for forgiveness for a crime I hadn't committed, or just for today I could make peace with the fact that for now we were broken and couldn't be fixed.

"Just for today," I whispered, tears burning in my eyes.

Then I walked out.

I fought with myself the entire way, but I stayed strong. I gave myself grace for once.

Twenty minutes later, as I waited in Newark Penn Station for a train back to the city, I heard my cell chime in my purse. My stomach did a little kick when I saw it was a text from Mom.

> **I can't believe you walked out without apologizing. You owe me lunch next weekend, young lady.**

With an aggravated sigh, I hung my head, wondering for the

millionth time how it was possible to love someone this much who irritated the hell out of me. I would never understand my mom. And I guess I just had to make peace with that too.

"I want to set you up with someone— Ooh, who is that hottie? He looks familiar."

Feeling caught, I wanted to click Christopher's image off the page, but I knew that would only encourage Althea's curiosity. "It's Darcy Hawthorne's ex-boyfriend. The astronaut. Captain Ortiz." I couldn't look as she bent over my computer screen. "He suddenly RSVPed to the engagement party, and I just wanted to learn a little more about him . . . just in case. It's not every day the ex-boyfriend shows up."

"Oh my God, you're such an overachiever. Though this is pretty nice extracurricular work. That boy is fine." Althea sat down on the edge of my desk. "Darcy Hawthorne has it all. Fine fiancé, fine ex-boyfriend. And an astronaut to boot, so you know he's smart and brave too. Some people have all the luck."

"Aren't you one of them?" I relaxed back in my office chair, relieved Althea hadn't picked up on my crush. The truth was, I *was* brushing up on details about Christopher. The engagement party was in two days.

"Yes, I am." She wore that secret smile that appeared on her face when Michelle's name came up. "And speaking of Michelle, her brother is newly single . . ."

Realization dawned. "No. Nope. Not ready."

"Oh, come on, Hallie. Derek is beautiful, and he's sexy, and he's actually a really nice guy. He got out of a long-term relationship a few months ago and is only now ready to get back on the horse."

"And you want me to be the horse?"

"I want the first woman he goes on a date with to be classy, kind, and sweet."

I felt my cheeks turn hot. "Don't do that. Now how am I supposed to say no?"

She grinned mischievously. "You can't. C'mon. We'll make it a double date."

A double date sounded better than a blind date.

Still.

"I don't know."

"Okay, wait, wait." She hurried out of my office and returned a minute later, cell clutched in her hand. "Look, look." After she tapped the screen a few times, she held it up to my face. On it was a picture of gorgeous Michelle with an equally gorgeous man at her side.

"You know looks aren't important to me."

"I know. But this one comes with the personality to match. I promise."

My gaze surreptitiously flickered back to the picture of Christopher in the article I'd found on him in the *New York Times*.

"Say yes, Hallie."

The engagement party was in two days.

"Um . . ." I looked back at Althea. "Let me think about it."

She wrinkled her nose in disappointment but nodded reluctantly. "Fine. But don't wait too long. You have no idea how many women just in his building alone have been waiting for him to break up with his fiancée."

"That's awful. Why would anyone wish that kind of unhappiness on someone?"

"See!" Althea pointed at me. "That! That right there is why you're perfect for him. You can both be nice people together."

I gave a huff of amusement. "I said I'd think about it."

"I'll leave you alone to do that."

Five minutes later, I got an intraoffice email from Althea. When I clicked it open, another photograph of Derek popped up on my screen.

I snorted at Althea's antics and hit Reply.

I said I'll think about it.

In response, she sent another photo.

Okay, Derek was definitely hot.

But, truthfully, someone else had my undivided attention. I enjoyed having a crush on Christopher. Maybe because it was fun to be crushing on someone when I hadn't experienced that feeling in such a long time. Also, because having this crush distracted me from the parts of my life that were difficult at the moment. From my parents, from the friends I was growing increasingly distant from, and from the fact that my last boyfriend made me feel insignificant and inferior.

I wasn't ready to give up my wonderfully distracting crush just yet.

Or the hope that maybe when we met, and I explained what had happened, Christopher might *not* hate me . . . and maybe, just maybe, he might even like me a little.

Yup, I groaned at my ridiculousness. I'd reverted to my teenage self, who had fantasized daily that one day I'd meet the Kings of Leon and one of them would fall in love with me.

"Grow up, Hallie," I muttered to myself, even as a stupid little smirk prodded my lips.

# TWELVE

## Chris

Standing beneath a tent on the rooftop of the turn-of-the-century hotel on Broadway, I couldn't help but admire the work that had gone into making it look this good. I'd attended swanky events in my life, but I'd usually been so desperate to leave that I'd never noticed or thought about the work that went into it. The guests at Darcy's party mingled beyond the tent in the open air of the rooftop, where classical musicians played. I stood inside the tented dining area as people passed me by. If my ears didn't deceive me, the musicians were playing instrumental versions of rock songs. That made me smirk as I nodded at people I knew and nursed the beer in my hand.

A few people murmured, "Thank you for your service" in my direction, and I nodded to acknowledge them, even though it was still discomfiting to have a face that strangers knew.

A man and his date approached me, and I braced myself. "Where did you get the beer?" he asked.

Relaxing, I tipped my head toward a server. "I just asked."

Servers mingled unobtrusively with the guests to offer them

flutes of champagne and canapés. I wasn't in the mood for champagne. I wasn't a champagne kind of guy.

Looking up at the ceiling of the tent, I realized it wasn't an average outdoor awning. This thing was wired with electricity. Large brass chandeliers and lanterns hung above our heads. Round tables were positioned inside the tent. Smaller lanterns sat in the middle of the tables, along with white floral arrangements. The decor was classy, simple, and unfussy. Just like Darcy.

Hallie had nailed it.

Speaking of . . .

I kept searching the crowds, hoping to spot the pink-haired event planner.

"You showed."

At the sound of her husky, familiar voice, I tensed and then forced myself to relax and turn to her.

"Darcy."

She hadn't changed. Still beautiful.

I suddenly saw her again in my memories, that night we first met four years ago. I was serving as an exchange officer with the US Navy and working as a test pilot for Patuxent River Naval Air Station. When I met Darcy, I'd just been selected to train to become an astronaut. She thought this was fascinating. I thought *she* was fascinating. Her confidence was incredibly appealing. While Darcy was privileged, she was aware of her privilege. She didn't apologize for it, but she was also cognizant of the fact that she had a responsibility to make a difference because of it.

The light from the chandelier above us glittered in her gray eyes.

Her floral perfume enveloped me as she leaned in to kiss my cheek, and as I expected, I didn't feel a hint of longing.

I'd realized some time ago that my feelings for my ex had

grown platonic. Despite how things ended, I knew she had a good heart, and I felt nothing but affection for her. We'd spent most of our relationship apart, with me training in Houston and her in Manhattan. Then, of course, I spent five and a half months in space. Five and a half months too long for Darce.

"You look great."

"Thanks. You too. But then you always knew how to wear a suit," she murmured flirtatiously, and I grinned. The woman just couldn't help herself.

"Where's the groom?" I glanced around, pretending I was looking for the guy who stole my girl and not the girl who'd planned this shindig.

"The soon-to-be groom. He's in the hotel, wrangling his parents. They flew in from Paris last night and are taking their sweet time getting to the party. They're minutes away in a hotel room here but can't make it to the party in time."

Hearing the strain in her words, I grimaced. "In-law issues?"

Darcy sighed. "They accused Matthias of selling out by marrying me, an heiress."

Stupidity like that never failed to surprise me. "Reverse snobbery?"

"Exactly." She shrugged. "I'll win them over eventually."

"You will." I squeezed her arm.

Her expression softened. "Chris, it's so good to see you. I mean it when I say that you being here means so much to me. You're one of the best people I know. I hope we'll always remain friends."

Once upon a time, those words would have made me wince. Now I replied easily, "You have my friendship for life, Darce."

She grinned, kissed my cheek again, and straightened her shoulders. "Into the breach I must go."

Chuckling, I nodded and watched her dive into the crowds to attend to her guests.

As I turned my head, a flash of pink caught my eye.

My breath hitched in my throat as I looked out toward the rooftop and saw her.

Hallie Goodman.

She was in profile to me, murmuring with a server, who nodded at whatever she had to say and strode away. Hallie turned to survey the party, and suddenly I felt nervous. I couldn't remember the last time I'd felt nervous about a woman. In fact, I think the last time I was seventeen and it was a *girl*.

I couldn't resist a smile as I stared at Hallie in the flesh for the first time.

Her cotton candy hair was styled in long waves that spilled over her shoulders. She wore a conservative silver-gray cocktail dress and impressively high-heeled shoes.

It was strange to look at a woman I'd never met before and feel this overwhelming sense of familiarity and closeness.

A throb in my throat drew my attention to the fact that my heart raced really fucking hard.

Then our eyes met across the rooftop.

Her lips parted in shock, and I tried to keep my expression as neutral as possible, but it was difficult. There was a sense of urgency in me. To go to her.

As if she read my mind, Hallie strode toward me.

My feet moved to meet her, and I skirted around guests, trying not to lose sight of her.

Then bam.

She was there.

Inches from me.

In those strappy heels, she was only a few inches shorter than me. Those big blue eyes were even more amazing in real life. A heady, sweet scent drifted over me as the breeze ruffled through my hair, and I knew it was her perfume. My gaze dropped to her neck, and I imagined pressing my lips against her throat, inhaling her fragrance.

Fuck.

A little dumbfounded, I couldn't find any words to say aloud and Hallie spoke before I could.

"I know who you are." She wrung her hands in front of her body, eyebrows drawn together in anxiety. "I'm Hallie Goodman. I'm Darcy and Matthias's event planner, and Darcy sent me files I asked for but accidentally included video letters you sent her home from the International Space Station, and I'm sorry, but I watched them. All of them. And it was so wrong of me, I can't even . . . There are not enough apologies in the world for invading your privacy like that. I'm so, so sorry."

Her eyes were wide with genuine remorse, and I wondered how I could have been so pissed at her just a few weeks ago. Now I knew, from watching her own videos, that Hallie was one of the good ones. It said a lot about her character that she would approach me, a guy she thought a stranger, and just blurt out the truth. That pureness of heart moved me. Wanting to alleviate her guilt, I opened my mouth to tell her I, too, had watched her videos, but she started talking rapidly again.

"If someone did that to me, a stranger watched my private video letters without my knowledge, I'd be so beyond mad, and I don't know if I could forgive them, so I understand if you can't forgive me. Or if you have to tell Darcy." Her expression blanched at the thought.

*Fuck.*

In that split second, I made a calculated decision. Disaster risk management. If I told her the truth now, when we hadn't had a chance to even move past initial introductions, then I was risking any chance of getting to know her in person.

I'd lose Hallie before I even had time to really know her.

The thought made me feel off-kilter.

So . . . it left me with only one choice. I'd tell her later. Once she knew me. Once she realized my intentions were well meaning.

Swallowing my guilt, I held her worried gaze and replied, "Honesty is a virtue I just happen to admire, so let's try this again." I held out a hand to her. "I'm Christopher Ortiz, friend of the bride."

# THIRTEEN

## Hallie

He wasn't angry?

In fact, his expression almost looked as if I intrigued him.

Me?

Christopher cleared his throat, and I realized I was just staring, stupefied at his outstretched hand.

Oh my God!

Like a reflex, I slipped my hand into his without thinking of the consequences, and as soon as his strong fingers curled around mine, I felt his touch everywhere. My whole body tensed with awareness, and a rush of heat filled my cheeks. Hopefully not visibly. Gaping into his handsome face, those shining dark eyes, I found my voice and the wherewithal to shake his hand in return. "Hallie Goodman. It's a pleasure to meet you."

A smile pushed up the corners of his spectacular mouth, and I felt the loss as he released me. When I'd spotted him across the room, it was like the entire party faded out.

There he was.

And shock of all shocks, he was looking at me.

When he crossed the room to meet me, my first thought was that he knew what I'd done—I was busted.

But nope.

Did that mean he was drawn to me before he even knew who I was?

The thought thrilled me.

"You've done an amazing job planning Darcy's engagement party. It looks great." He gestured with a beer bottle.

I frowned at it. Where did he get that? "Uh, yeah, thank you."

"I wanted to talk with you about working on a retirement party with me."

What? Party? Retirement?

Oh.

He approached me about work. *Not* because he was drawn to me. I deflated with the disappointed. "I'm sorry, for whose retirement?"

"Mine. From the air force." He smiled self-deprecatingly. "I'm not usually the social-butterfly type, but my aunt suggested it might be a nice sense of closure to invite some old comrades, friends, to a small party to celebrate the end of that chapter."

Christopher was retiring from the air force? "Oh. Well, sure, I mean—" Wait, didn't I just tell this guy I'd breached his privacy and trust? "I'm sorry, I'm confused. You heard me earlier, right?" I gestured behind me, indicating the past few minutes. "The part where I told you I watched your video letters to Darcy?"

His lips twitched, those dark eyes glittering in the fading light. I'd never seen eyes so dark yet so full of warmth. "I heard you, and I'm processing. But what I'm mostly processing is that you didn't need to tell me. In fact, for the sake of your job"—he gestured to the party—"you shouldn't have told me. Now unless you've shown those videos to other people or told all your friends about it, I think we can put it behind us and start over."

Oh my God, was he perfect? *Please don't be perfect.* The intensity of my crush on him already couldn't handle it.

"I haven't told a soul," I promised truthfully.

Christopher studied my face for a second. "I believe you."

"Just like that?"

He grinned, and it made me feel like butter on hot toast, my knees trembling as if they were ready to give out. This was ridiculous!

"Should I not believe you?"

"What? Of course you should."

His expression sobered. "I'm sure working together will give us enough time to get to know each other better."

Amazed at his forgiving nature, I shook my head. "Wow. Okay. I . . . It's more than I deserve, so thank you."

"You're welcome." He gestured to a server. "Can I flag you down a drink?"

"No, I don't drink while I'm working."

"Right. You're working."

Was that disappointment in his eyes, or was I just hoping it was disappointment?

"Speaking of." I nodded to his nearly empty beer bottle. "Where did you get that?"

"I just asked a server."

I chuckled, realizing what had happened. "My servers are under strict orders not to serve anything but the champagne until after dinner. Most of the guests know the protocol at these things, so it's rarely an issue. But who can deny a national hero and social media star if all he asks for is a beer?"

Realization dawned on Christopher's face. "Ah. Sorry, I didn't know. I didn't pressure him for it."

"No, I know." I grinned at his uncomfortable expression. He didn't like the fame? Interesting, considering he still posted regularly to Instagram. "You don't need to. And I would have given you the beer too, even if I hadn't watched those videos."

"I don't expect to be treated differently." He shifted on his feet, not meeting my gaze anymore.

He was humble too? *Thank you, Fates! Why don't you just rip out my heart and give it to him now?* "That's admirable. But you've done something few people in the world have ever done. You've served your country here and up there." I pointed upward. "That's pretty impressive, Captain."

His gaze zeroed in on me, something working behind his eyes. "Do you feel you know me?" he asked in a soft tone, curious, not accusatory. "Having watched those videos?"

Embarrassed but feeling I owed him, I answered honestly. "In a way."

"Just in a way? I shared some personal things on there."

"Some things. Mostly your thoughts on the world and on what you were doing. Yet, despite them being for Darcy, the whole time I kept thinking you were holding something back from her. It felt like you weren't giving her all of you." As soon as the words were out of my mouth, I wanted to die of mortification. How could I just blurt that out?

He raised his eyebrows, and an apology was just about to burst forth from me when he replied, "Maybe you're right."

I sucked in a breath of relief and then, as he held my gaze, staring at me like I was a puzzle he wanted to figure out, I think I stopped breathing.

Jesus, this whole situation was so surreal.

"Hallie, there you are." Darcy's voice jolted me, and I reluctantly tore my eyes from Christopher's.

Darcy sidled up to us, leaning into Christopher with familiarity, her hand resting on his shoulder. I fought the urge to shove her hand off him.

Whoa.

I was feeling territorial.

Wonderful.

That was sarcasm, FYI.

Seeing them together was like a bucket of cold reality. In her high heels, Darcy was taller than Christopher, whom I might have read somewhere was just an inch shy of six feet. Yet, it didn't look odd. He exuded too much charisma for anyone to care about the fact that his ex-girlfriend was taller than him when she wore heels.

They were striking together.

Her so fair and him so dark.

"Darcy." I shook myself from my stupor. "Is everything all right?"

"One of my more irritating guests is complaining because the servers wouldn't provide him with a beer."

Christopher grimaced. "Ah, that might be my fault. I fear I might have set a precedent."

"Sweetheart, you've earned your beer." Darcy patted his shoulder, then turned to me. "What shall we do? Shall we forgo the champagne-only rule for now?"

"If that's what you'd like, I can let the servers know."

"Yes, to keep the peace. Jeffrey really isn't one to understand the difference between himself, useless playboy heir to a fortune made by his parents, and national goddamn hero." Her smile strained. "But my mother did insist I invite him."

"Invite whom?" a sharp voice interrupted.

We all turned to admit the newcomer to our small group.

Darcy's mother.

Mrs. Violet Prendergast-Hawthorne. Daughter of an oil baron. Old money. And she'd married into a lot of new money when she married Charles Hawthorne. Mother and daughter were uncannily alike, despite the age difference.

The frostiness on Violet's face, however, melted as soon as she saw Christopher.

"Christopher, my darling boy, how wonderful to see you." She pushed through us to take hold of his free hand between both of hers, and Chris kissed her cheek, his expression warm.

"Violet, it's great to see you."

She didn't release his hand, standing close as she studied his face. "How are you? Your father says you haven't yet made a decision about your future?"

Intense conversation for an engagement party.

"Mother." Darcy gently eased between them. "Please don't harass Chris at my engagement party."

"Well, perhaps things would be different if he were the groom-to-be at this engagement party." She patted his hand again, oblivious or indifferent to the tension she created. "It is wonderful to see you. Charles and I must have you over for dinner so we can catch up. Charles is full of questions about your time on the station."

"I'd like that."

"Okay, I'll have Rosanna call you to arrange it." The affection in her expression disappeared in an instant as she turned to her daughter. "Where are your fiancé and his parents? It is rude to keep your guests waiting."

Suddenly desperate to be away from this cozy reunion and the reminder that Christopher Ortiz was way out of my league, I offered, "I'll go check on them. I'll also speak to the servers, Darcy."

My client threw me a sweet, grateful smile. "Thank you. You're a godsend, Hallie."

As I walked away without looking at Christopher, I heard Violet Hawthorne say, "Excellent planner, terrible hair."

I tried not to let her words affect me as I let the servers know they could serve any drinks that were requested and hurried into the hotel to find Matthias and his parents.

The rest of the evening I worked harder than ever to focus on the job at hand and did my very best not to search out Christopher. Yet, when the guests were all seated for dinner, and I'd faded into the background, I couldn't help but look for him.

When it was time for the engagement toasts, my gaze found Christopher, and I watched his expression as the bride and groom took turns thanking their guests and speaking of their love for each other.

Either Christopher was an excellent actor, or he was genuinely happy for Darcy.

The job of clearing up after dinner soon held my attention. The guests were out on the rooftop, which sparkled with the fairy lights wrapped around artificial topiary. Efficiently and quietly, we cleared away the tables as my servers walked among the guests with trays of petit fours and more champagne.

Within half an hour, we'd transformed the tent into a bar and dance floor. The musicians relocated inside, and the guests followed. I sent my assistant planner, Bree, home for the night, since the biggest part of the event had passed.

"You should have everything you require," I told the hired bartenders as the guests immediately zeroed in on them. "But if you run out of anything, let me know. There are more supplies inside."

The bartenders nodded, and I got out of the way. I was at the back of the rooftop, making sure the dirty champagne flutes were returned inside carefully when I felt a shiver skate down my neck.

I turned, and another stupid flutter made itself known in my stomach. Christopher.

It was still so surreal to see him standing in front of me. "Hi."

He smiled like I amused him. "Hi."

"Do you . . . do you need anything?"

"Well"—he stepped toward me, looking far too delicious in his three-piece suit—"your number might be helpful."

My . . . what? Holy . . . really? I mean . . . what?

"To arrange a lunch to discuss my retirement party."

Oh.

Right.

Could everyone hear the air hissing out of my hope-filled balloon?

I didn't keep cards on my person because Lia thought it was tacky to hand out cards at clients' events. "I don't have a card with me, but if you ask Darcy for my information, I'm sure she'll provide it, and we can arrange a meeting."

Christopher shook his head. "I don't want Darcy knowing about this just yet. She'll try to hijack the planning."

I gave a huff of laughter because she seemed like a person who would do that. "Okay. Do you have your cell with you?"

He pulled it out of his inside jacket pocket and said, "If it's not too much hassle, I'd prefer your direct line. I don't want to have to jump through hoops at your office to get to you."

I was planning on giving him *my* number anyway. Opportunist that I was. I rattled it off, and he saved it on his phone. "It's Hallie with an *ie* at the end."

"I know." He flashed me a quick, boyish grin. "I'm done here tonight, so I'll call, and hopefully we can arrange something for Monday."

My day was completely jam-packed on Monday. "Absolutely."

"It was nice meeting you, Hallie." His voice was all deep and rumbly.

Way too sexy for a client. Way too sexy. Bad idea! "You too. We'll talk soon."

And then he was walking away, and I most definitely ogled his ass.

Great ass.

"Bad idea, Goodman," I whispered. "This will not end well for you."

# FOURTEEN

## Hallie

I was sweating.

I hadn't even left the office yet, and there was perspiration under my arms, between my boobs, and across my upper lip. Glowering at myself in the mirror above the sink in the ladies' room, I patted my face with a powder puff to eliminate shine.

"This is just a lunch," I reminded myself. "A simple work lunch."

This morning had been a flurry of activity as I sped through tasks and rearranged a lunch I had scheduled with another prospective client. They hadn't been happy about it, which made me feel so guilty, but I was a little too overwhelmed with excited nervousness to give in to the people-pleasing spiral of agony such a situation would normally send me into.

Christopher had texted me yesterday morning to ask me to lunch. He'd named the place and time, and I'd agreed. Hoping it might be a long lunch, I'd attempted to get a full day's work done in one morning.

Hence the sweating.

At least, it was partly to blame.

A quick glance at my phone told me I needed to move. I stuffed my makeup back into my purse and marched out of the ladies' room only to almost collide with my boss. I stumbled away from her.

Lia crossed her arms over her chest. Her expression was suspicious and displeased.

Wonderful.

"Lia. Hi. I'm just on my way to a client lunch."

She raised an eyebrow. "Oh really? Surprising, because I just received an irate phone call from Julia Gardner-Smith about how unprofessional my staff are for canceling a lunch date last minute and how she'll have to rethink using my company at all for her wedding."

"I can explain."

"I'm breathless with anticipation."

Ignoring her sarcasm, I continued, "Have you heard of the astronaut Captain Christopher Ortiz?"

She frowned. "I'm sure I know the name."

"You will, because his face was plastered all over the news last year when he was sent on a mission to the International Space Station. He's only thirty-five years old, son of distinguished Manhattan businessman Javier Ortiz, and was one of the youngest captains in the United States Air Force. He made a bit of splash because he's garnered millions of followers on social media, is very handsome, and he dated Darcy Hawthorne for a few years before she met Matthias."

Lia's arms dropped from her chest. "Go on."

"He was at Darcy's engagement party on Saturday, and he asked to meet me for lunch to discuss the possibility of *us* planning a party to commemorate his retirement from the air force. He could only do today, and I used my judgment and decided he was a bigger fish to catch than Julia Gardner-Smith." I tried not to grimace at my tiny little lie, my heart racing. I was pretty sure Christopher would have been happy to meet on another day.

But the lie was necessary. There was nothing I hated more than pissing off my boss. Thankfully, it didn't happen often.

"Excellent judgment call." Lia nodded, her lips unpinching. "And if he's a friend of the Hawthornes, it's important we nourish that relationship. Every time that family hosts an event, I want it to be a Lia Zhang event."

I relaxed but tried not to be obvious. "Agreed. Well, he's expecting me, so . . ."

"Go, go." She shooed me with her hands. "Reel in that fish."

---

Christopher had arrived at the restaurant before me. It was around a fifteen-minute walk to the Victorian building that housed the restaurant. I'd eaten there a few times and liked the food and the laid-back vibe. I was pleased Christopher chose somewhere like this to eat rather than somewhere people went "to be seen."

Unfortunately the walk had just made me sweatier. Spring was fast fading into summer, and although it had rained all day yesterday, today the sun was back out. There was a slight chance I'd chosen my cute, sleeveless wrap dress out of my closet this morning, not just because of the sun shining outside but because of the man who would see me in it. The dress turned out to be a superb choice because it was so horribly humid out. I hoped there weren't sweat patches beneath my arms and tried to surreptitiously look as the waiter led me to our table.

I'd just ascertained I was okay in the armpit department and looked up only to be caught in Christopher's warm brown gaze. His lips curled at the corner in a slight smile, his expression welcoming.

Before the waiter could pull out my chair, Christopher rounded it and did it for me. For a moment, the gesture stunned me.

When was the last time a man pulled out my chair for me?

It was such an old-fashioned gesture.

And it completely charmed me.

"Thank you," I murmured as I slipped into the chair. It was so considerate and well-mannered. I couldn't even remember the last time George had held a door open for me. I'd held plenty of doors open for him, that was for sure.

"Hallie, are you okay?"

I blinked out of my reverie and wanted to melt into a puddle of gooey embarrassment at the concerned frown between Christopher's brows. "Oh God, I spaced out, didn't I?"

His lips twitched. "A little." He flicked a look at our server. "Lawrence here was just asking you what you'd like to drink."

I gave our server an apologetic smile. "A soda water and lime, please."

"Just water for me," Christopher said.

As soon as the server left, I blurted out, "You pulled my chair out for me."

Those dark eyes of his glittered with confusion. "And?"

"It surprised me. In a good way. Hence the woolgathering. Sorry." *I am such a dork.*

Christopher grinned. "I don't think I've ever met anyone who just says what's on their mind like you do."

"Oh, I don't. I frequently withhold feelings in order to protect the feelings of others." Did I just say that? I hung my head in mortification. "I seem to have a slight filter issue around you, Christopher, apologies."

"You can call me Chris, please." He was still smiling. "And I think you're very refreshing."

Something about his tone made my cheeks hot. "Thank you."

I pulled my seat a little closer to the table and knocked my knee against his. My pulse throbbed in my neck as I tucked my legs back under my seat.

"You look a little flushed. Are you okay?"

"Uh, I walked here. That's probably why." *It has nothing to do with my knee touching your knee, or the fact that I've reverted to a fourteen-year-old.*

"In those shoes?" Chris raised a brow.

He noticed my shoes? When? "I'm used to walking in them. My mom put me in my first pair of heels when I was fourteen and told me I better get used to them because they would help me overcome the disadvantage of being short."

"Is your mother short?"

"Nope."

"So how did she know you were done growing at fourteen? For all she knew, you might have grown into supermodel height."

"That's what I said." I replied a little loudly in my enthusiasm because it was *exactly* what I used to say to her when I was a teen. I flushed at my volume-control issue while Chris chuckled.

"Well," I continued more quietly. "She was right. Five foot four is not exactly tall. And I am now very used to walking in high heels. They hurt by the end of the day, but you grow used to the ache, you know." And why was I still talking about high heels?

Embarrassed by my rambling, I turned to why we were here. Work.

"So let's talk about your retirement party." I pulled my tablet out of my purse and tapped its pen on the screen to quickly open up my notes. "The first thing I need to know is budget. Do you have a budget in mind?"

"Ah, okay. Um . . . I have to admit I am clueless to how much it costs to throw a party. I don't want to spend crazy amounts of money . . ."

Seeing how lost he looked, I countered to rescue him. "What's most important to you? Food or venue?"

"Food. Always food." He grinned.

I grinned back. "Good choice. Okay, well, let's just discuss what you're looking for, and we'll come back to budget."

He nodded for me to continue.

"Most people want to jump right into discussing and nailing down the venue. However, I like to discuss food and music because those things actually give me a much better sense of the kind of energy you'd like at your event. So, Chris, what are you thinking?" I looked him directly in the eyes as he leaned toward me. "Food: Do you want a formal sit-down dinner, or would you prefer something more relaxed, where food is served sporadically throughout?"

"The latter. Definitely the latter."

I noted that. "Do you want to do a buffet, canapés, and snacks . . . Or we could even do something along the lines of a relaxed cookout. We could hire a chef who is a master of the grill, and we could do burgers, hot dogs, maybe even some seafood?"

"That sounds perfect actually. The cookout idea. I think it would appeal to a lot of my guests." He frowned. "Maybe not all though."

Scrawling on my tablet, I made another list heading. "Let's talk about guests, then. Who in general—I don't need names right now, though I will need a guest list as soon as possible—will be attending? Give me the generalized groups."

Chris's gaze never left my face. "Friends from the air force, from NASA. College buddies. All of whom I'm sure would love the cookout. But I'll also be inviting the Hawthornes, my father . . ."

I smiled to myself as I wrote. "Okay, I understand. I think, however, we're going to concentrate on the fact that this is *your* retirement party, a celebration of you, and it should reflect who you are. If a cookout is what you want, I can come up with ways to refine how it's served to guests who might not want to stand in a line at a grill or eat messy food with their hands."

"Sounds great."

"Okay, fantastic. That was easy." I smiled. "What about music? Do you want live music? A deejay? Or are you happy for us just to use a sound system to play a prearranged playlist?"

"A sound system is fine."

"Genre of music?"

Chris shook his head. "I don't want classical music. Too formal. A relaxed playlist. Maybe a mix of classic rock and pop. No techno, no dance, nothing too divisive that might grate on some people."

I wrote all that down too. "So, it's obvious." I looked at him now. "You want something very relaxed and informal, and I think we should let that inform your venue choice. Did you have somewhere in mind?"

"Actually my aunt offered her place in the Hamptons for the party. It's right on the beach, and I think that might play really well into a cookout."

My little event-planner heart jumped with glee. All the pieces were coming together beautifully and easily. I wished every client were like Chris. For more reasons than one. "It sounds perfect. Not to come across as too forward, but I'd need to see it to understand the space so I can plan appropriately."

"Of course. How about a weekend soon? I'll take you out there myself."

Ignoring the answering flutter in my stomach, I tried to nod coolly.

Suddenly I remembered the imaginary conversation I'd recited over and over in my head as I'd walked here. The one I needed to have with him before our lunch went any further.

The server returned with our drinks and to take our order. Once he departed again, I jumped right into it. "I hate to bring this up, but I really feel like I must because I'm a little confused by how easily I've been forgiven."

Chris's brows drew together. "The videos?"

"It's not something I really want to remind you of, but I do feel like we breezed past it at the party, and I wanted the chance to fully explain myself."

"Okay." He relaxed back in his chair and waited.

"I was . . ." I halted because I'd promised myself that I wouldn't get too personal. "There were, are"—*No, don't let him think you're too distracted by your personal stuff to work on his party*—"were things going on in my life at that time and . . . Jesus, this is going to sound so cheesy."

"I can handle cheesy," he teased.

Why was he so damn nice? My heart fluttered.

"At first your videos really drew me in because of the whole fascinating astronaut-in-space thing."

Chris nodded like he understood.

"And I know I should have stopped watching as soon as I realized these were personal videos for Darcy." I lowered my gaze and took a minute to draw up the courage to meet his eyes again. I did. Immediately I was snared in them, my breath hitching a little. What the hell was that? I pushed past the overwhelming feeling. "But you talked a lot about things I worry about, things I thought no one else was thinking about or philosophizing over, and I just really appreciated your viewpoint. Not just because you have a wisdom beyond your years, but because you have such a distinctive and rare perspective on the world because of your unique experiences. I know it's not a good excuse for invading your privacy, but I found solace in your videos, and while I'm sorry for watching them when I shouldn't have, I also want to thank you."

My pulse felt like an animal beating in my neck to get out. My palms were slick.

Eyes shining, Chris let me out of my misery by inclining his head. "I forgive you. And you're welcome. I know that feeling and, though it wasn't my intention, I'm humbled that you got something worthwhile from watching them."

Nicest. Guy. Ever.

I was so in trouble with this one.

"Thank you for being so gracious." I exhaled, trying to relax.

Humor flashed in his eyes, but he saved me with a subject change. "So I'll call Aunt Richelle and, uh, ask her which upcoming weekend works for her for you to see the place."

"That would be great. So your aunt Richelle? Paternal or maternal?"

"Maternal. She was my mom's younger sister. She's an artist, and despite being so much younger, she really stepped up to be there for me and my brother when my mother died."

Shit, why did I bring this up? Stupid, stupid. "I'm so sorry about your mother. And your brother. You don't have to talk about it if you don't—"

"It's fine," he cut me off with a small, humorless smile. "Everyone skirts around people's losses like loss is contagious and they don't want to get infected. Ever notice that?"

"Yes. However, I don't think it's entirely for selfish reasons. I know I always worry that I might cause a person unnecessary pain by bringing up the subject of a lost loved one."

Chris considered that. "I want to talk about them. There are people in my life who don't want to talk about them, and it's frustrating."

"I can imagine that would be extremely frustrating." I wondered which people he referred to. His father, perhaps? "Well . . . you can talk to me about them anytime." I rolled my eyes inwardly at myself. Sure, Chris Ortiz was going to choose *me* to confide in.

The left corner of his mouth lifted as if he found the thought just as silly. But then he surprised me by replying, "Thank you. And I hope we will. But first tell me about yourself. How long have you worked as an event organizer?"

I beamed at his word choice. "I love how you exchanged the term 'party planner' for 'event organizer.' Nicely handled, Captain."

Chris chuckled. "After seeing what you did for Darcy's engagement party, I feel like your job deserves more gravitas. It looked amazing. And surely, you're juggling several events at once all the time, right?"

More charmed than I could say by his appreciation, my cheeks ached from my stupid grin. "Yeah, I am. It's a lot more stressful than people think. Often we're dealing with massive budgets, and people want to know that the money is being used appropriately and in a way that appeals to their aesthetic, you know."

"Oh, for sure. You couldn't throw half your budget at a rock band for Darcy's engagement, for instance, or Violet would metaphorically separate your head from your neck."

"Violet. There it is. You did it again."

"Did what?"

"When you called Mrs. Hawthorne Violet to her face, I almost died. Only a famous astronaut could get away with that. It's like calling the Queen Lizzy."

Chris gave a bark of laughter. "Not quite. I'm pretty sure to the Brits that's blasphemy."

"Okay, fine. But she actually smiled at you. I mean, she was nicer to you than she was to her own daughter. And don't even get started on me. The three times I've met her, she's asked me each time if I colored my hair for a charity fundraising event and if it was ending anytime soon."

His deep laughter rang out through the restaurant, and it was infectious. "That sounds like Violet."

"Stop it. Just you saying her name makes me sweat with nerves."

"She's not that scary."

"She's terrifying. I do not know how Darcy came out of her. And you're right about the rock music. Matthias really wanted rock music at the party, and I thought Darcy didn't because it wasn't to her taste, but now you've got me thinking it was because of Mrs. Hawthorne."

"Uh, it's possibly a part of that, but I've known Darcy a few years, and she's definitely more of a classical music lover."

Suddenly it occurred to me we were talking about his stunning ex-girlfriend. Beyond the bite of jealousy I experienced, I felt like an insensitive twit. "I'm sorry. I probably shouldn't have brought them up."

"Why?"

I raised an eyebrow.

Chris sighed. "Look, Darcy and I are just friends. I'm genuinely happy for her, or I wouldn't have attended the party on Saturday."

"Okay." I wouldn't overanalyze why I really needed to believe that. "Anyway, my job involves solving problems like that."

"So you came up with the classical musicians playing rock music?"

"Yeah."

"It was good. It didn't even bother *Violet*."

I visibly shuddered. "That's never going to sit right with me."

He chuckled. "I think you have an issue with authority."

"Yes, I absolutely do. I was the kid who felt nauseated if a teacher so much as snapped at me."

"I was the kid who left an apple on the teacher's desk every morning."

I giggled. "I can totally see that. Christopher Ortiz, charming people since . . . 1987."

Chris confirmed his birth year with a nod. "I learned from the best." He shrugged unrepentant. "My brother, Miguel, taught me a thing or two about how to treat women."

I wanted to blurt out the question, *Not your father?* but I was enjoying our light banter and didn't want to ruin it. "Was he a ladies' man?"

"Oh yeah. While I was happy to leave an apple on a desk, I *was* a pretty shy kid, but Miguel was coaxing girls behind the bleachers from the age of ten."

"No way."

"Seriously, he was girl crazy from almost the beginning. He used to rib me constantly for being a serial monogamist. Was always trying to convince me to play the field."

"But that wasn't you?" I really, really didn't want that to be him.

"It wasn't me." He gave me a boyish smile. "I've always enjoyed being in a relationship. I mean, I don't need to be in one, but to me, one-night stands just feel . . ."

"*Empty,*" I supplied.

"Right."

*I'm in love.*

*Shut up. You're being silly.*

*You're infatuated, and there's a difference.*

"How did I get to one-night stands?" He shook his head at himself. "Sorry, we were talking about your issue with authority."

"Is it an issue?" I cocked my head to the side in thought. "I respect authority figures. I would think as a captain in the United States Air Force and a NASA astronaut that you have a very healthy respect for authority figures. So why is *mine* an 'issue'?"

His answering smile was appreciative, and the little hairs on the back of my neck rose. "As much as it might offend Violet Hawthorne, I think there's a relatively vast difference between her and my allegiance to the United States."

"Don't let her hear you say that, or she'll have Rosanna disinvite you to afternoon tea in the parlor."

He smirked. "Are you mocking the wealthy, Ms. Goodman?"

The usual spike of fear that I'd feel at anyone taking my teasing seriously didn't flare to life. Instead I held my finger and thumb up and replied, "Maybe a little. But I'm an equal opportunist mocker if that makes it any better."

"Oh really? Who else do you mock?"

"Me, frequently. Do you know just a few weeks ago I found myself in the ridiculous situation of buying a stranger several pairs of kitten socks?"

Eyes alight with amusement. "Oh, do tell."

I laughed. "It's a long story."

His expression said, *I've got time.* He gestured for me to continue.

And I did. Without the usual moronic shame I'd felt around George or Gabby or even my parents.

Ninety minutes flew by like five, and there was never a lull in conversation.

# FIFTEEN

## Chris

The one-bedroom apartment I was considering in Brooklyn was two hundred square feet smaller than my apartment in Manhattan and cost considerably less. It didn't have anything like the corner window looking out over the city, yet it was well designed, well maintained, and nothing more or less than what I required. It was definitely on the top of my list, I decided, promising my Realtor I'd be in touch before leaving her to walk to the subway.

Now I had to tell my father I was going to rent out Mom's apartment, and I knew how well that conversation would go. Whether because of the level of fame I'd reached with NASA or the fact that I'd dated a society princess, he incorrectly assumed it meant I wanted to be a part of his world now. And being a part of Javier Ortiz's world meant caring about appearances. Living in the right apartment, in the right area, meant something to him. He used to complain all the time about living in Bedford as if it weren't an extremely nice place to live. But it was the one thing Mom would not budge on. She didn't want us growing up in a world so far removed from what she'd grown up in. From what most people grew up in. Although it had a very small Latinx community, Bedford wasn't just for the upper middle class, and Mom liked that. She thought it was a good compromise between what my father wanted and what she wanted.

I couldn't give a shit about that materialistic stuff. I'd seen too much of the real world to know none of it mattered in the end. I wasn't the New York society guy, no matter what the internet tried to say about me.

It was best to tell my father about the apartment now anyway, while he was already angry with me. There was no more avoiding him. Aunt Richelle was right. I had to face my father. I just hated doing that when I was so uncertain about my future. Uncertainty was something that ambitious son of a bitch seemed incapable of feeling.

My father and Benjamin Clairmont's company was housed in an impressive building in Lower Manhattan that also held a law firm and a tech company, but my father had the prime upper floors. Including the best view. His staff greeted me with a warm welcome as his assistant led me toward his office.

"It's been a while, Christopher," Mena said with a smile thrown over her shoulder. "Your father will be pleased to see you."

Right.

Co-owning a conglomerate meant my father was an incredibly busy man. Work was his life. His company was a multi-industry, multinational one, which meant he knew a lot about many things. To his despair, neither Miguel nor I showed any interest in what he did. Miguel, he'd forgiven. Me not so much. Not until I became an astronaut.

Mena stopped in at her office, a small space attached to my father's, and picked up her phone. "Mr. Ortiz, your son is here to see you." After a second she replied, "Right away, sir," and hung up. She gave me a bright smile. "This way."

My father had the best office in the entire building. Any view from the South Street side entrance was pretty good, but Javier Ortiz's office was near the top floor, and his windows looked out across the East River toward Brooklyn.

"Thank you, Mena." I inclined my head toward her as I stepped into my father's space. His home, really. The sofa on the left side of his office was big enough for him to sleep on, which I assumed he did frequently. There was an attached private restroom with a shower. There were a lot of bookshelves filled with books in my father's office. I'd never seen him reading anything but paperwork, but I couldn't assume they were just for show. There were many things, I guessed, that I didn't know about him.

Once his assistant closed the door behind her, I finally met my father's gaze. He stood by his desk, his expression neutral. Javier Ortiz was a distinguished, handsome man in his sixties. There were deeper wrinkles around his eyes and mouth than there used to be, and his black hair was now salt and pepper, but he still did not look his age. Perhaps it was the way he held himself.

I'd never seen my father in anything but a sharp, tailored suit, other than a tuxedo. I couldn't remember a time when I woke up to breakfast to find him sitting in the kitchen in his pajamas, drinking coffee, and shooting the shit with Mom. That never happened. Even on the Christmas mornings he attended (and there were only a few) he was already dressed in a shirt and suit pants when Miguel and I got up to open presents. It was like he wasn't a real person. More work robot than human.

"He finally deigns to come see his father," he said as he rounded his desk.

I didn't bother taking a seat. "How are you?"

"How am I? More to the point, how are you? I've been calling and getting no answer. Is that any way to treat your father? Did I raise you to be so disrespectful of my time?"

"No. I apologize."

He raised an eyebrow. "Is that it?"

"What else do you want me to say?"

His expression hardened. "Why don't you start with what the hell is going on with your career? Why are you gallivanting around the Hamptons with your aunt? Shouldn't you be in Houston?"

Here goes nothing. "I turned down their mission offer. And I've retired from the air force."

The atmosphere in the office went from cool to freezing in zero point two seconds.

"You did what?"

I sighed. "I don't want to go back into space, and I'm absolutely certain that I no longer want to fly jets for the air force."

My father's dark eyes ran all over my face like he'd never seen me before. I was familiar with the expression. "Why are you so set toward destroying your own life?"

Another question of his I was familiar with. He'd said it to me when I told him I'd applied to the US Air Force Academy instead of the Ivys. The irritating thing was, he'd probably been right about that one. I had followed Miguel instead of following my own path.

Frustration burned in my throat, but I pushed past it. "I'm not set toward destroying anything. I'm just taking time to regroup."

"What kind of man takes time to regroup?" he spat the last word like it was filthy. "How can my son be so brave as to fly fighter jets and travel into space and yet be such a lazy disappointment now?"

Though his words physically hurt, like a punch in my chest, I showed no outward appearance of them bothering me in the slightest. "I'm sorry you feel that way. But I'm doing what I have to do."

"What is that exactly?"

I'd promised myself I wouldn't cave to his interrogation, but like always, Javier Ortiz had a way of making me feel like that nine-year-old who'd got caught stealing his father's watch. I'd only done it because I wanted to feel closer to him. To have something of his. And he'd treated me like a common thief. Suddenly the words were coming up out of me before I could stop them. "NASA received some interest in me writing a book, so that's what I'm working on right now."

My father's frown relaxed. "A book?"

"Yes." Shit. Why did I tell him?

"As in an autobiography?"

"Yes."

He nodded. "Fine. I'll want to read it first. And I'd also like you to publish it through one of my companies."

My father's company was the parent company of several publishing houses.

And this was why I shouldn't have said a damn word.

"NASA is going to deal with all of that." We hadn't discussed it thoroughly, but I was pretty certain from my conversation with them they would.

"I'll still want to read it first. I need to make sure that any mention of me or our family isn't damaging to the company's public image. And I'll want to make sure you're getting the best deal, so I'll need your contact at NASA."

There was his arrogance, thinking he could manage this over the efforts of an agency like NASA. I drew myself up for a possible explosive reaction. "You're not reading it, and you will have nothing to do with its publication. But don't worry, you're barely mentioned."

"Excuse me?" He cut me a dark look.

"The book is about my journey to becoming an astronaut." It was more than that, but he didn't need to know that. "You don't factor into it."

"I'll still want to read it first."

"And I said no."

"Why?" He took a step toward me, eyes flashing with his growing anger. "Why wouldn't you let me read it unless you were intending to say damaging things about me?"

Refusing to be intimidated, I replied calmly, "I don't want you reading it first because it's got nothing to do with you."

"I'm your father."

"Only in the biological sense."

"What the hell does that mean, you disrespectful little shit?"

I refused to flinch as he raised his voice. I'd learned long ago that the calmer I was during an argument, the more it pissed him off, and I was just spiteful enough to enjoy it. "I'm grateful for the opportunities the money you worked hard to make afforded us, but let's not pretend that you had any hand in raising me. Beyond your controlling interest in my education, you weren't there to raise me as other fathers are there to raise their sons. I'm not complaining." That was a lie. Mom was there for us emotionally and always had time for us in the evenings, but she worked extremely hard on her business too, so we had a lot of babysitters when we were kids. Miguel and I saw more of those babysitters than we ever saw of our father. "I'm just stating a fact. You and I are not close. Writing this book is very personal to me, and you are the last person I would think to come to about it."

"Always disrespecting me. Since you were a boy. Talking back, disagreeing with me, asking questions you should not be asking." He spat out each of these as if they were a crime and strode around his desk to stand behind it. "You were always ungrateful. Why couldn't you be more like Miguel?"

I lowered my gaze so he wouldn't see me flinch.

*Why can't you be more like Miguel?*

I'd joked to my brother once that I was going to get the question tattooed on my body because our father asked it so many times. The joke covered up the trauma the question inflicted on me.

Miguel was the charmer of the two of us. He always knew what to say to get around our father. Miguel was the one who convinced him to allow me to attend the academy.

"For just a moment, I was proud to be your father. To say my son was an astronaut. But, like always, you cannot stick to something once you commit. You even let Darcy Hawthorne slip through your fingers, and now she's marrying a fucking French artist, of all things. You should have proposed to that girl before you went up into space. I might have forgiven this current fuckup if you'd made a useful connection with the Hawthornes. You know I am interested in investing in the hotel business, but no, you had to screw that up too."

Hurt seized me. But I'd never let him see. Instead I gave a huff of amusement. "We're in the twenty-first century now. Maybe you should join us there."

"You impudent little fuck," he said in quiet fury. "Get out of my office. And don't bother coming back until you have your life together."

Shaking my head, knowing that wasn't the end of it because he was too much of a controlling bastard to let it go, I turned and reached for the door. I glanced back at him. "You'll find out soon enough, but I'm putting the Midtown East apartment up for rent and taking something more affordable elsewhere."

He muttered a series of curse words, glaring at me. "It wouldn't be an issue if you had a respectable job."

I lifted my chin, unsurprised by his answer, and yanked open his office door. The pulse in my neck throbbed hard and fast as I marched out of there, refusing to meet anyone's gaze. Unspent exasperation burned hot in my blood, along with dejection and disappointment. The conversation between me and my father never changed. I knew that going in. And yet, I hadn't quite figured out a way to stop caring.

I needed a distraction.

As if on cue, my cell buzzed inside my jacket pocket as I stepped outside my father's office building. When I pulled it out, I found a few texts from Hallie.

**Theme options for your party:**

**Red, white, and blue (sounds cheesy, but I can make it classy)**

**Hampton beach style**

**Space theme but for adults (not "adults" as in kinky but as in maturity)**

Chuckling at the last one, I texted back:

I don't know enough about any of this to understand these themes. I'm still in the city. Can we meet over dinner tonight so we can discuss?

Keeping my phone in hand, I walked toward the subway at Bowling Green. Obviously dinner was just an excuse to see Hallie again. Our lunch a few days ago had been the best afternoon I'd had in a long time. The conversation between us flowed easily. I couldn't stop staring into her gorgeous blue eyes, and every time she smiled I wanted to kiss her.

And I was pretty sure the sexual tension was mutual. She stared at my mouth a lot. That wasn't easy to ignore.

Despite knowing I was feeling something toward her after watching her videos (I wouldn't have gone to Darcy's party otherwise), I hadn't expected to feel this attracted to Hallie in person.

Yet, I knew doing anything about it was a terrible idea.

I was in a weird place in my life.

Starting a relationship with someone was not a smart thing to do right now, and I had no intention of pursuing anything romantic between us. But I couldn't help but want to be around Hallie. I definitely wanted to be friends with her. There was something about her. . . . I felt like I could trust her, and there weren't many people who came into my life I felt certain about like that. That seemed worth exploring, even if only in a friendship.

More than all my other reasons for not pursuing a romantic relationship with Hallie was the fact that I still hadn't told her the truth about *her* videos. Until I did that, friendship could be the only thing on my mind.

My cell buzzed.

It was Hallie.

**Sure. I'm free. Where will I meet you?**

The grin stretched my lips wide as a wave of anticipation flooded over me.

She'd distracted me just when I most needed it.

# SIXTEEN

## Hallie

The sun hadn't fully set as I walked toward the tapas bar on the Upper East Side. It wasn't a long walk from the subway, but just long enough to get the old nerves going again. My knees shook, and my palms were ridiculously clammy. When Chris asked to meet me again so soon, I'd been ecstatic. I'd even fantasized that perhaps he longed for my company and not just to discuss his party. We'd had such a good time at our lunch that I thought the nervousness, the fluttering anticipation, would have dissipated by now.

I was wrong.

The tapas bar had a very traditional Spanish taverna appearance with its dark red painted exterior and small windows. It had a casual outdoor seating area, and I was glad everything about it looked laid-back because I was still dressed in my clothes from work. I hadn't seen the point of going home to Brooklyn only to have to return to the city, so I'd stayed at the office.

"Hallie!"

The hair on the nape of my neck rose, and I turned.

Chris strolled down the sidewalk toward me, coming from the

same direction I'd just come from. He wore a blue shirt beneath a black sweater that showed off his powerful arms, and he wore suit pants. He was preppy but in a really hot way.

I smiled and gave a little wave.

He grinned, slowing down to a halt, and I noted he hadn't shaved in a few days. The stubble was good. Very good.

"I thought I saw you heading out of the subway before me. I was right."

Chris traveled the subway? I'd assumed he was a cab kinda guy. "You didn't call out to me before now, did you? I can be oblivious sometimes."

"No." He shook his head. "How are you?"

"Good. You?"

"I'm good now." He gestured to the restaurant. "Shall we?"

"Sure."

I turned to walk toward the entrance and almost stumbled at the feel of his warm hand pressing against the base of my spine. A flutter in my throat alerted me to the fact my heart had picked up pace. Trying not to tense or seem like I wasn't enjoying his guiding hand on my back, I focused on putting one high-heeled foot in front of the other.

Without letting go of me, Chris reached out with his free hand and opened the door. Music and the hum of conversation, laughter, and dishes clattering spilled out. It was cozy inside, and I was momentarily distracted from Chris's touch by the assault on my senses. The food aroma was heady and amazing, making me salivate. The Latin music was upbeat but not so loud that you couldn't talk or hear yourself think. People sat at a bar eating tapas, as well at bistro tables and booths scattered throughout the room.

"Hola." A dark-haired waiter approached us. "*Bienvenido a Valeria's*. How may I help?"

Chris replied, "Hi. We have a table booked under Ortiz."

The man's eyes widened. "*Sí, sí. Es un placer conocerle, Capitán Ortiz. Mi nombre es Víctor. Seré su mesero esta noche. Por aquí, por favor.*" He gestured with his arm and then started walking in that direction.

I couldn't speak Spanish beyond the basics, but it was clear from Victor's expression that he knew who Chris was. I hadn't expected people to recognize him, but apparently they did. As we followed, I noted Chris's hand felt like it weighed heavier against my back.

I glanced up at him and saw a small frown between his brows, and his mouth was a little pinched, like he was tense.

What on earth?

Victor pulled out my chair, and I reluctantly moved away from Chris's touch to sit. I murmured my thank-you and observed Chris as he sat across from me at the small, intimate table in the back corner of the room.

"*Es una velada perfecta para tapas. ¿Ha cenado antes con nosotros o le gustaría ver el menú?*" Victor directed his question at Chris, and we both waited for a reply.

Instead Chris's nostrils flared and he shifted uncomfortably in his seat.

Realization dawned and I jumped in. "Victor, while Spanish is music to my ears, it's also music I can't understand." I smiled with pretend sheepishness. "I don't want to make Chris translate everything for me tonight, so if we could converse in English, I'd so appreciate it."

Victor looked mortified that he might have offended Chris by speaking in a language his "date" didn't understand. "Forgive me, I should not have presumed." He continued to take our drink order and provide us with a menu. There was a tension at the table I did not like.

"I'm going to defer to your opinion and order what you recommend," I said, trying to alleviate the thick atmosphere.

"Why don't we order a sharing platter?"

"Sounds good."

"I can tell you what I've enjoyed in the past."

We pondered the menu for a few minutes, made our selections, and, as if he'd been watching us, Victor returned to take our orders.

As soon as he was gone, Chris's gaze darted around the restaurant as he took a sip of his wine.

And my lack of a filter kicked in. "You don't speak Spanish?"

His eyes came back to me. "Because I'm half Mexican, it's a requirement? And I didn't need you to cover for me like I should be ashamed I don't speak Spanish."

I almost flinched at the sharpness in his tone.

Feeling awful, I shook my head. "No . . . I'm sorry, I didn't mean it like that. I thought . . . Never mind. It was a genuine question. I know you speak Russian from your videos, so I just assumed you were this wicked smart linguist."

Chris studied me for a second, the blood rushing in my ears the longer he did it. Then, finally, his shoulders relaxed and his expression softened. "I'm sorry. I shouldn't have spoken to you like that. I know you were just trying to be kind."

"I'm sorry." I felt extremely awkward. In all his video letters Chris had come across as perpetually calm and even-tempered. But he was human, so it was unfair of me to hold him to an impossible standard of behavior.

"You have nothing to be sorry for, Hallie. I . . . uh . . . It's been a difficult day. The truth is I was never taught Spanish. And my father discouraged us from choosing a language as a subject at school. He thought it was a waste of our time because he could surround himself with paid translators and just assumed that would be our future too. I learned some basic Spanish from my brother, who learned it from friends in the military, and I learned some more from men I later served with. But it's very basic. I understood what Victor said to us, but my Spanish isn't good enough to reply fluently or hold an entire conversation with him."

Something like discomfort flickered in his gaze.

Did he think it was a failing that he couldn't speak Spanish? I hated that idea. "Why wouldn't your father teach you?"

"I don't know. When I bring up the subject, he shuts it down. All I know is that he was raised in foster care, and so I have no connection to my Mexican heritage."

"Do you want a connection?"

"As I get older, I definitely do. It was always something my brother and I talked about doing together. Learning Spanish. Going to Mexico. Maybe even trying to find our family. We knew our father would disapprove, but we were always stronger as a unit. We could withstand his disapproval together."

The sadness—which was obviously grief—in his eyes made me want to reach out and squeeze his hand. Before I could stop myself, I did it. My palm tingled as I held his warm, dark gaze. "You should do it." I squeezed his hand and released him before he could react. "If it would mean something to you, do it. It must seem so strange to have literally been on top of the world, to watch it turn and feel a part of this constantly expanding universe, and yet feel disconnected to something so intrinsically a part of you, something small in the grand scheme of things but big to you."

Chris's lips parted; his eyes grew round. He studied me like he'd never seen me before, and I suddenly cursed my overfamiliarity with a client. Just as I was about to apologize, he replied, his voice hoarse, "Exactly."

Knowing I hadn't crossed some line with him, I should have relaxed. Yet our eyes held, and I could practically feel the electricity sparking in the air.

Oh boy.

Chris broke our staring contest and cleared his throat. "So . . . uh . . . themes, huh?"

"Hmm?" It took me a second to understand the question. "Oh, right. Themes." I pulled out my phone and leaned toward him as he leaned into me. He smelled good. Clean and sharp, with a hint of something smoky. Like a crisp fall day in the woods.

I showed him a couple of inspiration pics on my phone and sat back in my seat just as our food arrived.

Any discussion about the party ended as we ate.

I moaned under my breath as the spicy piquillo truffle sauce wreaked wonderful havoc on my taste buds.

Chris smirked around a bite of food and wiped sauce off his lips with a napkin. "Good?"

I nodded, still chewing, my eyes wide with pleasure.

He laughed and dove back into his food.

You always knew food was good if you couldn't even make conversation.

"Amazing recommendation," I finally managed as I reached for more.

"I'm glad you're enjoying it."

We smiled at each other, and I sighed inwardly as I realized I really had to discuss the party with him. "So I'm leaning toward a laid-back beach style to fit with the cookout. I can keep it gender-neutral, leaning more toward an elegant, softer palette rather than anything too colorful and too theme-like. But we can add touches to individualize it."

"Agreed."

I narrowed my eyes. "You really don't care, do you?"

Chris huffed in amusement. "Hallie, I don't know anything about this stuff. I'm trusting you with it."

I swear I got goose bumps every time he said my name. "Okay, Captain. But I will be double-checking all my choices with you."

"That's fine by me."

"So does this mean you're staying in the city for a while, or do you return to Houston soon?"

*Please say no.*

Chris exhaled heavily, as if he were burdened by a physical weight on his chest. "Honestly, I don't know what I'm doing. I quit the air force, I turned down a second mission with NASA, and I have no clear direction. I spend my days uploading photos of me drinking coffee or playing with my aunt's dog to Instagram." He smirked unhappily. "I'm thirty-five years old, and I feel a little lost." His features hardened. "I can't believe I admitted that to you. I'm . . . Fuck."

"Hey." I ducked my head to meet his gaze. The turmoil in his eyes disturbed me. And it perturbed me how much I hated seeing this man upset. "It makes absolute sense to me you're struggling to figure out which direction you want to go in. What you experienced must have been beyond overwhelming. I imagine it was a jolt to your sense of perspective."

He shook his head. "Are you in my head or something?"

I smiled, feeling flush with pleasure. "I just imagine how I might feel if I were in your shoes."

"I feel like I've failed. I was focused on my goal before and after I went up there. Now I'm back and . . . I just don't know."

"You don't need to know yet."

"It's been almost seven months since I got back."

"I don't think this is something you can measure in time, Chris. You can't force this. You just have to take each day at a time and your life will come together. Don't let anyone pressure you, including yourself."

He smiled at me, that gorgeous, boyish, sexy smile I'd grown infatuated with via his video letters. I felt that answering flutter in my stomach. I hoped my attraction didn't show in my face, but I somehow thought that it might. "We have these meetings to discuss a party and somehow end up in deeper conversations."

"Do you mind?" I held my breath.

Chris slowly shook his head. "Not at all."

Trying not to grin like a kid at Christmas, I shrugged, attempting to be casual. "Then maybe we can be friends *and* event planner and client."

"I'd like that. Very much."

# SEVENTEEN

## Hallie

Wednesday 08:17

Captain, there's a man with a large husky tucked into his backpack on my subway this morning. I'm still trying to figure out how he got him in there.

Wednesday 08:48

I need photo evidence, or I'll never believe you. Also, are you going to start all of our correspondence with Captain?

Wednesday 09:32

Yes. It makes me feel like I'm on Star Trek. Also, do you think I'm a subway rookie? Attaching pic . . .

Wednesday 09:36

Husky in a backpack. I believe you. My morning was less exciting. Signed a lease on a new apartment. In Brooklyn.

Wednesday 10:51

Really? I live in Brooklyn too. Maybe we're neighbors.

Wednesday 11:11

Wouldn't that be nice.

Focus.

I'd had to tell myself to do that numerous times over the course of the day as Chris's text from this morning lingered in my mind. Had it sounded flirty? Why did the word "nice" sound dirty in my head?

"So what do you think?"

The question brought me from my musings back to present day and the very important client standing in front of me. I smiled at Natalia Pisano, owner of the Manhattan restaurant we now stood in. It hadn't opened yet, and it wouldn't until Lia Zhang Events pulled off an opening night to remember. Natalia successfully ran an earthy Italian restaurant in Brooklyn with her chef best friend, Paola, and they'd decided to open a fine-dining restaurant in the city. Of course, running a restaurant was a precarious undertaking, and my client wanted to give hers its very best chance.

Hence why she'd hired us to open it with a splash.

"It's beautiful," I said honestly. Polished floors I could see my reflection in, chunky oak tables with angled shapes and legs, oak pillars between dark wood screens that created a booth-like dining experience and privacy, soft mood lighting . . .

Simple, modern, elegant.

We had plans to add lighted faux topiary, and our team was working on swag to give to guests, but mostly I'd been working alongside Althea to get the "right" people into the restaurant on opening night. We'd tasted Natalia and Paola's menu. The food would speak for itself.

I tapped my tablet. "Shall we go over the plans?"

Natalia gestured to the nearest table. "Can I get you anything?"

"Oh." I gestured to the jug of water and glasses that were already on the table. "Water is fine, thanks."

As my client poured me a glass, I jumped right into it. "So here is my proposal: we start with a soft opening. We invite your friends and family, especially those willing to be honest, and we'll send out a survey to them afterward so they can give you feedback anonymously. When do you think you'd be ready for that?"

"Two weeks," she said without hesitation.

"Great. That gives us time to send out invitations for the soft opening. Once we get the survey back, you can work out any of the issues that guests might have raised."

"I actually did that with Pisano's." She referred to the Brooklyn restaurant. "But not the anonymous thing. That makes a lot more sense."

I nodded. "People tend to be more honest if it's anonymous. And once you have the kinks worked out, that's when we can move on to a grand opening. We're already working on decor, which you've signed off on."

Natalia murmured in the affirmative.

"And good news. Althea, who has been working very hard on the marketing side of the event, has come up with two great opportunities. First is for swag to give away at the grand opening. People love free stuff, and you want to give them something they'll use often that will also regularly remind them of the amazing food they experienced here. Althea talked with Key Buddy, the tech company behind the key-holder tracker that connects to your smartphone. We can customize the Key Buddy with the restaurant's logo, and the company will give us a bunch of those at cost for cross-promotion. We'll also add a few gender-neutral gifts with your logo on it, but Althea and I really feel like the Key Buddy is a winner. Their sales have seen an exponential rise this year, and consumers are really attracted to the product. I can send you the costs if you're interested, along with all our other swag suggestions?"

She seemed to think about it. "You know a few people in my family have those key-tracker things. I think that's actually a pretty cool idea and not anything I would have thought of. Yeah, send me the information."

Buzzed that she liked the idea, I continued on. "Althea has also reached out to two influencers with a combined following of more than three million people. Both regularly review restaurants on their posts, one of them is based in Brooklyn, the other Boston. We'd have to pay for their expenses, but I think that would be worth it to have them attend."

I continued as Natalia nodded along. "We'd also like to invite a few local politicians, a couple of chiefs from the New York Fire Department, same with the police department, et cetera."

She frowned. "Why?"

"They tend to know a lot of people and do a lot of networking, so they can spread word of mouth. You should obviously put as much energy as possible into your social media, but for the grand opening we want the people who were here to do the work for us too, because the food is just so damn good."

"I get it. Again, I wouldn't have thought of it."

"Great. And last but not least, I want you to think of a charity that means something to you, because I think it would be a wonderful idea if we make the grand opening a fundraiser for your charity. It makes your business look good, it creates positive energy around the restaurant from the offset, and your guests will be donating to a cause that means something to you."

"A local charity for cancer perhaps," Natalia said instantly. "My grandmother died last year of lung cancer."

A pang of sympathy echoed in my chest. "I'm sorry to hear that."

Her eyes brightened. "She was a wonderful lady and so proud of Pisano's. She would be amazed to see me opening a fine-dining restaurant in Manhattan."

"I'll have Althea look into local charities and send a list for you to choose from. I'll also email you over the budget breakdown. You'll see a significant amount is going into swag, advertising on social media, banners, sidewalk boards, et cetera. After seeing the completed article"—I gestured to the dining room—"I'm glad we're going light on party decor. We need to let this beautiful space shine."

Natalia grinned as she exhaled a dramatic sigh of relief. "I've been so stressed about . . . well, everything. I have so much to handle, so much on my mind, and I have difficulty giving up control, but listening to you, these amazing plans, I feel like I'm in safe hands here, Hallie. Thank you. You have no idea how much this means to me."

And that was why I loved my job.

Tuesday 10:02

**So I was thinking, if we are going to be neighbors, maybe you can come around for dinner one night?**

Althea and I had just slipped out of the office to grab a quick lunch we could bring back to the office because we were, as usual, swamped, when I saw the text from Chris. We'd been texting back and forth since last week, sometimes about his party, but mostly we just sent each other fun, random thoughts. We bantered well.

And now this. A dinner invite.

I didn't tell Althea about the text and pretended my preoccupation was with work as we waited in line at a local deli. But my mind raced with what to say. Would dinner with Chris count as overstepping with a client? Would Lia be disappointed and concerned? Or was I overthinking it? Chris counted as a friend now, right? Dinner with a friend was okay.

Althea and I returned to the office, and I sat down at my desk, lunch forgotten beside me as I stared at his text. I shouldn't.

Yet, somehow, I couldn't help myself. My fingers started to move before I could stop them.

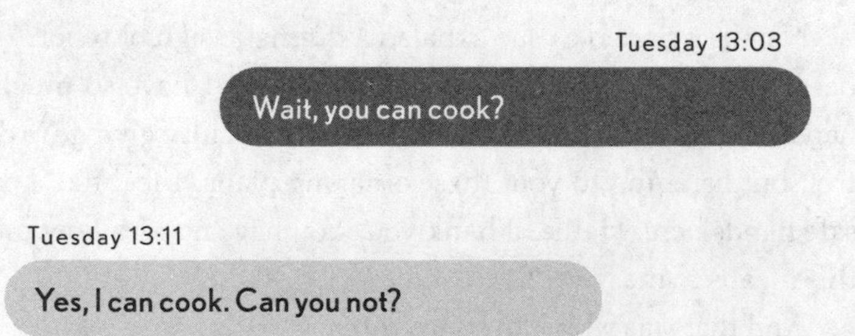

Tuesday 13:12

Um, it depends on your definition.

Tuesday 13:12

Gotchya, you can't cook. You can bring the beers.

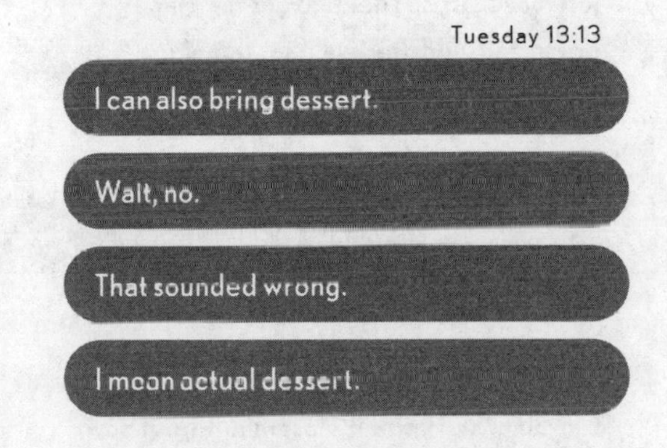


Tuesday 13:13

Is your face on fire right now?

Tuesday 13:14

No, but I have taste-tested many bakeries in the area and know all the best treats from all the best ones.

Tuesday 13:15

**Okay, you can bring the beer and dessert. I just moved in, so I need to get the place organized, and then we'll set that up.**

Tuesday 13:15

Sounds great.

Thursday 08:12

**Morning. So I know it's last minute, but how would you feel about visiting my aunt's place in the Hamptons this weekend?**

Thursday 08:44

Good morning, Captain. How fortuitous. I have no events this weekend. Saturday?

Thursday 08:46

**Yeah, this Saturday. I'm renting a car, so I'll pick you up. I was thinking early so we can beat the traffic. 7am good?**

Thursday 11:31

That works. I'm on Ocean Parkway.

Friday 07:48

**My new apartment is opposite Prospect Park, so we're not even a 10 min drive apart.**

Friday 12:05

You live near a really good bakery.

Friday 12:07

**You have a very naughty one-track mind.**

Friday 12:08

Naughty?

Friday 12:09

**Baked goods are naughty.**

Friday 12:11

Stop using that word. It makes baked goods sound dirty. You can't dirty up baked goods.

Friday 12:11

I beg to differ.

Baked goods are already dirty.

ROUGH PUFF pastry?

Filo (FEEL OH) pastry?

Friday 12:13

LOL. Stop it. You'll ruin desserts for me.

Friday 12:14

I was in a bakery in Brooklyn that sold chocolate nipple cupcakes.

Friday 12:14

Now you're making this up.

Friday 12:15

I'll prove it. Anytime I go into a bakery now, I promise I will find a dirty-sounding cake and send you a pic.

Friday 12:15

That is a lofty task indeed. It makes what you did on the ISS look like child's play.

Friday 12:16

Right?!

Friday 14:23

Okay. You've ruined bakeries for me forever. I just stopped in at my favorite Manhattan bakery, and they sell something called a summer berry grunt.

Friday 15:12

I told you.

Friday 17:06

You're awful for opening my eyes to this. I feel like a kid who just realized their parents had sex to have me.

Friday 17:08

Oh, that is a far worse realization than discovering a bakery sells grunt cakes.

Friday 17:42

Truth. But still. Baked goods do sound dirty to me now.

Friday 17:50

And my work is done.

Friday 18:01

Find a loftier enterprise than ruining my innocence.

Wait.

That sounded wrong.

Dammit.

Friday 18:03

You're funny, Goodman.

And I'm writing a book.

Does that count as lofty?

Friday 18:03

Seriously? Like fiction or an autobiography?

Friday 18:03

An autobiography. I think. I'm just writing whatever comes out at the moment. It just . . . happened. I've never thought of myself as a writer until now.

Friday 18:04

It makes sense to me. I thought you described what you saw from the ISS so well in your videos. This is great. I'm excited for you.

Friday 18:04

**Thanks. I don't know how it'll turn out, but I think it's a good thing. I think it might help me figure some things out.**

Friday 18:05

Definitely. I'd love to hear more about it when you feel like sharing.

Friday 18:05

**Absolutely.**

**I haven't told a lot of people about this.**

Friday 18:05

I won't tell anyone.

Friday 18:05

**Thanks. I appreciate it.**

Friday 18:06

I'm looking forward to tomorrow.

Friday 18:06

Me too.

# EIGHTEEN

## Chris

I was playing with fire.

When it came to Hallie Goodman, I was definitely playing with fire. She'd gotten into the rental car dressed in jeans, a T-shirt tucked into them, and an oversized cardigan. Her hair was styled, but she wore less makeup than I'd seen her wear before. I didn't care what she wore, I realized. She appealed to me in all her guises. Therefore, as I'd leaned against the car, waiting for her, I'd wanted to cross the distance between us. I wanted to greet her with a kiss on that luscious mouth of hers.

She'd approached me, a radiant smile on her face, and I felt a strong flicker of guilt that I still hadn't told her about the videos. I'd shoved it down, not wanting to ruin this weekend, and grinned at her as she stopped before me.

"Wow. You're short in those Converses," I'd teased.

Hallie had rolled her eyes. "I'm average height."

"*I'm* average height."

"For a woman. I'm average height for a woman." She'd tilted her head to the side, her hair shimmering in the morning sunlight. "And good morning, Captain."

I'd chuckled. "Good morning, Goodman. You ready for the Hamptons?"

She'd lifted a large purse that looked heavy. "Got my notebook, my tablet, essentials. Ready to do this."

The two-hour drive with Hallie was easy. Too easy. It seemed we were drawn to each other like binary stars. It was addictive and disorienting. We discovered within five minutes of the drive that we shared the same taste in music, and that got us talking for a huge part of the journey about concerts we'd been to. We swapped stories about our musical adventures, and Hallie played a couple of bands I hadn't heard of. Unsurprisingly, I liked them a lot. It was much less intense conversation than we'd had previously, and while the heavy conversation drew me deeply to her, this was nice too.

I liked the way she talked with her hands, always in motion, always animated and enthusiastic. She was refreshing and reminded me a little of my aunt Richelle.

We were on the highway, nearing East Hampton, when Hallie turned to me and confessed, "I've never visited the Hamptons. Grew up in Newark, then lived in New York my whole adult life except for when I was at college in Massachusetts. And I've never been to the Hamptons. If we wanted to go to a local-ish beach, we drove to Long Beach."

I threw her a smile. "You'll like it here. Aunt Richelle's house sits right on the water. It's quiet this time of year."

"Not that I'll be able to enjoy it. I'm here to work," she reminded me.

"I'm sure we can fit in a walk along the beach. Oh, and you're good with dogs, right?"

"Sure." Her smile turned sad. "I had a golden retriever growing up called Mike. When he died, my mom didn't want another dog. And I can't have one now because I work so much."

"I'm sorry about your dog."

"Thanks."

"You named him Mike?" My lips twitched against the urge to laugh.

Hallie laughed and it was a sweet sound. "What is wrong with Mike?"

"It's just an unusual name for a dog."

"My parents said I could name him, and I wanted to name him Mike." She shrugged. "I have no reasoning. Or at least I can't remember it."

She was so fucking adorable. I grinned at her, and she laughed again.

This felt good. Being here with her.

In fact, it felt great.

A little while later, I announced we were officially in East Hampton. Hallie watched the tree-lined streets pass by. "It's so pretty. I'd love to see it in the fall."

"Is that your favorite season?"

"I also love summer. Not so much summer in the city, but just the nostalgia of summer, I guess. We spent a lot of our summers in the Florida Keys, and those were the few times in my childhood where my parents seemed to get along. It was three weeks of palm trees, turquoise water, and white sand. Mom and Dad weren't arguing all the time, and I could just relax and be a kid." She frowned suddenly. "I'm sorry. I don't know where that came from. Excuse the downer."

I wanted to ask more about her parents. How she was doing with their crazy postdivorce antics, but I couldn't. Because I wasn't supposed to know. "Hey, I've talked to you about personal stuff. It's cool. I'm sorry they were like that."

She shrugged. "Other kids have it worse. Okay, so some of these houses are not what I expected."

"Did you imagine big colonial-style houses everywhere?"

"Yes."

"They're here too."

We turned down the hedged lane toward Aunt Richelle's, which was somewhere in the middle between the modest homes and those bigger houses Hallie had been expecting.

"This is idyllic," Hallie opined quietly.

"I'm glad the weather's good so you can see it like this."

"I bet it's melting hot in the height of summer."

"It is. But Aunt Richelle has a pool."

Her lips made a little *oh*. I had to drag my eyes off them and back on the road. I swung the car left into Aunt Richelle's driveway and drew to a halt.

Hallie stared at the house. "This is beautiful."

Grinning, I got out of the car, rounding the hood to her side, just as the front door opened.

Bandit bounded past Aunt Richelle just as I helped Hallie out of the car. His enormous paws landed on my back, the full weight of him shoving me, stumbling into Hallie, who fell against the car, crushed by us both.

"Bandit!" I heard my aunt shout, and the dog's weight fell away.

"Shit, are you okay?" I asked Hallie.

She gaped up at me, her cheeks a little flushed, her face too close to mine. "I'm fine," she whispered.

Feeling nothing but her soft body against mine, heat licked down my spine. I quickly stepped back, releasing her.

"Sorry, so sorry." Aunt Richelle was suddenly there, her fingers wrapped around Bandit's collar. "He gets a little overzealous."

"Oh my God, he's beautiful." Hallie seemed over her shock as she grinned at my aunt's dog, who desperately pulled to get to me.

"You can let him go," I said.

"What about your guest?"

"Oh, it's fine," Hallie assured her.

Aunt Richelle studied her as she released Bandit. He attacked me with love, and I hugged and petted him, trying to introduce my aunt to Hallie at the same time.

"It's so nice to meet you." Hallie held out her hand. "Thank you for inviting me."

"Oh, we don't do handshakes in this house. I'm a hugger. Is that okay?" Aunt Richelle smiled.

Hallie laughed, her whole body seeming to relax. "Yeah, of course."

I watched them hug and felt more than a little off-balance by how much I liked having Hallie here.

Once Bandit was done with me, he wanted to meet my guest, and I wasn't even aware of the massive grin on my face as I listened to Hallie's laughter. Bandit smothered her in love.

I caught my aunt's eye.

She studied me knowingly. And I got the impression she liked what she saw.

Aunt Richelle led us into the house, and Hallie's expression changed. She appeared pensive as she took everything in, and I could see the gears turning in her mind.

She was in event-planning mode already.

Chuckling, I pressed a hand to her back to guide her toward the kitchen where my aunt led. No doubt she had breakfast ready for us. Sure enough, the dining table was covered in a small buffet of pastries, waffles, and pancakes.

"You can think about the party later. Let's just have breakfast first," I said to Hallie. I kissed my aunt on the cheek. "You didn't need to do all this."

"I wanted to. It's nice to have company. Coffee?"

"Please." Hallie nodded, eyeing the food. "This is so nice of you, thank you. It was too early to eat when we left the city, but now I'm starving."

We settled at the table.

"You have a beautiful home," Hallie commented as Aunt Richelle joined us.

"Thank you. I never thought I'd stay in a place like this, but the first time I saw it, I just couldn't resist living by the beach. I love it here."

"I can see why." Hallie stared out of the window toward the beach. "It's in a beautiful spot. Chris tells me you're an artist, a painter. This must be such a magical place to paint."

"It is." Aunt Richelle smiled at her. "Every day the weather changes the landscape."

"I bet. I'd love to see your work sometime."

"Really? I'd be happy to show you my studio later."

I raised an eyebrow. Not everyone got that offer from my aunt. I wondered if she felt the same thing I did around Hallie: the instinctive gut feeling that she could be trusted. I didn't understand it, but I wouldn't second-guess it either.

"So do you think this place could be party central?" Aunt Richelle asked.

Hallie swallowed a bite of waffle and looked around the room. "I'll have to check out the rest of the house, but it's a wonderful space. Perfect for a cookout. We could open the doors so the party flows from yard to house. Maybe even put up a tent out there for shade and to keep refreshments cool. The smell and sound of the ocean add great atmosphere, and we should definitely cash in on the uniqueness of the location."

"That makes sense to me," my aunt murmured.

I nodded. I didn't care about the party, but I liked the way Hallie's face lit up as she talked about her work and her ideas.

"Hey." I approached Hallie, who stood in the backyard, scribbling on her tablet. We'd been at the house for a few hours. After breakfast, Aunt Richelle took Hallie into her studio, and they were in there longer than I'd expected them to be. When they returned, I took Hallie on a tour of the house and then left her to it because I could tell how distracted she'd grown as ideas started percolating in her head.

Soon I grew impatient for her company again though.

"Hey." She smiled up at me, her eyes hidden behind sunglasses she'd pulled out from her massive purse. "Bored?"

I shrugged. "Just wondering if you felt like a break. I'm taking Bandit for a walk down the beach."

"Sure." She grinned, and I fought the urge to reach out and trace her lower lip with my thumb. "Let me just put this"—she waved her tablet—"back inside."

"I'll get Bandit."

A few minutes later, we walked barefoot down the backyard and onto the beach. As soon as I opened the gate, Bandit took off toward the water. The beach was busier than it was a few weeks ago. Summer approached.

"Your aunt is awesome. I wish I was more like her," Hallie said.

"In what way?"

"Just some of the things she said while we were in her studio—they tell me she doesn't care what people think. I want to be more like that. Less of a people pleaser. Richelle seems so free and content. So independent. It's amazing."

"Her life isn't perfect." I needed to assure Hallie. "The grass isn't always greener."

"I get that. But this is a pretty nice life." She gestured around us.

"It is. And it brings her peace."

I felt Hallie's eyes on me as I watched Bandit jump in and out of the waves as we walked along the hard-packed sand of the shore.

"Is she okay? Sorry, you don't need to answer that. I'm being nosy."

"No, it's fine. I . . . I worry about her," I confessed. "She's a special person, and she stepped in to be what I needed after I lost my mom. But she's alone, and I don't think that's ever going to change."

"Why?" Hallie frowned. "She's talented and beautiful and really down-to-earth. Why would she remain alone?"

"She wants to." The frustration was evident in my voice. "There was someone. Her college sweetheart. They bought this house together. He died in a motorbike accident fifteen years ago. They'd decided they didn't want to get married and have kids, but that they were each other's for life. Then one day he was gone. I was in the academy, but they let me come be with her for a little while. Not long enough. Miguel was already on active duty and couldn't get back in time. It was not good. Anyway, as far as I'm aware, there's never been anyone since Akio, and I don't think there ever will be, and that kills me. I don't want that for her."

Tears shone in Hallie's eyes. "That's so sad. I'm sorry. I hate that that's her story."

"Me too."

We shared a few minutes of silence listening to the gulls in the sky, to Bandit's joyous barks, and to the ocean lapping around our ankles.

Then Hallie's voice cut through it all. "Maybe she's okay with that though. Your aunt Richelle. Maybe she's made peace with it.

Decided that what she had with him for the time she had was more than what most folks get."

"Isn't that something people just say to make themselves feel better about the fact that they're unhappy?"

"I don't know. I don't even know what happy is."

A spike of alarm cut through me. "You're unhappy?"

"No, that's not what I meant." She assured me. "I think we're taught to create goals and expect to achieve those goals if we work hard enough. Yet it's always human nature to want more. To expect more and more and more. And don't get me wrong, part of being human, part of what makes being a human a joy, is having dreams. Having hope. But I think there's a fine line between that and the perpetual hunger for more and inevitable dissatisfaction with our lives because of it."

Engaged, I asked, "Do you think that's true of everyone though? And shouldn't we expect to be *happy* in life?"

"Isn't happiness subjective? Two hundred years ago, being fed, healthy, warm, and safe *would* have made an everyday Joe happy."

"You don't know that."

"True. But it's likely. In some ways, life was less complicated back then. More difficult in a lot of ways, but less complicated." She shrugged. "I guess, I'm just saying that even with all of my family mess, sometimes I sit back and evaluate the good stuff I do have compared to other people. It's all about perspective, you know."

She was right, but still I pointed out, "It doesn't mean you can't be unhappy with your life."

"No. But maybe it means I can be happy with what I have, even if I'm a little unhappy about what I *don't* have. *You* can be happy with what you have, Captain, even if you're feeling a little lost right now."

I considered all I'd seen during my time in the military. "You're right. Perspective is key."

"I don't mean to sound all preachy and self-righteous. Perspective helps me cope, that's all."

"No, you don't sound preachy and self-righteous." I gazed down at her, watching the breeze blow strands of pink hair back from her pretty face. "I have the most interesting conversations with you."

She looked at me, those blue eyes bright with humor. "You mean intensely deep, heavy conversations entirely out of proportion to the length of time we've known each other?"

I chuckled. "There's nothing wrong with getting a little deep, getting a little philosophical. You're empathetic and wise, Hallie. I enjoy talking with you."

A little flush brightened her cheeks. "I think you're the only person in my life who has ever called me wise."

"Then I guess most people in your life haven't taken the time to truly know you."

She bit her lower lip as if to contain her pleased grin. I swallowed hard and forced myself to look away before I did something stupid, like kiss the hell out of her. Hallie Goodman remained off-limits romantically while my future was still up in the air . . . and definitely while she remained ignorant to the fact that I'd watched the video diaries she'd made.

Hours had passed since our walk on the beach, and Richelle had talked Hallie into staying for dinner too.

It was dark out, the night air cool as the sea breeze blew into the dining room from an open window. Aunt Richelle had cooked, and we'd spent the evening talking nonstop. My aunt had shared stories about me as a kid that she clearly found adorable. I didn't embarrass easily, and I enjoyed the camaraderie between her and Hallie. I'd never seen her like that with any of my girlfriends. Definitely not with Darcy.

And Hallie wasn't even my girl.

"Shouldn't we get back to Brooklyn?" Hallie suddenly asked, her eyes bright with alcohol. Aunt Richelle kept topping up her wineglass and Hallie hadn't seemed to notice.

"Oh, you can't. Chris has had one too many beers, and you've had too much wine. You'll have to stay," Richelle insisted.

"I couldn't intrude like that." Hallie waved off the invitation.

"Don't be silly. I keep clean extra pj's. There are even unopened toothbrushes in the guest bath."

At Hallie's uncertainty, I said, "I have had too much to drink. You okay if we stay?"

"Uh, sure, if it's really all right."

"Absolutely." Aunt Richelle suddenly yawned. "In fact, I'm a little too wined up myself. I think I'll head to bed. Chris, you can show Hallie to her room, right?"

I knew that twinkle in my aunt's eye. She was matchmaking. Under her own goddamn roof. I smirked at her antics. "Sure."

She winked at me. "Night, kiddos."

"Night!" Hallie called after her. "And thanks for dinner!"

Aunt Richelle threw a wave over her shoulder and disappeared out of the room, Bandit hurrying after her.

Hallie turned back to me. "That was an abrupt departure."

I laughed. "That's Aunt Richelle."

She nodded, her cheeks flushed as she stared at me. Something I didn't understand flickered across her expression, and she looked away. "I guess I better hit the hay, then."

"I'll show you the way."

As we walked out of the room, I raised my arm to rest my hand on her back and then thought better of it. I was a little buzzed. She was definitely buzzed. And I wasn't sure I could trust myself to keep things purely platonic between us. Instead I kept a little distance between us, heading upstairs first.

"Is this your mom?"

I glanced over my shoulder to see Hallie had stopped midway up to stare at the photos on the wall.

Returning to her side, I looked at the photo she studied. It was one of me, Miguel, and Mom. I was about eight or nine, and it was taken in the backyard of our house in Bedford, her arms wrapped around me, her head thrown back in laughter. I clutched her arms, grinning at the camera. Miguel leaned into Mom's side, laughing too. Aunt Richelle had probably said something hilarious. It was a great photo and one of my favorites.

"Yeah," I confirmed, my throat a little tight.

"She was beautiful." Hallie looked around at the other photos. "You all are. Is this Miguel?" She gestured to a photo of him in his uniform upon his graduation from the academy. He was only twenty-two.

"Yeah, that's him."

Hallie glanced up at me. "You look like him."

I smirked. "If Miguel were here, he'd say, 'He must be a handsome son of a bitch, then.'"

She chuckled. "I like the sound of him."

"He was the best." I touched the photo of the three of us. "She was too."

I felt her squeeze my shoulder. "I'm so sorry, Chris. I can't imagine what losing them must feel like."

It took me a minute to fight back a surge of emotion. "I've made peace with it. I have. But that doesn't make missing them any easier. I've talked about them in therapy," I confessed. "But I don't get to talk about them much outside of that. Sometimes it makes it feel like they were never here. You know, maybe I was already lost before I went up in space, 'cause I lost a piece of me when she died and another when he was killed."

Hallie tugged on my hand, and I looked at her, confused, as she settled down on a step. "Will you sit with me and tell me about them?"

Staring into her kind eyes, a sensation of falling came over me. I slowly sat down on the steps above her and leaned against the stair railing. "Let me see . . . my mom was funny. She had a mischievous sense of humor. One Christmas, she realized by the lack of surprise on our faces that my brother and I had discovered our presents before she'd wrapped them and put them under the tree. So the next year, when Miguel and I went hunting, she left fake presents with booby traps in them." I chuckled as I remembered. "One of them exploded and covered both of our heads in pink glitter. It took us days to get rid of it."

Hallie laughed softly and I kept talking. In fact, once I started, I couldn't seem to stop.

# NINETEEN

## Hallie

The sound of seagulls crying infiltrated my consciousness, followed by the gentle, rhythmic whoosh of the ocean. My eyes flew open, and it took me a moment to figure out where I was. The room was dim, with heavy curtains drawn over the large window.

It was the guest room Chris had shown me to last night.

Pushing up into a sitting position, my mouth felt a little dry and my stomach grumbled, but otherwise I felt okay considering the amount of wine I'd consumed.

Reaching for my phone on the nightstand, I switched it on. I'd switched it off at some point yesterday to conserve the battery. A minute later, my phone told me it was only a few minutes past 8:00 a.m. That meant I'd had very little sleep because Chris and I had talked on the stairs for ages about his mom and Miguel, about the distance between him and his father, and how it had always been that way.

Sliding out of bed, I wandered into the bathroom and grimaced at the ghostly pale face staring back at me in the mirror. Deciding to have a quick shower, hoping to rid myself of any toxins leaking through my pores, I tried not to overanalyze this weekend.

Or the past two weeks.

Had it really been only two weeks since I started spending

time with Chris? That didn't seem right. It couldn't be. It felt like we'd known each other much longer.

Smiling to myself, I kept the jets off my hair, scrubbed myself down, and got out. Not wanting to waste time in case Chris was already awake and eating breakfast without me, I hurried through my makeup routine, using the supplies I carried with me everywhere in my purse. I knotted my hair on top of my head in a messy bun and changed back into my clothes from yesterday. My T-shirt smelled a little. Yuck. It would just have to do, I supposed. I wondered if there was a way to stay upwind of Chris for the rest of the day. Feeling self-conscious about it, I reluctantly opened the bedroom door and almost stepped onto folded black fabric. There was a piece of paper on top. Reaching down, I smiled as I read it.

*Yours if you need it. Chris.*

I lifted the fabric, and a man's black T-shirt unfolded. It had the logo of one of our favorite bands on it. Grinning so big my cheeks hurt, I stepped back inside the room and closed the door. Bringing the T-shirt to my nose, I inhaled the scent of fresh laundry, but it didn't have Chris's cologne on it. Still, it was Chris's shirt.

Feeling stupidly giddy, I whipped off my sweater and T-shirt and shrugged on his. It hung way too big on the shoulders, but I didn't care. I tucked it into my jeans as best I could and slipped my sweater back on over it.

I was wearing Chris Ortiz's T-shirt.

It was like being fifteen all over again and the cutest guy in school gave me his jacket to wear on a chilly night. I stuffed Chris's little note in my purse like a fangirl.

Shaking my head at myself, I slipped out of the bedroom and hurried downstairs.

Richelle sat at the table in the kitchen, sipping coffee, her plate half-empty of French toast. She looked up as I strolled in and smiled warmly. Bandit had been sitting at her side, but he dashed across the room to greet me. He really was a beauty. And he'd been responsible for shoving Chris into me upon our arrival, so I had him to thank for that delightful moment.

At my exuberant greeting, Bandit got excited and jumped up, putting his paws on my shoulders in order to lick my face. I burst into a fit of giggles, trying to avoid his kisses and not stumble under his weight.

"Bandit, get down!" Richelle yelled, laughter in her voice.

The dog obeyed, and I shot her a grin.

"He didn't get you, did he?"

"Nope, but not for want of trying."

"He likes you."

"He's friendly."

"Not with everyone, believe it or not. He must sense something about you, like I do."

That was so nice. "Thanks," I murmured, warmed by the comment.

I had to admit I'd been nervous about meeting Chris's aunt, even more so when we pulled up to this beautiful house. But I shouldn't have been. Richelle was as down-to-earth as her nephew. I wondered, however, if she'd be as nice and forgiving as Chris was about the videos if she knew.

"Let me get you a coffee and some French toast."

"No, I can do it," I tried to insist, but she ignored me.

"Just sit down and help yourself to some orange juice."

Since I was parched, that sounded like an excellent idea. "Thank you."

"Is that Chris's shirt?"

I gave a huff of laughter. Of course she'd notice that. "Yeah, he left it outside my room for me."

"That sounds like Chris. He's always been an incredibly considerate person."

*I think he's wonderful and sexy and complicated and beautiful and so smart I'm pretty sure he'd fascinate me until the day I die.* "Yeah, he's great."

"It's amazing to me you've only known each other such a short time. He's so comfortable around you. You seem like you've been friends your whole lives."

I couldn't meet her gaze, instead I stared out the window to avoid it. "It seems that way to me too. Where is Chris?"

"Out jogging."

I looked back at her. "Seriously?"

Richelle chuckled. "Seriously. He runs on the beach every morning whenever he's here."

"He's big into his fitness, huh?" Damn, I was so not into working out.

"It's a part of him. He's had to be physically fit for his career most of his life. Hard habit to break. I don't know where he gets the motivation. I like long walks, but that's about as energetic as it gets for me. Plus, I like my hearty breakfasts, and I've been blessed with a good metabolism. Chris has a treat now and then, but he had a green smoothie before he went for his run." She made a face.

My expression fell. "I'm so not a green smoothie, working-out kinda gal." I bet Darcy was.

Richelle shrugged. "We're all made different, I guess. That makes life beautiful."

We chatted a little as she made French toast, and I dove on the food like a wolf, even though the thought crossed my mind that maybe I should try harder to eat more healthy. The French toast just tasted so good.

Richelle chuckled and took the seat opposite me. "Hungover?"

I swallowed, giving her a sheepish smile. "Not really. I'm just always so hungry the morning after drinking alcohol. Thank you for hosting me."

"You don't have to thank me again. I've loved having you here. I like the way my nephew is around you." Her gaze was penetrating.

I felt the blood heat under my cheeks. "I hope I can plan a party he'll like. He doesn't really seem that into the idea."

"I may have talked him into it. But I'm sure whatever you do, he'll love."

I gave her a grateful nod, and we talked a little about the painting she was working on as I ate. Someone had commissioned her to paint a portrait, which wasn't her usual style, as she loved working on landscapes, but the client was a big fan. I could see why. Richelle used a palette knife to paint, so her work had texture and a vivid sense of movement that was truly appealing.

It seemed there was an unending well of smarts and talents in the family.

We heard a door open and shut, and a few seconds later Chris walked into the kitchen via the laundry room. His hair was windswept, his cheeks flushed, and his shirt stuck to him with perspiration.

My belly flipped low and deep.

Oh boy.

Bandit dove at him first, and Chris showered him with attention before striding over to us. "Morning." He grinned at me. "You sleep okay?"

I struggled to find my voice for a second. "I . . . I uh, I slept great."

His gaze dipped to my chest before flicking back to my face. "You got the T-shirt."

"Yes." My cheeks blazed, or at least felt like they did. "Thanks for that. It was really thoughtful of you."

"Not a problem." He glanced at his aunt and then back at me. "I'm going to take a shower, but I'll be down soon."

I nodded, his hotness rendering me nonverbal.

I'd never been such a sucker for good looks before. It was Chris. It was everything about him.

Richelle cleared her throat, and I realized I'd been staring after him.

Whoops.

I gave her a strained smile, and she returned it with an embarrassingly knowing one.

"Maybe I can look at your ideas so far?" Richelle asked. "While we wait on Chris."

"Oh. Sure. Um . . . let me just . . ." I pushed back from the table, grateful for the distraction. "My tablet is upstairs in my purse. I'll be a second."

I hurried from the room and her too-knowing gaze, shaking my head at my obviousness.

As I approached the guest room, the sound of Chris humming "Hooked on a Feeling" by Blue Swede slowed my steps. He'd put me in the bedroom opposite his. I think I stopped breathing when I realized his door was open.

I definitely stopped breathing when he came into view. His attention was on his cell, not on the voyeur out in the hall, gawking at him in his boxer briefs.

Chris was almost naked.

My throat went dry as I drank in the sight of his muscular body. He had abs. Like actual definition.

And those shoulders. So broad and strong. He looked taller half-naked.

Then he turned, giving me his back, and threw the cell on his bed. Before I could talk myself into doing the decent thing and moving away, he curled his fingers into the waistband of his boxer briefs and suddenly they were around his ankles and he was kicking them off.

His ass.

Oh my.

It was a gift from the gods.

I flushed from head to toe as the muscles in his ass flexed as he strolled across the room to open a drawer in a dresser.

Reality returned, and I realized if his bedroom was set up like the room I'd slept in, he would see me as he walked past the door to get to the bathroom. I could not get caught ogling a client.

I shouldn't be ogling a client, period!

Hurriedly tiptoeing backward down the hall, my heart pounding in my chest, I was about to release a sigh of relief when my calves hit something big and warm. Suddenly the floor moved beneath my feet, and I let out a yelp of surprise as a bark echoed it.

And I was falling.

I put my hand out to catch myself and felt the pain lash up my wrist from taking the brunt of my impact with the floor. Bandit's face was suddenly in mine, and I groaned as I tried to avoid his kisses.

"Everything all right out there?" Chris called out.

Oh my God.

I'd just tripped over Bandit because I'd been staring at Chris naked.

"I'm fine." It sounded weak even to my ears.

Chris hurried out of his room, wearing only a pair of pajama pants, his brows drawn together. He let out a curse at the sight of me on the floor and lowered himself beside me as I pushed myself up. My wrist throbbed, and I flinched.

"Bandit, get off." Chris gently pulled the dog away by the collar. "What happened? Are you okay?" He brushed my hair off my face, my skin sensitive to the touch of his fingertips.

Mortified, I couldn't meet his gaze. "I'm a klutz. Tripped over the dog. I'm fine."

"If you're fine, why are you holding your wrist like that? Let me see."

He took hold of it, and I winced as a burn of pain flared down the outside of my wrist and arm. I finally allowed myself to meet his concerned gaze. I felt awful for spying on him. An apology was on the tip of my tongue, but I couldn't get the words out. It was much too embarrassing.

"I think you've sprained it. We need to get some ice on it."

"I'm okay." I tried to push to my feet, but Chris took over.

I sucked in a breath as he took hold of my good hand and wrapped his other arm around my waist to help me up. It put me against his naked chest. He was still warm and damp from his run.

Swallowing hard, trying to breathe normally, I forced a little distance between us as soon as I was on my feet. "I'm really okay."

"You will be when we get ice on it," he replied firmly, not letting go of my hand.

He led me downstairs as I cradled my sore wrist against my chest.

Of course this would happen to me.

The universe was always watching. Karma was always there to give you a swift kick on the ass for ogling a gorgeous, naked astronaut (and *client*) without his permission.

"Oh no, what happened?" Richelle was loading the dishwasher as Chris pulled me into the kitchen.

"She tripped over Bandit."

"That damn big goofball. He's taken me out in the past too. I'm sorry, Hallie."

"No, it's okay. It was my fault." I ducked my head. "I wasn't looking where I was going."

Chris released me but only to grab a tea towel and hold it under the ice dispenser in the freezer. He folded the towel around the ice and then handed it to me. "Sit. Ice it for twenty minutes. We'll see how it is then."

"I told you I'm fine. Just embarrassed for causing a fuss."

He lifted my chin with the gentle touch of his fingers until our eyes met. He smiled warmly into mine. "You've got nothing to be embarrassed about. Bandit, on the other hand, should feel pretty sheepish."

I chuckled, relaxing a little.

Until I remembered he was half-naked.

My gaze unwillingly dropped to his chest.

The memory of his full nakedness made me hot all over again.

Chris took a step back, and the hoarseness in his voice when he said he'd return after his shower forced me to look at him.

I was pretty sure the heat in his eyes was not my imagination.

Oh.

Oh okay.

Hope unfurled in my chest.

Then he pivoted and strode out of the room, and I tried not to picture his naked ass again and failed.

"Another coffee? Maybe an aspirin for the pain?" Richelle's voice reminded me I wasn't alone.

She grinned at me in a way I knew my thoughts were written all over my face.

Crap.

Covering my discomfiture, I turned away, pressing the ice to my wrist. "Sure, thanks." I squeaked out.

# TWENTY

## Hallie

The ice helped, but my wrist was still a little sore as we sat outside to enjoy lunch on the backyard patio. It had turned into a warm day, reminding me that summer really was just around the corner. We'd decided to grab some lunch before driving back to Brooklyn.

Culinary master that she was, Richelle served these amazing homemade crab cake sandwiches with bread she'd baked herself. I needed to learn how to cook and bake. Or at least marry someone who could.

"I've never asked, but how exactly does one become an astronaut?" I said to Chris after swallowing a bite of my sandwich. "Specifically, how did you become an astronaut from being a pilot in the air force?"

Chris shrugged and wiped the corner of his mouth with his napkin before he replied, "I was a test pilot and worked with NASA. It happened from there."

Richelle snorted. "I think Hallie wants the entire story." She turned to me. "Everyone expected, with his genius-level grades, he would attend MIT or Harvard or Stanford, but he followed his brother into the Air Force Academy."

Chris smirked at her before turning those swoony dark brown eyes on me. "I graduated as a systems engineer from the academy. An important qualification in my selection to NASA."

Fascinated, I asked, "And you made captain in the air force really young, right?"

"In four years, which is the shortest time period you can make captain," Richelle answered proudly. "He trained as a tactical fighter pilot, was on active duty for four years, and made captain by the age of twenty-seven."

I grinned at his aunt, who was practically bursting with pride.

Staring out at the water, Chris ate but said nothing. I wondered how he felt about his time on active duty. What he'd seen. Who he'd lost. Then he spoke. "I enjoyed flying, but combat wasn't for me." He turned back to me. "So I applied to Pax."

"Pax?"

"Naval Test Pilot School at Patuxent River in Maryland. I was there for three years, and I got involved in test-piloting for NASA. Miguel was the one who dreamed of being an astronaut. He was fascinated with space since he was a kid, and it rubbed off on me. When he died, having never pursued what he'd really wanted, I decided I'd try to make that dream come true for him. That's what got me interested in the astronaut-training program, so I applied and was selected when I was thirty-one. Trained for three years and then went on my first mission, as you know."

Awed and feeling like I'd done very little of significance with my life in comparison, I gaped at him.

Richelle laughed beside me. "Impressive and intimidating, I know."

He frowned. "How? All I did was work hard. People work hard all the time."

"Yes, but not all people are bona fide astronauts who live in space for *five* months." I shook my head at him. "You've packed so much into your life, and you're only thirty-five." No wonder he was floundering now. He'd literally reached for the stars and achieved it. What came next? I suddenly remembered his confession. "And now you're writing a book. I feel the desperate need to go home and reevaluate all my life choices."

Chris narrowed his eyes. "You shouldn't compare your achievements to anyone else. Look at your success. You're excellent at your job, Hallie, and that's why you work for one of the best event-management companies in the country. Never undervalue yourself."

I softened my cheeky grin, moved by his praise. "Thank you for saying that. As for your book, you know I think it's amazing."

"I can't believe you told her about the book," Richelle murmured.

She and Chris shared a look I didn't understand.

Eventually he shrugged. "Hallie knows to keep it to herself."

"Did you tell your father about it?"

Just like that, it felt like Richelle's words had conjured this wall between us and Chris. The tension radiating off him was palpable, and I knew from our discussion last night that things between him and his dad were awful.

And I thought my relationship with my parents was a mess.

As if on cue, my cell rang on the table beside my plate. I'd changed my ringtone Friday night to "Keep Moving" by Jungle, so it was pretty loud. It felt incredibly inappropriate at the moment. Seeing that it was Dad, I winced and muttered an apology before I left the table. I answered as I stepped away, hoping maybe the interruption would dissolve the tension the mention of Chris's father had created.

"Hey, Dad, can I call—"

"You need to call your mother right now," my father barked furiously in my ear.

In all the arguments I'd been stuck in the middle of, Dad had never spoken to me like that. My stomach dropped. "What's going on?"

"Your mother and Jenna were drunk and toilet-papered our yard last night. This is beyond acceptable behavior, Hallie! This is intimidation! Miranda is in tears, Alison is mortified, and my neighbors are affronted. I can't—"

"Dad, Dad, slow down. Are you sure it was Mom?" Of all the crazy stuff she'd done, I just couldn't imagine her toilet-papering Dad's yard.

"I saw her!" he raged. "I woke up because I heard them laughing, and when I went to investigate, they took off in that cheap lime-green monstrosity Jenna refuses to stop driving. I checked the security camera on the front door to make sure, and there was your mom, laughing it up and stumbling all over the fucking yard with rolls of toilet paper in hand."

Oh my God.

"Dad, I'm sorry. That is ridiculous." What was she thinking?

"It's beyond ridiculous, Hallie. It's criminal. Now you get on the phone to your mother and tell her to get her ass over here and clean this up, or I am pressing charges. She puts me through hell, and just when I'm getting back on track, she starts harassing my family? That's not happening!"

I winced at him calling Miranda and Alison his family.

"Right. I'll call her."

He hung up on me.

Like it was my fault too.

Resentful tears filled my eyes, and I squeezed the bridge of my nose to stop them. My wrist throbbed, and I released the pressure with a hiss of frustration. Despite the stumble over Bandit, I'd been having the best weekend I'd had for as long as I could remember.

But, of course, my parents would ruin it.

A firm hand settled on my shoulder. "Hallie, you okay?"

The hair on my nape rose.

I turned to face a concerned Chris. "I have to call my mom. I'll be two seconds."

He nodded, a deep frown between his brows, but he returned to the table while my phone rang out. Just as I was about to hang up, Mom answered.

"So you remembered you were supposed to be here for lunch?" she snapped, her tone hurt.

*What?* "When? We didn't make plans."

"I texted you."

"I didn't get your— Mom, that's not why I'm calling. Dad just called me, and he's furious at you and Jenna. You have to get over there and clean up his yard."

There was silence, then a petulant "I don't know what you're talking about."

Frustration squeezed my throat, and I gritted out, "You toilet-papered Dad's yard last night."

"I did no such thing."

"Mom, he'll press charges if you don't get over there and clean it up."

"Why should I clean up something I didn't do?" She raised her voice.

"You're on camera, Mom."

I heard her intake of breath.

"Mom?"

"I didn't do it," she insisted angrily. "And it's so like you to take that bastard's side in this!" She hung up on me, making her the second parent to do so.

Stomach churning, I hurried over to the table, where Chris and Richelle waited, wearing worried expressions. Mortified, I gave a quick explanation. "So," I continued after stumbling through the embarrassing details, "I have to get to Ridgewood and clean up the yard. I don't want to spoil your Sunday, Chris, so do you have a cab number? I can get a cab to the station."

"No, I'll drive you." Chris stood up from the table.

"No, really, I don't—"

"Hallie, of course I'm driving you," he interrupted, his tone stern. Then he leaned down to kiss Richelle's cheek. "I'm sorry to cut this short. I'll see you soon."

"Of course, go, go." She stood to hug him and then rounded the table to embrace me. "I hope you work things out with your family."

My smile was pained. "Thank you for this weekend. I've had such a good time. I'm sorry to rush out on you like this."

"Don't be silly. Family comes first. It was so good to meet you, and I can't wait to see you again." She gave me a broad smile. "Let me wrap up these sandwiches while you grab your things."

Ten minutes later we were in Chris's car, wrapped sandwiches on my lap, as we drove out of Richelle's driveway.

"I'm sorry," I apologized again.

"Stop saying you're sorry," Chris replied softly. "It's not your fault."

My resentment grew as we drove down the tree-lined highway, heading out of East Hampton. It had been so refreshing to get away from the city, to be by the sea, but more so to spend time in the company of two people I clicked with. For the first time in a long time, I felt like myself, and maybe that wasn't such a bad thing after all.

The reminder that my parents were a mess and didn't seem to

care about dragging me into their chaos made me so mad, I wanted to leap out of the car and just run back to the beach.

"I can feel you stewing from here," Chris said. "You can talk to me, you know. If it'll help."

Embarrassed by the whole situation, it took me a while to answer. "My parents' divorce has been the extra-messy kind, and I find myself stuck in the middle a lot." I looked over at him.

He scowled. "I'm sorry to hear that. Can I ask what caused the divorce? You don't have to tell me if it's too personal."

Where to even start?

"My parents are complicated together," I sighed heavily, remembering the thousands of fights. "I didn't realize it then, but looking back as an adult, I can see that I grew up in a very tense, unstable home. My parents veered between being the best of friends, mortifying me with public make-outs one weekend and then with public arguments the next. They fought a lot. My dad is—was—a sweet guy, but I think he was always insecure about my mom. Like he thought she could do better. So he was jealous of a lot of other men, and my mom found that hard to deal with. On the flip side, Mom is kind of materialistic, and they argued about money a lot too. Mom always seemed to want more, and Dad was very practical about finances and didn't think we should spend it on luxury items like a big house or a pool. They also argued about how much my dad worked. Mom was a real estate agent before she opened up her own real estate company, but she always was there for me. Every school event, every parents' evening, every birthday. Dad couldn't seem to manage that. While I knew he loved us, he prioritized his work a lot. So they fought about that too.

"I spent a lot of my childhood trying to defuse their arguments because I was so scared they'd get a divorce. I'd seen what that had done to friends' families, and I didn't want that."

God, how I'd worried about that as a kid, how I worried if I saw a man smiling at Mom too long, or if I had a school thing Dad couldn't make, and how those things might lead to an argument. A kid shouldn't have to worry about that stuff.

"I kind of thought by the time I graduated from college that parents just didn't divorce after a certain age." I laughed humorlessly. "So naive of me. About two years ago, something happened with my mom that I still don't quite understand because she won't talk about it. I suspect it was some kind of depression, but Mom isn't one for talking about feelings. So she just did things we didn't understand, and the biggest was asking Dad to move out." Emotion thickened my throat. "He was so devastated, Chris. Even with all the arguing, my dad adored my mom. He would tell me all the time that he thought there was no one as beautiful or as funny as my mom. And she just seemed to throw him away. I know it can't have been that simple, and he knew that too, but goddammit, she won't talk about it. It went on for about a year, and Dad decided he needed closure, so he asked for a divorce. It rattled my mom. She broke down in front of me, and I'd never seen her like that. She told me how much she loved him, how much she hated herself for what she'd put him through. But then afterward she pretended it never happened, and she was too proud to tell my dad she'd made a mistake and wanted him back.

"Six months ago, he met Miranda. She's a little younger, forty, and has a teenage daughter. She's nice. She seems nice. Her daughter is kind of a brat, but Miranda seems kind . . . and yet I still resent her because her presence is killing my mom." A tear slipped free and I swiped angrily at it. "And I know my mother did this to herself, and she's not exactly the nicest person to me sometimes, but all this crap she's pulling is because she's heartbroken. No matter what, she's my mom, and I want to fix things for her, but I can't. And now I'm just playing referee, and neither of them seem to care what this is doing to me, and I can't tell them because I'm so busy trying to please everyone. My dad thinks I'm on her side, and Mom thinks I'm on his side, and it's my feelings that get kicked around." I was crying. Full-on crying. Embarrassed, I covered my face. "I'm so sorry I'm unloading all of this on you."

Suddenly the car slowed, and I removed my hands to see Chris had pulled over. "What are you —"

I shut up abruptly as he released his seat belt and reached over to pull me into his arms.

He felt solid and strong, his embrace tight and reassuring. That strange sense of familiarity I felt around him overwhelmed me as I drew in his scent, as his warmth seeped into me. Why did he feel like such a safe place?

His comforting hold made me cry even harder.

"It's okay," he murmured, smoothing a hand down my hair.

After a little while, mortification returned, and I pulled out of his embrace even though his arms felt wonderful. Flushed, I couldn't meet his gaze. "I'm so sorry. I'm acting like a whiny teenager."

"Hey." Chris brushed my hair off my face so he could look into my eyes. I felt myself falling into his. "It doesn't matter what age you are, parents can still fuck you up."

I gave a huff of humorless laughter, wiping at my eyes. "Ain't that the truth."

"You okay?"

"I'm fine," I promised. "Thank you."

"No problem." He clipped his seat belt in and drove back onto the road. "Sometimes we bottle things up for so long that they just come pouring out when we least expect it."

"Thank you for understanding." I tried not to let my growing adoration for the man show. "For comforting me."

He gave me a soft look. "Anytime."

We drove for a little while in silence, and then Chris spoke. "I think your parents are probably the reason you're a people pleaser."

I nodded, feeling that resentment rise in me again. "Yeah, I think so. I hate confrontation, I hate upsetting people, and I end up dragging out friendships and relationships I'm not happy with because I don't want to deal with the fallout. I don't need a therapist to tell me my parents' behavior created that."

"That's not good for you, Hallie. Or for the people in your life. Sometimes being nice so you don't hurt feelings or get into an argument with someone is worse than just being honest. Sometimes there's kindness in brutal honesty, even if it doesn't feel like it at the time." He winced suddenly. "Anyway, it's not your job to police their war. Like you said, in the end no one is happy when you're too busy trying to please everyone."

My brows drew together. "Are you suggesting I pick a side?"

"Yeah. *Your* side."

"Isn't that selfish?"

"In this case, no. Your parents are adults. They should be able to handle the divorce themselves, and that includes this toilet-paper incident."

Despite the nervous fluttering in my stomach at the mere thought of leaving them to deal with the toilet-papered yard, the guilt that flushed through me at the thought of my dad pressing charges, my anger overtook those feelings. Would Dad really call the police, or was he just trying to force me into fixing the problem? And did Mom not care about the threat because she knew I'd cover her ass to keep the peace?

Did they not respect me at all?

"You're right," I blurted out. "Why the hell should I clean up the yard? I'm not doing it. I'm sweating at the mere thought of recusing myself from the situation, but I'm not doing it."

Chris grinned at me.

His smile made me feel stronger.

"You can drop me off at my apartment instead."

His gaze flicked back to me from the road, and I could have sworn there was pride in it. "I think that's an excellent plan. So that means you're free for the rest of the day?"

My heart leaped. "Uh, yeah, I guess."

"Me too. How about a movie and takeout?"

I thought it sounded like the perfect distraction from my parents. I also didn't know what it meant. Were we friends, or was this heading in a new direction? I didn't know. Chris hadn't made any romantic overtures, but there definitely seemed to be an attraction between us, right? Or was it all one-sided?

My brain hurt from overthinking it.

So I stopped.

Chris wanted to spend time with me and I him, and for now that was all that mattered.

"That sounds great. Favorite movie of all time?"

Going with the subject change, Chris shrugged. "*Back to the Future.*"

I gaped at him for so long he turned to give me a quick look.

"What?" He frowned. "You hate *Back to the Future?*"

"I love *Back to the Future.* It's just every guy I've ever asked that question to answered with a movie I suspected they felt was the correct answer instead of the movie they truly loved. Like *Taxi Driver* or *The Grapes of Wrath.* I think yours might be the first honest answer I've ever heard."

He shrugged. "I don't believe in lying about something to impress people. I don't believe in trying to impress people, period."

"Well, you're an astronaut. You never have to do anything else impressive ever again," I teased.

He grinned boyishly. "That's true."

"And so modest too." I laughed. "You're a real Marty McFly."

Chris chuckled like he was in on a secret I wasn't.

"What?"

"Nothing. It was just my nickname in the Air Force."

"McFly?"

He nodded. "My roommate at the academy found out *Back to the Future* was my favorite movie, and he started calling me McFly. It stuck until I went to Pax."

"You know *Back to the Future* is kind of a nerdy favorite movie."

"I'm a systems engineer and astronaut," he reminded me pointedly.

"You're also a fighter pilot and test pilot. You're like the toughest nerd ever."

He took my teasing in the good spirit I intended. "What about you? Favorite movie?"

"It's not very original, but I watch *It's a Wonderful Life* every Christmas."

"I haven't seen it," Chris confessed. "To be honest, I haven't had a lot of time for movies in my life. But if it's Hallie Goodman's favorite movie, then I'll watch it this Christmas."

*I hope you watch it with me this Christmas.* The thought snuck into my brain and heart before I could stop it.

# TWENTY-ONE

## Chris

I just don't know how you can give this place up," my Realtor, Megan, said as she followed the photographer around my Midtown apartment. Tomorrow, the place would go on the rental market.

"I'm not giving it up. I'm renting it out," I replied with a slight bite to my tone. Surely, it was obvious I needed to rent it for financial reasons. And it wasn't as if I was happy about it. "Your vetting process is solid?"

Megan turned from her spot behind the photographer, who was currently taking snapshots of my open living space. "Chris, of course we'll vet all prospective renters. No one but the most exemplary renter will get the keys. I promise you that."

Still not assured, I ignored the knot in my gut and nodded. My phone vibrated in my back pocket, and when I pulled it out, Hallie's name flashed on the screen. The knot eased a little. "I need to take this." I walked down the hall and closed myself in the bedroom. "Hey," I answered. "How are you?"

It had been several weeks since our weekend at my aunt's house. We'd seen each other merely hours before. Hallie had an event Saturday and during the day on Sunday, but she was free

Sunday night, so I'd gone to her place. After watching two comedies together, I'd left her apartment around midnight. Like the last few times I'd seen her since our weekend in the Hamptons, I'd kept a physical distance between us as much as possible. I was afraid if I got a whiff of her perfume, I'd remember what it felt like to hold her, and I'd be too tempted to break my promise: that I would not ask Hallie Goodman on an official date until I felt more certain about my future and until after I'd told her the truth about watching her videos.

Which apparently was becoming harder to do, not easier.

So much for my disaster-risk-management theory.

"My morning is going okay, I guess."

I liked the sound of her soft voice in my ear.

"I finally found out what happened with the toilet-paper incident. Dad didn't have my mom arrested, but I only know that because he left me a furious voice mail this morning about my continued absence as if I'm to blame for not controlling her actions."

Indignation flushed hot through me. "I think you need a break from them. Maybe don't answer their calls for a while until you're ready." That's what I did with my father.

"That's what I have been doing. I will have to answer eventually. Anyway, that's not why I'm calling. The invitation samples for your party arrived this morning, and I wondered if you were free at some point this week to look at them? We really should start making headway on this party if you want to host it next month, and these invitations need to go out ASAP."

The reason we hadn't made progress was because I kept deflecting any mention of it. Now seemed as good a time as any to break the news of my change of heart to Hallie. I'd decided a week ago that I didn't want to go through with the retirement party now that we were in each other's lives. I rebelled against the thought of asking people to go out of their way to attend, and also I disliked being the center of attention. I just hadn't known how to bring it up to Hallie, but I couldn't keep stringing her along when I no longer wanted to do an event. It wasn't fair. "I was, uh, going to talk to you about this when I saw you, but I don't want you wasting any more time or resources, so . . . I've decided not to have the retirement party."

"Oh no, why? I can come up with a better theme if that's the problem."

I grinned. "It's not that. I know you'd put together a fantastic party. It's just that the party was Aunt Richelle's idea. She gave me this speech about how it would bring me closure, and that seemed reasonable at the time. But the more I think about it, the more it makes me uncomfortable. I don't want to drag my friends from all over the country for a party. They would come out of respect, make time in their lives for it, and I don't think that's right. I think I'd seem like a big shot who thought he deserved a send-off."

"You won't seem like a big shot, but you do deserve a send-off."

"Not at the expense of wasting people's time."

"I'm sure your friends don't think you'd be wasting their time. They'd be happy to see you."

Hearing the disappointment in her voice, I sighed. "I've wasted *your* time. I'm sorry, Hallie." It was a jerk move on my part to put her through all that trouble only to back out.

"No, it's okay. I get it. You're not really the center-of-attention type. Um . . . you do know we still charge you for the time spent on planning, though, right?"

"Of course. I wouldn't expect you not to. You deserve to be paid for your time."

"Right. So . . . I guess . . . that's it."

Realizing why she sounded so forlorn, my mood lifted. "Let me make it up to you. I'll cook as an apology. We can have dinner at my old place tonight before some asshole with too much money to burn rents it out. I'll text you the address."

Her laugh was breathy, and my cheeks hurt from grinning at how relieved she sounded as she agreed. "That sounds great. Should I just text you when I'm leaving work?"

"Yeah absolutely. Can't wait."

"Me too."

We hung up, and I stared at my phone for a bit. It took me a second to realize I was still grinning like an idiot. The phone rang suddenly again, and I raised an eyebrow at the sight of Darcy's name. Wondering what she could want, I answered after a couple of rings.

"Chris!" She yelled my name, and I could hear the traffic of the city loud in the background. "How are you?"

"I'm good. How are you? Everything okay?"

"So good. I'm just on my way to a meeting with my wedding planner. We decided to go with the same company who did the engagement party. Right move?"

Meaning Hallie? She hadn't said anything about that. "Excellent move. The party was fantastic."

"Yes, we thought so. Anyway, I'm just calling because it was so wonderful to see you at the party, and I wanted to call right away, but then I thought maybe you'd find it too weird, and I kept going back and forth—"

"Darce," I cut her off because it wasn't like her to ramble. "You sure you're okay?"

"What I'm trying to say—and managing it poorly—is that I miss your friendship. I don't know if I'm allowed to miss your friendship, so you can absolutely tell me if I'm not."

"I miss our friendship too," I answered honestly.

"You do? It's okay I called?"

"Absolutely."

"Great! So how are you? What are you up to?"

"Uh, I'm in the middle of getting ready to rent out my apartment."

"No," she gasped. "Chris, I'm sorry. I know you love that place."

"Yeah."

"Where are you moving? Oh my God, are you going back to Houston?"

"Uh, no. Brooklyn."

"Fantastic. They say Brooklyn is the new Manhattan."

I chuckled. "Is that what they say?"

"Sure, why not. You know, we should grab drinks sometime. Catch up. We didn't really get to talk at the party."

The door to the bedroom opened, and Megan appeared with the photographer. "We need to photograph in here, Chris."

"Darce, I need to go but, yeah, call me and we'll set something up."

"Great! Talk soon."

I hung up, and Megan narrowed her eyes.

"What?" I asked at her pensive expression.

"Do you think it would be crass to advertise the fact that this is an astronaut's apartment?"

*What the fuck?*

She exhaled heavily at my expression. "You're right." Her gaze moved to the bed. "But I imagine there are plenty of guys out there who'd love to tell their dates that Captain Christopher Ortiz *slept* in that bed."

Hearing the innuendo in her voice, I shook my head and marched past her. "My name does not come into it, Megan. We're renting an apartment, not selling sex."

"When the apartment is as sexy as its owner, sometimes we are!" she called after me.

"No!"

I was pretty sure I heard her mutter "spoilsport" under her breath.

# TWENTY-TWO

## Hallie

It was difficult to concentrate on my lunch date with Darcy Hawthorne. As she looked over my digital inspiration boards for her wedding, I'd sometimes lose focus thinking about Chris. When he told me he was canceling the retirement party, it gutted me. I thought that meant the end of whatever had sparked between us, but then he'd invited me to dinner, and my hopes rose again.

I still wasn't sure what he wanted from me, and studying Darcy made me wonder if I really was imagining the sexual chemistry between us. She was just so my opposite in every way someone could be, and yet Chris had dated her.

My own insecurities were to blame for my reaction to her. I knew that. But I still couldn't help but feel relieved when the lunch was over so I could get out of her space and hopefully out of the shitty headspace being around her put me into. I had enough messy thoughts about my parents cluttering up my mind. The first few weeks after the toilet-paper incident, no one called me. Then my mom called me last weekend, but I was working, so I didn't answer. Then Dad tried, and Mom called again. Finally Dad left that voice mail this morning about how disappointed he was in me. While I felt vindicated in my choice to recuse myself from their craziness, I also felt guilty for not talking to them. However, I was afraid I'd start apologizing and doing anything to calm the storm, when what I really wanted to do was tell them how I truly felt about their treatment of me.

So for now, I was taking Chris's advice and ignoring their calls.

As I strode into our offices, Althea popped up from her desk and marched over to me. "How was lunch?"

"Productive. How was yours?"

"Boring. You know who isn't boring?" She followed me into my office.

"Ooh, let me guess. Derek?"

She gaped at me. "I haven't mentioned him that much."

I raised an eyebrow as I shrugged out of my jacket. "Just every day."

Her hands flew to her slender hips. "Well, he saw another picture of you this weekend, and he said again how he thinks you're hot. I didn't even have to prompt him this time."

"He did not say that. And how did he see my picture? *Again.*"

She shrugged. "I was scrolling casually through the photo gallery on my phone, and he's nosy."

"Althea."

"Okay, so I might have shown him another picture. Or five. But I couldn't not show him the photo of us at last Christmas's office party."

Now it was my turn to gape. "I was dressed as an elf."

"A sexy-as-hell elf."

"Althea." I slumped into my chair. "Please stop trying to matchmake me with Michelle's brother. I don't think it's a good idea."

"What is with the reluctance?" My friend sat down on my desk with a suspicious gaze. "Is it perhaps because you're crushing on a client?"

What the . . . ?

"Yeah, don't think I haven't noticed all these extracurricular activities with the hot astronaut these past few weeks."

I sniffed haughtily. "He's no longer a client. He canceled the retirement party."

"Oh. Shit. I'm sorry."

I couldn't help my stupid little grin. "Don't be. I'm going to his apartment tonight. He's making me dinner."

Althea's mouth dropped open. "Girl, nice! And no conflict of interest. I like it. Well, enjoy." She sighed dramatically. "I can't say I'm not disappointed about Derek, but if you have to throw him over for someone, you bet your ass it better be a sexy astronaut."

I shrugged. "I don't know if it means anything with Chris other than friendship. He hasn't made a move."

"He sounds like a stand-up guy, so he was probably waiting to cancel the party. Asking you over for dinner tonight . . . straight-up move."

"You think?" Hope swelled dramatically inside me.

"Oh yeah." Her eyes wandered over my face. "Look at you, grinning like a Cheshire cat."

I slapped my hands over my burning cheeks. "I know. I can't help it. I like him. A lot."

Her expression softened at my confession. "I've never seen you like this. This is good. You deserve to feel excited about someone."

"I am sorry about Derek, but I'm sure you have plenty of other choices for him."

"None quite like my Hallie."

Emotion clogged in my throat. "What did I do to deserve you?"

"Michelle asks me that same question every day. All I can say is you're damn lucky." She winked at me before standing up to strut out of my office.

I *was* lucky.

I'd never felt that way before, but finally I had people in my life who cared for me.

There was something about Chris's apartment that spoke to me. It was spacious, with a tremendous amount of light spilling in from the huge corner window that made up much of two walls in the living space.

Yet there was an easiness to it, a lack of pretension. While the furnishings were stylish, they were also comfortable and welcoming. The leather corner sofa looked expensive but also worn in, like you just wanted to curl up on it with a blanket and watch a movie. Or with a naked Chris. Now and then I'd get flashbacks to that moment of voyeurism and watching Chris's muscular ass walk across his bedroom. It would get me so hot and bothered I'd force myself to remember tripping over Bandit and spraining my wrist during the whole thing. Embarrassment killed my lady boner.

At least my wrist had healed nicely.

Shaking those thoughts away, I took in the incredible apartment and remembered this was Chris's last night in it. I felt terrible for him.

"This apartment is amazing," I told him honestly as he gestured for me to sit on a stool at the island. The aromas were also amazing. Chris could cook. Another very large tick on his pro column.

"It was my mom's. She left it to me and Miguel."

Wow. "I can only imagine how important this place is to you."

"It is."

"You'll be back here someday, Captain."

His expression softened. "Thank you for saying so." Then he seemed to shake himself and leaned toward me with a wooden spoon. It had a dollop of sauce on it. "Taste it and tell me if it's too spicy for you."

Feeling suddenly bold, I held his gaze as I wrapped my lips around the spoon. He swallowed hard, his gaze on my mouth, and I felt like wiggling triumphantly in my seat. A layered heat hit my tongue in waves as I sat back to focus on the taste. It was spicy but not overly so.

"Perfect," I replied.

Chris gazed at me a little too long before turning away. "Great."

I smiled to myself. "Where did you learn to cook? When did you have time?"

"My aunt taught me a lot growing up, but I really got into it while I was training for my mission. Any downtime I had, I screwed around in the kitchen, trying different things. It's relaxing."

"I can't cook, so I'm always impressed by anyone who can."

"I'm sure you could if you tried."

"Oh, I've tried. The last time was for my ex-boyfriend, George. I burned the pasta sauce, and I also put too much sugar in it instead of salt, but I didn't want to tell him because he'd lecture me, so I pretended like I thought the sauce was the greatest thing in the world. I'm pretty sure he must have thought I was crazy."

Chris kept his eyes on the food as he worked but asked, "Was that a while ago?"

"A few months ago. He dumped me." I felt my cheeks turn hot as the actual dumping event came back to me in full-color surround sound. "He said I was ridiculous, not serious enough for someone like him, that my job was a joke, that I was a joke, and the only reason he'd stayed with me so long was because the sex was great. Maybe for him, not for me." The latter I blurted out before I could stop myself. I groaned into my hands. "Why do I have no filter around you?"

"Hey." His large hand wrapped around my wrist and tugged.

I reluctantly revealed my face again, only to find Chris leaning across the island with an outraged expression. "He's an asshole. You know that, right?"

I nodded, somewhat taken aback by his vehemence. "I know. I told him as much."

"Good." He released me to stand back, his expression still thunderous. "That's all about him and has nothing to do with you. He didn't deserve you."

Flutters of desire made themselves known in my belly. "I know. But thank you."

His dark gaze met mine, cutting right through me with his intensity. "Hallie, I hate that someone would say that to you. I think you're amazing. I've only known you a few weeks . . . but I can't believe we've become such good friends in so little time. You're one of my closest friends now."

Those flutters died dramatically in my stomach, gasping for a last breath like they'd just been shot

Closest friends.

*Friend.*

I'd just been friend-zoned.

"Hallie?"

*Pull your shit together. Do not let him see how much this hurts.* I forced a smile I hoped seemed natural. "I guess there are people who meet and they just get each other."

"Exactly." His warm eyes glittered at me, and a confused dismay filled me.

Had I imagined the heated look just a few minutes ago? Or the one he'd given me when he was half-naked and pulling me up off his aunt's hallway floor?

What about the hot little smiles we shared now and then?

Or the way the air seemed to thicken between us when we got too close.

Had I really imagined all of that?

Fuck!

How pathetic did that make me?

"Dinner is almost ready. Can I get you a drink? I have beer or wine."

"Wine!" I practically yelled, hopping off the stool. My heels clicked loudly as I moved across his hardwood floors. "Let me help you. You want beer?"

"Yeah, sure. Thanks."

I poured myself a large glass of red wine as Chris plated the food and led me over to his dining table.

"My Realtor would kill me if she knew I'd made curry the night before viewings start."

Glad for the subject distraction, I nodded. "Just open the windows. Try spritzing some cologne or something. Where did you learn how to cook curry, anyway?"

"Aunt Richelle went backpacking with Akio after college, and they spent a lot of time in Southeast Asia. This is a Cambodian red curry chicken dish. She got the recipe from a local she befriended."

"Ooh, that's exciting. I've never tried an authentic Cambodian dish before."

It was delicious. Of course it was. Anything Chris put his mind to turned out well, right? Twenty minutes ago, that would have made me smile with giddiness. Now I resented him for it. He was too perfect.

And he didn't want me.

That really shouldn't have surprised me as much as it did.

Gulping down the wine, I tried to think of anything else and went with, "I've always wanted to go backpacking. I planned to during the summer before my senior year of college."

"Yeah?" Chris's eyes lit up. "I've always wanted to backpack too. Why didn't you go?"

I shrugged. "Everyone who has ever met me talked me out of it."

"Why would they do that?"

"Because apparently I'm not savvy or responsible enough to take care of myself on a backpacking trip."

He dropped his fork, his expression disbelieving. "Who the hell said that to you?"

My heart stopped at how annoyed he seemed on my behalf. "Chris, it's fine. A few friends. My mom. Ex-boyfriends. They kind of laughed at the thought, and when that many people share the same opinion, you start to think maybe they're right."

"Or maybe they're assholes."

"I do get myself into weird situations sometimes."

"Hallie." His tone was hard. "You can do anything you put your mind to. Ignore those so-called friends and family and this bullshit narrative they're trying to create for you. You are an extremely capable woman. You know you are. Go backpacking if you want to go backpacking. Don't let anyone stop you."

Tears rushed into my eyes, and I bowed my head to my plate so he wouldn't see them. I batted the emotion back, loving him for believing in me and hating him a little for only wanting to be my friend. I wasn't sure I could handle this. If he'd just stop being so perfect for me, I might be able to deal with the friend-zoning.

"Hallie, are you okay?"

Tears successfully fought back, I looked at him but smiled wearily. "I'm just exhausted. It's been a long day, and I'm still a little upset about the voice mail from my dad."

"Why didn't you say?"

"You went to all this trouble, and I didn't want to ruin your last night in the apartment . . . I'm sorry." I pushed away from the table. "But I think I just need some rest."

"Of course." He moved to stand up, but I gestured for him to stop. "Do you want to stay? You can take the bedroom. I'll take the couch."

*Ugh, stop being so nice!* "Nah, I'm going to head home."

"Right. Let me grab my keys. You're not taking the subway alone at this hour."

"Chris, no. I'll help you clean up, and then I'm going to treat myself to a cab home."

"You don't have to help me clean up."

"No, I—"

"I insist, Hallie. If you're not feeling yourself, you should go home. Rest up." He rounded the table, and I braced myself for proximity. Sure enough, he reached out to brush an errant strand of hair behind my ear, and I held back an answering shiver. "Are you sure you're okay? We can talk about your dad some more if you want?"

*Stop it!*

I shook my head, my smile tight. "Maybe later." I reached up to press a swift kiss to his cheek because I didn't want him to think anything was wrong between us. "I'll call you." I hurried around him to swipe my purse off the side table. "Thanks again."

"Hallie, wait—"

But I was already in the hall, yanking open his apartment door. "Night!"

"Hallie—"

I banged it shut behind me and rushed for the elevator. It was as if the elevator gods were on my side because the doors opened right away and shut just as I heard Chris's apartment door opening. The elevator descended before he ever made it to me.

Five minutes later, I miraculously grabbed a cab. Once inside the cab, which smelled of Cheetos, holding back my desolation, I rummaged in my purse for my cell to distract myself. Except there was a missed call from Chris, along with a text.

I'm worried about you. Text me when you get home.

I waited until I was in my apartment, until I'd kicked off my shoes and poured an enormous glass of water to counteract the enormous glass of wine I'd consumed, to text him back.

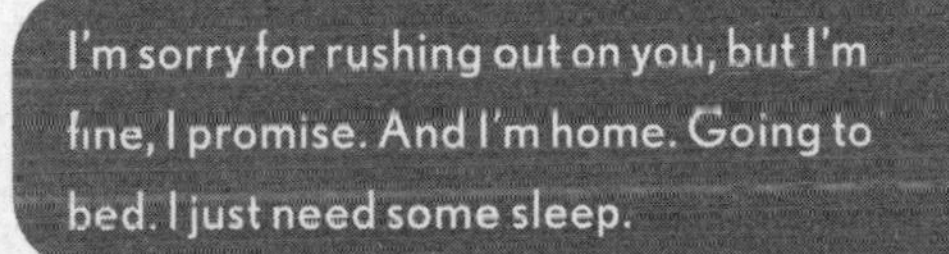


His answering text was instant.

Sleep well. I'll call you.

Did I want him to call me?

As I crawled into bed and my tears fell, I considered setting up my laptop so I could pour all my feelings out into a video letter. I hadn't done that since meeting Chris. Because I'd had the real person to talk to and we had been growing close. Now I couldn't voice my feelings. Maybe because they felt too big, too dramatic, considering how little time I'd known him.

Yet, I couldn't remember feeling this bad when any of my boyfriends dumped me, and Chris wasn't even a boyfriend.

Maybe it would be better to create some distance between us? Give myself some space.

But Chris had called me one of his closest friends.

I couldn't imagine that wasn't a big deal for him to admit. It wasn't something thirty-five-year-old men went around spouting willy-nilly.

My chest ached at the thought of hurting him.

He needed me.

Not in the way I wanted him to, but he still needed me, and he was one of less than a handful of people in my life who treated me with respect and believed in me.

I wasn't sure I could give that up for anything.

# TWENTY-THREE

## Chris

When I returned to Earth, the only thing that took longer to get used to than gravity was New York City. Up there, the humming machine sounds of the ISS were the only source of constant noise, and it was the kind of noise I easily adjusted to.

The first night I spent back in New York after five months in space and weeks in the calm environment of the physical therapy center in Houston was the hardest. I couldn't believe I'd never noticed how incredibly noisy the city was. How I'd never paid much attention to the almost constant sound of sirens and movement of people and vehicles. It had always just been a part of the city's soul. Its music. But when I got back, it was too much at first. Too loud. Too chaotic. Too everything. However, eventually the sound of New York City became like the machine noise on the station. It disappeared into the background, and I barely noticed it again.

Waiting outside the restaurant not far from Hallie's office building, I wasn't aware of the foot or road traffic, the music spilling out of restaurants and bars, the laughter and conversation of people passing by. I gazed down the street, anticipating Hallie's appearance.

I hadn't seen her in a week. We'd only talked through texts, and even then, she'd been off with me.

I'd fucked up with the friend comment.

As soon as it came out of my mouth, I regretted it, but then I'd thought it didn't matter because until I admitted the truth about the videos, I couldn't explain I was interested in taking her out on an actual date anyway.

But then she couldn't get out of my apartment fast enough, and afterward she wouldn't answer my calls.

Never in my life had I chased anyone. I didn't know if it was the stubborn pride I'd inherited from my father, but I abhorred the idea of chasing after someone who didn't want to spend time with me. I'd never done it with anyone, friends or women I was interested in romantically. Not even overtly my father.

Yet I was on the verge of dropping by Hallie's apartment and telling her everything, laying my cards on the table, when she texted me last night to apologize for not being around. She gave me excuses about her work and then asked if I wanted to have dinner with her the next evening near her office. More relieved than I could say, I of course agreed.

And tonight I would tell her everything.

Hopefully, she'd forgive me long enough to let me kiss her, because I didn't think I could go much longer without kissing the hell out of Hallie Goodman.

The only distraction I had from the woman was my writing. The book was coming along better than I'd expected.

The sight of pink hair in the distance drew me from my thoughts. The pulse throbbed in my neck as anticipation zinged through my every nerve ending.

I'd never felt like this, I realized.

It stunned me for a second.

Hallie spotted me outside the restaurant, smiled, and gave me that familiar little wave.

I swear that gorgeous smile of hers caused my heart to turn over in my chest.

It was warm enough to move around the city without a coat or sweater now, and she wore a long-sleeved dress that hit her mid-thigh. Despite her height, Hallie's legs were so perfectly formed they always looked long. This evening was no different, as she walked toward me in sexy high heels. I admired the way she walked in those things, like they were merely sneakers.

Too busy reeling from the sudden overwhelming realization of the depth of my feelings for this woman, I hadn't responded to her wave and still hadn't greeted her as she drew to a stop in front of me.

She gazed up at me with those big dark blue eyes, and relief filled me.

Hallie was here.

I'd missed her.

"Captain." She rested a hand on my arm, brows drawn together. "Are you okay?"

Reaching for her hand, I took it in both of mine. "I just missed you," I confessed.

Her face lit up, and I knew I couldn't dance around this any longer. It was obvious what we both wanted, and life was too damn short to mess around. Concerned but determined, I opened my mouth to tell her everything right there and then but was cut off by a booming voice.

"Hallie? Is that you?"

Hallie winced and muttered, "Oh God, no." Then she pasted on a smile and turned around to look up at the guy and woman who approached us. "George, hi."

George?

Her ex-boyfriend George?

I moved into Hallie's side and grabbed hold of her hand. She shot me a quick look of surprise but squeezed my hand.

People made their way around us on the sidewalk as George's eyes flickered to me for a second in confusion. He pulled the woman at his side closer to him. "Hallie, this is my girlfriend, Reese. She's a *financial analyst*." He drawled it, like Hallie might not understand what a financial analyst was, and with a puffed-up chest like he'd just announced Reese was president.

Also, he bumped into his ex-girlfriend, and the first thing he did was introduce his new girlfriend rather than asking after Hallie's well-being? Yeah, this guy was some gentleman.

I studied him like he was one of the irritating sand flies that had tormented me and my unit while we were in the Middle East. George was taller than me by a good few inches. There was nothing extraordinary about him physically, and I knew from how he treated Hallie that he was a dick. So what the hell had Hallie seen in this guy?

"Hi." Reese smiled sweetly. "George has told me a lot about you, Hallie. I like your hair. I'd never be so bold, but I wish I had the confidence to pull that off. And your dress. So cute. It goes with your hair. Is it a rinse?"

Hallie gaped at the rambling woman for a second and then gestured to me. "This is—"

"Oh, Hallie can get away with crazy hair since she works as a party planner." George grinned like he'd told the best joke on the fucking planet.

I shifted toward him and felt Hallie squeeze my hand so hard it was almost painful. Looking at her, I watched her lift her chin and physically draw herself up.

"Actually, I'm an event planner for one of the most elite event-management companies in New York. And self-expression at Lia Zhang Events is almost a requirement. It's important clients have a good sense of our creativity."

"Lia Zhang?" Reese gaped, wide-eyed. "I've heard of Lia Zhang Events. Didn't you guys plan Alicia Keys's fortieth birthday?"

"I can't talk about clients." Hallie shrugged with an insouciant confidence that made my lips twitch with pride. "Anyway, George, before you rudely interrupted, I was going to introduce you to—"

"Her boyfriend," I blurted before I could stop myself. I held out my hand to the prick. "Chris Ortiz."

George frowned but shook my hand, and I dropped it immediately, feeling tainted. "Ortiz? Is that Mexican?"

"It is." I narrowed my gaze on him as he smirked, as if this somehow pleased him. And that wasn't me being paranoid. I could read this asshole like a book.

"And what is it you do?" George asked, his nose practically in the air.

"I'm an astronaut."

His girlfriend's eyes lit with recognition. "Oh my God, I thought you were familiar." She hit her boyfriend's chest. "George, this is Captain Christopher Ortiz! He's famous on Instagram! I've never met an astronaut before." She smiled flirtatiously at me.

Jesus.

George gawked at me and then Hallie as if he'd never seen her before.

"Well, we have reservations." Hallie nudged me toward the restaurant. "See you around."

While I was trained to compartmentalize and stay calm in any situation, the thought of this guy thinking he'd somehow been better than Hallie just stuck in my craw. I stopped and called back to George.

He stopped midturn and gazed back at me, looking like a petulant child who'd lost a game. "What?"

I sneered at his snippy tone. "You belittled Hallie, and I would never make a mistake like that. She's amazing. She's kind; she's smart, loyal, creative, funny. Man, you were lucky Hallie even talked to you, let alone touched you."

Hallie choked at my side as George turned purple with indignation.

"Well, as Hallie said, we have reservations. Enjoy your evening." With my arm still around Hallie's waist, I guided her away toward the restaurant entrance.

She didn't say a word.

My reaction to George had been instinctual. I hadn't thought beyond putting him in his place. Hoping I hadn't embarrassed her, I glanced down and gave her waist a little squeeze. "Did I cross the line?"

Hallie looked over her shoulder to make sure George was gone and then turned to me. Laughter lit her eyes as we stopped at the restaurant door, and her body shook against me as she gave into her amusement.

Relieved, I grinned, holding her closer to me. I wanted to kiss the laughter off her lips.

She rested a palm on my chest, and I wondered if she could feel my heart pounding beneath it. With her free hand, she wiped tears of amusement from the corners of her eyes. "Seriously, that felt good to see him put in his place." Her expression changed, softening to something I liked a whole fucking lot. "Also those were the nicest things anyone has ever said about me."

*I'm going to kiss her.* "I wish that weren't true," I murmured, eyes dropping to her mouth. "You deserve people to say nice things about you all the time."

"Chris . . ."

Her sad tone brought my gaze back to her eyes.

She stared up at me, looking guilty and worried. "I hope you don't judge me for dating him. He wasn't like that at first. His superiority kind of got worse over time. I thought it was just about me, but the way he looked at you when he asked about your name . . ." Anger flashed in her eyes. "I think I was so wrapped up in my own stuff while I dated him that I didn't really see him. That's not an excuse, I know. But I want you to know, I plan to do better in the future. To make better choices. To treat myself with more respect and surround myself with people I can respect too. Like you."

This was it. I needed to tell her. "Hallie—"

The jarring burst of joy that was "Mr. Blue Sky" by ELO shattered the moment between us, and Hallie stepped away from me with a muttered curse. "That's me, sorry." She rummaged in her purse for her cell.

She'd had a different ringtone every week that I'd known her. I smiled at how loud this one was, despite being irritated it had interrupted us.

"It's my mom." Hallie chewed her bottom lip.

"Ignore it."

"She's called me eight times today. It isn't like her."

Shit. "Then answer it."

We moved away from the restaurant entrance as Hallie held her phone to her ear and covered her other so she could hear better. "Hey, Mom, is everything okay?"

I observed her face as she frowned.

"Mom . . . Slow down. . . . Mom . . . Where are you? . . . Okay, good. . . . How much have you had to drink?"

Oh hell. I ran a hand through my hair as Hallie's lips trembled. I placed a comforting hand on her shoulder.

"I know, Mom. . . . Okay, just stay there, I'm coming. . . . I know, I know. . . . I'm coming. I'll be there soon." She hung up, tears in her eyes. "My mom is wasted and sobbing hysterically about this mess with my dad. I need to go to her."

"Of course. Do you want me to come?"

"I appreciate it, Chris, but I don't think she'd like anyone else seeing her like this."

I hated feeling useless. "Let me at least walk you to the station."

She nodded, already miles away in New Jersey with her mom. I wrapped my arm around her shoulders, and she relaxed into me. "She'll be okay."

We walked, arms around each other, in silence to Penn Station.

"You sure you don't want me to come?" I asked when we reached the entrance.

Hallie turned, breaking our physical contact. "I might need you, but my mom just needs me."

I hated this.

I hated seeing her this upset and not being able to do anything about it.

"You take care of your mom, Hallie. . . . But remember, take care of you too."

Her mouth trembled. "I just . . . uh . . . I haven't heard her like this in a while."

I wasn't callous. I felt for Hallie's mom. But I'd also learned some things about how her parents treated her, and I didn't like a lot of it. At all. Hallie was the one *I* cared about, and I didn't want her lost in her parents' messed-up relationship anymore. Drawing her into my arms, I hugged her hard and she sank into me.

We stayed like that longer than I meant to.

"I better go," she murmured.

Nodding, I pressed a kiss to her temple and released her. "Let me know when you get there."

"I will." She smiled gratefully. "Thank *you* for being such a great friend, Chris."

I returned her smile with a small one of my own and watched her walk away.

The next time I saw her, I would come clean and hope that not only did I still rank as a great friend but that she'd still be open to something more.

Something that involved me kissing every perfect inch of her.

# TWENTY-FOUR

## Hallie

It was late by the time I pulled up to my father's new house. I'd borrowed mom's car since she was passed out on her bed. Exhausted and more nervous than I could remember being in a long time, I sat outside my dad's house trying to talk myself out of the car.

After listening to my mom drunkenly sob about her heartbreak for over an hour before she passed out, I felt anger building bigger and bigger inside me. Anger that had always been there, simmering. Not just at my dad. At Mom too. However, she was too drunk and upset for me to say what needed to be said.

And I had to get this out.

Perhaps it was the embarrassment of standing next to Chris, watching the distaste in his eyes as he realized I'd dated someone as abhorrent as George, or perhaps it was both that and years of resentment. Whatever had led me to jump into Mom's car and drive to my father's house, I knew I couldn't bottle it up anymore.

I'd turned a blind eye to who George was because it was easier than having to deal with a confrontation or a breakup. I'd let Gabby treat me like crap since high school. I'd allowed my parents to pass me back and forth in this stupid war, and I let all of them make me feel like an inept child. *I* allowed them to do that, and that was on me. But now it needed to stop.

Lia was the first person who ever made me feel competent and good at something, and that meant a lot to me, coming from someone as smart and as driven as her.

Althea was the first friend who made me feel like a person worth having in their life, and that meant a lot because she was a no-bullshitter and did not suffer fools easily.

And Chris made me feel special, important, and like I could take on the world if I wanted to. Chris, who was intelligent and brave and didn't do what other people wanted him to do. He made choices because they were *his* choices, and he was honest to a fault, no matter the consequences. He was right about my habit of people-pleasing in every situation. It didn't get me anywhere, and all it did was give my parents the license to take me for granted, to use me to clean up their messes.

I'd heard a lot about how they were feeling these past few years.

Not once had either of them asked how it affected me.

And if I didn't tell one of them, I was going to explode.

I pushed out of the car, slamming the door behind me. By the time I made it to the door, it was already opening. Miranda squinted at me under the light of their front porch. "Hallie? Is everything okay?"

"Is my dad home?"

"Yeah, yeah, come in." She stepped aside, and I noted she was in her pajamas. "It's late, are you okay?"

Sensing her genuine concern, I nodded. "I just need to talk to my dad."

"Hallie?" My father walked into the hallway from the living room. He was still in his dress shirt and pants, though he'd discarded his tie, and his hair was mussed. I could hear the murmur of the TV in the background. "What are you doing here?" His voice was low. "Is everything okay?"

I stared at the guy who had missed so many events in my life because of his work but who had shown me in other ways that he had my back. I'd bounced around from baseball to swimming to gymnastics to skating to art class to piano lessons . . . My entire childhood he'd indulged me in my whims and defended them to my mom when she said I gave up too easily. Honestly, I hadn't. I was just always excited to try something different. Dad had understood that about me back then. As I grew older, I lost that thirst for adventure because I'd been too busy trying not to ruffle any feathers and be a good girl and do whatever would keep the peace.

When I brought up the idea of backpacking before my senior year of college, my dad had said he'd double whatever money I made in the summers running up to it so I could do that. Then Mom found out and lost her shit. She said she would not spend weeks worrying about something awful happening to her kid overseas somewhere. My parents had such a huge fight about it, I eventually told them I'd changed my mind and didn't want to do it. By that point, Gabby and a few friends from college had made it seem like I didn't have the personality to do something so adventurous. So I scrubbed that one off my bucket list, and peace reigned in the Goodman household. For a while.

My fault for letting friends feed my insecurity and allowing my parents' relationship to dictate my life.

But it was their fault too for not seeing how their actions affected me.

I didn't recognize this guy in front of me as the guy who had supported my dreams growing up.

"I need to talk to you in private."

Concerned, he flicked a look at Miranda. "Okay. Let's go into the kitchen, but try to keep your voice down because Alison's sleeping, and she has an early flight tomorrow. She's going to stay with her dad in Florida for the summer."

I nodded, brittle at the reminder he was playing happy blended family.

Glancing over my shoulder, I saw Miranda peering curiously after us before she ducked into the living room, out of sight. My dad closed the kitchen door, not quite shutting it.

"What's going on? You haven't answered my calls for weeks, and then you show up here unannounced close to midnight."

I narrowed my eyes. "I didn't know I needed to announce myself to stop by my dad's house."

Something in my tone made his head jerk. His expression softened. "Of course you don't. I didn't mean it like that."

"Didn't you?" My hands shook at my sides, so I curled them into fists. "I just came from Mom's. She called me, drunk and inconsolable."

Dad sighed. "Your mother isn't my problem anymore."

"Your *problem*? Am I your problem? Do you even care what it's been like for me being tossed around in your whole moronic, childish divorce drama?"

"Excuse me?" he spat angrily.

His anger fired mine. "Not once have you asked me how I'm doing or how I feel. Every time you have an issue with Mom, you drag me into it like she's my responsibility. And the fact is, Dad, you're the reason she's messed up."

"Lower your voice," he hissed. "And may I remind you, your mother left me."

"Yeah, she did." Tears burned in my throat. "And I don't know why, and she doesn't even know why, but all this crap she's pulling now is because she's heartbroken!"

Dad looked away, the muscle in his jaw ticking.

"And I'm not asking you to feel sorry for her, because I know she broke your heart first . . . but everything you've done since has been to get back at her, and you haven't cared who you hurt to do it."

"What the hell are you talking about?"

"This house! Miranda, Alison!" I gestured around me. "You can't afford this house, Dad! This is the kind of house you always told Mom we couldn't have because it was a waste of money, but you could have afforded it then on both your incomes. I know you can't afford it on your own. But you bought this to impress Miranda because you knew it would hurt Mom!"

The color leached from my father's face.

Tears slipped freely down mine. "I might be a grown woman, but I'm still your daughter, and you threw me away. I only ever get a phone call if you need me to deal with Mom or if you need something from me . . . like throwing a sixteenth-birthday party for a girl I barely know when you never even bothered to show up to mine! You talk to me about Miranda and Alison like they're your priority and I'm no longer your family, like you divorced me when you divorced Mom. And I never said anything," I cried. "Because I was too busy trying to make everything okay for everyone else. But I'm not okay! I'm tired of your bullshit. Both of you." I swiped angrily at my tears, turning to stare out at the pool lit up in the dark. "Does Miranda even know this place is probably crippling you?"

"No, I don't."

I spun around. Miranda had stepped into the room. She glared up at my father, and my stomach sank as my father turned his back on us both. His shoulders rose and fell in shallow breaths as he leaned into the kitchen counter.

Remorse prodded me, but for once I refused to cave to it.

"I'm sorry for interrupting, but you were yelling, so I couldn't help but hear everything." Miranda's eyes brightened. "I'm sorry for how you've been made to feel, Hallie. I want you to know that I was not aware, and it was never my intention for you to feel pushed out of your father's life."

I shook my head at her, my gaze returning to Dad, who still wouldn't look at either of us. "I didn't come here for your apology. I only came here to tell the truth for once and to say I . . ." I took a shuddering breath as more tears welled up from my chest. "I don't want you to call me anymore, Dad. Not unless you're ready to stop involving me in your divorce, to be my dad again. And to start respecting me and my time."

When he still didn't look at me, I moved toward the door.

Miranda blocked the way, glowering at my father's back.

"Excuse me," I whispered.

She looked like she wanted to reach out and comfort me, but I didn't want comfort. I shook my head and strode past her and toward the door. Every step I took, I waited for my dad to call out to me, to stop me and hold me and to tell me he was sorry.

By the time I got into the car and pulled away from his house, I was crying again, this time with crushing disappointment.

# TWENTY-FIVE

## Hallie

**Call me tomorrow. I want to hear that you're okay.**

I stared at the text from Chris the entire subway ride to work the next morning. Last night, I'd texted him when I arrived at my mom's and then again when I returned home late. I hadn't told him what happened. I'd wanted to. In fact, I'd wanted to call him and cry from a distance on his shoulder. Yet, I also needed to sit alone with what I'd done. There was a possibility my dad and I would never recover from what I'd said to him, and I had this horrible knot in my stomach.

Yet I also felt strong and in control in a way that I hadn't in a long time. If ever.

It was overwhelming.

On the way into the office, I bumped into Althea.

"Hey, gorgeous, how are you this morning?" she asked, sashaying toward me with a hot drink in one hand, her phone in the other, and a large purse dangling from her elbow.

I took one look at her face, and without warning, tears welled in my eyes.

"Oh shit, okay. Follow me." Althea veered past the elevator and into the ladies' restroom. Trying to hold back actual sobbing, I hurried after her and watched as she kicked at all the stall doors with her six-inch heels to make sure the place was empty. Then she returned to the main door and locked it.

"Can you do that?"

"I just did." Her eyes ran over my face. "Okay, why the hell do you look like you're the only person on the planet who knows we're all about to die in a meteor strike that no Ben Affleck–Bruce Willis deep-core-drilling team can save us from?"

"That was intensely specific."

"Your expression is intensely *Armageddon*-like. Am I at least in the ballpark?"

"Perhaps in my own private universe." I sniffed, holding my head back and pinching the bridge of my nose. "I cannot cry and ruin my makeup."

"Hallie, what happened?"

I sucked in a breath and shook out my hands. "I kind of snapped last night and may have irrevocably destroyed my relationship with my dad."

"Did you tell him you were pansexual?"

Feeling awful, I closed my eyes. "Althea, I should not be complaining about this to you."

"Stop, stop. I'm sorry. You know I have an offbeat sense of humor." She'd explained to her parents about her sexuality when she was nineteen. They were both much older, Althea being the youngest of five, and the gap between her and her eldest sibling was fifteen years. While her mom had been nothing but supportive, it had taken a few years before her dad accepted her relationship with Michelle. He apologized for making her feel unloved, and now their relationship was good. But I knew from what Althea had told me that those few years in between had strained everyone in the family's relationship with her father. "This isn't about me. I'm just saying, if anyone can empathize with shitty arguments with your dad, it's me."

I leaned against a sink. "I just . . . I've been thinking a lot lately about how I people-please to a ludicrous extent."

Althea raised an eyebrow.

"You disagree?"

"Hell no. I'm just surprised you've finally realized that it's adversely affecting your life."

I snorted. "Chris helped me figure some things out about myself. Anyway, it all came to a head last night, and I finally called my dad out for buying that house to deliberately hurt Mom and shoving me out of his life unless he needed something from me."

"Good for you." Althea nodded. "I mean it. Hallie, that took guts, and it needed to be said. Do you know how badly I wanted to say that to him at that fucking birthday party?"

"Thank you. I told him not to . . ." My mouth trembled, and I put my head back again to stem the tears. "Ah, I told him not to call me unless it was to be my dad again and respect me."

Her slow clapping drew my head back down.

"Are you being sarcastic?"

"What?" she frowned. "No! I'm clapping. I'm proud."

"I usually consider slow clapping sarcastic."

"I have a drink in one hand and a cell in the other. I can only slow clap."

"Okay. Apologies. I accept your slow clapping. Thank you."

She leaned into me, expression serious. "Hallie, your dad isn't a bad guy. He's just sort of clueless and self-involved. He'll come around."

"You think? He let me walk out without saying anything."

"Sometimes when a person needs their head pulled out of their ass, it can be painful. It can take a while for them to process it, you know. Give him a minute."

I nodded, hoping she was right.

"So." She studied me again. "How are things going with Chris?"

The door to the restroom rattled. "Hey, why is this locked?" a voice called from the other side of the door.

"Shit. Let's take this conversation outside."

We got out of the restroom, ignoring the ferocious scowl of the woman who wanted in, and headed for the elevator. Making sure there was no one from our office around, I picked up our conversation as if we hadn't stopped talking. "I am very confused about him," I answered honestly. "He . . . uh . . . he friend-zoned me, but I'm getting mixed signals."

"Take it from the top. Start with the friend-zoning."

I explained to her what he'd said to me in his old apartment.

"And those were his exact words?" she asked as we got on the elevator and crowded into the back.

"Exact words."

Althea frowned. "So what are the mixed signals?"

I told her what he'd said and done with George last night, pretending to be my boyfriend. Her eyes got rounder, filling with more and more delight as my story went on. By the time we got off the elevator, she grinned from ear to ear. "Oh, okay, I gotta meet this guy and shake his damn hand."

"He's pretty amazing."

"Is that the mixed signal though? Because I would do that kind of thing for a friend I care about."

I loved Althea's blunt honesty, but sometimes it stung. "Right. Okay. Well, also, sometimes I think I catch him *looking* at me."

"Looking at you, how?" Althea stopped at her desk.

"You're ten minutes late," Dominic said at us snippily as he marched past.

"Fuck you too, Dom," Althea called out in a pleasant tone.

The surrounding staff tittered as Dominic almost collided with a wall. He glowered at Althea before hurrying down the hallway, out of sight.

"You need to watch out," I warned her. "Please don't get fired. You keep me sane."

"I'm just sick of his bitchiness. Yesterday he kept listening to my phone calls and correcting everything I said to throw me off. I wanted to kill him. But I'll do better," she promised, sitting on her desk. "I'll rise above. So continue. Chris looks at you, how?"

"Like he's interested." I squirmed in embarrassment. "I feel like there's this tension between us."

"But that could be because you like him."

"You said you thought he was interested."

"I did until he called you the best friend he ever had. That is straight up friend-zoning." Seeing my destroyed expression, Althea reached for my hand. "It's better to know that now, before your feelings grow any deeper. I'm sorry."

"No. You're right. I let my stupid hopes get in the way again." I squeezed her hand. "Thanks."

"Anytime. Always here for you. Hey, are you free this Friday night? Michelle and I are going to a new bar opening. We'd love for you to come."

"I'll think about it."

"You do that."

I started to walk away and heard Althea call my name again. Turning toward her, I grew still at her expression.

"I'm proud of you, Hallie. It takes guts to do what you did last night."

"I'm proud of you too. In fact, I'm going to start calling you my super-duper bestie."

"You had to ruin it." She sighed heavily and slumped into her chair.

"I've already ordered us T-shirts!" I called as I walked away, grinning. "And mugs! They have the words 'You're My Best-Tea!' written on them! You're gonna love it!"

"I'm gonna smash it!"

Our colleagues laughed with me as I strolled toward my office, feeling pretty lucky I had a friend who could make me feel grateful after the night I'd had.

"Knock knock."

I looked toward the door; the phone pressed to my ear as Althea hovered on the threshold of my office. Holding up a finger to silence her, I listened to the estate manager at the Blenheim estate on Martha's Vineyard try to talk me into a different date for Darcy Hawthorne's wedding. "Oh, I understand you close for the season the weekend before the weekend we're looking to book, but this date has a significance for Ms. Hawthorne and Mr. Lemieux, and they're adamant about marrying then. We've looked at numerous venues, and after paying you a visit this weekend, Ms. Hawthorne has her heart set on Blenheim for their wedding—"

"I understand that, but we're closed for the season on those dates."

"Ms. Hawthorne and Mr. Lemieux are willing to compensate you for the inconvenience."

There was silence. Then, "I see. I'd have to discuss it with Mr. and Mrs. Blenheim."

"Why don't I email you regarding the compensation? You can share it with the Blenheims and get back to me." I was pretty sure as soon as the Blenheims realized Darcy wanted to marry on their estate, they'd offer it up without asking for compensation, but Darcy authorized me to make the offer anyhow. The compensation offer was really just a way to get past the manager and talk directly to the owners, who were part of Darcy's parents' social circle.

"All right. I'll get back to you as soon as possible."

We hung up, and Althea smirked. "Look at you, working your charm."

"When Darcy Hawthorne wants a venue on a specific date, you do anything short of selling a kidney to make it happen."

"Maybe even then," we said in unison.

"Jinx." I relaxed back in my seat as Althea took her usual spot on my desk. "What's up?"

"I've been thinking all morning about your Chris problem."

"Is it a problem?"

"The look on your face says you're either close to falling in love with him or you're already there, so, yeah, that tells me it's a problem."

My cheeks grew hot, and I couldn't quite meet her gaze.

"Mm-hmm." She tapped the desk to get my attention. "Now this isn't me trying to be a pain in the ass, but I really think you might need a distraction."

"What kind of— You mean Derek?" I made a face.

"How do you do that? Am I that predictable?"

"You're a broken record." I stared at her, thinking about her doggedness with Michelle's brother. I trusted my friend. "Do you really want to set me up with him when I have feelings for someone else? Because that sounds disastrous to me."

"Confession: it turns out Derek, after dating a little, has decided that's all he wants to do for a while—casual dating. He's not ready for serious. And you're not ready for serious, so I don't see the harm in it. Maybe nothing will come of it, but maybe you'll meet and hit it off."

"Fine." I decided on impulse.

Althea's eyes popped out. "For real? You'll go on a date with him?"

"Sure." My stomach flipped at the thought. "I'm being bold these days and trying to do what's best for me. If Chris has friend-zoned me, I think dating other people might help me get over him."

"Friday night." Althea jumped off my desk. "I'll set it up. Something casual, like drinks. Dinner is too much pressure." She wiggled her butt as she hurried across the room. "Oooh, this is exciting!"

I laughed. "Don't get your hopes up!"

"Wear that ivory boyfriend sweater that looks like a dress on you." Althea shot back. "It looks great with your hair, and you can match it with those gold strappy Jimmy Choos you bought last summer."

"You pay way too much attention to my wardrobe, and I'll wear what I want."

"Okay, okay. But that outfit screams sexy casual."

*Dammit,* I thought as she disappeared out of sight. She was right. That *was* a hot outfit.

# TWENTY-SIX

## Chris

Scott Rose <SRose@Roselit.com>
To: Christopher_ortiz@bmail.com

Hi Christopher,

I'm Scott Rose, President of Rose Literary Management here in New York. As you might know, your aunt Richelle and I are friends, and she reached out to me regarding a book you're writing about your life and your much-publicized space mission with NASA. I have to say I'm fascinated to know more and would love to read what you've written so far. If you're interested, you can contact me at the number at the bottom of this email so we can discuss it a little further.

All best,
Scott

I pondered my options. Aunt Richelle hadn't gone behind my back to do this. We'd talked about it, but I hadn't been sure Scott

Rose would be interested. He owned one of the biggest literary agencies in New York with a West Coast division in Los Angeles. My whole life, I'd never felt uncertain of the work I'd done. Sure, the first time I went on a space walk I was half-terrified something might go wrong, but I was equipped with the knowledge to decrease the chances of that happening.

Writing this book was as far outside my comfort zone as I could get. Mostly because I'd never considered myself a writer.

There was a huge chance that Scott Rose would think what I'd written was a piece of shit.

If I'd had more time to finish it, to play around with it more, be certain of it to some extent, I wouldn't feel so apprehensive about sending Scott the partial manuscript. I talked openly in the book about my disconnection from the Latinx community and the desire to explore ways to connect—how I'd felt an uncomfortable mix of honor in being a leader for the Mexican community while struggling with the idea that I wasn't worthy of their pride in me because I hadn't been raised to embrace my culture. That was as vulnerable as it got, and I was, at heart, a very private person. So maybe that feeling of apprehension would always be there regarding this book.

My goddamn father, however, had taken the option to wait until I was ready out of my hands. At the beginning of the week, I'd received multiple calls from a publishing house under his conglomerate's ownership badgering me about my book and sending literary agents my way. I'd eventually had to block all their numbers on my phone. I knew these people weren't jumping to publish my book. They were being pressured by my father to get this done.

I knew my father's game.

He wanted to control this. He always tried.

I always outplayed him.

It didn't stop him from fucking with me.

The only way I knew how to stop it was to get ahead of him. He'd forced my hand. I'd wanted to talk to Hallie about it, but she'd been quiet ever since she'd gone to see her mother. We hadn't really spoken all week. I was worried about her too.

After speaking to Aunt Richelle about the manuscript situation, she'd suggested she contact her friend. The rest was history.

"Fuck," I muttered.

I reached for my phone and opened my texts. Last night I'd asked Hallie if she wanted to meet for drinks tonight, but she said she had plans and suggested we do something on Sunday instead. I wondered if she was working tonight at an event.

I wanted to ask her what happened with her mom and to get her opinion about the book. And, of course, finally tell her the truth. A week without a real connection to her felt too long, and I was feeling clingy, having initiated all of our recent contact.

Maybe if I had more friends here in the city, I wouldn't be so distracted by Hallie. My closest buddies, however, were on active duty or working at Johnson Space Center in Houston. We talked now and then, but I couldn't exactly call one of them up and ask them to meet me for a beer.

Maybe moving back to New York was a mistake.

As soon as I thought it, Hallie's pink hair and big blue eyes filled my mind.

It didn't feel like a mistake.

Dammit.

Shutting my laptop, I pushed up off the couch, thinking maybe I'd just go for an evening run instead. The thought had barely crossed my mind when my cell rang on the table, and I rushed to it, hoping to see Hallie's name on the screen.

I stalled at the sight of Darcy's name flashing on it.

Disappointed, I picked up and shoved the feeling out of my voice. "Darce, hey."

"Chris, hello, how are you?"

"I'm well. You?"

"I'm good. I know it's last minute, but I hoped you might be free to meet for a drink tonight. To catch up."

The thought of sitting around my apartment made me feel restless, and it might be nice to talk with Darcy. Have an actual friend in the city other than Hallie. "Sure. Just text me where and when."

"Wonderful!" She really sounded like she meant it, and I couldn't help but smile. "See you soon."

## Hallie

My smile was strained as I met Derek's eyes across the small, intimate table.

This felt nothing like how it felt to knock knees under the table with Chris at that tapas place. The bar was Derek's idea because it served food, so we had snacks and cocktails in front of us.

Derek gave me a pinched smile as our eyes met again.

Oh God, I was being a terrible date.

I just couldn't stop thinking about Chris and feeling guilty, like I was cheating. Which was ridiculous because he hadn't ever expressed any romantic interest in me.

*Think of something to say to the incredibly handsome man in front of you.*

"So . . . Althea tells me that as well as teaching high school history during the winter months, you're a baseball manager for one of the minors during the season?"

He nodded, sitting forward in his chair. "Yeah. I've been doing that for a few years now. I was assistant coach first, worked my way up."

"That's great. So do you get to travel?"

"We do, but not far. Our team doesn't have the budget for anything but a bus ride. We're not the majors." Derek had a dazzling smile that should have given me a stomach flip or butterflies or something. But it wasn't Chris's slightly crooked grin, so it didn't seem to do anything for me.

"You a baseball fan?" Derek asked, his spectacular hazel eyes glittering warmly under the intimate lighting of the bar. Those eyes looked almost green against his dark skin and were enough to make any woman swoon dramatically at his feet.

There was something seriously wrong with me.

Was I a baseball fan? "Um . . . I played when I was a kid. So I went through a phase of liking it."

"I'll take that as a no, then. It's okay, you don't have to like baseball."

"I'm sorry," I suddenly blurted out. "I feel like I'm making this so hard on you."

He chuckled. "It's okay. Are you nervous? Because you don't have to be nervous with me."

"Honestly?"

"Of course."

"My mind is elsewhere. Althea assured me you just want to casually date, right?"

His lips twitched. "Right. I need to thank her for laying that out for me."

I snorted at his sarcasm. "I said . . . I said yes to this date because I'm trying to get over someone else."

Derek raised an eyebrow and leaned toward me. "Do you want to talk about it?"

Everything in me relaxed.

Wow.

Althea was right.

He was so nice.

"You want to spend our date talking about another guy?"

"Well, you're just going to be thinking about him, so why not talk to me about it. We're here. We have drinks. Food. And I'm a guy. I might have a new perspective on the situation for you."

That was true!

Desperate to talk to someone other than Althea about what I was feeling, I opened up, and hundreds of words about Chris poured out.

## Chris

The bar Darcy had directed me to served food too, and the place was packed. Darcy had texted that she was in a small booth at the back of the restaurant, so my gaze moved there first.

Darcy smiled and waved from her spot, and I moved through the tables to get to her.

"Hey." I leaned down to kiss her proffered cheek. "How are you?"

"I'm great. I ordered you a beer." She gestured to a bottle of my favorite craft beer as I slid into the booth across from her.

I tapped the beer bottle against her cocktail glass. "Cheers to that."

Darcy smiled that sweet smile of hers. It was the first thing I noticed about her when we met. She was tall, beautiful, and elegant, but her smile wasn't glamorous or sultry. It was sweet, and her laugh was almost childish and completely infectious.

The incongruity was disarming and unexpected.

For a while I thought I was in love with her, but I knew now that what we had wasn't love. Even though it was mostly long-distance, we'd dated for several years, and I'd never shared myself with her the way I had with Hallie in the mere few weeks we'd spent together.

That didn't mean I didn't still feel affection toward Darcy. Despite the way things ended, I believed she was a good woman and intelligent and passionate about the things that mattered to her.

"How are you?" she asked.

Something about her tone was too probing. "What do you know?"

Darcy sighed. "Your father mentioned something to my father about you floundering and writing a book?"

"Floundering." I huffed, feeling the sting even though I wished I cared less.

She touched my arm. "You know I don't believe you're floundering."

I shrugged. "I'm just trying to figure out my next move."

"And the book?"

*My fucking father.* "Just something I'm thinking about doing," I lied. I didn't want to get into it with her. As great as she was, Darcy loved a project and could be pushy about it.

"Well, if you ever want to run ideas by someone, I'm here."

"Thank you." I took a chug of my beer. "What about you? How are the wedding plans going?"

She raised an eyebrow. "You want to hear about that?"

"Darce, we're good," I promised her. "I mean it."

Suddenly she exhaled slowly. "Oh, Chris, I'm exhausted. Matthias's family hated our engagement party. They hated New York and our friends. Now they're talking about not coming to the wedding, so days after we booked our venue on Martha's Vineyard, Matthias starts talking about eloping to Paris. I can't elope. I'm a Hawthorne. If I don't marry in New York, it will break my mother's heart. He doesn't get that . . . and"—frustration wrinkled her nose—"I think he thinks I'm a spoiled snob."

I didn't know how to answer that because, as much as I cared about her, Darcy sometimes could be a little pretentious. But she was never malicious about it. It was just a consequence of her upbringing.

"Great, I'm complaining to my ex-boyfriend about my fiancé. How classy." She mistook my silence for discomfort. "I'm sorry. You know it devastated Mother when she realized I was switching an astronaut for a French artist." She threw me a guilty look. "And not just because she was proud of you but because she genuinely loves you."

"You know I'm fond of your family too. But it wasn't meant to be. We're both where we're supposed to be now."

"You're the very best of men, Chris. Do you know that? So smart and kind and understanding."

Chuckling uncomfortably, I shrugged. "Did you just bring me here to get me drunk and lay compliments on me?"

"Oh, yes, I forgot you hate to be complimented. Do you want something to eat?" Darce changed the subject. "They do hot snacks. We'll need a menu though."

My gaze drifted over the table, looking for a menu. Finding none, I searched the tables behind us only to freeze at the sight of pink hair and a familiar profile.

Hallie.

Sitting in the middle of the room at a small table, leaning toward a guy I was secure enough to admit was *handsome* and laughing flirtatiously, was Hallie.

My Hallie.

On a date.

Suddenly my chest tightened with something like panic.

"I think that's Hallie Goodman," Darcy said beside me. "You remember her from my engagement party? She's planning my wedding— Chris?"

I was already out of my seat, moving around the tables, my feet taking me to her with a mind of their own. The pulse in my neck throbbed, and the heat that flushed through me shocked me. The heat that told me I was angry.

Listening to the voice in the back of my head that reminded me I had no right to be indignant because Hallie and I were just friends, I reined in the emotion and shoved it back down just in time.

Hallie and her date looked up as I stopped at their table.

My gaze locked on the face that had grown more familiar to me than any other. Her eyes rounded with surprise. "Chris."

Just like that, my irrational anger completely deflated.

My panic did not.

This woman was made for me.

I knew that deep in my bones.

And I'd been so wrapped up in my own problems, I'd taken too long to express that to her.

"Hey," I forced out.

"What are you doing here?" It might have been my imagination, but Hallie's gaze kept flickering between me and her date like she was guilty of some wrongdoing.

"I'm here with Darcy." I thumbed over my shoulder.

Hallie's gaze darted toward the back of the bar. "Oh."

"As friends." I felt the need to add pointedly.

Was that relief in her eyes?

"Um, Chris, this is Derek." Hallie gestured to the guy across from her.

I gave him a tight smile and held out my hand. After all, it wasn't his fault I'd screwed up, taking my damn time. "Nice to meet you."

Derek grinned at me like he knew a secret. He *was* a good-looking son of a bitch. "Hey, man, nice to meet you."

I released his hand, feeling a little desperate to make a claim on Hallie, to alert this guy to the fact that he had competition. Leaning down, I pressed a soft kiss to Hallie's cheek, my lips lingering a half second too long as I inhaled her perfume, a scent that would forever be synonymous with her.

"See you Sunday," I murmured in her ear before standing up.

I cut her date a quick look.

He smirked at me as if to say, *Oh, I hear ya loud and clear.*

Good.

Turning on my heel, I strode away, replaying what I'd just done in my head. It was infantile and so unfuckinglike me to act out of jealousy. To be jealous! I was not a jealous guy. What the hell was I doing?

My hands shook a little as I returned to Darcy, who gaped at me like she'd never seen me before.

"You *know* my wedding planner?"

I shrugged, my gaze drifting back toward Hallie. Derek was leaning across the table, grinning and talking as Hallie covered her face like she was embarrassed about something. Had I embarrassed her? The idea made me itch to go back over there and smooth things over. And also grab her hand and take her away from this guy immediately.

They looked cozy. Comfortable with each other. How long had she been seeing him? Why hadn't she talked to me about him?

My heart beat faster.

"Chris?"

Darcy's sharp tone brought my attention back to her and her question. "Uh, we met at your engagement party."

"And what? You're friends now?"

"I hired her to plan a retirement party, which I'm no longer doing, so don't even think about it," I hurried to say at the way her eyes lit up. "But Hallie and I became good friends. We've been spending time together." My gaze returned to the table.

Hallie laughed at something Derek said.

"Oh." Darcy's tone suggested confusion. "Okay. That's a little strange, but whatever."

At my silence, she continued, "Did you know Jen McIntyre is working for NASA now?"

"Who's Jen McIntyre again?" I asked distractedly, eyes still on Hallie and her date.

Darcy's voice became like ocean waves lapping at shore. I could hear her, but she was just background noise.

"Chris," she suddenly snapped.

Her tone dragged my gaze off Hallie. At her annoyed expression, I felt the sting of guilt. "Shit. Sorry."

Her eyes darted across the room. "You seem to be worrying over her. I'm sure she's fine." She considered Hallie. "I guess she's pretty cute and sweet and would easily provoke brotherly protective instincts in a man."

Really?

"I couldn't feel *less* brotherly toward Hallie Goodman. Believe me, that's not the feeling she provokes."

Darcy raised an eyebrow as understanding dawned on her face. "My wedding planner? Seriously?" She studied Hallie again, frowning. "She doesn't seem your type at all."

Irritated by what her comment insinuated, I asked coolly, "And what do you mean by that?"

She shrugged. "She's not really . . . well . . . extraordinary. You're extraordinary, Chris." Darcy touched my arm, her expression sincere. "And that's a quality you deserve in your life partner."

I rebelled at every word out of her mouth. "One: I struggle

with this concept that somehow we deserve and/or are entitled to anything."

"If we work hard enough for something, we certainly are entitled to and deserve it." Darcy disagreed vehemently.

"Two," I continued as if she hadn't spoken because I was goddamn annoyed by her judgment of Hallie. "Hallie Goodman is funny, sweet, compassionate, and the type of beautiful that comes from being *extraordinarily* kind. If anyone doesn't deserve someone in this scenario, it's me."

Lips parting in shock, Darcy slumped against the booth. "Wow. You really do like her. I'm . . . Chris, I'm sorry. What I said about her was awful and . . . Oh goodness, you know I try not to be my mother, and the snobbery is hard to beat back. Matthias is right! Forgive me."

She gave me big, remorseful eyes, making it hard to stay angry at her, even though I still felt this kernel of indignation in my gut. I tried to laugh it off because I'd never been the type to hold a grudge, and I wouldn't let my irritation with Hallie's date hurt my friendship with Darce. "Of course, I forgive you." My gaze drifted back to Hallie.

"Chris, you're clearly extremely bothered by the fact that she's on a date with another man. I think we should leave."

Hallie suddenly got up from the table and began heading toward a hallway that had a neon sign above the wall that read **RESTROOMS** with an arrow pointing the way.

"Darcy, I hate to be rude, but just give me a few minutes." I slid off my seat before she could protest and hurried around the tables. Derek had his phone out and was engrossed in whatever was on there. He didn't notice me hurrying after his date.

The hallway was low-lit, with two doors on the left for men and women. It made an L-shape as it turned left toward the end. I ducked my head around the corner and saw it led to an emergency exit. We were alone.

Leaning against the wall opposite the ladies' room, I waited for Hallie.

I didn't have to wait long.

She stepped out of the room, head down, as she rummaged through her purse.

I finally processed her outfit, and my fingers curled into fists as heat shot through me. Hallie wore an oversized sweater, an off-white color that made her pink hair pop.

And that was it.

It fell to her upper thighs like she'd just rolled out of a guy's bed and pulled on his sweater.

She wore it with a pair of the sexiest goddamn shoes I'd ever seen in my life. Her legs had a shimmer to them that drew the gaze. Jesus Christ, she had great legs. I wanted them wrapped around me.

I pushed off the wall, and her eyes flew up at the movement.

"Holy shit." Hallie gasped, clutching her chest. "You scared me." Her hand dropped as her round eyes got impossibly larger. "What are you doing here?"

Instead of answering, I took hold of her elbow and guided her around the corner, out of sight. I situated her against the wall and settled my hands on her hips, the fabric of her sweater sliding an inch up her thighs. She felt warm beneath my touch but also small and delicate. A renewed wave of something I didn't quite understand crashed over me.

It disconcerted me to consider it might be possessiveness.

That was not a quality I admired in anyone. My father had treated my mother like a possession.

Fuck.

Staring at her, dazed, overwhelmed, I reassured myself that I didn't see Hallie as a woman to possess.

The difference between me and my father was that I wanted to belong to Hallie as much as I wanted her to belong to me.

"Chris?" Her breath hitched on my name.

It took every ounce of willpower I had not to kiss her.

My hands flexed on her hips. "Why didn't you tell me you were dating someone?"

Hallie stared at me like she'd never seen me before. "I'm not. This is a first date. It just kind of happened. You know my friend Althea . . . Derek's her fiancée's brother. It's casual. Nothing serious."

I frowned at that. "So you're a casual dater?"

She stiffened and murmured, "I need to get back."

Her eyes dropped to my mouth.

Oh yeah, I was so done with this dance. "What if I asked you to end your date with him and come back to my place with me?"

She shifted beneath my hands, those gorgeous eyes searching my face. "You're a good guy, Chris, so I know this can't be some pissing contest, right? I mean . . . you friend-zoned me."

Dammit. I knew I'd messed up that night at my apartment. "I didn't friend-zone you. And I don't want to have this conversation at the back of a bar. But I promise you, I'm not screwing around. Please. Leave with me, Hallie."

She considered this and then slowly nodded her head.

Triumph and anticipation flushed through me.

I squeezed her hips and then forced myself to release her. "I'm going to put Darcy in a cab. Meet me outside when you're ready."

# TWENTY-SEVEN

## Hallie

"That's cool. I think I'll stay here, have another drink. You good?"

I gaped at Derek. Althea was right. He was awesome. "I'm g-good," I answered nervously. "I just feel bad."

"Don't be. Sometimes guys need to see what they're going to lose before they pull their heads out of their asses. Sorry we're morons that way."

I laughed, but I could hear how breathy it sounded. My nerves were shot to hell. I could still feel Chris's hands on my hips even now. Possessive. Wanting.

The way he'd looked at me in the hallway . . .

Oh wow.

Definitely not friend-zoning me.

Derek had said as much as Chris walked away from the table and back to Darcy earlier.

"Okay, you do realize he wanted to scare me off, right?" Derek had laughed as soon as Chris was out of earshot.

Hope had been blossoming and deflating in me so much these last few weeks that I didn't want to hope anymore. I'd waved off Derek's assurance that Chris definitely had more than friendly thoughts about me and attempted to concentrate on our date and not on the fact that Chris was in the same room. Impossible, considering I was hyperaware of him.

And now this?

It felt like a surreal dream.

"Althea's going to kill me."

"She won't." Derek stood up from the table and leaned down to kiss my cheek. "Go get him."

"Let me at least pay for my drinks and—"

He scowled at me. "Don't even think about it."

Damn, in another life, this guy . . . "I hope I'll see you again."

"I think Althea is close to adopting you, so I have no doubt we'll see each other again."

Impulsively, I hugged him. "Thanks, Derek."

He chuckled and gave me a quick squeeze. "Go, woman. I don't want to end up in a bar fight with a beloved national hero."

Laughing, cheeks flushed at the thought of Chris being jealous over me, I left Derek to his evening and strode on shaky legs toward the exit. As I stepped out, I caught sight of Chris on the sidewalk. A cab pulled away from him and he turned.

Our eyes met, and it felt like every inch of me, every nerve zinged with life like I'd just been shocked by electricity.

He'd never looked at me with such raw desire before.

My knees shook.

Suddenly he crossed the distance between us and took my free hand without a word. His grip tightened, his thumb brushing across the top of my hand in reassurance. He felt *right*. His hand in mine.

In my heels, I was almost the same height as him, but he slowed his stride so I wouldn't have to hurry at his side.

Assuming we were grabbing the subway back to his place, I was surprised when he hailed a cab. Well, I guess we were in a hurry.

Inside the cab, Chris sat close to me, my thigh pressed against his, his hand still in mine. Butterflies threw a rager in my belly. I hoped my palm didn't feel sweaty. Drawing my gaze up his strong throat, from his sharp jaw to his mouth, I bit my lip to stop myself from reaching for him.

Never had a mouth tempted me as much as Chris Ortiz's.

"Hallie," he whispered my name on a groan, and I lifted my eyes to his.

I squeezed my legs closer together as he swallowed hard.

How long would this goddamn cab take?

"I want you to touch me," I admitted in a whisper.

A muscle in Chris's jaw flexed, and he released my hand, only to settle it on my knee. My skin tingled beneath his palm. "Soon," he murmured as we watched his hand. He moved it, his fingertips caressing my inner thigh. I shivered, and I knew he felt it because his fingers flexed on my skin.

He didn't move it any farther, but he continued to make circles on my inner thigh until I was so ready to combust, it wasn't even funny. I let out a little moan and saw the cabdriver's head snap up toward the rearview.

I caught his suspicious gaze and flushed furiously.

Chris chuckled, but he didn't stop tormenting me.

I had never, in my entire life, felt the hazy, all-consuming control of my hormones. While I had a ton of questions for Chris, important ones I knew we should discuss before anything else happened, my priority was to get him naked.

"Oh, thank God," I choked out when the cab eventually pulled up outside Chris's Brooklyn apartment.

He laughed, releasing my thigh to pay the driver.

And then he was helping me out of the cab, my hand tight in his again as he hurried up the front stoop to let us into the building. The silence was thick, our breathing a little loud, a little shallow, as we took the stairs to the second floor.

Chris's scent hit me fully as we entered his place. It wasn't the apartment in Manhattan, but it was a good size, and it was furnished comfortably. He'd made it feel like his place already somehow. Maybe because it smelled like him.

Speaking of, I wanted to bury my face in his throat.

He released my hand to stride across the living room and drop his keys on the kitchen counter.

Disappointed by the sudden distance between us, I waited a little unsurely near the entrance.

Chris turned to me.

His expression was no less heated than before, so I attempted to relax.

"I didn't bring you up here for a casual night together," Chris said, his tone almost stern. "You need to know that now, because if that's all you want from me, I can't give it to you. I can't because . . ." He released a long breath, something beyond tender and special settling in his expression. "I care about you a lot, Hallie—I have real feelings for you. Serious *romantic* feelings. I was going to tell you before now. I wanted to tell you last weekend, in fact, before your mom called. So I want you to know that this isn't a jealous reaction to Derek. Yeah, I was jealous, but I was going to tell you how I felt before I saw you with him." Suddenly he looked fearful, which confused me. "Hallie, I need to tell you something, and I'm not afraid to admit that I'm terrified that once I do, you'll turn around and walk out of my life and I'll never see you again."

Stunned, apprehensive, the heat flushing my skin cooled. "You . . . you can tell me anything."

Chris took a deep breath, expression wary. "I knew you before we met at Darcy's engagement party. That first video you sent apologizing for watching my videos reached me. I was in a bad headspace when you sent that first video. All I heard you say is that you watched these private videos of mine, and it irritated me. I told Kate to make you think the email bounced so you wouldn't contact her or me again. But you sent another . . . and I couldn't help but be drawn to you."

A whole mix of emotions filled me—embarrassment, indignation, hurt—and I took a few steps back toward his front door. "But . . . my emails *kept* bouncing. You . . . made me think I wasn't sending them to anyone. I thought— I said some really personal things on there."

Remorse made his features haggard, and he took a pleading step toward me. "I know. I can't explain the instant pull I felt toward you, Hallie. I can't explain what it was like. I just knew that I wanted to be in your world a little longer, and I thought if you realized someone was watching, you would stop. It is the single most dishonest thing I've ever done, and I have no good excuse for it. Your videos just made me feel less alone."

Like his videos had made me feel less alone.

Oh my God.

He had kept this from me, but I was a hypocrite if I couldn't forgive him for watching the videos.

I nodded slowly, my head spinning. "Right. Okay. So we did that to each other. I can't be mad at you for doing to me what I did to you . . . but, Chris, I confessed to you. Right away. Before we were even friends. You've kept this from me for weeks, and you decide to tell me now?"

He took another step forward. "You said at Darcy's party that you didn't think you could forgive someone doing that to you."

"I didn't mean it." I threw my hands up in exasperation.

"I thought you did. And I thought that it would be better if I told you the truth once you'd gotten to know me. Once you knew that I would never maliciously keep this from you."

"Why tell me right now? When we're about to . . ." I gestured vaguely between us.

"I want you," Chris said gruffly. "So much. I wanted you from that very first video diary you sent. That's why I was afraid to tell you the truth because I didn't want to lose you before I even got the chance to really know you. It was wrong. I'm sorry. But I couldn't take this further between us without telling you. I would never do that."

I considered his words. Considered the truth. And while my cheeks still burned at the thought of Chris knowing all my private thoughts, I realized I'd told him everything I'd said in those diaries all over again to his face. I'd trusted him. His keeping this from me had thrown me.

"I will never lie to you again. Never. Believe me."

He *did* tell me the truth. Now. Before I slept with him. If he just wanted sex, or something casual, he'd have kept that to himself. Would I allow his mistake to erase the weeks of deep, caring conversation, of easy, fun banter, of a strong connection that made me feel less alone in the world?

Looking deep into Chris's dark eyes, I saw him.

I saw his genuine remorse.

I saw his kindness.

And I saw the way he saw me.

To Chris, I was special. I mattered.

I rushed him, throwing my purse on the floor as I dashed across the room. Wrapping my arms around his neck, I pulled his head to mine and finally, finally, his lips were on my lips.

Chris jerked his head back before I could even feast on them. "Hallie?"

Understanding, I gasped, "I forgive you, and I also have serious romantic feelings for you."

"Just like that? You're sure you forgive me?"

"How quickly did you forgive me?"

"Within a few hours."

My lips twitched, my fingers flexing on his nape. "Well, I could wait a few hours to pretend to consider it further if that would make you feel better or—"

The rest of my words were swallowed in his kiss.

His hungry, searching, desperate kiss. I felt the hem of my sweater dress ride upward as Chris bunched the fabric in his fists at my back. "You're killing me in this sweater," he panted against my mouth, walking me backward as he pressed kisses along my jaw. "It makes a man think very, very dirty thoughts."

Note to self: tell Althea she was right about this outfit.

"Get up here. I have more apologizing do," he growled, sliding his hands under my ass to lift me. I wrapped my legs around his waist with a girlish squeal that he once again swallowed with his mouth.

I clung to his body, to his lips, as he carried me.

When I came up for air, we were in his bedroom.

His bedroom.

Where we were about to have sex.

Chris laid me gently on the edge of his bed, and I unwrapped my legs, releasing him. He stared down at me with an intensely focused expression.

Nervousness returned as he whipped off his T-shirt.

Yup, he looked just as amazing as I remembered.

His body was hard and smooth and powerful.

It was intimidating.

There was no cuddly softness to him, like George.

Chris worked out and worked hard to keep his body in this godlike shape. He'd had to for his career.

I wasn't perfect like him.

My belly was soft, not toned, and it had a slight roundness to it, which I could probably eliminate with some sit-ups, but the very thought bored me to tears.

Until now, staring at this gorgeous man who wanted to have sex with me.

A man I was falling in love with, so I kinda wanted him to think I was the sexiest woman on the planet and that I was the best sex he'd ever had.

Fuck.

I should have done sit-ups.

Feeling myself slide out of the hot, hazy, mindless passionate place I'd been enjoying more than life, I jumped desperately off the bed to reach for Chris's pants. I needed back to that place pronto!

Unfortunately he bowed his head to unzip himself at the same time and our heads collided.

"Oof." I stumbled back, clutching my head, and Chris laughed, reaching out to steady me.

"You okay?"

While I flushed with mortification at my clumsiness, he kissed my head, his lips trailing across my temple as he murmured, "Better?"

I nodded, but the head bump firmly spiraled me into a full-blown panic.

While I was always an overthinker when it came to first-time sex, the stakes had never been higher. I couldn't be bad at sex with *Chris*.

"Let's get rid of this thing finally." His fingers curled under the hem of my sweater dress, and I braced myself, lifting my arms over my head so he could free me of it. My eyes slammed closed as the fabric brushed up over my face and cool air caused goose bumps to rise across my skin.

Would he think my tits were too small? They were average-sized boobs, but if Chris was a boob man, they might fall short of his expectations.

I tried to remember how big Darcy's were.

Why was he at the bar with Darcy tonight?

He kissed me again, and I curled my fingers around his nape, trying to fall back into the kiss. I was almost there when his hands slid possessively down my back to grip my ass. He squeezed, groaning into my mouth. Even though I could feel how hard he was against the zipper of his jeans, all I could think about was what he'd think when he clapped eyes on my backside in the far-too-bright lights of his bedroom. Would he see the cellulite at the back of my thighs? Chris's ass was rock-hard. Why hadn't I been doing those daily squats my mom suggested when she saw me in a bikini last summer? Why?! I bet Darcy did daily squat thrusts.

Why *was* he at the bar with Darcy tonight?

Chris caressed my ass, his fingers tickling around my hips and up across my belly as he continued to kiss me. My stomach trembled as his fingers teased the waistline of my lace underwear just before dipping inside.

Oh my God, when was the last time I waxed? It was last week, right? That was fine. But what if Chris prefers a full bush to my landing strip? Worse, what if he likes it bare?

Suddenly he broke the kiss and pulled his hand from my underwear. I swayed against him, resting my palms on his shoulders to steady myself.

Hell, he was glowering at me.

That was not the expression of a man having a good time. Did I suck at kissing?

Chris surprised me by cupping my cheek in his warm palm. His voice was gruff as he asked, "Where are you right now?"

Perturbed, I answered immediately and a little indignantly. "I'm right here."

He released me, his expression so far from happy, my heart nose-dived into my stomach as he stepped away from me. "You were here at first. In the living room when you kissed me. As soon as we got in here, you went somewhere else. If you're not sure you want this after what I told you, I understand. We can stop."

Flummoxed that he'd noticed my preoccupation (though unsurprised he cared), I crossed my arms over my waist to hide my half-nakedness. The first time (and often the second and third) with a guy was pretty much always like this. I was too riddled with insecurities and anxieties about making it good for *him*, I couldn't enjoy it myself. Once I grew comfortable with the notion that my partner was at least reaching satisfaction, I could enjoy sex enough to orgasm when we fooled around, but I had never come when a guy was inside me. And no one I'd been with until this point had noticed or cared about my preoccupation.

It was worse with Chris because I'd never been with someone I wanted this much or felt so much for.

*This is Chris.*

Exactly.

This was Chris. "It's not about that. I promise you, I'm not a grudge keeper. I do forgive you, and I appreciate that you told me the truth before we took this further."

"Then what is it?"

"I can't relax," I admitted.

His brow furrowed. "Why not?"

I laughed humorlessly because wasn't it obvious? "Because I'm always anxious about the first time with someone, and I've never wanted sex to go as well as I want this to go with you. I've already conked you on the head." I gestured in irritation at his body. "And you look like a sports ad! I only found out what a squat thrust is last summer. Until that point, I was pretty sure it was some kind of fruit."

Chris burst into laughter and choked on it at my mortified expression. His mouth trembled with renewed hilarity as he failed to talk through it.

Hurt, I reached for my clothes.

"No. Hallie." He reached for me again, this time tugging my arms away from my body. "I'm not laughing *at* you. You're just so funny and adorable and sexy, and it baffles me you don't know these things already. I could not care less about a conk to the head, and I could not care less if you work out or not."

"But . . ." I trailed off, realizing that admitting this was so unsexy. How could he think otherwise? A guy didn't want to be with a woman who was insecure in bed, right? They wanted a confident woman who could rock their freaking world.

"But?"

"Nothing." I moved into his body. "Let's try again."

Chris lifted his face away from my incoming kiss. "Hallie . . . talk to me."

I tried to pull away, but he wouldn't let me.

"This is me." He took the words from my head as he nibbled on my earlobe. That hazy feeling simmered inside me. "You can tell me anything."

His mouth trailed a delicious path down my throat, and I bowed into him, the words seduced from my lips.

"I can't stop thinking," I confessed on a sigh. "Do you like my body, my kiss? Am I too soft? Can I make this good for you? What will you like—"

Chris kissed me, his tongue licking at mine, the kiss deep and sexual and literally breath-stealing. All my worries went up in flames as the haze consumed me. I panted for air when he finally released me. My expression must have been something, because his was more than a little cocky. "That's better."

"Captain—"

"I have been fantasizing about this moment for weeks." He walked me back toward the bed and gently pushed me down on it. He reached around my back and unclipped my bra, sliding the straps down my arms. I shivered as the cups fell away, my nipples tight and hard as the cool air hit them.

Chris covered my right nipple with his mouth and sucked at it. Heat shot between my legs, and I let out a sharp cry.

He lifted his gaze to mine, his dark with hunger as he dropped the bra and curled his fingers into my underwear.

"My shoes," I whispered.

"I'd like to leave them on."

I shivered at what this said about how he felt about my shoes. Biting my lip against a grin, I lifted my hips off the bed to help him with my underwear.

The urge to cover myself was real, but then I saw the way Chris's breathing changed as he devoured the naked sight of me.

"You're beautiful," he said shakily, his eyes meeting mine so I could see the sincerity in them. "Beyond anything anyone could want. And I *want* you, Hallie. But this isn't just about me. You get that right? Sex is about two people, not just the guy and what he wants."

I raised an eyebrow because that wasn't what I'd experienced. The lovers I'd had had been pretty selfish. Or were they? Had I just been so focused on pleasing them *I'd* railroaded myself out of the experience?

Chris cursed under his breath at my expression and then abruptly kissed me with a fierceness that obliterated my brain cells.

When we came up for air, he said, "I know you have an issue with trying to please people, but here's how we get past it in here: it is doubtful that there is anything you can do in this bed that I won't like." He grinned boyishly, and I couldn't help but laugh. "But I promise to be one hundred percent honest and tell you if something is not working for me. Now you promise me that if something isn't working for you, you'll tell me. Promise me you'll be honest with me."

Oh man, this guy. I'd never met anyone who cared enough to be in my head like Chris was. "I promise."

"Good." He reached for another kiss.

I gently halted his progress, and he stood up straight, brow puckered. Then I confessed without thought, "I saw you naked at your aunt's house."

Seriously, what was with my lack of a filter around him?

Chris raised an eyebrow. "When?"

"You know how I tripped over Bandit?"

"You were spying on me?"

"Unintentionally." I stood up, my hands raised beseechingly. "Oh God, Chris, I'm so sorry. I came up the stairs, and your door was open, and you took off your underwear—and your ass, oh Jesus, your ass is mesmerizing, but then I realized I was perving on you, and I tried to back away, but I fell over the dog and— Oh!" I yelped in surprise as he lifted me by the waist and threw me with ease onto the bed.

I landed with an *oof* and sat up on my elbows to watch Chris unzip his jeans.

"You're not mad?"

"Did it make you hot?" he asked hoarsely, shoving down his jeans. "Watching me?"

"Yes. Very, very, very, very hot."

Then he was naked. Entirely naked.

And apparently he wanted me a *whole lot*.

"Oh boy." My gaze flew upward. "I'm sorry for being insecure earlier. Clearly, I had nothing to worry about."

His lips twitched as he approached the bed. "Still, I think we need to make sure you're back in the moment and not stuck in your head."

"How?"

"By giving you it." Chris wrapped his hands around my ankles and yanked me down the bed.

I laughed at the swiftness of the movement, but the sound petered off into a gasp as he kneeled at the end of the bed and spread my legs. His mouth settled between my thighs, and Chris proved he was a man of many, many talents. The tension coiled low and fiery in my belly, building as his tongue and fingers played me beautifully. He learned me, he paid attention, and when he discovered what worked, he kept at it with determination.

I came with a shattered cry, and as I shuddered on his bed with the release, I felt his fingers on the straps of my shoes. Within seconds, my shoes were gone, and I waited, all hot, damp skin and renewed need, as Chris grabbed a condom out of his bathroom and donned it.

Greedily, I reached for him, opening my legs to him as he settled his powerful body along mine and kissed me. Wanting to touch and feel every inch of him, my hands wandered over his back, down his stomach, and wrapped around him.

Chris groaned into my mouth, kissing me deeper.

He throbbed hotly in my hands as I guided him between my legs.

Then he pressed forward.

I widened my thighs and slid my hands across his smooth back, my fingers reaching for his ass, digging into the muscles there as Chris broke the kiss to brace himself on his hands. Our gazes locked as my body gave way to his.

"Hallie," he said my name like a prayer, as the fullness of him overwhelmed me. "Are you okay?"

I nodded, lifting my hips. "Don't stop."

He brushed his mouth across mine, a whisper of a kiss, each brush a tease of what he could give me, and he did the same with his hips. Gliding slowly in and out. I gasped at the delicious friction. I'd never climaxed during penetrative sex. But staring into Chris's eyes as he teased my mouth with kisses, as his biceps flexed with his slow thrusts, as his stomach brushed against my trembling belly, I felt it might be possible. No guy had ever made me feel more in the moment, more *needed*, and that was intoxicating.

I moaned as shivers rippled down my spine with the building tension.

"Oh fuck, Hallie." Chris bowed his head, gritting his teeth as his hips picked up pace. "Tell me you're close."

I was, but I wasn't going to come in time. "Just come." I squeezed his ass.

He bared his teeth at me. "Not before you." He slowed his thrusts.

"Chris, no, I'm good," I panted, lifting my hips to urge him on.

His eyes flashed with what I'd soon realize was that goddamn perceptiveness of his. "You promised. Tell me what you need."

"I, uh . . . Chris . . . oh . . . uh . . ." I moaned as he canted his hips at a certain angle. "Touch me, touch me . . . I can't without . . ." My explanation trailed off as he slipped a hand between my legs, his thumb easily finding my clit.

"Is this what you need?" he asked hoarsely against my mouth, his lips touching mine with each word.

I nodded.

Chris moved his hips as his thumb circled and pressed down on me.

There was no countdown, no warning.

Just like that, my astronaut successfully launched me into the stars, and I was still gasping Chris's name as he followed me into them.

# TWENTY-EIGHT

## Chris

A sound my brain couldn't quite process in that place between sleep and awake pushed me further toward consciousness. Opening my eyes, the hazy vision of Hallie climbing into my bed yanked me closer to waking.

I rolled into her as she rested her head on the pillow, her face becoming clearer as my vision sharpened. Memories of last night made my blood hot. "Where were you?" I asked, my voice gritty with sleep.

She smiled shyly. "Peeing."

I grinned. The toilet flushing had awoken me, I realized.

My gaze fell to her mouth. I loved her mouth. I wanted that mouth. So I took it. She tasted of mint. I pulled back to ask her if she'd brushed her teeth, but Hallie wasn't for breaking the kiss.

She kissed me hungrily in a way that took me from zero to a hundred in seconds. I let her roll me, wrapping my arms around her small waist as she straddled me.

Feeling the fabric in my hands, I broke the kiss, my gaze dipping down her body.

She wore my T-shirt.

"As sexy as this is, it needs to go." I whipped it off her before she could protest.

For a second, Hallie gazed a little unsurely down at me. Her pink hair fell wildly over her rounded breasts, her skin already a little flushed with arousal. Her lips were swollen from all the attention I'd given them last night.

It blew my mind that she had no idea how gorgeous she was. Who were these idiots she'd dated before me?

In fact, I didn't want to know.

Every woman I'd dated had a past except for my first girlfriend. It had never bothered me, the idea of other men in their beds.

It irritated me to think of Hallie with anyone for two reasons. One, for the first time in my life, I wanted someone so badly, I was jealous. Two, clearly, they'd all been assholes if Hallie felt sex should be all about the guy.

"You're staring," she whispered, her palms resting lightly on my chest.

"Hallie Goodman is naked and straddling me," I answered with a grin. "Of course I'm staring. I'd like to memorize this moment."

Her spine straightened, her breasts jutting out, nipples tight and tempting. Confidence crept into her touch as she caressed my chest and undulated slowly on me. "Do you need to memorize it?" Hallie leaned down to kiss me. "I was kind of hoping to straddle you naked a lot in the future."

The very thought made every inch of me tighten with a sense of desperation and need. I wanted that. I wanted her here for as long as she'd have me. "Sounds like an excellent plan to me," I replied hoarsely as I slid my hand around her nape to bring her lips back to mine.

Not long later, I was inside her again. Goddamn heaven. Watching her ride me, lost in the moment, free of worries, confident that I wanted her as badly as she wanted me was the sexiest thing I'd ever seen. I was just a guy at the end of the day, and the idea that Hallie was so hot for me she forgot her own anxieties and worries made me cocky (and turned on) as hell.

A while later, Hallie followed me into the kitchen wearing my T-shirt again.

"What would Ms. Goodman like for breakfast?" I inquired as I yanked open the refrigerator.

"It's very hard for me to concentrate when you're not wearing a shirt."

I glanced over my shoulder at her, catching her checking me out. I chuckled. "We can keep it together long enough to have breakfast, right?"

"We have to." She pouted. "I have an event tonight. I need to leave in a few hours."

Shit. I'd wanted the whole day with her.

"I'm free tomorrow though."

"Are you free the whole day?"

Hallie bit her lip against a smile. "You want me all day?"

"Yeah, I do. I wish I had you all day today."

"Me too." She shifted on the stool at my kitchen peninsula. "Should we talk about all of this?"

"Breakfast first. Then we'll talk."

"Okay. I could do pancakes if they're in your repertoire?"

"They are, and your wish is my command."

As I moved around the kitchen, I felt Hallie's gaze on me. When I looked at her, I saw a question in her eyes. "What is it?"

She straightened her shoulders, her sex-tousled hair falling down her back with the movement. "You said you wanted me from the first time you saw my video diary. Is that true? I wasn't sure you felt like that from the start. I thought maybe it grew into that for you."

"I wanted you then. Even more when I saw you at Darcy's engagement party. I thought your honesty was cute as hell, and I liked your pink hair and your beautiful eyes and your lips." My gaze dropped to her mouth as I swallowed down the guilt I still felt for taking so long to tell her the truth. "I wanted to kiss you that night and every night since."

Hallie's eyes lit with delight. "I've wanted to kiss you since I watched *your* video letters."

When I gazed into those sincere blue eyes, a quick slideshow of images filled my head—of her sitting on the stairs at the Hamptons house listening avidly to my stories about Miguel and my mom, of her laughing on the beach with Bandit, of us hanging out watching movies together, talking about things that didn't matter and things that mattered the most. No judgment. Just mutual kindness and support. Feeling not alone for the first time in as long as I could remember.

"I wanted you then," I murmured, "but not like I want you now. It's *more* now. This is real, right? You and me?"

Her smile softened. "I'd like it to be." Her expression tightened. "Though, without sounding like a jealous girlfriend, I think I would like to know why you were with Darcy last night."

Not expecting that at all, I flipped Hallie's pancakes onto a plate and pushed them toward her. "I told you. I was there as her friend. Just her friend."

"I know she's an important client, and I should probably not be saying this, but she cheated on you, Chris, while you were in space. She got engaged to the guy she cheated on you with after only a few months of dating him. Her actions had people gossiping about you online. How can you be friends with her? Unless . . . there are still feelings there?"

Wow, okay.

I rounded the counter and took the stool beside her, bracketing her knees between my thighs. Seeing the worry in her eyes made me take a minute. I hoped my keeping the truth from her hadn't permanently damaged her ability to trust me. Fuck. I guess only time would tell. For now, I wanted to find the right words to assure her. "If I still had feelings for Darcy, I would have already told you when you and I were just friends. She and I dated for a few years, but—and I didn't realize this until I met you—we didn't entirely share ourselves with each other. Or at least I didn't with her. I stopped trying."

Hallie nodded, her expression pensive. "I noticed you only got a little personal with her in your videos."

"Exactly." I reached for her hand, addicted to the idea of being able to touch her freely now. Our fingers twined together playfully as I continued. "She knew some real things. Things that were hard to ignore. Like my terrible relationship with my father. But when I realized she didn't want to talk about things that made her uncomfortable, like my mom and Miguel, I think I just shut off completely. I started seeing a therapist during my mission training, and I had her to talk through those things with, so I decided I didn't need Darcy's emotional support, especially if it discomfited her. Moreover, I didn't like going to fancy society events with her and socializing with her friends. Despite my father existing in that world because of his company, I'm not a part of it. I didn't grow up in that world, and I didn't know how to relate to it. Darcy acknowledges her privilege, she works incredibly hard at her career, but she grew up as a New York socialite, and she likes that lifestyle. That would eventually have become an issue for us. She didn't really have me, and I think she knew it. I don't think she was just scared about me being in space and didn't know how to process it. She was already pulling away before we even launched. Do I wish she'd waited to break up with me first before cheating on me? Yes. But I also know she didn't *intend* to meet Matthias and fall in love with him while I was on the ISS, and I know she didn't want me to lose focus while I was up there, and I appreciate that. People make mistakes, Hallie. Unless they're repeat offenders, I will try to forgive them. I won't hold someone to impossible standards that I myself can't be held to."

Her fingers tightened in mine.

I pulled her closer. "Let's be clear . . . I don't want Darcy. I don't want anyone else but you. I'm *in* this with you."

She bit her lip against a smile again, and I reached for her lower lip with my thumb, pulling gently to free it. "When you're happy, I'm happy, so don't hide it."

"You can't be real," Hallie whispered, searching my face. "You're too perfect."

Remorse kicked me in the gut, and I pulled away. "We both know I'm not perfect. Whatever you do, don't hold *me* to impossible standards. I'm not going to do that to you."

"I know you're not perfect." Hallie clambered onto my lap, straddling me on the stool. My blood rushed south. Fuck, I felt like a horny teenager with this woman. "You made a mistake. People make mistakes . . . but, Chris, you're perfect *for me*."

"Okay, I'll accept that take," I murmured, delighted as hell about it.

"I feel like I've known you forever," Hallie confessed against my lips.

"Me too," I answered honestly, my arms tightening around her waist.

"Breakfast can wait, right?"

Oh yeah, it could. I launched off the stool, holding her to me as

I marched toward the bedroom. "I have a feeling you might be late for work today."

"I have a feeling I don't care."

My chuckle rumbled into her mouth as she kissed me like tomorrow might never happen.

# TWENTY-NINE

## Hallie

Just like Saturday morning, my body seemed to have an internal alarm clock that woke me up before Chris on Monday morning. Anytime I spent the night with a man, I'd awoken before him. I blinked away the sleep as soft light filtered through my bedroom curtains.

A smile prodded my lips at the sight of *this* man in my bed. He snuggled close to me on the pillows, and giddiness made me wriggle my toes. It was surreal to me he was here. That we'd had crazy, awesome sex last night and fallen asleep in each other's arms. And that was after we'd gone out for dinner and drinks and I'd caught him up on my family saga. Chris had told me he was proud of me for being honest with my dad and admitted that he hadn't been strong enough himself to have hard conversations with his father. He told me I was inspiring. And I'd wanted to dive across the restaurant table and have my wicked way with him.

Didn't he realize he was one of the reasons I'd had the strength to be honest with my dad?

That I still hadn't heard from my father (or my mother!)

wouldn't diminish my happiness. I wouldn't let that fear and hurt buried beneath my happy thoughts push its way through.

I'd found something special with Chris.

Something I really deep down believed other people found, but I never would.

The whole point of waking up before him was to get ready first, but I couldn't help but take a second to study his handsome face. "Handsome." That felt like such an insipid word to describe Chris. He was so much more to me.

His lashes looked thicker and longer in his sleep. When he smiled or laughed, lines around his eyes crinkled sexily. But his naturally tan skin was smooth in sleep. There was stubble on his cheeks this morning, and I had to fight the urge to reach out and touch it.

Sucking in a breath, I forced myself to move, only to realize I couldn't.

Chris's arm rested over my waist in his sleep.

Shit.

Holding my breath, I gently took his wrist in hand and slowly, slowly, slooowly—

My breath hitched as he shifted.

His eyes didn't open.

Heart pounding, I gently rested his arm on top of the duvet and slid out of the bed.

Chris, thankfully, did not wake up as I took his T-shirt off the floor and slipped it on. I grabbed a bunch of the fabric at the neckline and sniffed it, inhaling his cologne. Biting back a giggle of girlish glee that this was not a dream, I tiptoed into my bathroom. Closing the door without fully shutting it, I made quick work of brushing my teeth and then reached for my face wash so I could start my makeup routine.

My hand hovered over the wash.

Since my very first sleepover with a boy, I'd snuck out of bed before the guy woke up. My motivation being that if my boyfriend believed for the rest of his life that I woke up looking naturally dewy and fresh-faced, it would make him happy.

People-pleasing at its finest.

Looking at my reflection, I tried not to wince. You see, I wasn't one of those women who looked great without makeup. I looked sun-deprived and exhausted. Unless I worked up a sweat, I rarely had color in my cheeks that wasn't manufactured, and I looked tired because I worked long hours.

But it was me.

Messy hair, makeup-less, au naturel me.

And Chris wanted *me*.

Not the people-pleasing version that thought she needed to be perfect for others, but just me.

Hallie Goodman.

In all my glory.

And if he didn't, if this version of me wasn't enough, then that was his problem.

Not mine.

I pulled my hand back from the face wash. A full face was not how I started my mornings when I was alone. My first priority was always coffee. Nodding to myself in the mirror, my eyes glimmered with pride. I'd come a long way. It felt good.

Just as I turned to leave the bathroom, the door opened and Chris stood in the doorway.

Naked.

My gaze drifted down his hard stomach to between his legs, and saliva filled my mouth.

"You're awake." His voice drew my eyes back to his. He studied me with a heated look in his eyes I knew well.

"Apparently you are too."

Chris grinned sexily. My skin flushed as he moved into the room and grasped my hips in his hands, moving me backward until I bumped into the counter.

"What are you doing?"

Without a word, he picked me up like I weighed nothing and settled my bare ass on my bathroom countertop.

His gaze roamed my face. "Making you late for work."

"Oh, okay." My breathing grew shallow, feeling him hard between my thighs. Our kiss was hungry, heart-wrenching, and arousing.

"You're so beautiful." He broke the kiss to murmur against my throat, his lips trailing down it. I smiled giddily to myself. Beautiful. With him I truly felt it. "Christ, I can't get enough of you." He wrapped his mouth around my nipple through the fabric of his T-shirt, growling as I cried out at the sensation.

His hand slipped between my legs, and I arched my hips into his touch. As I came from his masterful fingers, Chris took the opportunity to don protection, and seconds later he was inside me, right where I needed him.

It was fast, furious, and the kind of passionate sex I'd heard about but never really allowed myself to dream could happen for me. Suddenly the future really did fill me with true excitement and anticipation. Everything with Chris was different from any romantic relationship I'd ever had, and it made me hopeful and optimistic and ready for anything with him at my side.

The thought was as thrilling as it was terrifying because I'd never wanted a relationship to last as much as I wanted this one to last.

# THIRTY

## Chris

The last week with Hallie seemed almost dreamlike. It was as though we were lost in our own little world. I'd stayed at her apartment most nights at her bequest. Weirdly, with Hallie this didn't seem too fast, too much, or too anything except overwhelming. In a good way. In a fantastic way.

After a phone call with Aunt Richelle to let her know Hallie and I were together, she, of course, wanted us back at the Hamptons at some point. She was the only one who knew beyond Hallie's friend at work, Althea. We'd agreed I wouldn't post any of the photos I took of Hallie on my Instagram, though she took some shots of me around the city that I posted in between reposts of my photographs from space. It helped keep my followers engaged, especially since I'd decided to go ahead with trying to publish my book. I'd need my followers' support. But I did not want strangers knowing about me and Hallie before our families. Besides, I wasn't really a guy who wanted everybody knowing his personal business. And I didn't want people in Hallie's business either.

Hallie's parents still hadn't been in touch, and I could wring their goddamn necks. It was my purpose in life to keep her distracted from the fact that her parents were insensitive, selfish morons. We'd spent yesterday hanging out in the city, enjoying the weather in Central Park and the fact that Hallie didn't have an event she needed to be at until the next day.

While Hallie was at a Sunday brunch engagement party for work most of the day, I'd spent mine ignoring three calls from my father, working out, and then agonizing over every word in the sample chapters I'd decided to send to Scott Rose. The decision was cemented when Hallie offered to read a few chapters and surprised me with her honesty about what she loved and what she thought needed work. I loved that she felt comfortable enough to be real with me. And her confidence in me also gave me the push I needed to send Scott the work.

Well, I would send it tomorrow once I was sure it was as good as I could get it for now.

My buzzer rang and I filled with anticipation, shut my laptop, took off my reading glasses, and leaped over my couch. I hurried to the door. "Yeah?"

"It's your girlfriend, and I bring food," Hallie said into the intercom.

Grinning, I buzzed her in and unlocked my door. The clack of her heels coming up the stairs made my heart beat faster.

Then suddenly she was there, smiling a little wearily at me as she gestured with a large takeout bag in her arms. "I hope you're hungry."

Reaching out into the hall, I hooked my finger around the belt on her dress to pull her into me for a kiss and took the bag out of her arms with my free hand. Hallie's soft lips pressed hard against mine, and I tasted something sweet on her tongue. I broke the kiss and her breath hitched. "Orange juice?" I murmured, nipping playfully at her lower lip.

Hallie grinned. "Mimosa. I snuck in one toward the end of the event, and believe me, I needed it."

"I sense a story." I led her inside and took the takeout into the kitchen. "Plates or out of the containers?"

"Containers are fine." She kicked off her shoes and flattened her feet onto my hardwood floors with a groan that sounded so sexual my body couldn't help but react. "I've been dying to get out of those all day. New shoes are a bitch."

Any amorous thoughts I had dissipated at the sight of her slumped shoulders as she walked over to the counter to peer into the containers. "You okay?"

"Demanding bride and groom. Wait until you hear what my people-pleasing ways got me into today."

Once we had settled on the couch together, the TV on but just a murmur in the background, I asked her what happened.

Curled up on the end of my couch, knees drawn toward her chest, container of Chinese food in hand, Hallie looked tiny. A surge of protectiveness rushed through me at the way she squeezed her eyes closed, as if in pain. The feeling was not new to me when it came to her. In fact, it had been gathering momentum and strength ever since we started dating. I reached out to stroke her knee. "Now I'm worried."

Her eyes popped open, and I relaxed as she gave me a somewhat crooked smile. "Oh, no, it's not bad. It's embarrassing but not bad."

I waited patiently for her to continue.

"So . . . everything was going swimmingly at the engagement party when suddenly the bride and groom approached me and told me they had an issue to deal with and needed privacy in the ladies' restroom. Could I guard the door for them?"

Already suspecting what was coming next, I grimaced for her.

Hallie groaned. "God, you know already, which just makes me the most naive person on the planet."

I squeezed her knee, trying not to smile in sympathy and failing.

"I took them at their word, and they slipped into the restroom and I stood guard, turning people away, fibbing about a plumbing issue and that it would be resolved soon. That was fine. Until the sex sounds grew audible."

I almost choked on my kung pao chicken.

"Uh yeah. And they were loud. So loud that people were staring and were visibly outraged. I panicked."

"What does that mean?"

"I started to sing 'Sweet Caroline' at the top of my voice."

I couldn't stop a loud explosion of laughter because that mental image was hilarious.

"Stop!" Hallie's cheeks flushed red as she prodded me with her foot. "It's not funny. There I was, this lunatic, singing 'Sweet Caroline,' waving my hands and trying to get everyone to join in."

It was difficult to voice the question around my laughter, but I asked, "Why that song?"

"The bride's name is Caroline."

"Well, that makes sense."

"You're still laughing."

"It's really funn—" I couldn't finish as I gave another bark of laughter.

Hallie, thankfully, was laughing too.

Grinning adoringly at her, I eventually asked, "Did it at least work?"

"Yes. And by the way, kudos to the happy couple for their stamina, because I got through the entire song, and by the second verse, the guests joined in. So the bride and groom walked out of that restroom, looking thoroughly fucked, to a hundred people singing 'Sweet Caroline.' The bride was generous enough to share with me that the second chorus brought her to climax, and now 'Sweet Caroline' is forever tainted for me."

Still chuckling, I gestured to her. "Come here."

"What? Why?"

"Come here."

Looking bemused, Hallie set her food on the coffee table and crawled along the couch to me. I kissed her as soon as her lips were within reach. When I finally let her up for air, she gazed at me in a dreamy, dazed way that made me feel fifteen feet tall.

"What was that for?"

"Because you're adorable and sweet and funny, and your boss does not know just how lucky she is to have you working for her."

Hallie practically melted into my side. "You don't think I'm a people-pleasing moron?"

I frowned at her. "Never. Don't call yourself that. You're hilarious, and you went above and beyond at your job. All I care about is that you're okay. If today made you incredibly uncomfortable and unhappy, then that's not okay. But if it's just a funny story you can add to your repertoire, then who cares? You did a good job."

"It's just a funny story," she assured me with a small smile. "Thank you."

"For what?"

She pressed another soft kiss to my mouth. "For being you." Then she licked her lips. "Mmm, kung pao chicken. Any left?"

Grinning, I handed her the carton and reached for hers on the table.

She settled into my side, and I switched on a sci-fi TV show we'd started watching at her place this past week. However, once the food was eaten and we were curled up together, her head on my chest, I noticed Hallie lifting her phone to check it every fifteen minutes or so.

"Waiting on a call?" I asked.

"What?" She looked up at me with those long-lashed wide eyes.

"You keep checking your phone."

"Oh." Her gaze dropped back to the TV. "My aunt Julia has been calling me, but I haven't picked up. If it was an emergency, she'd leave a voice mail, but she hasn't, so clearly Mom, for whatever reason, is using her as a go-between."

"But you're waiting for her to call again?"

"No." Hallie sighed heavily. "I'm waiting for my mom or dad to call me. It's been weeks now and nothing. That's shitty." Her voice hitched.

Her fucking parents.

I pressed a kiss to the top of her head, tightening my arm around her. "They'll call."

And if they didn't, I guessed I'd just have to find a way to help them pull their heads out of their asses.

"I don't want to talk about them tonight, if that's okay."

"Of course."

"Did you send the chapters to Scott?"

"Uh, not yet. Tomorrow."

Hallie sat up. "Are you sure? Because you know you don't have to send him anything."

I smiled in reassurance. "I'm just being a perfectionist. But I want to send it to him."

Nodding, she sank back against the couch instead of on me. Between that and the fact that she kept shooting me glances out of the corner of her eye, I knew she wanted to say something.

"What is it?"

Hallie chewed on her lower lip in thought.

My brows drew together. "You can talk to me about anything."

"I know." She nodded. "I have to ask, and I really want an honest answer. I don't want you to think about us or anything else, just what's in your gut. . . ."

"Okay?"

"Do you . . . Do you *want* to go on another space mission? I know you didn't when you got back, but with some time and distance, I thought maybe—"

"No." I cut her off gently. And I meant it. "I have no doubts in that regard. I know with certainty I don't want to go back."

"But in your videos, you seemed to love it, and I can't get that out of my head. I'm afraid you're missing something without it."

"Hallie, I loved my time in space. I loved training for it. I loved my crew, and I miss them, and I miss the buzz and atmosphere at NASA. I miss being a part of something truly important to humanity's progress. I do miss all of that, and I would never trade that life-altering experience for anything. But I don't want to go back into space, and here's why: that first experience can never be replicated. So that's one reason. And two, and this is me being completely honest, I didn't love being an astronaut enough to deal with the toll continued space exploration would take on my body."

Her expression slackened with surprise. "How bad of a toll?"

"It can be bad," I told her honestly. "Never mind the fact that we're exposed to radiation, increasing the risk of cancer. There are other health risks. We exercise up there to slow the process, and it helps, but we still come home with a reduction in bone density and in muscle mass and strength. We can build that back up. My bone density is almost back to its normal levels. I check in with my doc every couple of weeks. I should hopefully be back to normal in another few months."

"What? How did I not know this?"

"It's not a big deal," I promised. "And I got my muscle and strength back up to where I was before I went on mission with a lot of therapy and hard work when I returned to Earth. All of that is fixable. What isn't is the ramifications on our cardiovascular system."

"What do you mean?"

"Zero gravity changes the way the blood flows around our body. Our blood pressure gets very low. My motor skills were off when I returned home, and I felt faint a lot. I had to get a transfusion of normal saline to get my blood pressure back up to where it needed to be. The big thing I was warned about and advised of, as we all are, is that over time we can develop heart and blood vessel problems that you'd expect in someone much older. That increases our chances of heart disease and strokes. I also didn't wear glasses before I went up into space. When I got back, I had blurriness that I didn't have before, and now I need reading glasses, and who knows if that's permanent or not." I shrugged.

Hallie processed this, slack-jawed. "But . . . but there are men who go up there all the time."

"Yeah." I nodded. "And they are very aware of the risks and what they're putting their bodies through in the name of science. We need to know what space travel does to our bodies so we can figure out ways to stop it in order to travel farther into space, in order to get to Mars, for instance."

"But you don't want to risk it."

I smirked. "I know it's not heroic to admit, but I didn't like how I felt when I got back. Up there, zero gravity is amazing and exhilarating, and I have never slept better in my life. But when I got back, my body felt foreign. It wouldn't do what I needed it to do and, yeah, I worked hard to find my normal, but it took some time. For someone like me, someone as physical as I am, I found that daunting. It was the reality of what they'd warned me about before I went up. And in all honesty, and I admitted this a little in my later videos, I wanted to come home by month four. I missed life on Earth." I chuckled at the thought because I never thought I'd say it after the shit I'd seen in the air force. "Don't get me wrong, I'd take that job over being a fighter pilot any day of the week. I'm always going to be a scientist over a soldier. So, yeah, I miss NASA. I do. I miss the mission. But I don't miss space as much as an astronaut should."

Hallie reached out to stroke my cheek, and I leaned into her touch. "You amaze me. You *are* heroic. And you'll find your way, Chris. I know it."

Words that felt like too much too soon to share bubbled up inside me, and so I kissed her, hard, before they poured out of me.

## Hallie

I was still reeling from what Chris had divulged about the toll on his body from his time in space as he switched the volume up on the TV and we settled back in. Barely paying attention, all I could think about was how selfishly glad I was he wasn't going into space. Not just because I'd miss the hell out of him and fear for his life every second of every day, but because I'd also worry constantly about what it was doing to his body.

Since the point was moot, I tried to shake it off and not worry about it.

When the TV show relocated to Thailand for a scene, I allowed myself to be distracted. "Thailand is on my bucket list," I commented. "It was going to be my first port of call on that backpacking trip I told you about."

"It's on my list too." Chris seemed to take a breath. "What if . . . what if we did it?"

"Did what?"

"What if we went backpacking together?"

A thrill shot through me, and I scrambled up into a sitting position to stare at him. I needed to know if he was serious. His expression said he was. "What? When? How?"

He grinned at my barely contained excitement. "We could take next summer off. You could ask for a sabbatical at work, and it would give us all year to save."

The prospect sounded as daunting as it did wonderful. "What if Lia won't let me do that?"

"Then we won't go. No pressure."

"But we could seriously try to figure out how to do it?"

"Absolutely." He tugged on my hand, his sexy smile giving me butterflies. "I want to travel the world with you."

*I love you so much.*

Swallowing the words I was afraid would send him fleeing, I confessed, "I want to travel the world with you." And there was a particular country that popped into my mind first. "What about Mexico?"

Chris's fingers tightened in mine. "What about it?"

Since his tone was neither defensive nor sharp, I forged ahead, "Maybe we could start there."

Something I didn't quite understand brightened his dark gaze. "Yeah," his voice was a little hoarse. "Yeah, I'd like that." He pulled me into him again, and I rested my head on his chest.

"So we're doing this? We're planning a three-month trip around the world? Mexico first . . . then Asia?"

"Sounds like a plan to me, *mi cielo*."

I raised my head at what sounded like an endearment. "*Mi* what?"

His eyes darted over my face, and there was no hiding his affection. I could only hope that his affection was as deep as mine. "I had a friend in the air force, Juan, second-generation Mexican and raised in a big Mexican American family. He's the one who taught me the basics of Spanish. And he called his fiancé '*mi cielo*' all the time. It means 'my sky,' 'my heaven.' I never really gave much thought to it—" He stared deeply into my eyes. "But now, every time I look at you, those words fill my mind. *Mi cielo*."

It took everything within me to stop myself from blurting out how I felt about him. I tried to hide the surge of emotions I was feeling by kissing him playfully. But as he murmured "*mi cielo*" again, my kiss turned hungrier, more desperate.

Chris groaned, guiding me onto my back. "I think I need to learn more Spanish if this is the reaction."

"I'm absolutely on board with that idea," I murmured before his lips found mine again.

# THIRTY-ONE

## Hallie

That I had clean clothes and toiletries at Chris's place didn't seem weird to him, and I was ecstatic to walk into my bathroom and see his stuff cluttering up my counter. Althea worried we were moving too fast, but it didn't feel fast for us. It felt right.

The Monday after my embarrassing rendition of "Sweet Caroline" had started like a regular Monday in Chris and Hallie's world. I woke up in his bed, he made it very difficult for me to leave it, we eventually did, he made me breakfast while I showered and then dressed in the clothes I'd dropped off at his place the morning before. I departed for work, and Chris went for his morning run before he'd return home to work on his book. Writing had started to occupy most of his day, which was exciting because it meant he was getting close to finishing it.

On cloud nine, not long later, I clung to a pole on the train and swayed with its movements, not paying any attention to the crowded car as I made my way into the city.

Until my phone vibrated continuously, distracting me from the podcast I half listened to through my earbuds. What if it was my mom or my dad? Hope blossomed within a confusing, icky tangle of resentment and hurt as I rummaged through my purse for my cell. When I pulled it out, however, I was shocked to find a bunch of texts and social media notifications from my friends. Seeing a text from Althea, I clicked on it.

Have you seen this? Are you okay?

Attached to her text was a link. I'd discover all my friends had also shared and tagged me in photos some random person had taken of Chris and me and posted to their social media.

A local New York paper had picked up the story in their gossip column.

Althea had sent me a link to that news piece. My stomach dropped.

**HAS OUR NATIONAL HERO FOUND A NEW HEROINE?**

And beneath the headline were photographs of Chris and me in Central Park on Saturday. In one we were holding hands and laughing, in another we were cuddling, and the pièce de résistance was a photo of us kissing. He cradled my face in his hands like I was precious, while classy me had my hands on his ass. It was a hot picture.

Cheeks burning, I skimmed the article, which outed who I was, where I worked, my college education, and that I was a surprising choice for Chris to move on with from Darcy Hawthorne. They then discussed Darcy breaking up with Chris to become engaged to Matthias. I could see from the tags on socials that a few big influencers had reposted the story on their feeds. Great.

Sweat dampened my hands and under my arms as I lifted my gaze in paranoia to see if anyone was looking at me. Thankfully, no one seemed to notice my existence.

I knew Chris still had his following on Instagram, but after the TV interviews upon his return from space, the media had pretty much left him alone. Why did anyone care anymore about whom he dated?

How did this happen?

Just as I climbed up the stairs out of the subway, my phone buzzed in my hand, and I startled. It was Chris.

Fumbling for the Answer Call button on my earbuds, I answered breathlessly, "Hi, hi, oh my God, hi."

"You saw the photos online?" he asked, his tone tense. "I've got a ton of comments on my last Instagram post about this, and apparently there's an article in a New York gossip rag."

I winced just imagining how cruel some of those comments might be. I'd had to stop scrolling through the comments on Chris's posts just because of the sheer amount of people who flirted with him. There was no doubt in my mind, some of those people had some not nice things to say about his choice of girlfriend. Shaking off the morose thought, I replied, "I saw the article. Althea sent it to me, and I've been tagged all over social media."

"Shit. Are you okay?"

"Um, yeah, I think so. I just . . . I don't understand why someone would take those photos." The idea of someone following us and watching us all day creeped me out.

"Some people don't have boundaries. As for the article, it's just a puff piece," Chris said, trying to assure me, but I could hear his agitation. "This will blow over."

"Are you sure? I mean, the media was pretty interested in you when you got home from the ISS."

"Yeah, because some of the social media posts from my mission went viral. The fact that I was dating Darcy only stoked the flames in New York at the time. We're not in the same situation here. This *will* blow over, Hallie," he repeated. "I'm sorry if this has upset you. I'm sorry this person violated your privacy."

"*Our* privacy. You have nothing to be sorry for," I assured him. "Are you at the office?"

"Almost. And no one is looking at me. No one cares."

"You sure? I could come get you."

He was so protective. I smiled, despite the swarm of butterflies in my gut. "I'm fine."

"Text me when you get into the office?"

"I will. Talk soon."

Despite my reassurances, I couldn't help but surreptitiously look around to make sure no one was watching me. They weren't. Chris was right. My friends were overreacting.

Nearing the office, I switched my phone to silent and hurried into the building, only to find Althea waiting for me in the lobby with a coffee.

"You're an angel." I sighed, taking it from her.

"You got my text, right?" Althea studied me carefully, like she was waiting for me to have a meltdown.

"I did." I took a deep breath as we stepped into the elevator. "Chris said I shouldn't freak out about it. That it'll blow over."

"I think he's right. I also think maybe you two should go social media official. Once Chris posts about you on Instagram, papers will struggle to sell pictures like that when the public can see it for free on his account."

It wasn't a bad idea, I supposed. I just didn't think he or I were ready for that.

"That doesn't mean this isn't weird for you though."

"It *is* weird," I admitted. "The idea of someone snapping pictures like that, watching us." I shuddered.

We stepped off the elevator.

"Those pictures were hot though," Althea teased.

I grinned through my embarrassment. "They had to print the one with my hands on his ass."

She chuckled. "That boy's ass is fine. Not one person in the world would look at that picture and judge you for the ass grab."

I chuckled. "Thank you."

"For what?"

"For making me feel better. I don't think it's quite sunk in yet, you know. The entire city woke up to pictures of me making out with my boyfriend, and even friends who don't live in the city have tagged me in this. Goddamn social media."

"It's so like you, Hallie, to pretend like you're not loving this," I heard Dominic say behind me.

Althea's eyes narrowed, but I shook my head at her and turned to face Dominic.

He wore a familiar ugly sneer on his handsome face. I refused to be intimidated by him or the fact that I could feel our colleagues staring at us from their desks.

"What is that supposed to mean?" I asked.

He raised an eyebrow, surprised by my sharp tone. "Uh, that no one here believes in your 'butter wouldn't melt' *gig*. You're just as ambitious as me, but at least I don't pretend otherwise."

"I'm sorry, what are you trying to say exactly?"

"That you acted unprofessionally by sleeping with a client in order to get ahead."

"You motherfucking—"

I reached behind me to stay Althea's angry rebuttal. "It's okay," I assured her, my eyes still on Dominic. "Dominic, your problem is that you think everyone thinks like you. But I don't use people, I don't tear them down, and I don't walk all over them and their feelings to get what I want. I also don't take out my own frustrations on them and blame other people for my failings."

His lips parted in shock, and it sounded like Althea was choking behind me.

"Now if you don't mind, I have work to do, and you're standing in the way of my office."

Dominic, blinking like he couldn't believe what I'd just said, stepped to the side to let me pass. With my head held high, I strutted past him and down the hall. As soon as I was inside my private space, I sagged against the wall, my heart pounding, my legs shaking.

The urge to burst back out there and apologize was real.

He probably hated me now.

The worry reverberated around in my mind for a few seconds until an internal voice yelled, *He already hated you!*

It was true. Dominic saw me as competition and weak competition at that.

Yet I'd just shown him I couldn't be pushed around anymore, and as sick as I felt, it also felt great! The world hadn't ended when I stood up for myself with Dad, and it wouldn't end today with Dominic.

Shaking off my nerves, I took a deep breath and crossed the room to my desk. Pulling out my tablet and phone, I was about to set them aside when I noticed the missed call notification on the screen. Five missed calls from my mom.

Coincidence?

I think not.

So I was only worth talking to now because she'd seen me kissing a famous astronaut?

A text popped up on the screen from Althea.

**You were magnificent!**

**I am so fucking proud of you!**

**I think Dominic is still in shock you stood up for yourself.**

This was followed by three "raise the roof" emojis and three "crying with laughter" emojis and a "blowing a kiss" emoji.

Heart still hammering with annoyance at my mother, I quickly texted Althea back.

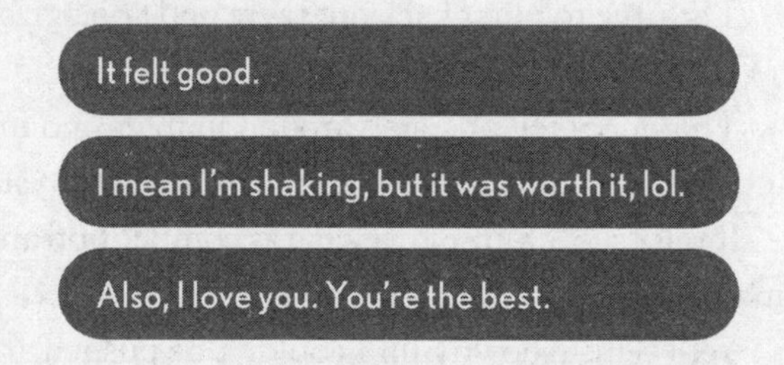


She texted back that she loved me too, and I tried to let that sentiment overpower the ugly feelings of resentment building in me toward my mom.

When I finally looked up from my phone, it was to find Lia standing mutely in my office.

Oh shit.

"Morning . . . Lia." I tried to smile, but it appeared more of a grimace. "How was your weekend?"

She crossed her arms over her chest and stared stonily at me. "Dominic sent me a link to an interesting article this morning."

Of course he did.

"Chris and I started seeing each other after he was no longer a client. No lines were crossed."

Lia relaxed, her arms dropping back to her sides. "I thought as much. I just needed to check."

"I understand."

She studied me for a moment. "Are you handling this okay? Do you need to take the day off?"

I smiled gratefully. "I appreciate the offer, but I'm fine. It's disconcerting and strange, but I'm fine."

"All right. Well, you know where I am if you need me."

"Thanks," I said to her back as she strode out of my office.

I sighed and took a massive gulp of the coffee Althea had given me. Work. I needed to concentrate on work.

Yet, I'd barely started when my office phone rang.

"Hallie Goodman, Lia Zhang Events," I answered.

"Ms. Goodman, Kyla Dell, *Uptown Magazine*. I wondered if I could ask you a few questions about your relationship with Captain Christopher Ortiz. How long have you been dating, and is it serious? How does Darcy Hawthorne feel about it considering you're planning her wedding?"

I gaped at my computer screen.

Was she for real?

"Ms. Goodman?"

"No comment." I hung up, glaring at the phone.

Shit.

I quickly called Chris and explained what happened. After he let loose a few curse words, he told me I did the right thing and, if they called again, to just keep saying, "No comment." In the end, I got two more phone calls from local journalists. Definitely freaked out, I informed Lia in case they started calling our main reception too. My boss was amazing. She handled it like it was no big deal and had her assistant, Amber, set up the phones so that my calls came to her first so she could vet them. Our receptionist, Navid, was directed to tell any journalists I was unavailable.

"This will die down," Lia assured me, repeating what Chris

had said. How it was just a puff piece and I would be yesterday's news tomorrow.

God, I hoped so.

It stressed me out. I hated the thought of our romance being picked apart by strangers.

Back at my desk, I couldn't help but look at Chris's Instagram account. It was masochistic, but the urge was too strong. Scrolling through the comments, my heart plummeted at some of the nasty things people said about me. Apparently Chris was out of his mind for jumping from an environmentalist lawyer to a "silly party planner." Most of the negative comments were sure I was just a "casual" thing. Other people said I wasn't pretty enough for him. And although there were lots of comments about how cute we were together, the positivity couldn't win against the way the negativity made me feel.

I closed the app like it had physically burned me and jerked back in my chair.

It took more focus and willpower than I knew I had to continue on with my work that day. Lunch with Althea in a café we liked across the street was fine, and no one paid any attention to me, which made me relax a lot. By the time I got back to the office, I was feeling more myself again, reassured that Chris and Lia were right and that this was just a blip.

Therefore, I was knocked on my ass when Navid came dashing into my office that afternoon, eyes wide with panic. "I tried to tell him he needed an appointment, but he just started searching for you, and he's out there—"

A man suddenly appeared in my doorway, his eyes on the nameplate on my door.

Navid gave me another wide-eyed look as he stepped aside and mouthed, "I'm so sorry."

Recognizing the man who was now in my office staring at me,

I stood on shaking knees and gestured to Navid. "It's okay, Navid."

"You're sure?"

"Yes."

He gave me a worried look but left us alone.

I stared at Chris's father, already knowing in my gut that it was not a good thing Javier Ortiz had taken time out of his very busy schedule to stop by my office on the same day photographs of me and his son kissing were splattered all over the internet.

"Mr. Ortiz." I couldn't round my desk without giving away my nervousness. "How can I help you?"

It was strange, as he looked me over like I was a bug, Chris's resemblance and non-resemblance to his father struck me. While objectively Javier was a very handsome man, his features, so similar to Chris's, seemed carved out of granite, and the dark brown eyes he'd given to Chris were nowhere near as beautiful. All because, where Chris's expression was open and warm and his eyes filled with kindness, his father's expression was severe, his eyes blacker, colder.

Javier's gaze dragged down what he could see of my body and then flickered around my small office. He sighed heavily, like he was exasperated. Then his gaze came back to mine, and I touched my desk to hold myself up against the distaste he couldn't hide. "While I'm sure you're perfectly good at your job and a capable young woman, it's obvious you and my son exist on entirely different planets. I don't know why your paths crossed, and I don't care. All I care about is that my son has the future he deserves. Being photographed with a party planner who clearly enjoys a good time—"

What the hell did that mean?

"—is a mar on his record that can easily be forgotten once the good-time girl goes away."

*"Good-time girl?"*

"We both know what you are, Ms. Goodman."

"You don't know anything about me."

"Oh, I know exactly who you are." He stepped forward and pulled something out of the inside of his suit pocket. "How much will it take to make you go away?"

My jaw literally dropped as I gaped at his checkbook.

It was like something out of a movie.

People did this in real life? "You want to pay me to break up with Chris?"

Javier stared at me, his eyes hard. "How much?"

I was horrified. And not because this man had insulted me, judged me, and decided in his outrageous arrogance that he knew me from a photograph. I was horrified for Chris. I was heartbroken that this was his father and that he would go behind his son's back and do this to him. What else had he done? What other parts of his life had he interfered in and manipulated and tainted?

"There isn't a number in the world you could get to, to make me break things off with Chris. Now, if you're done insulting me, I think you better leave before I call security."

He raised an eyebrow as if I was the audacious one. "You'll regret this."

"Is that a threat?"

"A warning. I can make your life very difficult."

"Go ahead," I dared him.

His eyes flashed in outrage, but he turned and stalked out of my office without another word.

Trembling, I practically fell back into my seat. What the hell just happened?

"Hallie? Hallie?"

I blinked, looking up past my computer to find Althea. She stared at me in concern. "Was that Chris's father?"

I nodded, barely hearing her over the rushing blood in my ears.

"What did he want?"

"To . . . uh . . . to pay me to break up with Chris." I laughed hollowly. "Who does that? He was like some pantomime villain."

"Hallie." Althea crossed the room, leaning over my desk to touch my hand. "Call Chris and tell him."

I bit my lip at the thought. It would hurt him.

My friend read me like a book. "Hallie, Javier Ortiz is a powerful man. He could do a lot of damage to your life, so you need to pick up the phone and call Chris right now."

Oh shit.

Oh shit, oh shit, oh shit, oh shit.

Feeling sick to my stomach, I grabbed my phone off my desk and hit Chris on speed dial.

# THIRTY-TWO

## Chris

"I'm going into a meeting in ten minutes, so I don't have time for whatever this is."

It took every ounce of self-control I'd ever gained over the years to stop myself from throwing a fist into my father's face as he glowered arrogantly at me.

As soon as I'd gotten off the phone with Hallie, who'd tried hard to hide the shaking in her voice but couldn't, I sped into the city. To *his* office. He had to know why I was here, but he just stood there like I was an inconvenience.

"You'll make time, you son of a bitch."

My father raised an eyebrow. "If you're going to be disrespectful, at least shut the door."

I slammed it shut behind me without even looking at it, and then I took a few steps toward him. It was shocking he couldn't hear how hard my heart was pounding. "Don't you ever come near Hallie again. And by that, I mean in any capacity. If she so much as has a client drop her, I'm going to blame you, and I'm going to blame you publicly."

For the first time in my life, my father seemed visibly stunned. "I hope you're joking."

"I've never been more serious in my life. Never mind the fact that you went behind my back and tried to pay Hallie to break up with me—I can't even think about that and if you've done it before—but you threatened her." My control slipped, and I was suddenly in his face. "You fucking threatened her, and it is taking everything in me not to put you on your ass right now. If you ever go anywhere near her again, I will let the entire world know what kind of bully you really are. And don't think they won't believe me—I'm the golden boy, and I'm not afraid to use it against you. I could give a shit how much money you have."

There was just a flicker, a slight slip of my father's control, that told me he hadn't expected this.

Stunned, I watched him nod slowly. My father cleared his throat and took a step away from me, his gaze just a bit wary. I didn't trust it. "I had no idea you felt seriously for this woman, and I was just trying to protect you and your reputation."

"From what?" I scoffed. "Hallie is the best person I've ever known. There are no skeletons in her closet."

"Her pictures and her job suggest a lack of seriousness."

"So what, because she has pink hair and is publicly affectionate, she's a—what did you call her? 'A good-time girl.'" Renewed anger surged within me, and I clenched my fists against it. "Hallie is one of the top event planners for one of the biggest management companies in the city. But even if she didn't work her ass off for her job, and trust me she does, she would still be too good for me."

I saw the slight sneer on my father's face, and I laughed humorlessly. "You think you're so above it. That money somehow makes you better than her and all these other people and, by way of blood, it makes me better. But how many people did you trample over to get to where you are? How many businesses have you fucked over? How many people despise you?"

My father scoffed. "You're wrong, but even if you were right, I don't need to be liked."

"Not even by your own son?"

A muscle flexing in his jaw was the only hint that he cared even one iota if I liked him. "I'll leave your girlfriend alone. I just hope you know what you're doing, because from here it looks like you're pissing your life away in every aspect."

"You know nothing about me."

"Oh, you'd like to think that. Poor Christopher. His father never cared."

I hadn't come here to do this, but for the first time in my life, I finally wanted to cut the bullshit between us. My father would never approve of me, and striving for approval I couldn't earn was the ultimate Sisyphean task. "Poor me nothing. But yes, I think beyond how it affects your own reputation, you could not care less about me or Mom or anyone. I don't know if you even cared about Miguel beyond grooming him to take over the company—"

"Enough!" My father slammed his fist on his desk, the objects on it bouncing upward with the impact.

Silence fell over the room.

"It doesn't feel nice, does it?" I finally said, my voice quiet. "To have someone come to your office and attack you."

"Well, she's certainly influenced you, hasn't she?" My father smoothed his hands over his hair and then straightened his tie, even though nothing was out of place. "Before her, you would never have been insolent enough to come in here and disrespect your father."

"You threatened someone I care about. Did you honestly think I'd let that go?"

"It was a warning." He sighed and looked out his office window. "And I suppose I don't know you as well as I think I do."

"You don't know me at all."

His gaze snapped back to mine. "I raised you."

"No. My mother and several babysitters raised me. You only got involved when it suited you."

He scoffed. "If you want to rewrite history and vilify me, go ahead. Can I expect the same in your book?"

"You don't think it's true?"

"Of course it's not true."

"I don't know who you are," I said, my voice a little louder with exasperation. "I don't even know my own father."

"More lies."

"Oh, it is? What have you ever shared with us about your life? Why did you prevent me and Miguel from exploring our Mexican heritage? Most of the Spanish I know, which isn't much, I learned from guys I served with. I know almost zero about my heritage. About your past."

"Why do you need to? I worked very hard to provide opportunities for you that you would never have otherwise, and look where it has taken you. What does my past have anything to do with your future?"

"I don't know . . . uh, maybe to feel connected to who I am," I replied sarcastically.

"Who you are is not your cultural heritage. It's the choices you make and the actions you take."

"See, I beg to differ. I have no idea about this whole side of me because you made sure I wouldn't, and I've been so afraid of disappointing or upsetting you that I haven't even learned to speak Spanish or visit Mexico, haven't tried to connect to an integral piece of me, even when I'm held up as a role model in the Latinx community."

"What do you mean *connect* to it? Everyone around you speaks English. You have no family that required you to speak Spanish. It would not have been a productive use of your time."

"I have you!"

"And what would be the point in our conversing in Spanish?"

And there it was. Proof that my father just didn't understand how to connect with his family. "For you! For me. Our heritage is something we have in common, and I know nothing about it!"

"What do you want to know?" My father yelled now, genuine emotion finally breaking through that granite facade of his. His accent, which was nonexistent these days, thickened with that emotion. "That my mother and father were immigrants who came to this country, worked hard to give us a good life, were the best parents a child could ask for, until one day my mother hid me in a closet when a stranger broke into our home and shot them to death for the money in their wallets?"

I stumbled back like *I'd* been shot.

My father cursed and gave me his back, his shoulders shuddering as he tried to gain control. Whatever I'd expected to find in this conversation that was long overdue, it was not such a painful truth.

"I'm sorry. I didn't know that."

He exhaled heavily, still not looking at me. "Why would you? Why would I tell you that? What use could come of it?"

"To share with me. To talk about it if you need to."

"I don't need to talk about it." He turned to me now, and I knew he was lying to himself. If therapy had taught me anything, it was that you didn't bottle trauma. Suddenly I felt like I was finally seeing my father for the first time. He was a product of his grief. Not dealing with it had made him who he was. "I was eleven years old." My father shrugged. "It's but a dream from another life."

I didn't believe that for a second. "How has this stayed hidden so long?"

"You mean how is it not public knowledge?"

I nodded.

"I buried it. Changing my name at eighteen helped. My real name is not Javier Ortiz."

Holy shit. "What is?"

"That's not information you require." He looked at his watch. "I really do have a meeting, Christopher."

Shaken, I could only nod.

Then my father shocked me even further by stopping in front of me. "I . . . I like control. I'm not a stupid man. I am self-aware enough to realize I like control. And sometimes I forget my son is a grown man and that he doesn't need me to protect him anymore. I shouldn't have visited Ms. Goodman today. It won't happen again."

"I appreciate that," I forced out through the emotion clogging my throat.

"I still want you to consider one of my publishers for your book."

And there he was.

I gave a huff of half frustration. "I'm handling it on my own."

My father's lips pinched in disapproval, but he nodded. "Fair enough. You can see yourself out, yes?"

And then he was gone, leaving me alone in his office, completely rocked by his revelations.

My cell rang in my pocket. Thinking it might be Hallie, I yanked it out even though I felt too off-kilter to hold a decent conversation.

It wasn't Hallie. It was Darcy.

"Hey, I just wondered if you were in the city so we can grab a coffee?" she said after I answered.

"Uh . . ." Now wasn't really the best time.

"I know it's not a great time for you, but I need someone to talk to. Someone I trust."

Hearing the vulnerability in her voice, I couldn't turn her down. "Yeah, sure. Where are you?"

Hallie gaped at me after I was done telling her what had happened at my father's office that day. After coffee with Darcy, I'd gone to collect Hallie from work. There I'd finally met her friend Althea, who seemed just as protective of her as I was, which was nice to know. She deserved to have the best people in her corner.

We didn't talk about what had happened, however, until we were safely back in Hallie's apartment. I still couldn't believe what my father had revealed, and my disbelief was mirrored on Hallie's face.

"Are you okay?"

It was the first thing she asked, and it made me fall for her even harder. I reached across the couch to take her hand in mine. "I'm reeling."

"No wonder." She scooted closer. "I'm so sorry about your grandparents."

"It's strange . . . What he did to you just brought up all this resentment and anger because my whole life I watched him keep us all at a distance, all the while trying to manipulate and control our lives. It didn't make sense. I was so angry when I went into his office, and I'm still pissed about what he did to you . . . but now I actually feel like I understand him better than I ever have. There was a part of me that hated him because I thought he was ashamed of his own heritage."

"Oh, Chris."

Remorse cut through me. "It wasn't shame. It was pain. And now I think I know why he pushed me even further away after Miguel was killed."

"Too much loss," Hallie whispered.

"Exactly." Emotion thickened my voice. "He's lost so much. Control is all he has."

"And if he doesn't get too close to you, somehow he thinks it'll hurt less if he loses you?"

"Maybe." I nodded, unbearably sad for my father. "Do you think that's why he kept my mother at arm's length?"

"I don't know."

"Did he love her, or did he marry someone he knew he would never really love?"

Hallie suddenly climbed into my lap, pressing her warm, soft body to mine in comfort. "I don't know the answers. And you could drive yourself crazy trying to figure him out. If he doesn't want to deal with the traumatic things that have happened in his life, you can't make him, and you have to accept the fact that he might never change because of it."

My arms tightened around her. "I know. I know you're right."

"But you have hope?"

I couldn't lie to her. "I can't help it. It feels like something shifted between us in his office. Maybe I should put a pause on the chapters in the book about exploring our Latino heritage while I figure things out with him? I don't want to stall any potential progress with him right now by blindsiding him with the publication of personal family history."

She cupped my face in her hand. "You should hope, Chris. It takes so much strength to not give up on the people you love, even when they make it difficult. You taught me that. But you can't let your dad's pain stop you from being who you want to be. If you want to learn Spanish, go to Mexico, research your family history; you should do all of that. And if you want to write about it, you should. I know you can find a way to do that without feeling like you're crossing a line with your father."

Leaning into her touch, staring into her eyes, eyes I knew I wanted to find refuge in for the rest of my life, I considered her advice. I wasn't quite sure what the right next move was, but I could promise one thing. "No matter how complicated the situation is between me and my father, he will never be allowed to hurt you or threaten you again."

"I know." Her kiss was soft, meant to console only. "I believe you."

Sighing wearily, I tucked her head under my chin and just held her for a while, taking the comfort she offered and hopefully giving it in return.

She traced soothing circles on my forearm, and my lids drooped with drowsiness as my body finally relaxed after the shit show that was this afternoon.

"Where did you go after your dad's?" Hallie broke the silence.

"I had coffee with Darcy."

The soothing circles stopped at the same time I felt the rigidity in her body. My eyes popped open, alert, even though she tried to hide her reaction by deliberately relaxing into me again.

Shit.

"It was just coffee," I assured her quietly.

"Did you tell her about what happened with your father?"

I leaned away and lifted her chin so I could look in her eyes. Her expression was too carefully neutral. She was hiding from me. Hiding her . . . jealousy?

"Hallie, why would I tell Darce? We rarely talked about him when we were together, so we're certainly not going to talk about it now. She had a huge fight with Matthias last night, and she wanted to talk to someone who wouldn't sell the story or spread it around town behind her back. She doesn't have a lot of friends she can trust in that respect."

"So you're her confidant?" Hallie tried to pull out of my arms, but I tightened my hold.

"You and I have a much stronger relationship than me and Darcy ever did, and I was also closer to you when we were just friends than I ever was with her. You can't be jealous of her."

The blank expression instantly slipped as she glared at me. "I can't? My boyfriend has rekindled his friendship with his gorgeous, smart, philanthropic ex-girlfriend whom his father loved, FYI, and I can't be jealous?"

"'Friendship' being the operative word. And if you trust me, you have to know that's all it is." Tiredness added a sharpness to my tone.

She flinched, and I had no choice but to release her or have her struggle in my embrace.

"Fuck, Hallie . . ." I bowed my head in exhaustion as she stood up from the couch.

"So you're saying that you wouldn't have a problem with me being friends with an ex?"

"No." I answered honestly, exasperated. "Hallie, I trust you. I trust you would never do that to me. She's a friend, and we have to trust each other with our friendships. Right?"

"You're making me feel like I'm a child for feeling this way."

My heart lurched at her hurt expression.

"If I was suddenly having coffees and cocktails with Derek or George or whomever . . . it wouldn't bother you just a little?"

I thought about my reaction to Derek, and remorse sliced through me. "Yeah," I acknowledged, pushing up off the couch. I hated the wary look on her face as I approached. "*Mi cielo*," I whispered, pulling her against me. "I'm sorry. You're right. It would bother me a little."

Pressing soothing kisses to her lips and along her jaw, I felt her relax into me again, and relief moved through me. Clasping her face in my hands, I stared into her eyes and said, "We're only human. So I get it that jealousy happens. But I promise you, you have no reason to be jealous of Darcy. And I need to know you trust me."

Hallie nodded slowly. "I do. Old insecurities kicking in there."

"You have no reason for them." I nipped playfully at her mouth. "You're all I think about. You're all I want." My kiss was hungrier now, deeper as my exhaustion gave way to something more powerful. I started walking her backward toward the bedroom. "And I'm going to show you just how much."

# THIRTY-THREE

## Hallie

It would seem this was the week for unannounced visitors to my office. When Navid informed me that my dad was at Reception, I had to ask him to repeat the information. But sure enough, my dad *was* at Reception.

Stomach rioting with butterflies, I walked out to meet him, and my heart lurched in my chest as our gazes caught. Dad's expression wasn't hard to read. He looked ill at ease and forlorn.

"What are you doing here?"

"I stopped by your place last night, but you weren't home."

The apartment buzzer had gone off last night, but Chris and I ignored it because he was passionately endeavoring to show me how little need I had to be jealous of Darcy, and there was no way either of us wanted to stop for a door buzzer.

Trying not to blush, I looked away. "Yeah, I was out."

"With your boyfriend?"

Disappointment crashed through me. "Is that why you're here?"

"No," he said hurriedly before glancing around. "Is there somewhere more private we can talk?"

Nodding, I told him to follow me and led him to my office. I caught Althea's eyes across the room and gave her a slight nod to reassure her I was all right.

Safely enclosed in my office, I leaned against my desk as my father took in my space.

"I've never been here before. The place looks great."

"Thanks." I studied him while he wasn't looking. Dad appeared exhausted. The vitality that had glowed from him these past few months had disappeared. He seemed dejected and weary again. "Why did you come?"

He exhaled slowly. "I had a conversation with your mother yesterday that woke me up."

Surprised, I could only raise my brows.

Dad chuckled humorlessly. "She called me yesterday to see if I knew anything about your relationship with this astronaut because you weren't answering her calls."

"Chris."

"Right. Chris. And I told her I hadn't spoken to you in weeks. I told her why. And I told her that because of your visit to the house, what you said, Miranda left me and that I was angry with you."

I flinched. Not from guilt.

From unbelievable hurt, that he would dare to blame anything in his life on me.

Dad grimaced. "Your mother tore me one like she never has before, and you know that's saying a lot. She told me I was a selfish asshole who'd neglected the one person in my life who had loved me and would always love me despite my many mistakes. The one person in both our lives who, until recently, never failed to show up. She also blamed me for you not calling her."

Wow. My mom had actually said that to my dad about me? "I

stopped taking her calls because I just wanted out of this wreckage you two have created."

He nodded, taking a step toward me. "I know you're right about all of that. I knew the night you came to the house. Your mother and I have been so unbelievably selfish with you, Hallie, and I recognized that. I was just . . . it was just easier to be angry at you once Miranda walked out than to deal with the fact that I had damaged my relationship with my daughter so badly."

"I'm sorry about Miranda."

Pain flickered in Dad's eyes. "I love her, but she was right. You were right. I wasn't myself with her. I was trying so hard to be someone else, someone your mother hadn't destroyed, that I lied about so many things." He scrubbed a hand down his face.

"Did you tell Miranda all of this?"

"She didn't want to hear it."

"She didn't want to hear it in that moment. Maybe she'll want to hear it now."

Dad huffed. "Even now you're being kind to me. I don't deserve you, Hallie."

I took a tentative step toward him. "Dad, Mom's right. I will always love you. And as long as you keep me out of the toxic relationship between you and Mom, you and I will be okay."

"Toxic?" He raised an eyebrow.

I nodded somberly. "Yeah, Dad, I realize now that it is pretty toxic. And it damaged your self-esteem. If it hadn't, you wouldn't have felt the need to buy that house and pretend to be something you weren't for Miranda."

The bleakness in his eyes turned into something more pensive. "I sold the house."

"You did?"

He nodded. "Got something more affordable back in Newark."

"Dad." I touched his arm. "Miranda loved you. Not the house."

He gave me a sad smirk. "I think Alison liked me better for that pool though."

"Alison is a spoiled brat and could do with a few less pools in her life."

Dad gave a bark of laughter. "You're not wrong." His smile died as he studied my face. "I am so sorry for taking you for granted. It shouldn't have taken your mother reaming me out for me to see that. Can you forgive me, Hallie?"

The tears welled up before I could stop them as I nodded, pinching my lips to stop the sob from breaking out.

"Oh, Cupcake." He pulled me into his arms, and I melted into my dad's familiar embrace. "I am so damn sorry for hurting you." His voice hitched with emotion. "I'm going to do my best to make it up to you, okay?"

I nodded, still unable to speak through my tears.

My body shook with the force of my relief. It wasn't until that moment that I realized how heavy my estrangement from my dad had been weighing on my heart.

My dad left a little while later, and we'd made plans for Chris and me to visit him in a few weeks once he settled into his new house. He'd also come by to check on me, to make sure I was okay after our relationship was outed online, and I told him a little about Chris. Seeing how happy I was, Dad seemed to relax about the whole thing.

It was difficult to concentrate on work after that, but I had a tour of venues with a client today, which kept me focused. I texted Chris in between to tell him about Dad's visit, promising him I'd fill him in later.

However, I had one thing still to do before I left the office that night.

Sitting on my desk, staring out the window to the street chock-full of people and vehicles during rush hour, I listened to my cell ring out.

On the fifth ring, my mom picked up. "I wondered when you'd finally call."

Pushing down my irritation with her, I replied, "Dad paid me a visit today. Thank you for what you said to him."

Mom sighed. "Hallie, none of us are perfect, but, except for the last few weeks, you're a good kid and your father treated you unfairly."

Though it was beyond nice to hear her say that, I pushed past the sudden pounding in my chest to say, "I can't be a part of your lives again if you're going to keep me in the middle of this war between you. I spent my whole life in the middle, Mom. I can't do it anymore."

She was silent so long I repeated, "Mom?"

"I'm here." Her sigh crackled the line. "While I think calling it a war is a little dramatic, I can agree to leave you out of it. Not that there's anything to be in anymore. I need to move on, and so does your dad. The toilet-paper incident made me realize how damn crazy it had gotten. And while I do think you should have picked up when I called you, I heard about what you said to your dad, and I know it was directed at both of us. And you're not wrong. We've been selfish. It'll stop. Anyway, your dad and I are holding on to stuff that doesn't even exist now."

The word "relieved" did not do my feelings justice, and I just had to hope they'd stand by this newfound perspective. "I think that's great, Mom. And thank you."

"Yeah. Well, I booked this retreat in the Catskills. Jenna is coming with me. We both feel we have some soul-searching to do."

"Mom, that sounds great."

"Can I count on seeing you when I get back?"

I nodded even though she couldn't see me. "We can do that."

"Not this weekend but next?"

"I have an event in the Hamptons that weekend. Weekend after?"

"All weekend?"

I rolled my eyes at her irritated tone. "Chris's aunt lives there, so we thought we'd stay with her since I'll already be there for this event."

"Ah, the astronaut. Well done, Hallie."

"Mom," I warned.

"What? I mean it. I'm impressed. He's very handsome."

"He's also brilliant and kind and considerate."

"Hmm. Just be careful. Does his aunt have a pool?"

"Yes, why?"

"Don't take that polka-dot bikini you wore during our spa break last year. It wasn't flattering. Or if you must, wear it with a sarong. And do you have beachy high-heeled sandals? Wedges maybe? Those will make you look taller and leaner in a bikini."

There she was. "Mom."

"What? You sound like you really, really like this one. I'm just trying to help you keep him."

"He's seen me naked, Mom. And he's still here, so I think I'm good. I have to go now."

"Okay. I'll let you know when I arrive in the Catskills. Oh, that's if they have a signal up there."

"Um, they might not. Send a carrier pigeon. It'll take you back to your childhood."

"Oh, aren't we Miss Sassy Pants now that we're dating an astronaut?"

Hearing the amusement in her voice, I smiled. "I hope you and Jenna have a wonderful time."

"Thank you, honey. Oh, and if you need to fix your hair color before you meet the astronaut's aunt, my stylist will fit you in last minute. You can't socialize with the Hamptons set with pink hair, Hallie. As cute as you looked in those pictures, your hair was really distracting."

I gritted my teeth to hold back my growl of annoyance. It was wonderful that Mom had agreed to leave me out of her relationship drama, and kind of her to stick up for me with my dad. However, she would always be Mom, and just as I'd have to learn to let go of my father's absences over the years and his behavior recently, I needed not to let Mom's nitpicking get to me if we were going to have a relationship. "Okay. Enjoy yourself. Bye!"

I hung up before she could say anything else that might put a dent in my self-esteem.

# THIRTY-FOUR

## Hallie

As I moved around my bedroom, packing my small overnight suitcase with essentials, I caught glimpses of Chris in my shower because the bathroom door was ajar. Forcing my thoughts elsewhere, for we had no time for shower hanky-panky, I looked away and assessed my bag.

To my everlasting gratitude, Chris had been right about the photos of us online. Interest died down within a few days because a well-known actor was photographed having sex with a married film director in a rooftop pool. Chris and I were promptly forgotten.

Almost two weeks had passed since that awful Monday, and despite my mistrust of his father and Darcy, we'd never felt closer. I'd told him all about hearing from my mom and dad, and he was relieved for me. He didn't seem to hold a grudge against them on my behalf and said he was happy to meet them whenever I was ready.

Chris wanted to meet my parents.

That shouldn't have seemed like such a big deal, considering we were practically living with each other. However, it was. I was excited to introduce him to them. To show them that despite the relationship trauma I'd witnessed between them, I'd chosen a man who was good to me. Our relationship was so far beyond the toxic kind, I felt almost like I was cheating at life. How did I get so lucky to end up with a man like Chris while other people floundered through their whole lives going from one car crash of a relationship to another? It didn't seem fair. But I wouldn't ruin my happiness by constantly looking over my shoulder for something bad that would take it away.

I had a sixtieth-birthday party at the golf club near Richelle's beach house, so Chris was going to drive me, drop me off, and then go to Richelle's. He'd pick me up once the party was over, and we'd spend the rest of the weekend together at the beach house. I was nervous to see Richelle again now that Chris and I were a couple, but he'd assured me his aunt thought it was wonderful we were dating.

"Bikini," I muttered to myself before rummaging through my bottom drawer. I pulled out the pink-and-white polka-dot bikini Mom mentioned last week. I'd thought I looked cute in it until my mom commented on the cellulite on the back of my thighs. We'd taken a spa weekend trip together, my treat, to shake off her depression. She'd complained about everything, including my body.

I'd never fully feel confident about how I looked, but I realized I couldn't let my mom's search for perfection poison my own self-esteem.

I would wear that damn bikini in front of Chris this weekend and do it with confidence!

Well . . . I'd try at least.

The bikini went into the bag, and I zipped it up just as Chris's cell rang on the bedside table.

"Captain, your phone!" I yelled so he could hear me over the shower.

"Who is it?"

I checked. "It doesn't say. It's a two-eight-one area code!"

The screen door on the shower squeaked open. "NASA! Can you take a message?"

What could NASA want? Maybe it was about his book. I hoped that's all it was about. I answered his phone, trying not to fangirl over the fact that I was about to talk to someone from NASA. Taking a deep breath, I answered calmly, "Chris's phone, Hallie speaking."

"Oh, hey . . . uh . . . Hallie Goodman?"

"Um, yes."

"Hi, Hallie, this is Kate from the tech department at JSC. Is Chris available to talk?"

JSC? Ah, Johnson Space Center. And this woman knew who I was? Eek!

Wait . . . Kate?

Wasn't it her email address I'd sent all my videos to? She was the one who forwarded my emails to Chris and made it look like they'd bounced.

"Hallie?"

"Chris is in the shower and asked me to take a message."

"Right. It's nothing that can't wait. Can you just ask him to call me back?"

"Of course, no problem."

"Great . . . and, uh . . . It's awesome how that all worked out between you. You know you could write a book about it."

I flushed, understanding her meaning. "The videos?"

"Yeah. Sorry about that. I didn't mean to deceive you. But when I forwarded him those videos you sent to my email, who would have thought you two would end up together? That's something cosmic if you ask me."

Her words caused butterflies and a pang of longing all at once. Because it felt cosmic to me. Probably because I was deeply in love with Chris. I was pretty sure I was going to tell him I loved him soon. Not this weekend, because we were going to the Hamptons, and when I said those three words to him, I wanted to escape easily if he didn't return the sentiment.

Shoving the worry away, I replied, "All is forgiven. Water under the bridge. I'll let Chris know you called."

## Chris

It had so far been one of the best weekends I could remember.

Hallie had attended her event last night, I'd brought her back to Aunt Richelle's, and we had a late-night supper together. I'd tried returning Kate's call but couldn't get her, so I decided to wait until Monday. That morning we'd gone for breakfast and enjoyed the seaside summer energy created by the tourists and then we'd returned to the house.

I wasn't sure I knew how to spend a lazy day by the pool, but when Hallie walked out of my bathroom in a tiny polka-dot bikini I decided I'd learn.

With Aunt Richelle around, I was forced to keep any amorous thoughts to myself (though I'd deviously started planning ahead for the moment I'd get Hallie alone). We swam, we talked, Hallie and Aunt Richelle did most of the talking because they got along amazingly, and I felt at peace. I wasn't itching to get up and do something, to be productive. I was just enjoying being with two of the most important people in my life.

And I knew I wanted more Sundays like this. With Hallie.

So many more.

Forever.

As much as I loved my aunt, I admit to feeling a rush of relief and anticipation when she announced she was taking Bandit on a lunch date with her friend who also had a dog. I waited until I was sure Richelle was gone.

The whole time my eyes were on Hallie, who flipped through an interior design magazine, her sunglasses perched on the end of her cute little nose.

It was a wonder she couldn't feel the heat of my stare as my gaze traveled down her body, heat—and not from the sun—flushing my skin.

"Hallie."

"Hmm?" She flipped another page.

"Let's go up to the bedroom."

She lifted her head to peer at me over her glasses. "Now?"

"Right now."

"Hell yeah." Hallie jumped off her lounger, throwing her shades and magazine on it.

I laughed at her enthusiasm, scrambled off my lounger, and grabbed her hand to hurry her toward the house.

As I led her over the threshold into the kitchen, I made the mistake of looking back at her. Her cheeks were flushed with anticipation, those beautiful blue eyes of hers hot with desire.

Suddenly it was imperative I make love to her immediately.

The bedroom was too far away.

Needing every inch of her wrapped around me, I turned and lifted Hallie into my arms, her little squeal of surprise making me grin. She instinctively clung to me, and I turned and took three long strides to the kitchen table and settled her on top of it.

Hallie squeezed her inner thighs against my hips, eyes wide. "Here?"

"I can't wait," I confessed, sliding my hand around her to cup her nape, to pull her up into my demanding kiss. She grasped on to me, her fingertips biting into my upper arms as I kissed her hard, deep. Needing to touch her everywhere, I caressed her body, frustrated even by the tiny scraps of her bikini that kept me from her bare skin.

Her moan vibrated in my mouth, making me feel more desperate.

Fuck, would this feeling ever go away?

How could I want her more and more as time went on? Cupping her breasts in my hands, massaging them through the thin damp fabric of her bikini, I rocked into her body, impatient to be inside her.

I reluctantly pulled away, panting against her now swollen lips as I pulled a condom out of my swim shorts before shucking them off to roll it on. The whole time I watched Hallie's expression, the way her lust-filled gaze turned incredulous. "You had a condom in your swim shorts?"

I grinned unrepentantly. "I slipped it in when I saw you walk out of the bathroom in that bikini."

Hallie giggled, the joyous sound hitting me in the chest like a deep ache. God, I was addicted to this woman. I reached for her mouth, wanting to capture the sound, as I curled my fingers around her bikini bottoms. Hallie arched her hips up, helping me to remove them, and they dropped to the floor by my shorts.

Then I checked her readiness, fingers searching gently. "*Mi cielo,*" I murmured thickly against her mouth before kissing her, licking at her tongue, desperate to deepen the kiss until she was overwhelmed with need.

Hallie drew me deeper between her legs, her fingers almost bruising on my back. She arched against me again, rubbing against me, beckoning me inside.

I gripped her by the thighs and pushed in.

*"Mi cielo, mi cielo,"* I murmured mindlessly as her heat surrounded me.

Hallie gasped, her inner thighs drawing up tight against my hips. I watched her, memorizing every feature, every expression, every shade of blue in her eyes as I thrust into her.

Her lips parted on a cry as I slipped my hand between our bodies and thumbed the bundle of nerves at her apex. Her head fell back, and I increased pressure as I circled her, glorying in the bite of her fingernails on my back, on the restless shifting of her hips as she reached for release.

"Fuck, you're so beautiful," I panted.

Hallie stiffened with a cry, and then she was throbbing in pulsing waves around me.

Anchoring her hips in my hands again, I lost myself in her. Hard, deep drives made Hallie cry out, prolonging her pleasure.

My climax hit with such force, my vision blurred as she took everything I had to give.

Everything.

Emotion made my heart race as I helped her off the table, as I wiped it down out of respect for my aunt, and then led Hallie upstairs to clean up in the shower. I gestured for her to go in first and followed her in.

Hallie turned under the spray as she smoothed her hair back off her face. She smiled softly at me, knowingly, her blue eyes filled with an expression that I was absolutely certain matched the feeling I could no longer deny.

I pulled her into me, sliding my hands around her small waist, needing to touch her. My mouth was suddenly dry, my pulse throbbed in my neck.

"I love you." My words were hoarse, gruff with the depth of the emotion. "I am so in love with you."

Tears brightened Hallie's eyes as she sank into me. "I love you too. So much."

Though I'd suspected it was mutual, I buried my face in her neck with relief, my arms tightening around her as we embraced. Water spilled over our heads and bodies, but we didn't move.

We just held each other, breathed each other in, as we tried to process the utter magnitude of our feelings.

# THIRTY-FIVE

## Chris

I have to go to work," Hallie moaned as I trailed kisses down her throat the next morning. "You are insatiable."

"I'm in love," I muttered, smiling against her skin.

"Aw, how am I supposed to get out of bed now?" she complained, rolling me onto my back. "You can't say that when I need to leave. It makes me want to stay."

I chuckled, trying to pull her over me, but she tensed, so I stopped.

"I mean it." Hallie pressed a quick kiss to my lips. "I can't be late."

Reluctantly I released her. Since we'd said we loved each other yesterday, I had been unable to stop touching her. It was a compulsion. But I vowed to reel it in. "I need to get back to my apartment and write too."

"Good. Now stay in bed. Do not come into that bathroom while I'm getting ready because you will easily convince me to indulge in shenanigans."

My body shook with amusement. "Why would you admit that? That just makes me want to commence shenanigans."

"I'm locking the door!" Hallie yelled, laughter in her voice as she did in fact hurry into the bathroom and lock the door behind her.

"You actually locked the door."

"I have no willpower with you!" she complained behind it.

Resting my hands behind my head, I couldn't help but feel smug about that.

I'd barely let myself into my apartment just over an hour later when my cell rang. It was another Houston number.

Remembering Kate's call from Saturday, I hurried to answer as I moved into the kitchen to make a coffee.

"Chris, it's Tom."

My commander's voice surprised me because I had him saved on my phone as a contact. "You're not calling from your cell."

"Calling from the office. Look, NASA is looking at their pool of active astronauts for someone who might be interested in working at JSC as a mission specialist. I want to recommend you for the job, and I will, if you think it's a position you might be interested in."

Shock rooted me to the spot. "Mission specialist?"

"Yes. What do you think?"

My first thought was yes, I was interested. Rejoining a team at NASA definitely appealed to me.

A gut instinctual thought.

But it was immediately followed by the thought of Hallie.

In fact it drowned that yes out like a tidal wave.

I was happy.

Finally happy, and she was the entire reason.

And Hallie was happy here in New York. She was amazing at her job, so talented, and doing great things. Work that satisfied her. Genuinely. How many people could say that about their work?

I could see her running her own company one day.

And I was there in that vision.

With her in New York.

What was *I* doing though?

What kind of work would I do that was productive and benefited people? What was my contribution? As mission specialist at NASA, I'd be working on missions to space that would not only push space exploration forward but also progress here on Earth.

Mission specialist.

Holy shit.

I closed my eyes and saw Hallie's face as I told her I loved her this morning.

"Chris? You there?"

"When do you need an answer?"

Tom replied, "I can give you a few weeks."

A few weeks.

Feeling more than a little agitated, I gruffly thanked him and told him I'd be in touch.

As soon as I hung up, my stomach knotted.

I couldn't ask Hallie to give up everything she'd worked for and move to Houston.

No way.

She'd worked too hard for me to ask her to leave her job behind.

That left long distance, and the thought of only seeing her now and then made me feel like hell.

So did I say no to the job offer? Give up the chance of doing something worthwhile and put Hallie's career first?

I didn't know what the right thing to do was.

I just knew I did not want to lose Hallie Goodman now that I'd miraculously found her.

# THIRTY-SIX

## Hallie

The TV flickered in the dark of my apartment, casting light over Chris as we watched the movie he'd chosen. We took turns picking a film for what I'd dubbed our Monday movie nights, and it was his choice that night. He'd distractedly chosen a dystopian horror movie starring Sandra Bullock. It had been a big deal a few years ago, but I'd been too nervous to watch it on my own.

Now I wasn't even paying attention to it.

It had been over a week since we'd returned from the Hamptons, and despite telling each other we loved each other, I felt like Chris had been a million miles away since last Monday. He'd seemed fine in the Hamptons. That first night we'd snuggled in bed, and we'd talked for hours about our plans for the future before drifting to sleep.

Then the next morning he could barely keep his hands off me, and everything was great when I left for work.

But he'd been strange at my apartment that night. Preoccupied.

And the next morning, I'd woken up alone. That wasn't surprising, because sometimes Chris did wake up early for his morning run. What was weird was that he texted me to say he'd gone straight to his apartment and would see me that night.

I tried not to overanalyze it. But he'd been distant ever since.

It was like he was here, but he wasn't.

And he hadn't touched me beyond a peck on the cheek or lips.

Yes, I'd had my period for much of the week, and then I was swamped at the weekend with a wedding rehearsal and wedding and subsequently a little too tired for sex. But Chris didn't even attempt to seduce me, and since I'd gotten home from work tonight, I'd dropped a million hints that I wanted him to. Hints my usually intelligent spaceman wasn't picking up on at all. I'd squeezed past him in the kitchen, brushing my breasts against his back, when there was two feet of space for me to walk in.

Nothing.

I'd deliberately dropped a spoon (and then my phone) so I could bend over in my tight dress because that had worked without me even trying in the past.

Nothing!

To say I was beyond confused at this point was an understatement. How could he go from telling me he loved me to being this distant almost immediately afterward?

Was he second-guessing his own feelings? Or was something else at play?

The mystery of it all was driving me nuts. If something didn't change soon, I was calling him on it.

Watching Chris, I could see he wasn't paying attention to the movie at all because his gaze was unfocused, like his thoughts were somewhere outside of this apartment. A few days ago, I tried to ask him about his quietness, but he told me he was just preoccupied now that he'd signed with Scott Rose. They were polishing his book proposal together, and that filled up most of his days right now. Somehow, though, despite the sensitivity of the subject of his father and their Latino heritage in the book, I didn't believe him when he said that was the cause of his preoccupation. He couldn't meet my eyes when he said it, which was out of character for Chris. I felt awful because I'd promised him I trusted him.

"I'm going to *bed*," I announced. Hint, hint.

Chris flicked me a distracted smile. "I'm going to finish watching this."

We were there already? A mere summer of loving, and that was it?

"I'm not really that tired tonight," I tried to be more obvious.

"Then stay and watch the rest of the film."

I glowered at him and pushed up off the couch. "Maybe I'll just read before bed." I lowered my voice to a mutter, "Maybe erotica, since no one else is getting me off tonight."

"Huh? What?"

I waved him off, walking away. "Night. Don't worry about me."

"Okay, night."

Usually I slept in one of Chris's tees, but I snagged a nightie out of my drawer instead. I chose a silk-and-lace one that left little to the imagination. I put my hands on my hips and stared dazedly at my wall as hurt echoed in pang after pang in my chest.

Was I being unreasonable to expect our sex life to still be exciting this early into our relationship? I didn't think so.

Was I being unreasonable to assume my boyfriend and I should be closer than ever after declaring our love instead of feeling like he was in space and I was on Earth?

"What are you doing?"

Startled, I jumped at the sound of Chris's voice at my back. Pivoting, I caught Chris's expression change from bemusement to appreciation as his gaze lowered down my body in my sexy nightie.

*Oh, hello, there he is.*

"Is that new?"

Crossing my arms over my chest, I huffed. "So this is what it takes to not be invisible to my boyfriend."

His gaze returned to mine. "What's going on?"

I stared at him, feeling an overwhelming amount of frustration and desire. "What's been going on with you, Chris? You've been distant with me ever since we said I love you. Did we move too fast?"

His face slackened with surprise, and he strode toward me to pull me into his arms. I couldn't quite relax into him as my palms rested on his hard chest. "No," he said, searching my gaze. "Hallie, no. I meant it when I said I love you. I'm just . . . I am preoccupied with the book and worrying about my future, but I'm sorry if that's come off as me being distant. I don't want to make you feel that way."

His hands smoothed over my back, and I shivered at his touch. I missed him.

"Forgive me?"

Relief filled me, and I curled my arms around his shoulders. "Of course. But you can talk to me about anything. If you need to talk through your worries about the future, about your plans, I want to be here for you."

"I know." He brushed his mouth over mine, his voice gruff now. "And we will. But first I have to make up for my obvious neglect."

I grinned between his kisses. "Well, my subtle hints finally got you, huh?"

Chris chuckled, nudging me toward the bed. "You know what's an excellent hint?"

"Hmm?"

"Saying the words 'Chris, I want to have sex with you tonight.'"

Laughing, I nodded. "I will consider that in the future."

"And heads up: my answer to that will always be to get you naked as fast as possible."

My amusement squeaked to a halt as Chris suddenly turned me in his arms so my back pressed to his chest. He reached for the hem of my nightie, and I lifted my arms above my head as he removed it. Chris gripped my hips, gently pulling me back against him so I could feel the rigid length of his arousal pushing against his jeans. My breathing grew shallow as goose bumps rose all over me at the exciting contrast of my nakedness against his fully clothed body. My nipples tightened, and I let out a little gasp as he rubbed against my bottom.

He swept my hair off to one side, and his hot lips brushed my ear. "Do you doubt I need you, that I want you?"

I shook my head, shivering in anticipation as he trailed light kisses down my neck. Chris smoothed his hands around my waist, caressing my stomach as he traveled upward. Then he cupped my breasts and squeezed.

I moaned, resting my head against his shoulder as I arched into his touch. Ripples of desire quivered low in my belly as he played with my breasts, sculpting and kneading them, stroking and pinching my nipples into hard buds. His name fell from my lips in breathless whispers, while his hips undulated against my ass.

"Kiss me," he growled in my ear.

I turned my head at Chris's demand, and his lips found mine. I opened my mouth, inviting him inside. He kissed me deeply, hungrily, but like we had all the time in the world to indulge in the taste of each other. As we kissed, he released my right breast to coast his hand down my stomach and between my legs. At the first touch on my clit, I broke the kiss, gripping his thigh to hold on as he played with me.

"Chris," I whimpered, my hips moving against his touch.

Our eyes held as my desire built to a crescendo, the mix of love and lust in his expression pushing me quickly toward climax. The tension shattered in me, and I cried out, shuddering, my stomach trembling and my knees threatening to give way.

Chris lifted me into his arms and carried me to the bed to brace himself over me. His kisses were rougher now, more desperate. My lips were swollen by the time he released them to scatter kisses down my throat and over my chest.

My thighs tightened against his hips, the scratch of denim strangely erotic against my naked skin, when his lips closed around my nipple. He sucked hard, a pleasurable pain rushing through me as he moved against me.

"Chris," I panted. "Come inside me."

He looked up, his features granite with need. "Not yet."

Moving down my body, Chris's lips followed an invisible path toward my clit. I melted into the mattress in anticipation as he nuzzled his mouth between my thighs. He licked at me, pressed his tongue down on my clit, sucked it, and when his fingers joined the party, sensation exploded through me.

"Oh God!" I arched back on the bed, my inner thighs trembling.

That coil of tension low, deep inside was unfurling, pulling apart until it grew tauter and tauter and taut—

"Chris!" My body tensed for a second, and then I shuddered in release against his mouth.

Panting for breath, I came down from my climax only to feel a surge of desperate want. Despite the exceptional orgasm, I needed more from him. Our eyes met as he stroked my quivering stomach.

"Please."

He nodded, the muscle in his jaw flexing as he pushed off the bed and undressed. I devoured the sight of him, his strong, beautiful body that protected an even more beautiful soul, and I felt a wave of overwhelming love rock through me. Eyes never leaving mine, he pulled a condom from the wallet that was in the back pocket of his jeans.

Ready for me, Chris put a knee to the bed, his arousal throbbing between his legs. His hands curled behind my knees, and I let out a little laugh as he pulled me toward him. Thighs gripped in his strong hands, Chris held me open to him and pushed inside me, his teeth clenching as he glided slowly through my tightness.

I relaxed into him, my spine melting into the bed, and suddenly I was overwhelmingly filled with him. We found a slow, sexy rhythm, and I watched him watch me. When his gaze dropped to where we met, and he watched himself move inside of me, I gasped with need—it was the sexiest thing I'd ever seen. Chris's chest moved up and down in shallow breaths as his excitement increased. Then his grip on my legs tightened, and he braced on his knees to drive into me faster, harder, his thumb finding my clit at the same time.

"I love you," he gasped, eyes fixed on mine. "I love every inch of you, Hallie."

I came before he even said my name.

"Fuck!" Chris fell over me, his forehead pressed to my shoulder, and tensed with his release seconds before he shook through it.

"I love you too." I whispered as I caressed his sweat-dampened back. "I love you so much."

Chris lifted his head to meet my gaze. Adoration lit his eyes, and I wrapped my legs around his hips, not wanting to lose him or that look on his face. "*Mi cielo*," he murmured, caressing my cheek.

It was a perfect moment.

Until his cell phone rang loudly in the living room.

"Ignore it." He kissed me.

As his mouth worked its way down my neck to my chest again, the phone stopped ringing.

Then started up again.

Chris groaned, resting his forehead against my stomach.

I sighed heavily. "Someone clearly wants you. You better answer it."

Grumbling, he kissed my stomach before rolling off me. "Be right back."

As satisfied as a cat lazing in a sunspot, I watched his fine naked ass walk out of my bedroom to retrieve his phone.

A few seconds later, he returned, phone in hand, frowning at it.

"Who is it?"

His wary look alerted me. Before he could reply, the phone rang again. "It's Darcy."

Ignoring the niggle of unease her name produced, I forced myself to be mature about it. "Well, she's called three times, so you better pick up."

That Chris looked genuinely put out that our moment had been interrupted eased my feelings of less than attractive possessiveness.

"Darce, hey." He answered as he crawled back into bed with me and pulled me into his arms. I felt his arm tense around me. "Whoa, okay, slow down."

Her voice was loud through his phone, her unintelligible words sounding fast and slightly hysterical. Concern filled me as I watched Chris's expression.

"Darce, are you drunk?"

*Uh-oh.*

"Okay, where are you? . . . Right . . . Stay there. . . . No, stay,

I'm coming to get you. . . . Yeah, stay there. I'll be there soon." He hung up and fell back against the pillows. "Fuck!"

"What's going on?"

"They broke up. Her and Matthias. She's wasted and suddenly panicked because she's so wasted and by herself at some bar in the city."

I tried not to be irritated that she'd called Chris and focused on my disbelief that she and Matthias had broken up. "But they seemed so in love." Every time I'd met with them, they were holding hands and staring adoringly into each other's eyes.

The wedding!

Oh my God, the wedding.

This would be all over the papers.

Poor Darcy.

"How did this happen?"

Chris pushed up off the bed and dressed. When he looked at me, his gaze darted down my naked body, and he started muttering curse words under his breath again.

"Chris?"

His eyes moved from my breasts to my face. "Their timing is the worst."

"So this just came out of nowhere?"

"No." He shrugged on his T-shirt. "Darcy's been calling these past few weeks because their relationship has been rocky."

Chris really was her confidant now? I swallowed down my irritation because I wasn't the one whose relationship had just imploded. "I hope she's okay. Will you text me when you find her?"

Chris's expression softened as he leaned down to kiss me. "Have I told you lately that I love you?"

"Yes. And it was very climactic."

He chuckled and pressed another kiss or three to my lips.

"Right. I need to go." He reluctantly straightened but winced in regret when he looked at me again. "Please be naked when I get back."

"You got it."

Then, a minute later, he was gone. To rescue his ex-girlfriend.

"I'm okay with that," I announced loudly and somewhat aggressively to my room. "I'm more than okay with that." Instead of dwelling, I distracted myself with optimistic thoughts of Matthias and Darcy getting back together. For their sake and mine.

And for the sake of the deposit they'd put down on the Blenheim estate.

But mostly for their sake.

Chris loved me.

I had zero to worry about.

# THIRTY-SEVEN

## Chris

Scott Rose <SRose@Roselit.com>
To: Christopher_ortiz@bmail.com

Hi Chris,

I've sent the book proposal to the editors we discussed. Now we just sit tight and see what offers come in. I'll call you as soon as I know more.

All best,
Scott

I reread Scott's email, trying to take heart in his optimism that offers would definitely come in for the book. Logically, I knew he was probably right. One, he understood the publishing industry better than I did, and two, I wouldn't be the first astronaut to have his autobiography published.

That didn't mean I wasn't nervous. I'd decided after all to include everything. Including my thoughts about being a trailblazer who felt an aching disconnection to his cultural heritage. I just hoped that by the time the book released, things would be in a place with my father where we could weather the fact that I'd put personal details like that in the book.

Those were *my* words on the page. What if these editors thought I was boring or a terrible writer?

It was an unusual sensation for me to feel so much uncertainty about something I'd worked hard on.

I didn't like it.

My cell beeped, drawing my focus. I was almost thankful until I saw it was a text from Tom.

**Chris, just checking in. Hope to hear from you soon. We have to choose someone in two weeks.**

Shit.

My hands shook a little as I texted back.

I'm interested, but there are outside factors to consider. I promise I'll let you know before the two weeks are up. I appreciate this offer more than I can say.

"Fuck." I threw my phone on the couch and scrubbed a hand over my face.

The only person I'd told about the job offer was Aunt Richelle. She'd confused me even more by telling me I needed to make a choice for myself and no one else. I knew she wasn't wrong about that. Logically I knew that. But I couldn't imagine life without Hallie, so she was a huge factor. End of story. Never mind the fact that I wasn't even sure I wanted the job. Which was why I hadn't told Hallie yet, because I felt like throwing that kind of wrench in our works should only be done when I was certain the job was something I really wanted. In not telling her for that reason, I was on my own to ponder the consequences if I took the job. If I decided I did, then we'd talk about how we'd make that work for us both. And by that I meant in a way that didn't disrupt Hallie's career or the life she wanted in the city she wanted.

"Fuck," I repeated.

I knew there were event companies in Houston. It wasn't the same as New York though, and her parents were here, and she was just starting to have a better relationship with them. In fact, I was meeting her parents separately for the first time this coming weekend.

We'd never discussed whether Hallie wanted to stay anywhere other than New York. She wanted to travel, but that wasn't the same thing. Was she tied to this place too much to live somewhere else for a few years? Maybe more than a few years?

As for traveling, if I took this job at NASA, I couldn't take Hallie on the summer backpacking trip we were planning next year. The thought of disappointing her sat like a brick in my gut. Then again, she might see starting over in a new city, in a new state, as an adventure.

The only way to know was to talk to her, and to talk to her, I had to decide about whether I wanted this job.

My apartment buzzer sounded, and I got up to answer it. My head pounded with all the overthinking. "Yeah?" I asked.

"It's your father."

Surprised, I pressed the button to let him into the building and then unlocked my apartment door to wait for him. What the hell was my dad doing here? We'd spoken on the phone once since our confrontation in his office, and it had been as friendly as a conversation with my father could be. It wasn't a lot, but it was something. I had to admit that the job offer was only part of my preoccupation. Learning about my grandparents' tragic demise naturally impacted me. I wanted to know more. Though I already knew I wouldn't learn anything from my father just yet. I hoped that with time, we could work our way up to that.

My father's footsteps echoed up the stairs, and then he appeared, dressed in his custom three-piece suit. "You need an elevator."

"Afternoon to you too," I replied dryly, stepping aside to let him into the apartment.

He nodded at me as he passed, and I studied him as he took in my new place. The sight of a pair of Hallie's high heels discarded near the coffee table seemed to arrest him for a moment. After a second or two, he flicked me a look. "It's not Midtown East."

I sighed, looking around the place. "No, it's not. But it's home for now."

"For now?"

"What are you doing here?" I evaded. "Coffee?"

"I came to ask a favor, and no, thanks. I have a meeting I need to get to."

He always did. "What favor?"

"I, uh, I know it's a little last minute, but I wasn't sure . . ." My father trailed off, his expression uneasy.

I'd never seen him so uncertain, which piqued my curiosity beyond measure. "What is it?"

"Well, there's this event. In my honor. An award for philanthropy."

My father was one of life's contradictions. He made a shit ton of money, he was ruthless, a crappy father, pretty sure he was a shitty husband, and yet not only had he donated millions to charities over the years, but he'd set up a foundation that helped children in the foster system seek higher education.

Admittedly, I often let myself forget about his philanthropy because the actions were so incongruous with the man I knew.

Yet after our enlightening discussion about my grandparents, and my realization he wasn't ashamed of his roots but clearly heartbroken by anything that reminded him of them, I wondered if I knew my father at all and if anyone would ever really know him.

I wasn't quite ready to give up trying. "That's great. Congratulations."

"Yes, well, I wondered if you might attend with me. I could take a date, but I think you being there would be better."

Had my father just offered an olive branch?

Attempting not to stare in disbelief at him, I forced a neutral expression on my face. "I'd be happy to."

My father's shoulders seemed to drop as if relieved. "Good. That's good. It's this Saturday night. My driver will pick you up around seven thirty."

Shit. I was supposed to have dinner with Hallie's dad on Saturday night. We were attending lunch with her mom on Sunday.

But my father had just requested my attendance, not out of some need to control me or make himself look good. He wanted me there. And he might never reach out like this again if I rejected him. "I'll be ready. Tux?"

"Of course. Good." He nodded, his gaze darting back to Hallie's shoes. "I do want to meet your young lady on better terms, but this event doesn't seem like the right place. I don't want her thinking I'm trying to prove I'm something I'm not."

"I get it. We'll do dinner, just the three of us, some other time. If Hallie is ready to."

"Right." My father cleared his throat. "I better get going."

When I closed the door behind him, I couldn't help but smile a little.

For a few minutes, my father had seemed like a real person for the first time in as long as I could remember.

I felt stupid snapping a photo of myself in a tux, but I'd promised Hallie I'd send her one since she was in New Jersey with her dad. I also hadn't posted to Instagram in a while, so I sent it to Hallie before I posted it to social media. Ignoring the slight chafing feeling I felt as I posted the photo, my mood lifted when I received Hallie's response.

**Oh my God, you better still be wearing this when I get home.**

There was so much to love about her text.

**You get that means we're having sex while you're still in that tux?**

I laughed and quickly texted back.

Despite your subtlety, I got it.

**Well, you're not good with hints, and you did tell me to be obvious.**

I did. And you were.

Good. Because I cannot say enough how hot I am for you in this tux.

I have to meet my father in five minutes.

So I'm putting the brakes on this conversation. Until tonight.

There will be no conversation tonight. Only me, you, that tux, and multiple orgasms.

Are you with your dad right now?

Ugh, no, he's in the restroom.

So as soon as he gets back, you'll stop sexting me?

Oh, you think this is sexting? Cute.

I'm pretty sure this is sexting.

No it's not, and to prove it to you, I plan on sending salacious text messages to you all night.

That would be highly inappropriate.

Exactly ;)

The beep of a horn drew my head up from my phone, and I realized I was grinning like a moron. I quickly sent her a text that my father had arrived and stuffed my phone into the inside pocket of my tux. Feeling it vibrate against my chest, I smirked, wondering what salacious text message I'd just received.

My father's driver stood by the passenger door of the town car.

"Ivan." I nodded in greeting.

"Captain Ortiz." He gave me a respectful nod before opening the door for me.

"Ivan, how many times do I have to ask you to call me Chris?"

He just gave me a nonanswer of a smile, so I thanked him and slipped inside. My father sat on the opposite bench, facing backward toward me. "For eternity," he answered for Ivan. "Good man, Ivan. Very professional."

"I'm not in the air force anymore." I reminded him.

"You made captain in four years and served your country well. It's your legal right to be addressed by your rank."

I sighed but didn't respond. "So where is your event held?"

"The Lower East Side."

"Do you have your speech memorized?" There was always a speech at these things.

My father nodded, his gaze sharp on my face. "Ms. Goodman didn't mind that we did not invite her?"

I frowned at his word choice. "Well, I explained my father wanted me to come as his date, and she agreed she didn't want to be a third wheel."

He rolled his eyes and sighed heavily. "Please refrain from calling yourself my date for the rest of the evening."

"No problem. And yes," I answered seriously. "Hallie has plans with her own father tonight, so it's fine." She'd been extremely understanding, in fact, and agreed this was an important moment between me and my father. I just hoped her dad was just as understanding. It wasn't the best impression, canceling on our first dinner together.

"How is your book coming along?"

"It's coming," I evaded.

"I heard NASA reached out to you about a position in Houston."

Shocked, I narrowed my gaze. "How did you hear about that?"

My father shrugged. "You know I have eyes and ears everywhere."

"Isn't that comforting."

His lips pinched together at my sarcasm. "Must you be defensive about everything? I only want to know what's happening in your life."

He was right. I couldn't fall back into old habits with him if I wanted us to have a better relationship. That didn't mean I fully trusted him, however. "I'm thinking about their offer. That's all I can say right now."

"I hope Ms. Goodman isn't the reason you haven't—"

"Stop." I said it firmly but gently. "Not tonight. Please."

My father agreed with a pinch-lipped nod, and we devolved into far less dangerous small talk.

It surprised me to see the media gathered outside the building on the Lower East Side while powerful people and some famous faces walked a short red carpet up to the entrance of the event.

"This is a bigger deal than you made out," I murmured, peering out of the tinted window.

"The event might also be tied to a feature on the company in *Mogul Magazine.* We ranked in the top for best corporate reputation."

That did shock me.

My father smirked. "I'm not quite the ruthless bastard you think I am. At least, I've been trying for the last few years not to be. We're turning the company around and attempting to do better."

Floored, I shook my head. "I didn't know." I hadn't paid attention. "That's great. I think that's great."

"When your son risks his life for the good of his country, it makes a man reevaluate his life."

Wow.

I didn't know what to say to that.

It completely bowled me over that my father said that, let alone thought it.

"Right, let's get out there." He brushed over it like it wasn't momentous and stepped outside to flashing camera bulbs as Ivan opened the door.

Still reeling, I took a minute before following him out.

"Christopher! Christopher, can you look this way! Christopher!"

I blinked against the lights and the cacophony of shouts from the journalists as my father put his arm around me and posed for their photographs. Forcing a smile on my face, I relaxed into it, having done this a few times in the past as Darcy's date at events like this.

"Oh, there's Darcy," I heard my father say, and then seconds later he greeted her in front of the press with a fatherly kiss on each of her cheeks. She looked statuesque and beautiful in her gold evening gown. It was a stark contrast to the drunken mess I'd found her in last weekend when I'd collected her from the bar in the Bowery.

Her gaze turned to me, and she held open her arms, her smile widening. "Chris!"

I accepted her embrace, ignoring the clamoring shouts of the paps behind us. "What are you doing here?" I asked in her ear.

"I was invited," she said, as if it were obvious. "You look wonderful." She smoothed a hand down my tux and then turned toward the cameras. "Smile, darling, and give them what they want so we can get inside, out of this hullabaloo."

I gave the press a few shots, and then gently nudged Darcy toward the entrance. My father had already disappeared into the building. "Let's get inside. You look better?" I framed it as a question.

She beamed at me. "I actually feel like an enormous weight has been lifted off my shoulders. Did Hallie tell you what a lifesaver she's been canceling everything?"

I knew Darcy well enough to know that her family wasn't good at showing weakness or vulnerability. There was no way in hell she was as okay with her breakup as she pretended, but I didn't press her. "Hallie didn't say. She's very protective of her clients' privacy, even with me."

"Isn't she a sweetheart? She couldn't come tonight?"

I shrugged. "It didn't seem like the best place to . . . introduce her to my father." I hadn't told Darcy about his treatment of Hallie. It was nobody's business but our own.

"I understand." She slipped her arm through mine and smiled. "Then I guess that means you can keep me company tonight. It's nice to have a friendly face here. This is my first big event since the breakup." Her voice shook, betraying her nerves.

"Hey, you're doing great."

"Thanks. For everything. I'm glad you're here." She gestured ahead of us. "Shall we?"

There was a slight niggle in the back of my mind that Hallie might not understand our accompanying each other tonight, considering I was supposed to be here for my dad, not Darcy. But there was a panicked look in her eyes, and I decided Hallie would understand Darcy needing some support. And I wouldn't keep it from her because that would just make her think there was something to hide.

Plus, Hallie had been great and supportive about Darcy last weekend. She'd get it.

She was wonderful like that.

# THIRTY-EIGHT

## Hallie

I want to kill him," I growled at Althea as I glared at my computer screen. "I'm right to feel this way, right? I'm not being a jealous girlfriend."

"Oh, you're being a jealous girlfriend. But you also are so within your right to want to kill him for this."

My heart pounded at Althea's confirmation. What Chris had done here *was* shitty and wrong. I'd barely left the apartment this morning when my phone buzzed with a text from Althea with a link to an article in the same gossip rag that posted the photos of Chris and me in Central Park.

Except this time, their speculation wasn't over me and Chris. It was over him and Darcy.

"Nothing is going on here, right?" Althea laid a comforting hand on my shoulder.

As furious as I was with Chris for lying to me about this event and the reason I couldn't come, I knew in my gut that his duplicity wasn't about cheating. Chris wasn't a cheater. I refused to believe he had that level of disloyalty in him after everything we'd talked about.

"Not overtly," I answered, holding back the sting of tears. "He told me she was at the event, that they spent some time together, but this looks like more than that, right?"

"Maybe. Maybe not. The papers will say anything."

Splashed across several New York gossip rags this morning were photographs of Chris and Darcy at his father's event on Saturday night. Headlines speculated Darcy had broken her engagement off for Chris and the two of them were back together. An anonymous source said they'd been spending lots of time together these past few weeks and that his relationship with me had just been a casual thing. Boy, did that burn, even if it was bullshit.

That Darcy had one arm draped around Chris's shoulder and her other hand resting intimately on his stomach, while his hand sat low on her spine didn't help. Their whole body language was way too cozy for my liking. I could be forgiven for thinking they'd just met on the red carpet, but there was also a photo from inside the event, and Darcy was sitting next to Chris at a table I knew as a planner would be assigned.

Like she was his date.

Was I not good enough to attend a fancy charity award ceremony?

While he'd been much more present with me lately, I thought of his preoccupied behavior before that and how his excuse that it was because of his book never really sat right.

My old insecurities started eating away at me.

"Hallie?"

I blinked owlishly up at my friend. "The papers are wrong. At least . . . they're premature."

Althea bit out a curse.

"It's okay." I reached for her hand and squeezed it. "Let's not jump to conclusions until I talk to him. Okay, until I yell at him and then talk to him."

By the time I got off the subway that evening, I'd worked myself into quite a furor. Chris hadn't called all day, even though he must have been alerted to the online attention. I had six missed calls from my mom, but nothing from my boyfriend! That he was avoiding me panicked me into thinking maybe the gossip wasn't far from the truth. I mean, Chris and Darcy had certainly looked the part of a couple.

Everyone and their grandmother seemed to think so.

It was a surprise then to find Chris in my apartment, typing away on my laptop. He lifted his head, wearing the reading glasses that made him even sexier somehow, and grinned in greeting. "Hey, gorgeous." He got up from the couch, removing the glasses. "How has your day been?"

Because I was a masochist, I'd bought a physical copy of one of the more well-known papers. I smacked it against his chest. "You tell me!"

Chris's eyebrows practically hit his hairline as he caught the paper. "What the . . ."

"Why didn't you call me about this?" I slammed my purse down on my kitchen counter before opening the cupboard that housed my wineglasses. "Something to hide?"

"I didn't call because I still can't find my phone. I think I might have left it at your mom's."

I thought of those six missed calls. Maybe they were about Chris's phone and not the articles. Or probably both. We'd had lunch with her yesterday and she'd been great. She made very few nitpicky comments about me and actually seemed to be protective of me, almost interrogating Chris. I'd expected her to be all over him and make me feel like he was too good for me. Afterward, I'd felt bad for thinking that of her because she'd been perfectly nice. That's why I hadn't answered her calls, because I didn't want her to say something to me like, *Well, I didn't want to say it, but this was to be expected.*

"Oh."

"Yeah, oh. Why are you so pi— Ah, I see."

Grabbing a bottle of wine, I tried not to slam it and the glass down on the counter as I faced him. He scowled at the half-page article on him and Darcy. The pulse in my neck throbbed, and my palms were clammy as I tried to open my bottle of wine.

Chris looked over at me. "You're upset about this? Hallie, I told you Darcy was there, and you know these New York gossip rags print bullshit."

"Oh, you think I'm upset they're insinuating you're cheating on me?"

He shrugged, baffled.

Which just pissed me off even more.

"Chris, I know you wouldn't cheat on me." I rounded the counter, ignoring the relief that flickered across his face. "But you clearly lied about why I couldn't attend this event. You blew off meeting my dad for this! Darcy wasn't just there. You were her date. She's at your table, and she was clinging all over you."

Anger darkened Chris's features as he threw the paper aside. "I did not lie to you. I didn't know she'd be there, and we met outside and took some photos for the press because apparently that's what happens at these events. And she wasn't sitting next to me as my date. She's pictured in my father's seat because he was barely in it all night, schmoozing the room, so we hung out. Just like I told you, it was her first appearance in public since the breakup. I was just being a friend, having a care for her feelings."

Ugly resentment filled me. "And it never crossed your mind that being pictured together like this might cause gossip?"

"Of course it crossed my mind, but it's not like it's true."

I gaped at him. "I have been fielding texts and social media notifications and calls all day offering me commiserations."

Chris blanched.

"So when you were standing there with your arms around another woman, your ex-girlfriend, and she's not only got her arms around you but her hand on your fucking stomach, it didn't occur to you, this might hurt Hallie? Or were you too busy caring for another woman's feelings to think about mine?" I held back the tears that shook my voice because I refused to let him see me cry over this.

My so-called boyfriend squeezed his eyes closed as if he were in pain. When he opened them, they were heavy with remorse. "Fuck. Hallie . . . I'm sorry. I really wasn't thinking. I'm so sorry." He crossed the room to pull me into his arms, and while I let him, I didn't return his embrace. There was stubble on his cheeks, and it scratched as he covered my face and mouth in kisses. "Please forgive me for being an inconsiderate asshole?"

It was hard to let go of the fury and resentment that had taken over my body all day, but as he murmured apologies repeatedly, I began to slowly melt, calming myself down.

I didn't want to fight with Chris.

It was the worst feeling in the world.

And as much as the still simmering hurt inside me made me want to yell at him some more, I read the truth in his eyes, and I believed him. "Okay," I whispered against his mouth. "I forgive you."

He clasped my face in his hands, his gaze intense and heated. "I would never want you to get hurt like this. And you're right. Another woman shouldn't have her arms around me like that, because I wouldn't like it if the situation were reversed. There was nothing in it, just two friends who are comfortable with each other, but I won't let it happen again. I promise. But I also caught the comment about me lying." Frustration tightened Chris's features. "I promised I never would again, and I meant it."

I sank into him with a weary sigh. "You're right. All the texts and calls and pitying messed with my head today."

"Shit." Chris hauled me against his chest, hugging me tightly. "I'm so sorry." He kissed my temple. "Hey, let's go somewhere really public and have sex there. That'll put an end to the speculation."

I giggled, so relieved I could cry. "Ooh, what about the Met?"

"Think it's been done before," he joked.

Laughing, I buried my head deeper against his chest. Breathing him in, I allowed myself to let go of all the poison that had slipped into my emotions today. "I just get scared about us," I admitted softly. "About losing you. I like you a lot, you know."

His biceps flexed reflexively around me. "You love me," he corrected. "And I love you. Everything is . . . everything is heightened right now. But we'll settle into the feelings."

I smiled at his usual wisdom and decided it was too reassuring not to believe him.

If only love were really that simple.

# THIRTY-NINE

## Chris

My father stood up from the table in the hotel restaurant, and I marveled when he greeted me with, "It's good to see you, son."

"You too." I tried not to look as surprised as I felt.

First the award ceremony and now lunch. He'd also called me twice since the award ceremony "just to talk."

He was trying.

This side of him was the side Miguel always got. The father who was interested in him beyond what he could do to enhance our family's reputation. My whole life, as much as I'd adored my brother, it had hurt to live within his shadow and to not know why there'd been such a vast difference in the way my father treated him to the way he'd treated me.

Sometimes I wondered if it was because I'd always been closer to my mother, and he'd thought trying would be the equivalent to competing for affection. I'd asked my therapist, and she'd said there was no way of knowing without asking.

One day I would.

Just not today.

The revelation about my grandparents had changed something between my father and me, and I wanted to do what I could to make sure the change was a good one.

We ordered lunch, and my father asked, "How is your young woman?"

"Hallie. She's well."

"The event-management company she works for . . . It would seem it's very successful."

"Yeah. They have a lot of high-profile clients. Hallie's job is extremely involved, much harder than people give credit for, and she handles the pressure with so much grace. She has fantastic instincts and cares about her job. I'm proud of her and what she's achieved in her career."

He nodded. "And I'm sure the feeling is mutual. Speaking of, have you thought any more about your future?"

I tensed.

"No pressure," my father insisted. "No judgment. Just a discussion. And the offer to help if I can. I just want you to succeed and be happy, Christopher."

Though he'd been increasingly congenial lately, it still took me aback.

"Thank you. I'm considering the offer from NASA."

"Good." He looked relieved. "Excellent. When do you need to get back to them with a decision?"

"I have some time," I replied vaguely.

His lips pinched together, a telltale sign he wasn't pleased with my answer. I waited for him to revert to character and say something condescending.

He didn't.

He just took a second and then nodded slowly.

Deciding to take advantage of this newly patient version of my father, I leaned across the table and said, "If you don't want to talk about it, just tell me, but I would like to hear more about your parents. Where they came from. What they were like."

I knew I was pushing it.

Yet my father surprised me again. Though his eyes flared with emotion, maybe even anger, he eventually responded, "One day, son. I *will* tell you one day. But not here, not now. When we're somewhere private and I can find the words."

This was a compassion I'd never experienced for my father, not even when my mother died—because one, I was consumed with my own grief, and two, he was so stoic I wasn't even sure what he'd felt at her loss. The loss of his parents, the way that it happened, and most likely the consequent years in foster care, had a profound effect on my father. On who he'd become.

Knowing that made his actions over the years a little more understandable. Maybe losing Miguel and Mom, and then seeing how close he'd come to losing me over his treatment of Hallie, had woken him up. Had exacted a change.

And I believed no matter who someone was or what age they were, people *were* capable of changing for the better.

If I could offer that faith to a stranger, I could certainly offer it to my father.

Sitting back in my seat, I let the subject of my grandparents go. "Did you catch the Yankees game?"

Baseball was the one sport my father followed religiously despite his busy schedule. He groaned, reaching for his glass of water. "Did I see it? Are you trying to upset me by bringing it up?" From there, he launched into an irritated diatribe that made me laugh, and for the first time in as long as I could remember, I had a good time in the company of my father.

# FORTY

## Hallie

Bad timing.

It could ruin everything, just as much as good timing could change a life.

Unfortunately today was all about the bad timing.

After Chris had let me into his apartment, he didn't even kiss me hello before he ducked into the bathroom to wash up for our dinner plans. That led me to standing in Chris's bedroom, staring at the bathroom door, trying to drum up the courage to confront him about how distant he was being once again. I thought his whole weird, distracted phase was over, but the day after our argument regarding those photos of him and Darcy, he returned to being off planet.

By the time Friday arrived, my worry over his behavior and mixed signals was making me a little frazzled.

I couldn't keep it in anymore. It was all I could think about, and it distracted me from work, from life, from everything. I'd tried to pay for lunch with my MetroCard today. Yesterday, I'd sent an "I love you" text to my client Christine instead of to Chris. She replied, "Thank you?"

So it was the ultimate in bad timing that Chris's phone (returned per my mother, who did want to talk about the photos and made an annoying disbelieving *hmm* noise when I explained them to her) *bing*ed on his bedside table.

And the name that flashed on his screen was "Darcy."

My heart lurched in my chest, and I reached over to tap his screen. And I didn't even need to think about invading his privacy because the preview on the banner was enough.

Her text started with **Today was fun . . .**

Blood whooshed in my ears.

*Today was fun?* He'd seen her today? Today when I'd asked him to join me for lunch because I hated the distance between us and he'd told me he had lunch plans with his father?

Okay.

Now I was way past worried.

Why would he not tell me he'd seen Darcy today unless he had something to hide?

Tears threatened, and I felt this itchy, panicky sensation.

I didn't think love was supposed to feel this way. Althea and Michelle didn't have this kind of drama in their lives.

Oh God, was I destined to repeat my parents' mistakes?

*NO!* a loud voice screamed from the back of my head.

No, I would not end up in a relationship like theirs.

The bathroom door suddenly opened, and Chris stepped out in just his underwear. I ignored how beautiful he was as he shot me a look of confusion. "Why are you just standing there?"

I waited for him to pull on his jeans before I lifted his phone and handed it to him.

Frowning, he took it and swiped up the screen. He froze at the sight of Darcy's text.

"You told me you were having lunch with your father today and that's why you couldn't meet me."

A muscle ticked in his jaw, and to my shock, Chris glowered as he looked up from his phone. As if he were the wronged party. "I *did* have lunch with my father today. Darcy showed up with a friend. My father asked them to join us. It was a coincidence."

"And you didn't think that was worth mentioning?"

He hauled a T-shirt on and left the bedroom. Chris spun around in the middle of the living room. "I would have told you tonight, but you saw the text before I could. I can't keep doing this with you, Hallie. I can't keep assuring you that there's nothing going on with Darcy."

I scoffed. "You think her turning up to the restaurant is a coincidence? Chris, there are over eight million people in this city and over twenty-six thousand restaurants, and she just happens to walk into the same one?"

He smirked at me. "How do you know those stats?"

Fury flamed through me. "This isn't a joke!"

Chris gritted his teeth and took a deep breath before answering. "I don't want to stand here and yell. That's not the relationship I want to be in. I've told you, nothing is going on."

"Then where are you?" I lowered my voice, taking a step closer to him. "I can feel you pulling away from me."

He shook his head in disbelief. "That's not true. You have no idea how much I think about you all the time. I'm here."

His words were pretty, but they didn't match his actions. I said as much and continued, "Before you, I would have just let it go. I would have shoved down this feeling and pretended like it wasn't happening. Like you weren't pushing at all my insecurities." But he and Althea and even Lia helped me learn to stand up and do what's best for me too. "Staying quiet in this relationship while you pull away and have secret lunches with your ex-girlfriend makes me feel bad about myself. I don't want to be in a relationship that feels like this one does. It's horrible."

Chris stared at me in disbelief. "Hallie . . . I didn't invite her, she just showed up in the same spot. As for the pulling away"—he took a step toward me—"I'm not pulling away. I got offered a job in Houston as a mission specialist for NASA. They offered it to me three weeks ago, and I only have a week left to give them my answer before the offer expires."

Renewed hurt and confusion filled me. And definitely anxiety too. Was he leaving New York? "And how come you haven't told me anything about that?"

"I wasn't sure I wanted the job, and I didn't see any point in bringing our future up for discussion until I thought more about whether the job was something I *really* wanted. It's a lot for you to consider. For us to discuss. Whether we'd do long-distance or . . . I didn't want to throw that at you unless I was seriously considering it."

"But how can you *ever* make a fully informed decision unless we discuss it? I mean, I would never stand in the way of what you wanted." Tears filled my eyes. "But if we're serious about each other, then surely that's a factor in whether you want the job. I don't think you can separate the two. You should have trusted me enough to handle it."

He huffed at my accusation, shaking his head. "It wasn't about not trusting you. I didn't want to burden you with the worry until *I* had a better handle on it. Besides, you're one to talk about trust. What about trusting me with Darcy?"

My patience snapped, and all the ugly suspicions I had just spewed out before I could stop them. "You cannot believe her turning up to lunch today was a coincidence? That her being at your father's event is a coincidence? That her calling you, of all people, while she was breaking things off with Matthias is a coincidence? She wants you back, Chris!" I ignored how furious his reaction made me—shaking his head like I was crazy. "And I think your father is helping facilitate a reunion."

There. I said it.

A muscle ticked in Chris's jaw as he glared at me. "You can't possibly think that."

Heart pounding, I felt him slip further and further away with each word, but I couldn't stop them. "He came to my office and made it clear I wasn't good enough for you. He *threatened* me. He's tried to control your life before, so, no, I don't think it's impossible that he and Darcy are colluding to get you back. I know, despite your dad, that you didn't grow up in that world. But I plan events for one-percenters all the time, and it is like nothing you can imagine. The social politics, the scheming. Everything is about making the right connections. Everything is a business. Even love. This is the kind of shit they pull. And if you're with Darcy, you're exactly where your father wants you. Ever since we got together though, you've been kind of a wild card for him."

Chris took a step toward me, and I flinched at the hurt in his eyes. "You know . . . you know what it means to me that my father is *trying* to have a relationship with me. I don't expect him to change overnight, but I believe he *is* trying."

The tears came, and I couldn't stop them this time. I looked away, swiping at my face with shaking hands as they fell quickly. Too many to catch.

Skirting past him, forcing down the sobs that wanted to rip out of me, I grabbed my purse and then shoved my feet into my heels.

"Where are you going?" he asked, sounding dejected.

Finally I met his gaze across the room. I'd known it all along.

It had been too good to be true.

"I can't do this, Chris," I choked out.

"Because of Darcy." He stepped toward me looking desperate. "I told you, I was going to tell you about the lunch as soon as I saw you."

"Maybe. But even though I get why you thought it best to

keep the job offer from me, you *were* wrong. You should have shared that with me instead of making me feel like something else was going on. And the weirdness, the distance between us, made me so insecure, which I hate! Now I tell you I have a problem with Darcy and with your father, and you're not willing to hear it. Which says to me that my feelings don't matter—"

"That's not true."

"But it feels true. And I've just gotten out of that place with my parents. Caught in the middle, unsteady, uncertain, and trying to make everyone else feel okay and no one giving a shit if I do."

"I give a shit."

A sob broke free before I could stop it. "It doesn't *feel* like it, and that's what matters. And this isn't something I feel because of a text from Darcy. It's been there in the background for weeks. Uncertainty. Insecurity. I think if I felt like I really *had* you I wouldn't feel this way. And I think I feel this way because *you* don't know what you really want. I deserve better than that."

"You're ending this?" Chris staggered back like I'd physically hit him.

I stuffed down another sob. "I . . . No . . . I just think we need some time apart. A break. We moved too fast. Practically living together. Got caught up in the attraction. But I won't be my parents. Passion isn't enough to build a life on."

"That's all you think we have?"

I gestured wearily at the distance between us. "I don't know. Maybe some time away from each other will answer that." I wrenched open his apartment door.

"Hallie . . ."

I glanced over my shoulder at him.

Chris stared incredulously. "I don't want to take a break. A break is just code for 'It's over but we can't admit it.' I love you. I don't want it to be over."

Clinging to his "I love you," walking back in there, hoping everything would just resolve itself, would hurt more than accepting this was what we needed right now. I'd spent my whole life hoping. Hoping for my parents to stop fighting. Hoping for my friends and boyfriends to see me as something more than an anecdote they told at a party.

Hoping to one day meet someone who really saw me and still thought I was the most special person in their universe.

I thought I'd finally found the latter, and from there I had hoped it would last.

Hope was a double-edged sword. It gave you the strength to get up out of bed during the worst times of your life, but it could also blind you and stop you from moving on from things that, in the end, weren't good for you.

I wouldn't spend the rest of my life yo-yoing between the highest highs and the lowest lows. "Sometimes love isn't enough, Chris."

# FORTY-ONE

## Hallie

Working through heartbreak was one of the hardest things I'd ever had to do. It was unbelievably challenging to plan weddings and engagement parties and be around touchy-feely couples who expected their planner to be thrilled for them. In truth, I had a ton of bitter thoughts I wanted to express and knew I'd self-sabotage if I did.

It had been five days since I walked out on Chris.

Five days and, although I'd been the one who initiated the break, it was a punch in the gut that he hadn't contacted me. He had only a few days left before he had to give his answer to NASA about the job. Maybe he already had, maybe I was no longer a factor.

When I closed my eyes at night, I had flashbacks to nights spent in Chris's arms. He'd made me feel so loved, so cherished. I couldn't believe that his affection wasn't genuine in those moments. I knew he thought he loved me.

But with some space, he'd obviously realized I was right. We'd moved too fast. I'd gotten caught in the middle of his intense relationship with his father, with his uncertainty about his career . . .

Clearly, this was just not the right time for Chris to be in a serious relationship.

"Sweetheart, you look exhausted."

I blinked, looking up from the water glass in front of me, as my mom slipped into the opposite seat at the small table. "Hello to you too."

Mom smiled, but I saw the concern in her eyes.

After I'd finally texted her that Chris and I were taking a break, Mom had insisted on meeting for lunch the next day in the city, and she apparently wouldn't take no for an answer. Althea was ready at the drop of a text to come rescue me if Mom decided to rub salt in my wounds.

"I'm fine. Just swamped at work."

"You're heartbroken," she said bluntly. "And pushing through despite it. I'm very proud of you."

I raised an eyebrow. "Thanks. I think."

"I saw how you two were together, which is why I'm so shocked by this." She leaned across the table. "I just . . . I can't imagine what could have torn you two apart. You seemed so together, so in sync. It made me so happy to see you had that."

It surprised the heck out of me to hear her say that just as much as each word felt like a bullet in my chest. "Well, we kept disagreeing about a few things, and I found myself arguing with him a lot and just got really terrified I'd turn into my parents and end up in a toxic decades-long relationship."

As soon as the words were out of my mouth, I regretted them.

Closing my eyes against the pained expression in hers, I shook my head. "I'm sorry."

"Is that what you really think? That arguing in a relationship somehow makes it toxic?"

"Doesn't it?" I opened my eyes.

"For goodness' sake, Hallie. I will admit that your father and I should have ended things a long time ago, but that doesn't mean other couples in healthier relationships don't argue."

"I know other couples argue. But this was not a small disagreement."

"Until recently, you've spent your whole life avoiding confrontation, and now that you're not afraid to avoid it, you somehow think a little confrontation in a relationship means it's doomed. How do you expect to communicate with your partner?"

"Peacefully and calmly."

She snorted. "So you plan on choosing a man you have lukewarm feelings for, then?"

Confused, I sighed. "What?"

"Sweetheart, whatever happened between you and Christopher was obviously due to tension, and I assume a very big argument."

"Several arguments. With repetitive themes."

"And you broke up with him instead of figuring it out together?"

"I didn't break up with him. We're taking a break because he doesn't seem to know what he wants in life. Besides, there are trust issues on either side, and I'm not sure they're surmountable."

Mom scrutinized me. "People make mistakes, Hallie. You'll make them; he'll make them. But you can't figure that out separately. You have to talk. Maybe even yell at each other. Maybe until you're blue in the face. But you can't figure out if you're right for each other if you never see each other."

Exasperated, I pushed back from the table. "I'm too raw to deal with this right now."

"Hallie." Mom reached across the table to cover my hand. "Please. I didn't come here to upset you. I just . . . I've done a lot of thinking and looking inward, and I have this habit of pushing people away when I'm feeling my most vulnerable."

I grew still.

"It's a habit that's done a lot of damage in my life, and I'm trying to be better." She gave me a tight-lipped smile. "And I would hate to think I've passed that quality on to my daughter."

"I've made myself vulnerable to people," I replied quietly.

"Most of whom didn't matter." She squeezed my hand. "Chris matters. And that is so much scarier, am I right?"

Tears filled my eyes as I nodded.

"I'm not telling you what to do about Chris. I just want you to realize that when you love someone with a lot of passion, fear of losing them can make you question everything. Maybe you and Chris do have some trust issues, but it's possible it's not a lack of trust in each other but a lack of trust in yourselves."

Whoa.

I sank back in my chair, blown away by her wisdom, her unexpected kindness and openness. Who was this version of my mother?

"Anyway, I didn't actually come here to say all that. I came here for you and me. Whatever you do about Chris, I want you to know that I am going to try to be better at *seeing* you. I've underestimated you in the past, and I want to make up for it." She pulled her purse up onto the table, rummaged through it and withdrew a piece of paper.

Mom held it out to me.

I stared in confusion at the check in my hands. The check written out to me for five thousand dollars.

"I know it's not a huge amount, but I thought it might be a start."

"For what?"

"You know, since you were a kid, all you talked about was traveling the world. It was the one thing that held your attention, your passion, until this job came along. But you stopped talking about it after college, and I let myself think it was because you were over it. Now, I suspect—with a little help from Jenna, who is far more perceptive than people give her credit for—that you just stopped talking about it because I didn't support the idea."

"Mom." I shook my head in disbelief. "I can't believe you even thought about this."

"You and Chris mentioned it last weekend. Your plans to travel. And after you left, I couldn't stop thinking about it because I didn't know you still wanted to do that. Chris made very pointed comments about how capable you were, and I realized they were a jab at me."

"Mom—"

"No, it's fine. He's not wrong." She gestured to the check. "But this is my way of saying that I trust you and I'm proud of you, and I don't think you should sit on this anymore. Travel, Hallie. Go out there and do it alone if you want to. Don't sit on anything you want, because you will one day turn fifty years old and look back at your life with so many regrets that they surmount any good thing you achieved. I don't want that for you."

Tears brightened my eyes. "Thank you, Mom."

"Don't cry, sweetheart. You'll ruin your makeup, and it's the only thing saving you from looking like hell right now."

And there she was.

My mother, ladies and gentleman.

I laughed because some things never changed.

And I tried not to cry because some things did.

# FORTY-TWO

## Chris

When my mother was diagnosed with cancer, I'd felt real panic for the first time in my life. It came from my powerlessness to stop this thing that was killing her. The panic took up residence in my chest for months, a pressure that pulled at the air in my lungs, making it hard to breathe. It was always there, this dreadful sensation of perpetual falling with nothing to grab on to to stop it. I'd wake up during the night gasping for breath.

Mom's death took away the panic. There was a relief in its absence until I realized that a new gnawing emptiness had replaced it. That ache was a million times worse than the panic.

It seemed ridiculous to feel a similar kind of panic because Hallie had asked for some time apart, but that panic dug its fucking claws in my chest, and I experienced an out-of-body sensation. Like everything was slipping away.

All because it terrified me that I could lose her forever over this.

Six days had passed since Hallie walked out.

There had not been a word from her since, and every time the phone rang or my door buzzed, my heart jumped so hard in my chest it physically jolted me.

It was never her.

I could have called her. I wanted to so many times. But she said I made her feel like what she wanted didn't matter. If she wanted this break, this torturous, hellish time apart, then that's what I'd give her. No matter what it cost me.

The urge to escape to the Hamptons came over me every second of every hour of every day, but I couldn't not be in the same place as Hallie. My hope was that she'd remember that I did know what I wanted—*her*. She'd see that things might have gotten blown out of proportion—that you didn't take a break over an argument. You stayed and you worked it out. Together.

But now that we were on day six, I panicked that waiting for her to come around would only lead me to losing her for good. So, I'd called my aunt for advice, and it had ignited a fire under my ass.

"You're waiting for her to come to you?" Aunt Richelle had asked with a tone I didn't like after I relayed, almost word for word, the argument Hallie and I had six days ago.

"Yes."

"But she broke up with you."

"She said we're taking a break. And it was said in the heat of the moment."

"Was it?" She'd sounded alarmingly skeptical. "Because to me it sounds like she had some valid suspicions about your father and Darcy, and you made her feel like her feelings didn't matter. So I'm thinking . . . she's not coming back to apologize."

The blood had rushed into my ears. "You think her suspicions are valid?"

"Chris," my aunt had huffed. "Oh, sweetheart, I know you've been on the defense with Javier your whole life. I know you've been overwhelmed with revelations about his past and it's made you see him differently. I get it. I do. But, Chris, look at the facts. Your father has interfered with your life in ways you know of and ways I'm sure we know nothing of. He ambushed Hallie at her job and threatened her."

I'd flinched at the reminder.

"And while I know you think Darcy is sweet, that's because, despite everything, you're an optimist and you try to see the best in people. You get that from your mom. It's how she ended up married to your father. But while Darcy surely has her good qualities, I never liked her for you. She's spoiled and determined, and I do think it's weird she chose you out of all her friends to be her confidant during her relationship crisis."

Hearing my aunt say everything out loud, things Hallie had said but I'd disputed because I thought she was simply jealous, made me feel like the world's biggest, most naive moron.

"Fuck." I'd sank back into my couch, feeling a little lightheaded. "I can't have been that blind. Surely?"

"Maybe I'm wrong. Maybe Hallie is wrong. But, Chris, out of Hallie, Darcy, and your father, which one of them has been nothing but honest, loyal, and supportive of you?"

Emotion had risen in a painful burn from my chest, and my vision blurred. "I've fucked up, haven't I?"

"I think so. But it's never too late to fix things."

I had missed calls from Tom about the job, but I couldn't think about that until I fixed things.

Because I was a fucking idiot for making Hallie Goodman feel like I wasn't completely devoted to her.

I'd let my hope blind me to the facts. If Hallie, the one person who I trusted above all others, felt like she was being maneuvered out of my life, then there was substance in that, and I had to make her believe in me again.

In us.

Truth first, then Hallie.

I scrolled through the contacts on my phone and hit Dial, not sure she'd pick up at this time of day.

Three rings later, the call connected.

"Chris, hi, it's so good to hear from you," Darcy sounded in good spirits.

Impatient, I had no time for pleasantries. "I'm going to ask you something, and you owe me an honest answer."

There was silence, then: "Okay. Are you all right?"

"Was it a coincidence . . . you attending my father's award event alone? Turning up to our lunch last week?"

More silence. Finally she responded. "No."

Shit. *Hallie, I'm so sorry.*

"Javier called me after Matthias and I broke things off. He told me that if I still had feelings for you, I should come to the event."

"Jesus Christ." My fucking fuck of a father!

For the first time, he'd outmaneuvered me. I was so blinded by my desperation to have some kind of relationship with him that I didn't see him playing me.

"Chris, he just wants you to be happy, and so do I. I never meant it to become a manipulation. When your father texted where you were meeting for lunch, I got caught up in the idea of there being an us again." Her tone hardened with determination. "We make sense, Chris. You and I."

"No, we don't," I replied as softly as I could manage, considering the fury I felt toward my father right now. "There will never be a you and me again, even if there weren't a Hallie and me. You cheated on me, Darcy."

"I'm so sorry, Chris. I don't know what I was thinking when I left you for Matthias."

"I know you're sorry. That's not the point."

"Maybe we could work at it. I could earn your trust again."

"We can't. I don't love you. You and I were never in love, because if we were, you couldn't have done that to me, and I wouldn't have gotten over it so damn easily."

"Chris—"

"You know what I won't get over? Losing Hallie. So thank you for your honesty, but I have somewhere I need to be now."

"Chris . . . I am sorry."

"I'm not going to call again, Darcy, and I don't want you to call me either."

"But—"

"Our friendship isn't good for either of us if I can't trust you and if you're holding out for something that will never happen. It's better if we end it now."

I waited for a response, and finally the line went dead.

In all my distractions over this whole NASA gig, I hadn't seen what I was doing to Hallie.

Choosing Darcy's feelings over hers. Not intentionally, but still.

Choosing to hope that Hallie had walked out of my door in the heat of the moment but would come back to me. Well, if her insecurities were really just spot-on gut instinct, then she wasn't coming back to a fool like me anytime soon. Not unless I righted my wrongs against her.

Renewed panic filled me as I slammed out of the apartment. I had to find Hallie. I would beg on my knees if I had to, because I couldn't let one more day pass without her knowing she was all that mattered to me.

"Left for the airport? What the hell do you mean she just left for the airport?" My chest felt too tight, and it wasn't from the fact that I'd run all the way from the subway to Hallie's office building.

Her friend Althea glared impressively at me. "Well, see, some asshole astronaut broke her heart, and she decided she needed as much distance from him as she could get." Her gaze flickered away before coming back to mine. "She's taken a sabbatical and is going on the trip she'd planned to take with you next summer. She's going alone. So because of you, I don't get to see my best friend for three months. Thanks for that."

Three months?

No.

No goddamn way.

"Which airport?"

Althea raised an eyebrow. "Excuuuuse me?"

"Which. Airport?" I enunciated impatiently.

"JFK. Her flight leaves . . ." She slowly lifted her phone to check it. "Her flight leaves in two hours. You might make it."

I was already running out the door before she finished.

"Uh, you're welcome!" Althea yelled at my back. "And you better grovel, Captain! Grovel like there's no tomorrow!"

If I hadn't been terrified of missing Hallie at the airport, I might have found her friend a little bit amusing.

# FORTY-THREE

## Hallie

The airport was crowded with people as I dragged my small suitcase behind me toward the check-in desk. I'd taken business trips over the last few years, and I'd learned it was better to arrive early and be bored at the airport than to be a hot, sweaty mess from running to catch your flight.

Lia had a client interested in a five-star hotel in Vermont as her venue. Usually one of the other field coordinators would fly out to look over the venue, schmooze the manager to see if there wasn't a deal to be had. Sometimes even Lia went herself if the client was big enough. This was a client she'd usually fly out to Vermont for, but with that sharp intuition of hers, she'd sent me instead.

"It'll give you something to focus on."

Yes. Something to focus on. Some space to think.

Mom had got me thinking a lot.

Maybe the reason I was functioning and not curled up in a sobbing ball in a dark room somewhere was because there was a part of me that knew I could have handled things differently. That if Chris and I could just talk, if he'd acknowledge his part in how things went wrong, and I could acknowledge maybe I should have trusted myself and him more, then maybe we could work things out.

A weekend away from the city to contemplate that was a great idea.

I didn't know what would happen next between us, especially with this job offer in Houston he might have already accepted.

My phone rang in my purse as I walked toward a self-check-in machine. Since it could be Lia, I rummaged quickly through the purse for it. It wasn't Lia.

It was Althea.

"Hey?" I answered. "I'm at the airport. I didn't forget anything, did I?"

"Um, yeah, but it's on its way to you."

I frowned. "What?"

"Yeah, so you're not through security yet, right?"

"No, I'm at the entrance."

"Good! Stay there! Whatever you do, don't go through security. I sent something you need. You'll know what it is when it arrives."

"Can I take it through security? Althea?"

She'd hung up.

What?

I tried calling her back, but it went straight to her voice mail. Huffing in exasperation, I shot off a quick text asking her what the hell she'd sent and how long it would be before it arrived.

**It's a surprise. But you need it. And it'll be there before you need to go through security. Promise.**

What the hell?

Sighing, I checked in so I'd at least have my ticket ready to go, and I rolled my carry-on suitcase behind me as I found a spot to stand near the entrance. Playing Candy Crush on my phone, I glanced up now and then to check if my surprise package had arrived. I wondered who was bringing it.

Forty minutes passed, and I was really getting antsy about my flight. Candy Crush had long lost its luster, and I just stood there glaring at the doors every time more people walked in.

Then suddenly the doors parted and Chris jogged through them, his hair askew, his cheeks flushed, his eyes darting in every direction.

What. The. Hell?

My suitcase clattered to the ground as I let go of the handle in shock.

Chris's eyes followed the sound, and our gazes locked.

He swallowed hard and crossed the distance between us.

Chris was here.

"Did Althea send you?"

His lips twitched as his eyes seemed to catalog every inch of my face, as if he was afraid he'd never see me again. "Yeah."

"What are you doing here?"

Chris's expression turned pained, and he said my name as if it the consonants and vowels had jagged edges.

"Chris?"

"I fucked up." He took a step closer to me, invading my personal space.

I didn't care.

"I was so distracted with this job offer and with the revelations about my father that I stopped seeing you clearly. You were right about him and Darcy. They were trying to manipulate me."

"I wish I hadn't been right, because I know how much you hoped your father was starting to change."

"I know." His eyes brightened with tears. "And that's why I

fucked up. Because even now, even after I hurt you, you still don't want anything to hurt me."

"I don't. I never want that."

He grasped my arms in his hands.

"Darcy is out of my life for good. No one gets to come between us. You're my priority. You're always my priority. I never want you to think your feelings don't matter to me, and I'm so sorry that you felt that way. Hallie, that will never happen again. And I'm so sorry for waiting like an asshole for you to come to me this week. I should have chased after you as soon as you left." Chris bowed his head to mine, his voice gravelly with fierceness. "I shouldn't have let you leave in the first place. Because we will probably argue in the future, Hallie. Over things that don't matter and things that do. That doesn't mean we're not meant for each other. It just means we're human."

"I know. I know that. I do."

Hope lit his eyes. "Does this mean you can forgive me and give me a second chance?"

"What about everything else? About the job?"

Chris smoothed his hands up my arms, along my shoulders, to clasp my face in his hands. I shivered at his touch, at the adoration in his eyes. "I would like to take the job. But it has to be *our* decision because I want us to be together. I've been a student and a soldier, an astronaut, a scientist, and a writer. And I've never felt a hundred percent certain that any of those things were something I wanted or needed to be." He touched his forehead to mine. "But being yours . . . that's the only thing in my life I am one hundred percent certain I want and need to be."

Tears slipped free as I wrapped my hands around his nape, holding on for dear life.

"So if you want me to drop everything right now and go on this sabbatical trip with you, I will do it. Because there is nowhere in the universe I'd rather be. I love you."

For a moment, his beautiful vows of love and commitment were all I could hear.

"I love you too." I reached for Chris's mouth, needing his lips on mine.

We kissed like we hadn't seen each other in years, hungry and desperate and so full of love we couldn't contain it.

Neither of us cared we were in public.

I don't think either of us were even really aware of anything but the other person.

Yet as his kisses slowed, growing softer, sweeter, his words penetrated.

I reluctantly released his mouth. "Uh . . . sabbatical trip?"

Chris brushed my hair off my face. "I understand, Hallie. You taking the trip without me."

"What trip?"

"The backpacking trip."

"I'm not going backpacking. Have you seen what I'm wearing?"

Glancing down at my pencil skirt, shirt, and heels, Chris frowned. "Okay. I'm confused. Althea told me you were at the airport because you were taking a three-month trip to get away from me."

That sneaky . . . Attempting not to grin and failing, I said, "I'm so sorry, Chris. I think maybe she was just trying to push us together. I'm just going to Vermont for the weekend. A business trip."

He let out a string of expletives that made me cover my mouth to hide my smile. Chris narrowed his gaze on me, though I saw the glitter of possible amusement in his eyes. "This isn't funny. I nearly had a heart attack trying to get here in time."

As if she were psychic, my phone rang and it was Althea. I waved my phone at Chris so he could see who was calling. He narrowed his eyes, and I saw the wheels turning in his mind. Poor Althea. I think a little revenge might be in her future.

"Did your package arrive?" she asked without preamble.

I smiled giddily at Chris as he snuggled me close. "He's here."

"And it's all good? He groveled? I specifically instructed him to grovel."

Laughing, I nodded. "There was sufficient groveling. And we're good. We're fantastic actually."

"Ah, thank God!" Althea cried dramatically. "I'm so happy for you."

"Thank you, my friend." I murmured, reaching out to stroke Chris's face because I just couldn't not touch him right now. He turned his mouth to press a kiss to my fingers.

"Lia is on her way to the airport, so you and Chris can leave. She's giving you the rest of the day off."

"But what about the trip?" I frowned.

"She decided it was best she dealt with it, considering how distracted you'd probably be with thoughts of your astronaut lover."

"Althea!"

"I'm not kidding. You can leave. Enjoy your weekend. Have lots of sex! Love ya." She hung up.

I stared at my phone for a second and then stared up at Chris.

Chris, who was mine.

Who didn't give up on us. Who would have given up his life in New York to follow me around the world. Who could admit when he was wrong and do everything he could to make it right.

My whole life I'd done the chasing, the people-pleasing. No one had ever chased me. No one had ever prioritized me the way I was willing to prioritize them.

Until now.

"Trip is off." I slipped my phone back into my purse and took a hold of his hand. "What do you say we take this back to my place?"

His hand tightened around mine. "I know that look in your eye. Shouldn't we talk first before you rip my clothes off?"

"No. We have lots to discuss about our future together. And I'd quite like to do that naked after several apology orgasms. Mine. Not yours."

Chris chuckled, pulling me into his side with one arm while he took my luggage with his free hand. "I thought you already accepted my apology?"

"The verbal one, yes. But we haven't had sex since our argument, so you owe me for all the sex we missed."

"Admit it," he teased as we walked outside. "You just love me for my body."

"Well, it contains all of my favorite things about you." I answered seriously.

Chris shot me a look, like he wasn't sure how to take that.

I pulled on his shirt to draw him to a halt. "Your mind, your heart, and your soul."

He relaxed, grinning. "You like my ass too though, right?"

"Oh, I love your ass. It's definitely up there on the list. There are lots of things to love about you, Captain. You're a complicated, fascinating man who is more than just one thing. And going forward, you can be anything you want to be. We both can. And we'll be those things and be together." I smiled, thinking about something his colleague Kate had said to me. "Something tells me that no matter where we end up, it will always be together. What we have is kind of cosmic like that."

Approximately ten minutes later we were in a cab heading back to Brooklyn. We sat close together, my hand clasped in Chris's as the driver sang along with his radio. Once he realized we were New Yorkers, he seemed to lose all interest in us. Which was fine by me.

I couldn't stop staring at Chris. Like he might disappear at any second.

Feeling my gaze, he looked down at me and squeezed my hand.

My heart lurched in my chest as I remembered he'd said he wanted to discuss taking the job with NASA. However, I didn't panic. Instead I pressed as close to him as I could get. Holding his gaze, I let everything I felt for him shine out. No outside forces would tear us apart this time. "About NASA."

He looked a little wary. "Yeah?"

"If it's what you want, we *will* figure it out. Together," I promised, and meant it.

Better yet, I *believed* it.

Chris's face relaxed into a smile, and he raised our hands to press a kiss to the top of mine. "Okay, *mi cielo.* We'll figure it out together."

# EPILOGUE

## Hallie

A FEW MONTHS LATER
CANCÚN, MEXICO

The resort was out of this world. I'd never been anywhere like it or imagined I ever would. Adults only, first-class service, swim-up bars, cabana beds galore, and white sand beaches kissed by the turquoise waters of the Caribbean.

It was the perfect end to our three-week adventure in Mexico.

Chris and I strolled back to our room, my hand clasped in his. We could hear the waves lapping at the shore in the distance, the cooling breeze ruffling through my hair, and our light footsteps on the sand-peppered walkway.

The bars and restaurants were on the other side of the resort, so we couldn't hear music or the sounds of other people. Just surf and ocean breeze.

After sixteen days of intensive travel from Mexico City to Puebla to Oaxaca to Tabasco, these last five days at a spa resort were a total surprise. Chris was an active guy. He liked to have something to do every day, so I'd expected our entire vacation to be jam-packed with activities. We hadn't exactly relaxed upon arriving in Cancún, but today had been our laziest day yet, and I'd loved it. I'd known we were coming to Cancún to see the Mayan ruins at Tulum and go swimming and snorkeling in Cenotes Dos Ojos, a diving site not far from the ruins.

But Chris had booked this part of the trip and surprised me with our accommodation.

A luxury spa resort.

"To decompress before real life starts again," Chris had said.

He also seemed to be enjoying the relaxing day after a few days of activity.

We'd used a guide the first day here to take us to the jungle to the diving caverns. Thankfully, our helpful guide warned us to wear plenty of bug spray because . . . jungle. The caverns were a little too busy for my liking, and there were bats.

Bats.

Nope.

Just nope.

But Chris had the time of his life, and I couldn't help but be a little proud of myself for participating in the diving, even if I was constantly aware of the bats.

The second day, we visited the ruins at Tulum. But today we'd lazed around the pool, drinking cocktails, reading and napping on our cabana bed. There were multiple restaurants on the resort that catered to different cuisines. We were returning from dinner at the seafood restaurant.

Tomorrow we had appointments for a couple's massage.

Now that to me was heaven.

When we returned home, I'd miss the smell of sunscreen and mojitos.

I squeezed Chris's hand. "I can't believe we only have a few days left before reality sets in."

Chris looked down at me and released my hand, but only to

slide his arm around my waist to draw me closer. "We'll have more trips like this in the future."

I wasn't sure about that. It would be difficult to top Mexico. We'd spent time in Mexico City, the highlight of which for both of us was a guided tour of the National Museum of History. It was outstanding. We toured Chapultepec Castle, and we did a food tour through a culinary neighborhood called Polanco—also a highlight. We'd ended the food tour with *churros con chocolate,* and I already suspected I'd be dreaming about those churros for years to come. Then we got a bus to Puebla so we could experience the safari. Our guide was friendly and knowledgeable and showed us how to feed and pet a rhino. And we cuddled kangaroos.

Cuddled kangaroos!

An experience that just couldn't be beaten.

From Puebla we got a flight to Oaxaca and spent a few days visiting the ruins of the ancient Zapotec capital. I got chills walking around those ruins, imagining ancient life here. Chris had been similarly blown away. Things with his father had returned to their usual strained fashion now that he knew Chris would never give him the opportunity to control his life. He didn't approve of me, but I had hope father and son could build bridges. So I'd keep trying for Chris's sake. While he still didn't have answers from his father about possible Mexican relatives, Chris admitted just being in Mexico was a good start. He said he felt connected to the country and couldn't explain why it felt so familiar to him. It was like he'd been there before. Perhaps it was psychosomatic or perhaps there really was this genetic bond between people and places. Whatever it was, I was just so thankful to experience his first time in Mexico by his side. We even brushed up on our Spanish together. I wouldn't lie. Chris speaking Spanish got me a little hot and bothered.

Okay, a *lot* hot and bothered.

From Oaxaca we flew to Tabasco, where we experienced more world heritage sites and waterfalls and awesomeness.

By the time we got to Cancún, I was exhausted.

But even though I was extremely glad these last few days would be nothing but lying around by the pool, I couldn't imagine us ever pulling off a trip like this again.

Chris seemed to sense my dubiousness. "We will," he insisted. "We might not be able to backpack for three months at a time, but we'll still travel and see the world the way we want to. We've just proven we can."

I snuggled into his side, nodding. "I'm just feeling a little melancholy because it's almost over."

He kissed the top of my head. "Let's enjoy this now. We'll worry about that when it comes."

By "it" he meant NASA. When we got back to New York, Chris would have to pack again. He'd taken the job with NASA, and he was finally expected in Houston next week. I would not be going with him. At first.

After spending weeks researching, I'd approached Lia with a proposal for me to open a division of the company in Houston. To my shock, she was already working on plans to open an office in Los Angeles and had been looking for a third city. Houston hadn't crossed her mind, but my research opened her up to the possibilities there. And while she'd miss having me in New York, she believed in me and had faith I could run a team.

We'd found an office a week before I'd left for my three-week vacation with Chris. I had a bunch of personal days saved up, and Lia had agreed to let me take the vacation once I assured her Dominic could handle my workload. He was only too happy to, considering once I left to run the Houston office, he'd have my job. But it was worth it. I'd miss New York, of course, my parents, Althea and Michelle . . . but I'd be taking a giant step up the ladder of my career, and Chris and I would be moving in together. A scary step—career- and relationship-wise—but also extremely exciting.

It would be a few months yet until Lia Zhang Events was ready for Houston, and until then Chris and I would do the long-distance thing. I tried not to hate the idea but failed.

We'd been inseparable for months. For instance, I'd been right by his side when he got the call from his agent that a big New York publisher made an offer on his book.

It wouldn't be for a while yet, but Chris took the deal and would be a published author.

A published author and a mission specialist with NASA.

I was so proud of him.

I already missed him even though I knew our separation was temporary. Dark thoughts crept into my mind now and then that somehow the distance would force us apart. I knew that would only happen if we let it and that both of us were committed to making our relationship work. Yet fear didn't often listen to sense.

Shoving the morose thoughts aside, I snuggled deeper into Chris's side, and we wandered into our room. Somehow, I think we both were more sleepy from a lazy day of eating and drinking than we were from all our adventures. We changed our clothes and readied for bed. A few gentle kisses good night later, we lay down and were out by the time our heads hit the pillow.

It was the cramps that woke me.

Despite the AC, my skin was slicked with sweat as I jolted up from sleep in a panic and launched myself off the bed toward the bathroom. I just made it in time to throw up the entire contents of my stomach.

"Oh, fuck," I heard behind me, and glanced up just in time to see Chris launch himself at the sink to do the same.

That set me off again.

Things only got worse from there.

To put it politely, our bodies wanted everything we'd consumed in that seafood restaurant to evacuate from wherever it could.

Hours later, exhausted, miserable, Chris and I lay on the cold tile of the bathroom floor, afraid to leave just in case. And honestly too weak to get up.

We stared hazily at each other in pale-faced shock.

"I think it was the seafood," I whispered hoarsely, my mouth and throat dry.

"Don't talk about it," Chris begged, squeezing his eyes shut.

"Of all the things we've eaten on this trip . . . the five-star resort got us."

Chris snorted and then cracked, "Now we really do know everything about each other."

Despite the misery of the situation, I started to laugh, shaking against the tiles as tears of hilarity brightened my eyes. Chris's laughter joined mine until we were gasping for air.

But when we grew quiet, I reached weakly across the floor for his hand, and he curled his sweat-dampened fingers around mine. "No one I'd rather go through epic food poisoning with."

He smiled wearily at me. "Back at you, *mi cielo*."

I must have drifted off, because the next thing I knew, Chris was lifting me gently to undress me and help me into the shower. My energy depleted, my head spinning, I could only hold on to him as he cleaned us from head to toe.

Out of the shower, I leaned against his back as I drank the bottled water he'd insisted I consume. All the while Chris brushed the tangles out of my wet hair and pulled it up into a bun so it was off my neck. I made sure he downed a bottle of water too, and then he helped me into a fresh silk nightie and led me back to bed. "Big spoon or little spoon?" he murmured in my ear as we got in.

"Big."

Sometimes when I was too hot, I preferred to be the big spoon.

So Chris turned, and I snuggled into his back, my head pounding, feeling like I might sleep for a year. I slid my arms around his waist, and he covered my hand with his.

After pressing a kiss to his naked back, I whispered, "Feel better. I love you."

"I love you too," he murmured.

My last thought before falling asleep was that weirdly after our ordeal I wasn't afraid of the temporary long-distance relationship looming in our immediate future. We loved each other. We took care of each other. I was pretty sure if we could experience this level of "intimacy" and come out of it closer than ever, we could deal with a little bit of distance.

Chris and I were in this for life.

Through all the epic adventures and through the very worst ones too.

As long as we had each other, we could handle anything the cosmos sent our way.

# ACKNOWLEDGMENTS

For as long as I can remember I have been simultaneously fascinated and terrified by space and its many mysteries. While reading an astronaut's biography one day, it occurred to me that I had never read a romance with an astronaut for a hero. As soon as the thought occurred to me, the idea for *A Cosmic Kind of Love* snowballed at speed until Hallie and Chris were living their story out in my head, demanding to be written.

While for the most part writing is a solitary endeavor, publishing most certainly is not. I have to thank my amazing editor, Kerry Donovan, for loving this idea, for believing in it, and for helping me bring this story to fruition. Moreover, thank you to all the team at Berkley for your hard work on Hallie and Chris's story.

A very special thank-you to Emma Renshaw and Jessica Galván for their contributions. I'm forever grateful.

Of course, a massive thank-you to my agent extraordinaire, Lauren Abramo. Thank you for always having my back and for making it possible for readers all over the world to read my stories. I'm so lucky to have you!

And thank you to my bestie and PA, Ashleen Walker, for handling all the things and supporting me through everything. There are no words for how much I appreciate and love you.

Thank you to the wonderful Elena Armas, Tessa Bailey, Staci Hart, and Chloe Liese for agreeing to read early copies of *Cosmic* and for saying such lovely things about it. I truly appreciate you!

To every single blogger, Bookstagrammer, BookToker, and booklover who has helped spread the word about my books, thank you! You all are appreciated so much. On that note, a massive thank-you to my ARC review team and the fantastic readers in my private Facebook group, Sam's Clan McBookish. You're the kindest, most supportive readers a girl could ask for, and I hope you know how much you all mean to me.

There aren't enough thank-yous in the world for the friends and family who put up with me and my writerly ways. I love you all so much.

Finally, to you, my reader, the biggest thank-you of all.

READERS GUIDE
A COSMIC KIND OF LOVE
SAMANTHA YOUNG
READERS GUIDE

# DISCUSSION QUESTIONS

1. If you were in Hallie's shoes, would you have continued to watch Chris's videos? Why or why not?

2. If you were in Chris's shoes, would you have told Hallie you knew she'd watched the videos immediately, or would you have kept it to yourself? Do you agree with Chris's decision not to tell Hallie immediately?

3. What elements of Hallie's personality make her a good event organizer?

4. Chris says he loves science because "there's always a solution to be sought." However, he recognizes that same finality can't always be applied to people and emotions. How do you see this logic play into his personality?

5. Hallie and Chris both have strained relationships with their parents. How do you think they handled their problems with their parents? Would you have done anything differently? And how do you think their issues with their parents affected their relationship with each other?

6. Would you rather work for NASA or Lia Zhang Events? Why? What are the stressful and rewarding elements of each career?

7. Hallie struggles with people-pleasing. Do you think she grows by the end of the novel? In what ways?

8. Which secondary characters do you think were the most supportive of Hallie and Chris throughout the book? Do you think those characters influenced Hallie's and Chris's growth as much as Hallie and Chris influenced each other?

9. Do you think Hallie and Chris came to a fair compromise at the end of the novel by moving to Houston? If the opportunity arose, would you start your life over in a new city if it meant being near a loved one?

10. What do you think Hallie and Chris are doing a year after the novel ends?

*Keep reading for a preview of*

# MUCH ADO ABOUT YOU

BY SAMANTHA YOUNG

*Available now*

There you are, Evie." My editor, Patrick, lifted his hand and curled his fingers, gesturing for me to follow him.

My boss had jolted me out of concentration mode. Outside of work hours, I offered freelance editing services to self-published authors to supplement my income, and one of my clients was a crime writer. An old friend of mine from Northwestern worked with the FBI, and I'd emailed him three days ago with facts I needed checked. The author had gotten her info online, and I just wanted to make sure it was correct. I'd received my friend's response minutes after coming into the office. Fascinated with the information he'd sent me, I'd forgotten I was at work.

Patrick's sudden appearance caused giddiness to fill me, swamping the melancholy that lingered. I strode through the open-plan office, smiling at my colleagues as I made my way toward Patrick's office. My desk sat in front of the glass cube that housed his space.

Picking up speed, I hurried to follow him inside.

"Close the door."

Despite everyone being able to see what was going on in the office, once that door closed, the cube was soundproof. It was pretty cool. I glanced around. Patrick's desk sat near the bank of windows that looked down over East Washington Street downtown.

Boxes containing my boss's belongings filled the space.

I'd worked for Patrick for ten years. He was a good enough boss. Thanked me for my work. Seemed to appreciate me. However, we'd had our differences over the years, mostly because he'd never championed me the three times an editor job opened up at the magazine.

Now he was retiring, and as I was his loyal, long-standing editorial assistant, everyone at the magazine predicted that I would get his job.

"You've packed up really early," I observed. "The job is still yours for six weeks."

Patrick nodded distractedly. "Evie, take a seat."

Not liking his tone, I slowly lowered myself onto the seat in front of his desk. "Is everything okay?"

Come to think of it, when was the last time Patrick beat me into work? I usually arrived at least fifteen minutes earlier than him every day.

"Evie . . . you know I think you're a great assistant. And you'll make a damn good editor one day . . . but the higher-ups have decided to hire an experienced editor. Young guy, twenty-five, certified as an editor, been working at a small press for two years. He's coming in next Monday so I can show him the ropes."

It was like the floor fell out from beneath my feet. "Wait . . . what?"

My boss frowned. "Gary Slater. He's going to be your new boss."

Was the room spinning?

Or was that just the anger building inside me so much that my body couldn't handle it? "More experience? Certified?" I stood up on shaking legs. Not only had I been editing here for seven years, Patrick knew I was a freelance editor too. Experienced? "*I'm* certified. You know I am." Although I'd come into the job with an English degree, I'd gotten into the editing program at the Graham School at the University of Chicago and worked my ass off after hours to get certified. "This guy is twenty-five. I've been doing this job for ten years, and they want to make this barely-out-of-college kid my boss?"

"Evie, lower your voice," Patrick scolded.

I struggled to calm down. "Is this a joke?"

He shook his head. "I'm afraid not."

"And you." I curled my lip in utter disappointment. "Did you even fight for me on this?"

Patrick sighed. "Of course I did. I told them you had enough experience, but they want someone who's been editing."

"*I've* been editing. I've been editing work you were supposed to edit for the last seven years. But I guess that doesn't matter because I lack the one appendage that apparently makes a person more qualified—I don't have a dick!"

My boss blanched. "Evie."

I didn't care if I was losing it. There were five editors at *Reel Films*—none of them were women. There was only one female critic. And you only needed one guess to know what kind of movies she was asked to review.

I was done, I realized.

"I quit."

"Evie." Patrick pushed back his chair. "I know you're upset, but don't do anything hasty."

"Hasty?" I guffawed and turned to throw open his door. "I've done this job for ten goddamn years, and this is the thanks I get? No."

Feeling my colleagues' burning stares, I ignored them as I swiped all of my belongings into my big slouchy purse.

"Evie, will you stop?" Patrick sidled up to me.

I closed my bulging purse and turned to glare at him. We were eye level. "I hope this stuck-in-the-nineteen-fifties publication goes down the toilet, Patrick. As for you . . . thanks for ten years of nothing." On that note, I stormed out of the office, not looking at anyone, focused entirely on getting the hell out of there.

As the elevator stopped on the ground floor, my legs began to tremble so badly, I thought they might just take me out. Splatter me right across the marble floor. It would be the perfect end to the grotesqueness of the last twenty-four hours.

Yet, somehow, I walked out of there.

I just kept walking.

Walking and walking.

My mind whirled as I attempted to figure out what I would do with my life. How had I ended up here—with no promising prospects for my future?

When I thought my despair couldn't get any worse, my cell rang. I pulled it out and saw it was my stepfather calling. I loved Phil, but his call was bad timing. Considering he rarely called me when he knew (or thought) I'd be at work, however, I felt compelled to answer.

"Evie, sweetheart, I just called your office and they told me you quit."

"Yes."

"Why didn't you tell me?"

"It was . . . kind of a recent decision." I stared around, realizing I was in Millennium Park, next to the Jay Pritzker Pavilion. A woman with a six-pack ran past me in workout gear, while a guy spilled his latte down the front of his shirt and started cursing profusely.

I couldn't even remember walking here.

I was losing it.

". . . so I thought I better call you right away," Phil said.

What?

"Sorry, Phil, what?"

"Your mother," he repeated patiently. "I just got off the phone with her. I'm picking her up from rehab this Saturday, and she wants me to take her to see you."

Feeling my stomach lurch, I staggered toward the nearest bench and slumped down onto it.

I loved my mom.

But this was shitty news on top of a shitty day.

I couldn't take any more disappointment from my mother.

"Phil, I can't talk about this right now. I need to go." I hung up, feeling bad about it because Phil was great. However, I couldn't concentrate on the guilt.

Instead, all I could think about was the need to escape.

I thought of the money sitting in several savings accounts. Life insurance money left to me when my dad died. I'd used a bit for tuition, but with interest my savings were substantial. I'd been holding on to the money to buy a house, for that day when I finally met Prince Fucking Charming and settled down.

Since that seemed like a dream that would never come true, I pulled up the search engine on my phone and typed in "vacation escapes in England." It was moronic considering I no longer had a full-time job and should probably be concentrating on finding another in Chicago. Besides, I doubted Patrick would give me a reference, so that was going to be a much harder feat than usual.

However, in that moment, nothing else mattered but getting away from my life.

As a fan of all things classic literature—Jane Austen, Charles

Dickens, Geoffrey Chaucer, Charlotte Brontë—England was on the top of my bucket list.

I scrolled somewhat frantically through the vacation listings until my eyes caught on a link.

MUCH ADO ABOUT BOOKS—A BOOKSHOP HOLIDAY!

The nod to Shakespeare made me click on the link.

The advertising copy made my hands shake with excitement.

Much Ado About Books was a small bookshop in the quaint fishing village of Alnster in Northumberland. I googled it, and that was Northern England, near the border with Scotland. At Much Ado About Books, not only did you rent the apartment above the bookstore, but the owner let you run her bookshop.

It was a booklover's dream vacation getaway.

I could do that.

I could totally run away from my life and manage a bookstore in a little village in England, where none of my troubles or worries could get to me. And come on, someone named the bookstore after a Shakespearean play. It was fate.

It had to be.

No more men who made me doubt myself.

No more job that made me feel like a failure.

In fact, no more entire life circumstances that made me feel like a failure.

And I wasn't just going to England for a two-week break either.

No way.

Hands shaking, I dialed the number on the ad after checking the country code for the UK. It rang five times before a woman with a wonderful English accent answered.

"Much Ado About Books, how can I help?"

"Uh, yes, hello, I'd like to speak to someone about booking a stay at the bookshop."

"Oh . . . okay. Well, I'm the owner, Penny Peterson."

Butterflies fluttered to life in my belly. "Hi, Penny, my name is Evie Starling, and I'd like to book the store for a whole month. Starting Monday. Please tell me that's doable?"

Photo by Mark Archibald

**SAMANTHA YOUNG** is the *New York Times* and *USA Today* bestselling author of the Hart's Boardwalk series and the On Dublin Street series, including *Moonlight on Nightingale Way*, *Echoes of Scotland Street*, *Fall from India Place*, *Before Jamaica Lane*, *Down London Road*, and *On Dublin Street*. She resides in Scotland.

CONNECT ONLINE

AuthorSamanthaYoung.com

AuthorSamanthaYoung